Ecstasy and Distress

by

Richard Shain Cohen

CCB Publishing
British Columbia, Canada

Ecstasy and Distress

Copyright ©2016 by Richard Shain Cohen
ISBN-13   978-1-77143-280-1
First Edition

Library and Archives Canada Cataloguing in Publication
Cohen, Richard Shain, 1928-, author
Ecstasy and distress / by Richard Shain Cohen – First edition.
Issued in print and electronic formats.
ISBN 978-1-77143-279-5 (hbk.).--ISBN 978-1-77143-280-1 (pbk).—
ISBN 978-1-77143-281-8 (pdf)
Additional cataloguing data available from Library and Archives Canada

Richard Shain Cohen may be contacted through: **www.richardshaincohen.com**

Cover artwork design by Rose Kennealy and Jack Kennealy.

Publisher: CCB Publishing
              British Columbia, Canada
              www.ccbpublishing.com

To my dearest wife, Arla,
who has always supported my writing.

Books by Richard Shain Cohen

Be Still, My Soul

Monday: End of the Week

Petal on a Black Bough

Only God Can Make a Tree
(Poetry co-authored with Alfred R. Cohen)

The Forgotten Longfellow: Man in the Shadows

Healing After Dark:
Pioneering Compassionate Medicine
at the Boston Evening Clinic
(Co-authored with Morris A. Cohen, M.D.)

Our Seas of Fear and Love

Ecstasy and Distress

CONTENTS

Part I

Part II

Part III

Part IV

Part V

Part VI

Part VII

ACKNOWLEDGMENTS

Jocelyn Ledbetter, Maine Medical Center Library, searched, found and forwarded to me much of the early Maine medical history that was so very helpful.

Allan M. Levinsky and I talked about his book, *The Night the Sky Turned Red*, (see the Bibliography), and agreed that I could use some literary license.

I wish to acknowledge my close friends who have read and edited my manuscript: Arthur J. Faber, PhD. and James T. Kenny, PhD. They have willingly done so without stinting on their comments and making suggestions that have helped make my writing better.

I also thank the Brown Library, Maine Historical Society, for the time spent there doing research and the help of the librarians.

This book would not have been offered for publication without the continual support and comments by my dear wife, Arla F. Cohen.

FAMILY TREE

17th CENTURY

Edmond & Ruth

19th CENTURY

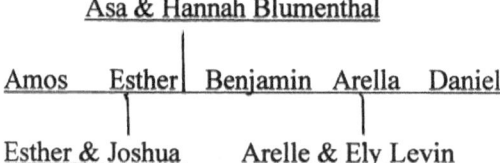

Asa & Hannah Blumenthal

Amos Esther Benjamin Arella Daniel

Esther & Joshua   Arelle & Ely Levin

Benjamin & Constance   Daniel & Riva Kaplan

Olivia   Millicent   Joseph

Olivia & Alexander Levine   Millicent & Ely Abrams   Joseph & Marie Lewis

Nathaniel Asa   Kathryn Anne   Sandra May

20th CENTURY

Nathaniel Asa & Evelyn Doris Blake   Kathryn Anne & Bryan Wilson

Mathew Robert Benjamin   Samantha Eleanor   Andrea Louise

Mathew & Mareen Meyer

Ruth

PREFACE

Ecstasy and Distress is a historic family saga and romance that spans several centuries. The story unfolds as a Jewish immigrant family settles in the busy and growing city of Portland, Maine in 1840. Here they find many hardships as they confront anti-Semitism, nativism, and adjustment difficulties as they gain acceptance as peddlers and shopkeepers. Their initial drive proves successful as they push forward in successive generations to enter professions such as medicine and law.

We are surprisingly drawn back to the family roots upon discovery of a painting of a married couple, a Jewish woman and a 17th Century Irish Catholic man who left a written letter that relates their history. He is a doctor who flees Ireland in 1607, during what was known as "The Flight of the Earls." He eventually meets his wife, Ruth, in Eastern Europe after traveling along the northern European coastline. The medical history then continues in Portland.

During the 1850s a medical school was established in Portland. Thus the professional story prevails when a son of the immigrants with the aid of a Protestant doctor gains admission to the school. The medical history of the family endures from this point through the Civil War and beyond.

The problems of the immigrants parallel the belligerence of male doctors objecting to females, including those from the family, who break these barriers to become physicians. Added is the same derision when females in the family seek to enter the profession of law.

Thus the story tells of Jewish marriages and intermarriages that continue to build the family tree. These characters are strong, self-assured women and men who reject family dismay as they find joy and regain acceptance and love within the various families along with their children.

The locus and tribulations of family life, growth, and struggles continue in Boston, Washington, D.C., the Southwest, and North Africa as the story enters the cloaked world of the wartime OSS. In this intelligence organization is a Christian family member who had been with the Department of Investigation, that became the FBI, for which he spied on the German-American Bund, a national band of Hitler admirers and anti-Semites. Now with the OSS he works along with The Jewish Brigade in helping to defeat the German General Rommel at El Alamein.

Part I

Chapter One

Ache and Kiss – The Past

I, Benjamin, am telling the story of my immigrant family. My twin sister Arella and I were in my mother's belly when my family arrived late in 1840. The ship with other refugees was crowded. The crew rarely helped with problems and left the people always feeling as though no one cared. What kept them from despair was their dream of America. My father had heard of a state named Maine that had many farmlands, mountains, lakes and a place where they felt they could be safe and perhaps flourish. Jews in Europe were often bitterly frowned upon, alienated, pariahs in their own lands, often harassed, beaten, or killed. So Maine was where my father, Asa, took my mother, Hannah, and my oldest sister, Esther, and oldest brother, Amos, to the city of Portland.

It is very peculiar, for I learned that soon after my family arrived in the United States not only Arella and I were born but also my youngest brother Daniel. I say peculiar for it was a number years before the great President Abraham Lincoln was saying goodbye to his friends in Springfield, Illinois. He could have been talking for many like my family from towns and villages where they had lived in Europe.

My Friends, no one, not in my situation, can appreciate my feeling of sadness at this parting. To this place, and the kindness of these people, I owe everything. Well, there was no kindness except for a few in my father's village. *Here I have lived for quarter of a century, and have passed from a young to an old man. Here my children have been born, and one is buried*. We had been there for centuries, and we buried who knows how many children and those older. *I now leave, not knowing when, or whether ever, I may return . . .* Well, my parents knew they would never return, nor did they care. Then the great President Lincoln referred to God, everyone's, no matter how we may worship. *Without the assistance of the Divine Being who ever attended him, I cannot succeed*. I believe this was also meant for us, for me. I mean being accepted in this, our country, in any endeavor we might choose. But there's more. *With that assistance I cannot fail. Trusting in Him who can go with me . . . and be everywhere for good, let us confidently hope that all will be well*. Then I think this was meant for the few friends and even family my parents left behind. *To His care commending you, as I hope in your prayers you will commend me, I bid you an affectionate farewell*.

Now you may wonder why I should quote this great compassionate man. Well, please bear with me, because there was still sadness to follow here in America that only he could righten. And even though we Jews served in the war, like I would do, or those who tried to help the government with, well, those with money – there was General Grant's order that all Jews be held and then thrown out of the South because they were moneygrubbers. He did not take into consideration that not that many Jews were selling cotton from the South, that the people selling cotton to the Northern army were for the most part Christians. So General Grant ordered that: *The Jews, as a class, violating every regulation of trade established by the Treasury Department, and also Department orders, are hereby expelled from the Department*. He was calling all of us Shylocks with our hooked noses and gleefully rubbing our hands over the money we collected out of a horrible blood bath. There were other generals like Sherman and Butler who were worse and wanted to see us suffer because I believe they despised us, we Jews who gave the world our one God. Yes, I know, others think of Jesus and God and I respect that. So why can't they respect us? So General Grant went on: *Within twenty-four hours from the receipt of this order by Post Commanders, they will see that all of this class of people are furnished with passes and required to leave, and anyone returning after such notification, will be arrested and held in confinement until an opportunity occurs of sending them out as prisoners unless furnished with permits from these Headquarters.* And finally, still thinking of the Jews he stated: *No permits will be given these people to visit Head Quarters for the purpose of making personal application for trade permits.*

Well isn't this just like Europe, "these people" a damnation of all Jews, when they were forced to leave homes in hideous Europe? Yes, General Grant was referring to the Jews profiting from making money on cotton. But what was the difference when so many Christians were involved? I suppose they may have been helping the North's enemy in a way, but I don't think so. Maybe some of them gave their earnings to the government to help fight that brutal slavery. Well, I don't know that. And inside me, I despised those who hurt their Jewish brethren. But they were my fellow Jews. What crime did they commit?

Anyhow it was our great President Lincoln who stopped this with his own order to General Grant: *It will be immediately revoked.* Well that's enough of this, because I have stories to tell from my time that I'm certain had to affect those of my blood who followed.

Well all this about General Grant came later as did my service.

And so, my people felt they had lightened their burden as Jews and became people like any of the others they saw and spoke to, even in their broken English they had made strong efforts to learn to speak before they landed in this great land.

How my father decided on Portland, Maine, I learned later. They had landed in Boston where they heard of Portland. In

3

Boston my father told us about his first contact with a man when he went to look for work. He wanted to save money to start his own business.

"Mister, do you have any work I could do?"

"What can you do?"

"Well I was a teacher where I came from?"

"What did you teach and where?"

"In the old country," father hesitated.

"Yeah and what did you teach, Jew boy?"

He felt like the man slapped his face. Even worse, his stomach felt the pain, like he was going to throw up. He faltered answering. "I sometimes helped teach reading to the boys."

"Ya did, huh. That's so impressive," he laughed. "And I suppose you can do that here in my store. I don't hire Jews. Now get outta here."

Father stared at him, shaking. He wanted to jump on him and beat him to the ground. Instead, "You know, Mr. you is no good. You is bad as in the Old Country."

He laughed more. "Is that so. This ain't the Old Country and I don't give a damn for any Jew being in my store. You'd probably steal me blind. Now get out!"

My father knew his face was red. He wanted to go back to where all the Jews were living and hide though there were fights even there. Well, of course there would be, but it wasn't to kill somebody, to insult him for being a Jew. That ignorant man. Didn't he know the Jews came before the Christians and even the Mohammedans, that he got Jesus from us, that great rabbi? Forgive me. I'm getting a bit off here. But I admire Jesus of Nazareth and am proud he was a Jew, just as I'm proud of being one myself, for everything good we gave the world. Everything good we offered thousands of years before, going back to the great Cyrus, and before him, and would in the years and centuries to come. Maybe my father should have told that rotten man just what I thought, but, to tell the truth, he scared

4

my father who ran out of his store not even bothering to go someplace else to look for a job. Was all of Boston like this? He didn't want to believe that. But he moved the family to Portland, Maine.

Then, after being a peddler my father did own a store. All this time I was growing up and in my brain a thought kept itching. My father's brother, who helped him come to the United States, lived in Portland and where to a bigger extent the Jews were respected.

Oh, the itch. Well it had suddenly occurred to me, Benjamin. A doctor - to be a doctor. Did I really want this? Soon I would settle it. I would be taking more of my high school subjects and include science. I had another year. I also decided I would have to find a doctor who would take me as his apprentice. There are medical schools, but would they accept me? I had heard that Jews were not welcome. So I would have to find a Jewish doctor, only I wished I could go to a school. So I made up my mind. I must also make money, but not for a horrid man like the one who called my father names. I would find something that would make enough that would allow me to save and let me do what I wanted most, now that my mind was made up.

My father's brother had become a house painter. The Jews in the part of Portland where he lived seemed to like him, and I heard he made money and hired people to help. I decided to see my uncle and ask for a job. My mother thought I was crazy. "And just what for? You'll be a doctor yet? A Jewish boy a doctor?"

"Mother, I know what I want. I'll finish high school and work my hardest to become a man who helps sick people. Wouldn't that make you proud?"

"I suppose. But Benjamin, who allows Jews to become doctors? But I'll pray for you. What about money? And what about your father?"

"No. I need to do this my way. I didn't mention Uncle."

* * *

"Uncle Moshe. I'm wondering whether you will let me help you paint houses. I need to make money and save it to become a doctor. Sure I have to finish school, but I will. Before you know it, I'll be finishing high school. And, oh, I don't know. But I'm pretty sure of myself, and I think you can help me. Would you?"

"You want to be a doctor, Benjamin?" It sounded sarcastic. It was. He was that way. I learned that from my father. "Do you know how to paint?"

"Well I never did it before."

"What did you do, anything except sit around and read books when you could get them? Books don't get you money or jobs."

"Well they will, uncle." He was making me angry, but I kept my voice from shouting, squeezing myself hard.

"Some joke. I suppose your mother told you to come see me."

"I did it myself. No one knows I came to see you and ask, and I'm not going to beg. Now are you going to give me a job or not?"

He laughed. "I suppose so. But what are we going to do about your learning?" So he put me to work, teaching me about colors, how to mix the paints, and eventually letting me paint the outside of a house, a board at a time. "No, not that way. You'll be makin' a mess. For a guy who thinks he's a doctor or will be, and who reads and reads, you're just a stupid kid. Do it this way." And he grabbed the brush from me and with it, he seemed to just glide over the wood. I have to say, I admired the way he could do it. He was almost like an artist. I might even like him, if he learned to keep his nasty mouth shut most of the time.

It was mostly Jews who hired him, of course. Seldom the Christians. But after I learned the trade, he began to allow me to start or finish a job, looking at my work with his appraising eyes full of sarcasm. Sometimes, I wondered if he even liked me. But I guess he did, because one day he came to me, placing his strong arm gently around my shoulders. "Ben, we got a job with a goyishe family. I'll let you go and start. But no foolin' around. You do a good job, hear, and take care of things before I get there."

Of course, I was surprised. My uncle liked what I did. That made me feel good inside. We had been working together for some time when this happened. It also made me feel swell, because by now I was close to finishing high school and doing well. My family was proud of me as I was, but I tried not to show it.

But then it happened. I went to the house, my uncle expecting me to make the arrangements for painting, my heart beating fast, not wanting to be talked to like that store keeper to my father. A young woman came to the door of the big house. It was also then I noticed a sign at the gate and in the window. It was a doctor's house. That made me think. I hesitated and she waited, then asked, "May I help you?"

I looked at her, swallowing, frankly stunned by her face and how she looked. She wore a day dress, long, almost down to the floor, her pomaded chestnut hair, parted in the middle like all girls. She had curls, two ringlets hanging down, the rest done up on top in a braid. And her hazel eyes. They were shining hazel. I tried not to stare. She was beautiful and so surprised me.

I had tried not to look at the girls who went to their side of Portland High School, mine, our side, all boys. I feared they would distract me. But they did. Getting older, like I was now, I thought about them, what they were like, what it was like seeing them with breasts that their dresses hardly emphasized, wondering what they looked like without clothes. I knew a little about those menstrual periods because of my two sisters and when I saw their underclothes when washed and hanging, and cloth pads sometimes. I even heard them, when they didn't know I was listening to them talking about *it*. My mother and they never talked in my presence and that of my brothers about menstruation or anything else about females. However, some of the guys at school drew pictures of naked women in the bathrooms. So how could a fellow ignore girls?

My mother had always told me how I was a handsome boy. Well, I didn't know about that, but right now, standing in front of her I hoped she thought so. I was tall now, with brown hair and blue eyes, somewhat filled out. I did notice when a girl looked at me and I did the same with her. So I guess I was growing into manhood. I was already wearing my long jacket and pants that fell to my black shoes. I hoped I looked good. Thinking about myself, she brought me back.

"Well, what can I do for you?" her voice gentle but firm as if knowing I was selling something or was supposed to work for her family.

"Uh, I am supposed to ask your father, I mean Dr. Sterling, when he would like my uncle to start painting your house. Oh, it's possible I may be the one. Is he busy? If so, I can come back when he's free." I stared at her. She was stunning. She seemed taller than she was standing there above me. I felt my face redden. That was stupid of me. I've talked to girls before. Well, like my sisters.

She grinned, maybe guessing what I was thinking, and softly told me, "Won't you come in? My father does have a patient, but my mother is here. I'm pretty sure she can help you."

I hesitated. She started to laugh. "Well come in. We aren't terrible people." I think she was talking about herself. At least, thinking back, that's what I believed. I stepped into the entranceway and noticed she was a few inches shorter than I, but I thought taller than, well, most women, because I didn't know about most. I was comparing her to my sisters, and I liked her. Maybe she could see that. I remembered, at least, to take off my hat, holding it nervously. I was mad at my uncle. He had never sent me on an errand like this, and I didn't like feeling uncomfortable, maybe because I wanted to keep looking at her. But a funny thing. She looked at me as if my presence pleased her. I was, of course, unconscious of her thoughts. *I like his blue eyes and brown hair, his chin with the dimple. His nose is so straight. He doesn't look like a Jew.* She had to look at me again, but quickly averted her eyes. *I don't want him to notice I am attracted to him.*

"I'll get my mother. Just a moment please. Just follow me." She led me to a smaller room I later learned was called a drawing room, past a living room, dining room and a tall curving stairway. It was a large, beautiful house. I looked about the room, "Well please have a seat. My mother will soon be here." Perhaps she thought because I wore good clothes it was all right to be inside and to sit on one of the chairs. I watched her walk away, her skirt seeming to float with her. It also occurred to me that if her father liked me, perhaps he would take me as an apprentice in medicine. Or maybe one day I would as I planned save enough money and get into the hospital medical college, if they overlook I'm Jewish.

While I was sitting, I heard softly from nearby, "Mother. There's a young man I took to the drawing room. He's here about painting. I think he's a Jew. He doesn't quite look it."

"Well, some people are and others aren't. So stop talking about them the way you do. We got the Lord Jesus from them. But . . ." and she hesitated, never saying what else she thought. "I suppose you took him there because he isn't covered in paint, I hope."

"No mother. He's dressed very nicely in a day suit and seems to have nice manners."

"Oh well, let's go see what he's like and if we can trust him to paint. We won't bother your father yet. I think he's with a patient. I heard the office door close."

They came to the room. I stood. Her mother had her hair done up the same way, was about the same height as her daughter. They looked so much alike to me. And the dress she wore. It had ruffles in the skirt and it was hooped. I stared at them, but especially at her daughter. I felt my heart beat faster.

"Young man, I hear you're thinking of our hiring you to paint. You don't look like one," she spoke firmly, but smiled a bit, I think looking at me who suddenly stopped staring at her and at her daughter.

"Well, yes, ma'am. My uncle is the painter. I help him when I have time from school and will probably be here some of the times. Oh, don't worry. It will be a very good job."

She watched me closely. "You go to school? Where?"

"Well, I'm in high school, almost done now. And then," I stopped, wondering whether I should say it. "Well, I want to become a doctor like your husband," and I looked at the young woman beside her unable to help myself, "and her father."

"Stop looking at my daughter. Her father makes the decisions." She spoke more sternly now. "Sit down, please. We'll talk about it." Then I sort of think she was making fun of me, as she smiled a little. "If my husband finishes with his patient, he'll join us."

I watched her daughter again seeming to glide. How like an angel. My sisters didn't appear to walk so gracefully. I liked her, but it made no difference. She would never look at me the way I did her. "Your clothes look clean, young man. So why don't you sit over there." It was near a fireplace. "I won't need you now, Constance. You have some duties to finish. I later found out she attended the Martin's Day School."

Constance left. I could not help but follow her with my eyes as she silently and proudly, her head tilted upward, left the room. She was so graceful, her dress showing off her hips and slim waist. I was fascinated. Her mother sitting opposite me, interrupted. "Young man." She brought me back and away from Constance. I'm sure she continued to notice the way I looked at her daughter. Then she sat silent for a while. "We need a good job. By the way, what is your name?"

"Ah, Benjamin, ah, Blumenthal, Ma'am."

"You're a Jew, are you not? I thought Jews were never at a loss for words," she spoke quietly, that slight smile upon her face again. Was she making fun of me, or did she like me? I couldn't tell. I had the feeling she did not like Jews but would use them to do the hard work in or on her beautiful house. Before she spoke again or while I was thinking her husband came in.

"Hello, dear. This is Benjamin Blumenthal. He represents his uncle the painter. Shall I leave you two to discuss business?" She was a typical woman of the time, nothing to do with business. It was the men's responsibility. She kept a house suitable for a doctor, raised her daughter to be a proper lady. Constance's father, however, being enlightened, saw to it that she would have an education. It was more than just reading and writing but learning languages and about the world she lives in and would when her parents were gone.

"Well, if you have other matters to attend to, then do so, Faith."

She rose. "Fine, Nathaniel. I'll go see how Lucy is making out in the kitchen." Lucy, I later found out, did some of the cooking and often answered the door.

I watched her leave, She was stately and a woman, from my perspective as a high schooler, who would fascinate a man. I kept watching her, her beautiful daytime hooped dress, her lovely arms below the mid-sleeves, watching the slight sway of her skirt as she walked. I tried not to stare, but I had never been in such a fine house nor seen a woman and her daughter like Dr. Sterling's family.

"Young man, would you tell me what your uncle intends and how much it will cost? I'm also wondering that someone apparently as young as you can paint, well, rather like I expect."

"I'm not that young, sir. I'm in my senior year of school and hoping by helping my uncle I'll have saved enough and have funds to help me as I continue my education."

For a moment it seemed as though he had forgotten about the house painting. "And what do you expect to do after high school?"

I looked at him, hesitant about telling him what I planned. "I want, I want to be a doctor, sir,"

"You mean you want to be like me."

"Yes, sir."

"That's admirable. I'll keep that in mind."

I didn't know exactly what he meant by that. Perhaps if he liked my work, if he liked me, he'd allow me to be his apprentice, even though I still wanted to attend a medical school, like the one in Portland. I knew it was hard for a Jew to be admitted. Perhaps that's the way Dr. Sterling also looked at me, as though I was someone inferior. But he didn't seem like that the way he conversed with me. Maybe that's because he was a doctor and spoke the way he did.

We talked some more, about the cost, the colors, and my uncle who obviously would do most of the work, because it was a doctor's house and had to be as good as possible. Frankly, when my uncle told me to come here, I couldn't imagine that he got a message from a Christian. I was so surprised. I trembled some going to the house. Yet, Dr. Sterling made me feel somewhat comfortable discussing the work and telling him more about me, as well as how expert my uncle is. Dr. Sterling seemed so patient and even respectful of my future plans. Maybe that helped him decide in my uncle's favor. I hoped so. You see, my uncle was always putting me down and sneering at my wish to be a doctor. Oh well.

Dr. Sterling said he would have us do the work and asked that we start by the next week. "Do you think that's possible?"

"I don't see why not, sir."

I started to rise from my chair.

"Just a minute. We're not done. You forgot to tell me the exact cost." He laughed. "I don't want to bargain. I don't believe in that unless I think someone is trying to take advantage of me."

I thought. *Oh, the Jewish thing again. I almost hate being a Jew.* He interrupted my terrible thinking. I then told him how much my uncle would charge and that I was certain one of us or both would be there the next week. Now I did rise from the chair.

Dr. Sterling smiled and thanked me. "The price is satisfactory. I'll expect you next week. I'll tell Mrs. Sterling to look for you in case I'm with a patient or at the medical school." He seemed to watch me more closely, as though examining a patient. "Sit a moment, Benjamin. May I call you that?"

"Of course, sir."

"I like the way you talk and your manners. Your parents must be proud of you and have taught you well."

"That's true, Dr. Sterling."

"What are your future plans? Are you going to take over your uncle's business?"

"Oh, no, sir. Truthfully," and I was almost fearful of repeating, "I want to become a doctor and have thought of both an apprenticeship and also applying to a medical college. I was thinking of trying the Portland School for Medical Instruction." It occurred to me most of the Jews here were in the trades. So what was I thinking? Because of that I added, "I know that will be hard to get into, but I'll see what happens." Yet I was so surprised by Dr. Sterling's interest in me.

Dr. Sterling, who I later realized was not given to quick judgments, especially from his experience in medicine, did something that startled me. "I've had a thought. If when you have time from your studies and your work, would you like to watch what I do? Be something like my apprentice. Although in some places," he laughed, "like Paris in France this is going out of fashion, but even here and in other parts of the country. Anyhow, you'll know what kind of profession you'll eventually become part of. I assure you, if you want that, I'll be hard on you. And another thing, Benjamin, there's much to learn. I'll also give you materials to read, and when I think you're ready, I may have you see patients with me. And when you finish high school, I'll expect you to attend The Portland School for Medical Instruction. Of course you'll see patients there, and it will mean even more reading, attending lectures like mine and those of other doctors." Dr. Sterling hesitated. *Would Benjamin be accepted at the new school? Well if he were good enough, I'll do my best to make certain he received acceptance, especially because I, Sterling, am one of the Lecturers.*

"I'd be honored to be something like your apprentice. I'd love it, and I promise you I'll work hard. I'm a good student too, and I will definitely apply to the school."

"I believe you, Benjamin. I have that impression by your manner and the way you talk with certainty. So, everything is settled, and I'll see you next week when you and your uncle can start painting. Then, if you still want to accept my offer, you know, of course, you'll have to give up working as much for your uncle. I hope it won't cause you problems with him." Then he thought of it, "When you're at the Medical College, you'll have to stop working, because it will take so much of your time. So be prepared for that." He now rose, came to me and took my hand, "I'm looking forward to your visit, as I imagine you are too. And, Benjamin, when you think you're ready, you and I will start. If you do really well, perhaps you'll be able to talk to some of the patients before I see them. And if you progress well enough, I may, but I'm not promising, let you do preliminary examinations. That will take time, of course. But we'll work that out. Remember, though, Benjamin, medicine is hard and sometimes disagreeable and at others very satisfying. It takes not only intelligence but ability to accept success with a patient and the gratification that offers but also the heartache of failure. We don't know enough yet. It's becoming a more exacting science, I believe. And there are people working on cures and the way we should treat people. We learn from past errors and from trying our best to be as certain as possible about what we do."

"I'll work hard, sir, and I understand what you have told me and what you expect. I promise you, you won't be sorry," a big smile on my face.

"I believe so, Benjamin," and with that he went to the door with me.

All my nervousness was gone. As I left the house, I thought of Constance, her beauty, the way she carried herself. Perhaps I would see her much more. I wanted to.

Dr. Sterling went to his office, aware he had patients waiting. Mrs. Sterling was there, asking the patients not to be anxious, that the doctor would soon be coming.

"Here I am. I finished arranging everything," looking at his wife and whispering in an almost conspiratorial tone, "Faith, I'll want to talk to you about what I decided."

* * *

Meanwhile, he could not believe that Dr. Sterling had asked him if he would want to become like an apprentice. A doctor. It was unimaginable when he asked his uncle for a job. How many Jewish doctors could there be? But he would become one someday. He would have to work hard and study and not disappoint anyone, meaning Dr. Sterling and his family. *And some day I am going to have a sign that reads Dr, Blumenthal. So what matter if it were only Jews that would be my patients?*

15

He joyfully walked as fast as he could, even ran, ignoring shortness of breath. He couldn't wait to tell his uncle the news and his family too. *Oh my uncle. He'll laugh at me, ask me what I was doing, making my future or helping his business? And what right did a Jewish boy have becoming a doctor, if he could? Would anyone in my family laugh at me? Oh, I don't care. I'm so happy.*

Then there was Constance. *Will I get to know her? She's so, well, so beautiful. The way she walks. So stately. Her eyes fascinate me, that shining hazel; and the way she looks at you, as if she sees into your soul. If she sees into my soul, she'll know what kind of person I am, what I'm thinking. Oh, oh. I just hope I might have a chance to get to know her. But her mother will keep me away from her. She's nice but so stern. Anyhow, if I'm with Dr. Sterling and at the medical college, I'll be so busy, we'll never get to know one another. She's everything I see in her. I know it. But she's a Christian.*

He wouldn't admit it to himself, but suddenly he wondered what she would look like without clothes. He was ashamed of his thought, even though sometimes he tried to imagine the same about his sisters. He could feel his face redden and turned to watch the street, the buildings, listening now to the murmurings of some people about him. The happy feelings inside him, though, were so far beyond his dreams. It was deep within him. He remembered his father telling him grandfather's belief that when a person felt as Benjamin suddenly had it was God speaking to him. But he wasn't even sure he believed in God after the terrible experience with the Rabbi who taught him for his Bar Mitzvah.

I'd rather think of Constance and hope someday when I'm a doctor I'll find a Jewish girl like her. Yes, I am old enough to think about such things. This is my last year of high school. I'm a man. I'll be graduating in 1858.

He stopped, not far from his uncle's, hesitating, except then he started again to his shop. "Uncle," he yelled. His uncle turned toward him. "What's the hollerin' about, Benjamin? You think I can't hear?"

16

"Oh, it's just that I got so excited. They gave us the job, and we're to start as soon as possible. I mean next week."

"You think I never had a job before?"

"It's just that I didn't think a Christian family would be so willing to have us paint."

"You also think I never had anything to do with the goyem. Where's that head of yours?"

"Where it's always been, uncle." He was smiling. He didn't tell his uncle about Dr. Sterling and becoming, well, his apprentice. Studying and painting and school. How would he manage it all? He knew he could work it out. "We're to start next week."

"All right already. When you finish school day you come help me. All right?"

"I do have to study, but I'll get that done at night." Night. Benjamin started thinking of Constance again, wondering how he would ever get to know her. She and her mother were so distant. Anyhow, Dr. Sterling was nice and he *would* be like his apprentice. He would not tell his uncle yet. First, he wanted to tell his mother and father.

He left his uncle and soon was with his family. "Mother. Is father home yet?' His father had shown the way by peddling, saving enough money and buying his own store where he sold clothes. It kept his father very busy.

"Of course he's here. Don't you see it's dark out?" his mother answered. "Papa. Your son Benjamin is all excited about something. Leave your paper and come to the kitchen. His father appeared, his sisters and his brothers.

"What's all the excitement?" his mother and father almost simultaneously questioned.

Before answering he looked at his sisters, wondering whether they would ever be as appealing as Constance. They were most certainly attractive and almost women now. Esther, the older, had blonde hair and blue eyes and was tall, the other,

Arella, being almost as tall with green eyes and auburn hair. They were very close despite their occasional arguments, choosing clothes that suited them. He loved his entire family, his brothers, sisters, and parents. His mother and father had always been supportive of their children, worrying only when they talked of the future that they might be prevented in some way because of their religion. Benjamin began to doubt that. This was the United States. His parents interrupted his thoughts. "Papa, look at him. Come now, tell us what happened to so excite you."

"You know I want to be a doctor. Well today, I went for Uncle Moshe to talk to a doctor who wants his house painted. I didn't know he was a doctor until I saw the sign." He was talking rapidly, stopped to catch his breath. "His wife is nice, and he also has a daughter." He wished he could add what he thought of Constance. "Anyhow the whole family is just wonderful."

"And so," his father interrupted. "Moshe is always painting and making lots of money. So why so breathless about that, Ben? What, you liked the daughter?"

His father surprised him referring to Constance. He looked at his mother who suddenly was serious. "Benjamin, no *Goyishe* girls, only for looking. What about it? Is she what excites you? You remember what I'm telling you. You can get hurt. So nu, go on."

His father was seriously looking at him. "Wait, mamma. I think it's not just a girl. What else? Tell us."

"Well, their name is Sterling. And he's a doctor. He told me he would be willing to teach me some medicine, you know, something like an apprentice. But I have to apply to the Portland School for Medical Instruction. Of course that will cost for the time I'm there. But I am saving money." He hesitated. "I may have to ask you for some help, Father."

"This Doctor Sterling talked to you like that?" his father

continued. "Do they accept Jews in the school? I wonder. But living here has been a good experience. I even have goyem come in the store every so often. But to get into a school," he wondered aloud. "Well, all they can say is 'no.' Ach. Let's not worry about that. You'll just have to try when it's time. Oh, it's already time I think. Here it is late in the spring. You get an application and fill it out. And we'll see what happens. And, Benjamin, if they take you and you need some help, don't worry. Imagine, Mamma, a doctor in the family. Now don't worry until there's something to worry about. He'd be busy with relatives and the people who know about the store and Moshe. I approve and hope that Dr. Sterling will always be nice to you. *Gott tsu danken.*"

* * *

Faith Sterling and Constance busied themselves helping some with Lucy preparing supper, knowing Nathaniel was usually busy with a late patient that could delay eating. Now, however, Faith was curious about her husband whispering to her and hoped he would for once be on time. She was a rather impatient person who, on this night, did not wish to be kept waiting. She knew from the manner in which he approached her after Benjamin left he would not talk in front of Constance. Momentarily, she thought of her daughter and not only her love for Constance, a loyal daughter, but her thankfulness she lived and was now seventeen years old.

She still felt as though perhaps she failed after her beautiful daughter; for the next birth, a dead boy, became a tragedy in her life that made her feel for many years she was a failure. The birth of the second child was not only extremely painful but one that almost killed her. She suffered so, doctors claiming what they knew, that she had an occluded vagina and a pierced cervix with excessive bleeding. From the effects upon her organs that never fully recovered, according to her doctor, she could never have another child.

She gave her time and love to Constance's upbringing, fearful every time her daughter became ill, despite Dr. Sterling's assurances and watchfulness of both his wife and daughter. Both parents assured that Constance would have an education and be a credit to her sex. When she told her parents she wanted to attend college, they were hesitant. It meant she would leave home, be in another state where they would be unable to guide her and assure that nothing ill happened to her. There was still time before she was ready for such a venture.

Thinking about this, Faith became a bit unsettled. She was unprepared for thoughts of Constance away from home, another loss. However, forcing her attention to her husband, she was now curious about Nathaniel's apparent secret. She moved about the kitchen impatiently directing and making certain Lucy prepared the evening meal well. Lucy becoming irritated started to object to Faith's instructions. "Mrs. Sterling. Please. Haven't I been doing this for the family for how many years now?" Constance, making biscuits, laughed loudly. Lucy turned toward her, smiling, but then, looking angrily at Mrs. Sterling, she pursed her lips, preventing herself from saying anything nasty. Now Faith was smiling. They all loved Lucy, this now graying, plumper woman who had been with the family for how many years? "Twenty-five. That's it," Lucy thought. "Mrs. Sterling. Do leave me alone. I just counted in my head. I've been here since before Constance was born." She bit her lower lip, suddenly, looking away, thinking of how she had tried so hard to help Faith through her trying times after the stillborn baby.

Still smiling, Faith answered, "Yes. You're right. But you know I have to interfere as lady of the house." Soon they were all in a good mood. Only now, Constance, looking at her mother, began thinking of how she would approach not only her mother but her father about her plans. Well that would wait.

Dr. Sterling finished seeing patients earlier than usual. Faith hurried to him before he could become part of a family conversation. "Nathaniel, tell me why you sounded so secretive."

"I wasn't secretive.'

"You were, the way you whispered to me."

He started to answer but thought better to just come out and tell her what he decided. "Well, while I was talking to the boy, Benjamin Blumenthal, I liked his manner and asked about his future plans. He told me this was his last year in high school and that he wanted to be a doctor."

"A doctor. Oh, Nathaniel, a Jewish doctor."

"Well, there must be some in the country. Why not here in Maine, even Portland? There's a nice Jewish population here. Come to think of it, I didn't ask him if that clothing store was his father's."

"So what if it is? That doesn't make the boy special."

"I don't know if he's special, but he strikes me that he is."

"From a conversation about painting? Nathaniel! Please! He's a Jew. And he wants to be a doctor. That takes nerve." She had never thought too much about Jews. They had never been in her life until this day. Yet, as much as she usually respected her husband's opinions, when she didn't, she would argue. Now she began to wonder.

Nathaniel interrupted. "You're right. Nerve. Not only that, it takes a good and curious brain, sensitivity, and humaneness. And I think he has all these."

"So just what are you trying to tell me, Nathaniel?" She felt her heart beating a little faster. She knew her husband quite well. He was describing himself. Suddenly she felt a pain, thinking of Benjamin and the agony of birthing a dead boy. Was her husband trying to make a son out her inability ever to have had a child again, especially a boy?

A bit exasperated, he replied, "What I'm trying to tell you is that I told him that he could be like an apprentice but that he would have to apply to the medical school."

Faith was growing angry. "How could you do this? You bring him into our home without even consulting me." She was quite well aware that women were supposed to accept their husband's wishes, but she was not most women. This was a bit too much. "And you are going to have this boy in the house with a grown daughter." Listening to herself, she wanted to laugh. Benjamin would not be in contact with Constance unless it was absolutely necessary. Yet she could not erase her thoughts. It was not that he was a Jew. It was about that son that died at birth, the hellish agony she had endured, that kept troubling her. Yet, that wasn't her husband to hurt her in such a way. But the pain she now experienced was real.

"Faith, I know I'm doing something good. I feel it."

"And if you are wrong?" her voice had grown husky, anger rising.

"Stop. Now. You're being unreasonable. I want to do something that would not only please me but that is right. And you come up with," he started to say ridiculous, but instead he told her, "objection. Listen to yourself, dear. You're getting angry." He went to her, bringing her closer, about to hug her, and she yielded. "It's just that you took me by such surprise, Nathaniel." There were tears in her eyes because of the horrible thoughts she had had. She refused to allow herself to cry, rubbing her face against his shoulder. He did, however, feel a shudder.

"Dearest," in almost a whisper, "I would never do anything to make you uncomfortable. I believe that you will come to like the boy. And please. I feel good about this. Perhaps I'm overreaching. But I have to do it."

She moved from him to look at him. "I know. And I'll try to help however I can. But you know, Nathaniel, applying to the medical institute, I just don't know. How will they ever accept a

Jew?"

"Perhaps I'm being precipitous, but if he's what I think, I'll do what I can to help."

Faith understood her husband well, and she would have to support him. She loved him too much, something for which she had never been sorry. Would she regret this support after what she had heard about these strange immigrants with whom she had never come into contact until earlier this day? What would her neighbors think or say? Thus, as of this day, the home of Nathaniel Sterling seemed to have changed.

* * *

Benjamin ate his dinner silently, ignoring his parents and siblings. He usually was the most talkative among the children. Esther and Arella whispered between them. Suddenly Esther giggled.

"What's so funny?" their father in a gruff voice wanted to know.

"Oh, come now, Asa. Why are you always picking on the girls? So they had something to laugh about. You should be happy they laugh," Hannah interrupted.

"Well, Papa, we thought," she hesitated, laughing now, digging her finger into Arella's side, who also began to laugh.

"Stop and tell me what's so funny."

"We just thought, Esther continued, still laughing, "What, what, if it's just a joke but funny. We just thought about the doctor's daughter and thought of Benjamin following her around, maybe asking a Goyeh girl to marry him." They both laughed now.

"That's funny? Stop. Now." Their father was becoming irritated by their silliness. "It would be shameful for this family, and I don't see anything funny about it.

Hannah gulped some food she had been chewing, almost

choking. "Asa, the girls are having fun. Don't be so mad. Benjamin would never do that."

Benjamin's tried to keep from blushing but couldn't. He had been too astonished by Constance. He was about to speak, when Amos started. "You'd never do something like that, would you, Ben?" mocking his mother.

By now, Benjamin was becoming angry. "Why don't you all leave me alone," as he rubbed his face in a gesture to rub away the red. "Dr. Sterling is nice enough to help me some learning about medicine. And who knows? Maybe I will get into the school. Won't that give all of you something to talk about? The doctor's daughter. I'll probably never see her. Anyhow, she seemed nice and that's that. What's with you all? She met me at the door. Maybe I'll never see her again," he repeated in an angry voice. "Shut up and leave me alone. There's nothing funny about God helping me to become a doctor."

"Oh. But you told me one day, Ben, you don't believe in God," Daniel challenged.

"Did you say that?" their mother asked. "How could you?"

Benjamin refused to answer and began to rise from his chair. "You make fun of me because you're all jealous that a nice man wants me to learn something. Who knows? Maybe someday I'll be able to help one of you." He started to leave the table.

"Enough!" their father yelled. "And you sit. That's enough of this foolishness. Just stop and eat."

That night Benjamin, before going to bed, got his dictionary and began to look for medical words that described illnesses of which he had heard. Some were absent. It frustrated him. He wondered if his father would help him buy a medical book. He wanted to read. He fell back on his pillow, ignoring his brothers, and as he closed his eyes, his thoughts were of Constance, her beautiful, shining hazel eyes and lovely figure. If he could only get to know her. But he was almost certain that was an impossibility. He was, as he said at the supper table, going to study with Dr. Sterling. Yes, he was going to study and some day he would, somehow, become a doctor and treat his Jewish neighbors and perhaps some Gentiles, if they liked him enough. He would be a good doctor. "A good doctor," as he fell asleep.

* * *

At the end of the week, after I had helped my uncle as much as possible after school, I was painting the frame of the carved glass front doors. Lazily I brushed, my mind wandering, thinking of what I had learned in school today and what I would have to study that night. Suddenly the door opened. Without looking I spoke loudly, "Be careful. The paint's wet."

She laughed. Surprised, I looked from her so lovely face to her blue dress with white about the sleeves, the skirt with white trim about the bottom of the pleated skirt, unable to say anything, stopped my painting. In my work clothes, I thought how terrible I must look next to her.

Smiling, she softly told me, "My father wishes to see you."

"Oh. Thank you." The brush almost slipped from my hand, because she made me slightly nervous, as did seeing Dr. Sterling. I also started to wipe my hands against my paint pants but quickly realized that would look bad and would truly soil me. I had been as careful as possible about keeping paint from my clothes and face. After I dried my hands on a cloth, I told her, "Well, I think I'm ready," my hand going automatically to my face, hoping there was no paint there. As she saw my movement, she laughed. "Benjamin." All I could think was. "She called me Benjamin." She stopped laughing but a smile stayed with her. The smile faded as she seemed to scrutinize me. *He is handsome. His eyes are so beautiful. Tall and solid.* She felt her face warming in a blush that she stopped by turning sideways to him.

"I'm a bit soiled, but I know I won't get any paint inside."

25

"Well, I wouldn't expect you to carry a can of paint into the house, Benjamin." She was enjoying herself, aware of his embarrassment and the hope that she had upset him.

"I'll follow you, of course, Miss Sterling."

For some reason, astonished by her attraction to Benjamin, she said, "You may call me Constance." She steadied herself, turned from him, "Come. I'll take you to my father."

"Oh." I stumbled, and recovering, repeated, "Thank you. I'm coming." Constance. The name reverberated through me.

Dr. Sterling sat, watching the young man walk steadily toward him. He admired what appeared his confidence.

"Have a seat here by the desk, Benjamin. I have a book I want you to look at." I looked at the title, *Gray's Anatomy*. I bought this from its European distributor. It is the best I have seen regarding the human body. This will give you some idea of how much you must and will learn. I shan't give it to you to take home, but when you have time and you are here, I want you to go through it. I'll also explain what you don't understand. Beyond this we'll talk about medicines, women having children and diseases of women and children, as well as those that can infect males and females and whole populations. You have to learn also not to be embarrassed about studying the differences between the sexes. So, Benjamin, this is your first lesson. Why don't you spend some time now looking though this book? O.K.? I'm going to see a patient or two in the examining room, but we can talk until then." He patted Benjamin on the shoulder who felt a pleasure throughout his body at the touch.

"Thank you Dr. Sterling. I'll start now," a smile on my face.

Dr. Sterling going to his waiting room, stopped. "Call me if you want some explanation. I think you'll need it."

* * *

I sat in the chair, lifting the heavy book and placed it in my lap. Slowly, with almost a religious feeling I opened to the first page, then fingered through several more. I then went more quickly, surprised by the human body from about the waist up that showed no skin but the muscles of the body. It absolutely fascinated me. I traced along the illustration, following the anatomy, somewhat stunned to learn that it was what I looked like without skin, more so that all people looked like that, a woman too, but perhaps not so muscular as what I thought was a man looked like. It was a man's head. I studied the picture, still tracing. Suddenly my mind wandered. Constance. My sisters. I wanted to know if it had about females. I thumbed through the Index and found "Female Organs of Generation." I was no longer the student but the ordinary curious male. Vagina, Uterus, Mammary Glands . . . I became excited and looked for pictures, seeing them, what I only imagined or heard the guys at school talking about. Then I saw something about nipples and fallopian tubes and ovaries, uterus, cervix. My hands trembled as I went quickly to these pages, my heart beating faster. These were all the hidden parts of my mother, sisters, and Constance. It looked so strange to me. It would be something to see what they looked like in a real female. Now I knew but not how they worked. Suddenly I stopped. I thought I heard Dr. Sterling coming. I quickly turned many pages toward the beginning.

"Well, Benjamin, what do you think? Do you still want to learn how we all function and why and all that a doctor has to learn to be able to treat people properly?"

"I do," hoping he would not notice my red face after what I had looked at. "I have no question whatsoever. I want to be like you, to treat people and bring them back to health. Imagine being able to do all that."

"Well, it isn't just like that. We have so many diseases and still so many questions. We don't have all the medicines we ought to have. That means we are ignorant about much regarding illnesses and injuries. Also," and he hesitated it seemed, "Death. We wish we could prevent it, but so often we fail. So you will learn that our profession is filled with much sadness, as well as joy. You have to be willing to face all of that. You have to be strong, Benjamin, as well as intelligent along with accepting your ignorance and desire to fight against our ailments. Can you do it? Are you strong enough?"

"Dr. Sterling, after having come from where my parents did and having to learn about their new country, and struggling at first, if they could do it, I know I can and want to do it."

"Then it's settled. Come into my office."

I followed him into his office. Hidden from his patients in a closet sized room was a human form on a rod I later learned could be disassembled in certain ways to show the skeletal bones, and what composed our whole bodies. It did surprise me but made me curious. We all came down to this. All those muscles and other parts covered what was hidden. I later learned Dr. Sterling had bought one of these after a trip to Europe.

Dr. Sterling noticed me somewhat studying that form. "Does this make you curious?"

"It, it does. Looking at the book I skimmed, it's just absolutely amazing." I was excited and wanted even more strongly to know as much as possible. It also suddenly hit me how it would take hours and hours of study. I would have to pay attention to everything Dr. Sterling told me and read all he wanted me to. I would do it.

He interrupted my thoughts. "Benjamin, you're going to learn about different medicines we use to try to help people, but sometimes they don't work. That's something you'll learn when we talk about *Materia Medica*. It's frustrating, but we are learning new treatments. And there is one thing I want you to know. Wash your hands before and after you treat someone. We have learned that much, at least some of us have. What causes infections, though, we aren't sure. For example, lots of doctors when they deliver a child don't do that. Well, we know now that it helps keep the woman safer during the delivery and that hopefully they won't die from puerperal fever." As soon as he said that, I felt my face redden. He noticed. "Now, Benjamin, you have to learn not to be embarrassed by what we talk about or what you see. In time you'll get used to it." He smiled, and continued. "That hand washing also pertains to surgery on men and women and anything you may touch that is impure. There is something called carbolic acid that helps prevent infection. In the United States we don't see this widely used, but it is in Europe. One has to be opened minded to learn good ideas from others. Well that's one lesson for you right now. An easy one. Now I'll have you come into the room where I examine patients and show you about there."

We walked into his examining room. There was a narrow table there with a sheet on it. There were also oil lamps about for more light. Against one wall was his desk, a chair in front for a patient I imagine. There was also a cabinet with glass windows where there were some bottles of medicines. On another wall was a bookcase with medical books and some printed journals.

"Benjamin, this is the inner sanctum. Here I am able to examine my patients in private, of course. One thing, when you talk to a patient, you do not disclose to the public anything private or names. You may discuss your episodes with other doctors and may perhaps say something general to someone like your wife, for example, say 'I saw an interesting case today,' after which you may describe it in general terms. Remember, when a patient comes to you, it is a trust that is sacred."

"Yes, sir, I'll remember."

"Now what we'll do today is look at the anatomy book's

beginning, and I'll tell you about such matters of auscultation, and about various diseases, how I treated them or tried to. A failure may depress you, but eventually you will learn that you sometimes win or lose. Remember that also.

"Note I used the word auscultation. Hop on the examining table. Unbutton your shirt. That's it. Lie back. Now suppose I believe a patient may have a heart problem or perhaps that terrible disease tuberculosis. We don't have all the medicines, unfortunately, for cures though there are some we use to help alleviate the patient's illness. Anyhow, let's leave that for now.

"I am going to tap on your chest. As I do this, I'll be listening to the sound. Then I'll place my ear to your chest, listen for unusual sounds either of the heart or the chest. What I've shown you is the older way of listening and perhaps discovering a patient has a heart disease or tuberculosis."

He pulled from a drawer in the table an instrument that had two tubes and at the end a device to hear sounds. He leaned over, listening to my heart's regular beat.

"Now I want you to do that to me. I obeyed and listened to Dr. Sterling's chest and then his heart, thinking its beat was not the exciting one I felt in my chest when I would see or hear Constance speak or as when she led me to her father's office. I was glad that Dr. Sterling could not hear that one but only my normal inquisitive heart.

* * *

That was an interesting thought, he told himself. Not his inquisitive knowledge seeking mind but his heart. He had thrown his life into the world of medicine, he realized. And one day he wondered, despite religion, whether he could become well acquainted with Constance. She was always within him now. He even dreamed of her. And one night when he had a discharge and woke with his nightshirt and leg sticky, it was a vision in which he had been kissing and hugging her while she ran her hands soothingly over his body. He would never tell anyone, not even his oldest brother, Amos. He thought back to the first one he ever experienced and how it scared him until Amos told him to expect those every so often. This one, though, was so exciting and pleasing he wanted it to happen again, to have her with him as they made love. He did wonder what his mother thought when she found his nightshirts dried, showing the dried patch when she did the laundry. His sisters Arella and Esther had asked about that once when helping their mother, but she avoided the inquiry and just said their brothers must have spilled something. Arella thought to her menstrual periods and how she tried to hide the blood stains.

Benjamin's mind stopped wandering when Dr. Sterling rose and looked at him curiously. "Well, that's one lesson for you. Others will come. Take the Gray's book with you when you go home tonight and study the first ten pages of anatomy. We'll go over them together so I can answer your questions. Perhaps I'll also test you."

So it was that Benjamin had his introduction to the wonders of medicine. Some time had passed when one day Constance again led him to her father, smiling and talking about her day and asking how his studies were progressing. She had heard her father and mother talking about Benjamin but did not tell him exactly what she heard. She just wanted to have fun watching his reaction. "Benjamin, something different is going to happen today when you see my father." She bit her lower lip to stifle a laugh. She so enjoyed teasing him. Just being near him did something to her, feeling inside the thrill while imagining what it would be like to have him touch her in private places or even holding her hand. She wanted to grasp his. She looked away trying to hide her blush, feeling the warmth not only of her face but its seeping thrillingly to her belly. It reminded her how she had often looked at her nipples and the surrounding brownness, and played her fingers about them so they hardened sending electrification downward between her thighs, her most intimate self.

Once, though, her mother warned her not to touch herself, that it was known to be bad. Inquisitive, she ignored the injunction, played with her nipples, feeling them stiffen, sending exhilarating warmth between her thighs, dared to run her fingers below and felt the excitement throughout her body and the shuddering orgasm. She lay as her heaving subsided, her breathing returning to normal. She focused on the unimaginable feelings and pleasure she never dreamed her body possessed. When relaxed, she smiled at the unbelievable satisfaction. Yes, she would arouse herself when she pleased, learning soon more of her sensitive folds, fingering, and separating them to insert her fingers into her sex. She would never again hear her mother's words.

She forced herself from her fantasizing of those arousals and back to her parents' conversation.

"Faith," she heard her father softly say, "I've decided to have Benjamin apply to the medical school."

"You can't be serious. He's a lovely boy I have to admit. He's even the kind someday I'd like Constance to meet, but Christian mind you. I've gotten over his being Jewish. You know because of that he won't be accepted. Why place him in that situation that will be so embarrassing?"

"I want him to have the benefit of regular schooling where he can learn most of what he must. You forget I'm one of the professors there and believe that it is where he belongs."

"I haven't forgotten, dear," she spoke softly, suddenly aware Constance could hear them from where she was standing.

"Constance, please leave us. This is private."

Constance pretended to leave but stood close enough to listen, hiding by the parlor door.

"I don't care what he is. And, yes, I'm aware how many

people feel about Jews. But I'm telling you, Faith, this boy is exceptional. He's handsome, tall, makes a good appearance. He speaks well, no accent that I often hear my friends mocking. They ask me how I could have taken him in, if I'm a secret Jew." Nathaniel's voice rose, growing louder with anger. "I'm sick of all this nonsense about Jews are only money grubbers. Mark me, Faith. I'm right about this."

"Well you think you're right. I don't. And don't get mad. He's a Jew. Accept it. They'll turn him down."

"Let them try." He liked Benjamin, treated him almost like a son. And if Faith thought that was the kind of man she would want for Constance, he agreed, but Christian. And he whispered to himself, "Hopefully." He had noticed a change in her when she was near Benjamin. Faith must have also. Perhaps she had warned Constance to stay away from him. She had.

Thinking of that conversation, the occasional anger and word Jew, her mother's reaction to him when they talked, she looked closely at Benjamin. He seemed like any other person to whom her parents had introduced her. Yes. She did like him. No one, not even she, could stop her feeling that way.

"Benjamin," this time a slight laugh, "Father," she started, now blushing openly, only this time because she had listened secretly to her parents. "Father will surprise you."

Benjamin, of course, saw her red face that she was trying to hide by turning. *Do I love her? Is that what I feel? This hollowness and almost like a pain in my heart, when I think of her.*

Suddenly he felt her hand touch his arm, an involuntary movement. "Good luck, Ben." She had never used his name that way. No one did.

Aware she had touched him and feeling his slight shudder and movement toward her to feel her more, her mind restlessly told her, *I like him too much. My parents would be furious with me, perhaps disown me. I'm almost of marriageable age after this year. He and I are the same age. I don't want to marry. I'm going to college. I know father wants more for me. Mother hesitates, but father will bring her around. I'm going to college, and I'll marry when I'm ready and who? Whom? I wish . . .*

Just then they came to the office door. "Well, Benjamin," formal again, "Here you are at your destiny."

"What?"

"Oh, just go in." She wanted to shove him, turned away, smiling, happy for him.

Chapter Two

Apprehension and Confirmation

Benjamin told his father and mother he was applying to the Portland School of Medical Instruction. He had the application.

"Benjamin, I think you've lost your mind," his mother proudly warned. His father nodded, smiling, but afraid of the disappointment his son was about to face. They talked some, and Benjamin left for his room. He filled out the application and would mail it. He then changed his mind. He would take it to the office on Middle Street, so that he would be able to start school in 1858.

Thus Benjamin took his first nervous steps toward the building that for him had a holiness about it. Dr. Sterling had told him he would study with perhaps six other students, that there would be lectures and demonstrations, as well as recitations. He would have to remember that he would never receive selective attention from him, that once in school he would have to compete with the other students and learn from doctors he had never met.

So he entered the building and went to the second floor, knocking on a closed door. He heard "Enter." A doctor sitting at a desk, looked up, smiling when he saw Benjamin. He handed the doctor his application which, after seeing the name, gave it a cursory glance. Suddenly, placing the paper on his desk, the doctor told him, "We are now full for the next year. I doubt you will be able to take your place with the others."

"Well," Benjamin answered, trying to hide his disappointment, "I imagine the next year then."

"No." Abrupt, gruff.

"But why not, sir?" he asked, trying hard to hide his discomfort.

"You just will not fit. You haven't all the qualifications we seek. Thank you for considering our distinguished profession, but I'm sorry."

As Benjamin, trying to hide tears, turned from the man, the physician grumbled to himself, "The damn Jews think they can do anything they want, be welcome like our good people." It made no difference to him knowing that Jews had studied medicine in Germany or that Baron Rothschild with all that ill-gained money. Jews were peddlers, storekeepers. That's where they belonged and welcomed in Portland."

Benjamin, once on the street, tried hard not openly to cry. "I do belong," he spoke softly. "I am smart. I would be an excellent doctor. Dr. Sterling told me so." He would have to tell Dr. Sterling of the rejection. His parents. They'd probably say, "I told you so."

Where should he go first? He started toward Dr. Sterling's but then turned toward home. His father was still in his store with his brothers. His mother was in the kitchen baking with Arella and Esther. They seemed to be babbling to Benjamin until he heard Esther yell out, "Ouch. Oh, it hurts." She held her two fingers, shaking them, tears forming. "Come now, Esther. Be a big woman. Come here. I'll put some grease on them," her mother urged, running her hand softly on her daughters face. As her mother touched the edge of a pan, she saw Benjamin, the saddened look of his face. While she spread the grease on her older daughter, murmuring, "There now. You'll be healed," her face showed concern. Turning from Esther, she asked, "Benjamin. What has happened you look as though somebody beat on you." His sisters turned, Esther forgetting her fingers. "What now?"

"They turned me down. The man told me I was not smart

enough for them, or at least that's what it sounded like."

"The goy at the medical place?"

"Yes, Mamma."

"And he told you aren't smart enough for them? *Goyishe Dum kopf.* Forget them. Go with your father. You'll be happier."

Arella looked sternly at her mother. "Mamma, no. Never no. He's no store keeper."

Before she could continue, her mother interrupted. "You're telling me your papa is nothing. You stop. Now. Apologize. *Dum Kopf.*"

"No. He is smart. Maybe the smartest of all of us. He wants to be a doctor. Who are they to turn him out, telling him he's not smart enough?"

"Yes, Mamma, Arella is right. You know it. He was not insulting papa."

Benjamin, unable to hold back his tears, unembarrassed before his sisters and mother, interrupted. "Stop. Don't argue. Please. Not now. I did not insult papa. I was meant to be a doctor," and he ran from the kitchen to his bedroom, falling on his bed.

Arella and Esther left their mother and followed, Arella placing her hand on his head, rubbing his hair. "Ben. Don't cry. That doctor isn't the only one in the place." Esther sat on the bed, rubbing his back. "Ben, Arella is right. We all know you love us. Even papa. You don't belong in a store. You're a doctor."

Arella continued. "You've been with Dr. Sterling. You are going to be a doctor. We all know that. Go to Dr. Sterling."

Benjamin turned over, lying on his back, rubbing his hands over his eyes, wanting to hide his tears from his sisters. "I will. I have to tell him." Looking at his sisters, he could not hold back. "You know I love you both, the whole family. I want you to be proud of me. And if you need a doctor someday, I want to be able to get you the best care." He smiled. "I feel foolish. Look at me, crying."

"Oh, and young men don't ever, ever cry. They're just big and strong, put here to protect us weak females," Arella laughed.

Benjamin sat up and suddenly hugged one then the other.

"Go see mama. Tell her you love papa and didn't mean anything bad. You just feel hurt," Esther urged. "And then go see Dr. Sterling."

"You're both right." He laughed. "Weak females. You two are the strongest of us all." He looked at his sisters. "I don't know what I'd do without you."

Now Arella and Esther had tears, not caring to hold them back. The three of them sat on the bed, hugging, crying, and laughing.

* * *

The following morning Benjamin went to Dr. Sterling. Mrs. Sterling met him at the door.

"Ben, you're so early." He was now accustomed to people shortening his name. It was not like the first time Constance had said that.

"I couldn't help it, Mrs. Sterling. I have to see the doctor. Something happened."

"I'll see if he's busy. Go in the parlor and wait. All right?" She hesitated." You look sad, like something happened. Is your family all right?"

"Oh, yes, ma'am. It's me. I, I mean."

"Mrs. Sterling smiled. "I'm aware you know grammar. Now off with you. See if Constance is free. She could sit with you and talk." Mrs. Sterling, hesitated, wishing she could retract her words. She was aware of the attraction between them, Constance once telling her mother how handsome and tall Benjamin was and the allure of and honesty in his bright blue eyes.

Once more she heard a repeat admonition from her mother about male attraction, reminding her again, "Constance, he's a good boy. I see it in him, feel it about him. But you remember. He's Jewish."

"Oh, mother, of course. I know all that," and she laughed. "I know what you have taught me. Don't worry. I'll be careful around them and *him*."

Constance had been in the drawing room, but when she heard the front door, she rose to go, heard her mother. She quickly went to the parlor.

"Benjamin. You're here in the morning. Won't your uncle be angry?"

He hesitated, having been looking at her, the ringlets and part in her chestnut hair, her violet day dress as she swept to a chair. She smiled, aware of her attraction to him.

"Come, sit over there, near me. You haven't answered, Ben."

He smiled. She called him Ben. She liked him. He just knew. They sat, at first silently, looking at one another, wanting to touch.

"You haven't answered me."

"I suppose he'll be upset. I don't care, Constance. There are more important things in the world than my uncle's painting."

"Benjamin. That's impolite," smiling as she said it.

"Well, look at what your father does."

"Yes. But you are going to be something like him. I know you will." She stood, as if to smooth her day hooped skirt. He quickly looked at her hips and upward, hoping she wouldn't notice. He didn't realize she was aware, would be and that she was pleased by the way he always looked at her, as though she were matchless to him.

"Well, you haven't told me why you are so early at our house."

"I had a bad time at the School for Medical Instruction."

"Something's wrong, Ben. Tell me." Her face showed her concern. She reached for him, held back. She thought quickly, knowing it had something to do with being Jewish. Suddenly within her was a hatred of all religion. *Who were we*, she asked herself, *to think we're so special? Ben is so, so intelligent, so gentle. Oh. I think I may love him. Is that what this is? I hate what is happening to him. I want to hold him.* She held back tears, wiped at an eye.

"I think I should tell your father first, Constance. But it's bad. It is about me, something the man didn't like." She thrilled when he used her name but was now very angry, hurting because he was.

She rose to her full height. "I'm going to tell my mother to get father quickly.

"I'm here, Constance. Benjamin, come to my office."

"Father, I want to . . ."

He gently stopped her, noticing her glistening eyes. "Please, dear, go see if your mother needs you. Come, Benjamin."

Constance appeared to droop, silently left, turning to watch them walk toward her father's rooms.

In the office, Dr. Sterling did not sit behind the desk but drew a chair facing Benjamin.

"Now, young man, what happened at the Institute?"

"The doctor I saw looked at my application. He said I wasn't fit, that I was . . . was not the kind of person they are looking for. That's not exactly what he said, but close, Dr. Sterling."

"He told you *that*? Who was it? Do you know his name?"

"He never told me. Truthfully, Dr. Sterling, I suppose I shouldn't say this, but he was rude and gruff. He never asked me any questions, just looked briefly at my application and told me I'm not fit. I'll apologize if you wish, but I think he saw something he didn't care for from the time he saw my name. My religion, sir. Is that why I'm not fit? How can he be so mean?"

"I know how, Benjamin. You need not apologize to me. You

stay here the rest of the day. Try to study some. Look at the microscope I bought." He laughed a bit. "It cost quite a bit. That's between you and me, for now.

"Meanwhile, I have no patients coming until near noon. I'm going to have a talk with Dr. Erstwhile."

With that he left, found Faith, his face red with anger, told Faith what he was going to do.

* * *

Nathaniel went to the barn and took his carriage from his driver, Ambrose, whipping the horses, riding rapidly from the West End to the Middle Street classrooms. Women in their fashionable hoop dresses and men accompanying them stared at the driver, some recognizing him, others scared out of the way so as not to be hit.

Once there, Nathaniel pulled the horse team up short. He sat for a while to calm himself as much as possible, but still angry he walked quickly to the second floor. Dr. Erstwhile still sat at the desk. Seeing Nathaniel, he began to smile, until he was told, "Take that smile from your face."

"What?"

"You have so much to be proud of, don't you John? You lecture to our students, so proud of yourself, in particular about the students we choose."

"Well, yes. And why not?"

"There was a Benjamin Blumenthal here yesterday. You turned him down, told him he was not good enough to be among the student body."

"Oh, that Jew boy. He does not fit, Nathaniel. He doesn't belong in our student body."

"That Jew boy, as you call him, is my apprentice who I sent here."

"Oh, c'mon, Nathaniel. They're all peddlers and shop

41

owners. That's their stock in trade."

Nathaniel could feel his face growing warmer and redder with his previous anger. He was almost shaking. "You know, John, if we weren't civilized men, I'd thrash you." Nathaniel tried to calm himself. He noticed John's face becoming red. "You had better calm down, Doctor. You don't tell me what to do, who we should accept."

"I don't?" Nathaniel took several deep breaths to calm himself. "John, you just turned away in tears one of the most brilliant young men we will probably have in the school of Medical Instruction. That's your Jew boy, John."

Dr. Erstwhile, rose from his chair. "No one talks to me this way. You are completely unprofessional. In fact, you may think he's brilliant, but I've yet to meet a Jew I thought about that way."

"You go to hell, John. Your ignorance overwhelms me. I'll have you brought before the entire faculty. So help me, I will, John." Sterling was practically shouting now.

Erstwhile, smiled sardonically, yet fear appearing on his face. "You settle down, Nathaniel. I did the right thing. That boy would only be in for disappointment later."

"He's already disappointed. He also thinks I let him down. I won't allow it. You are going to write him and tell him . . . no, better still. He is going to come here, and you are going to inform him you were mistaken and that he will be welcome in the fall class."

"Who do you thin . . ."

"Before you finish, John," Nathaniel quickly interrupted. By now they were almost facing one another. "Benjamin Blumenthal is probably going to become one of our outstanding doctors. I promise you that. Let's just call the whole faculty and have Benjamin here for a recitation on anatomy, on microscopes and what one sees through them. You want more?"

"Microscope?"

"Yes, Erstwhile, you've heard of them."

"Heard of them? Of course. But what good?"

By now Nathaniel was becoming calmer, smiling because of the fright and ignorance the word microscope caused.

"Listen to me, John. I don't want us to become enemies over this young man. Just do this." Then it hit Sterling. "And I never, NEVER want to hear one of our faculty speak the words, 'Jew boy.'"

"They may not, but they'll be thinking it. Moreover, Nathaniel Sterling. Our students. Have you thought about them? They'll be hard on him, perhaps won't accept him either. I won't. You hear me. I won't."

"I don't give a damn about what you won't. But you will accept him into this school, if I have to drag you and him into a room to face one another, the entire student body. You hear me," Nathaniel's voice rising unintentionally again.

Erstwhile smiled as though he had won, though more from nervousness. "Your face is red, Nathaniel. Settle down before I have to treat you."

"Look, John. Let's get this over with. I want that boy in the next entering class. I happen to believe you will end up liking him. Also, you treat him fairly, and I know you won't be disappointed. Your beliefs are your own. But when it comes to medicine, we either have open minds for learning, or we not only fail our patients, but society."

"All right. Let's not argue anymore. Tell him to see me. I'll say I didn't read his application closely enough. I was too busy." Erstwhile turned his back to Sterling, trying to hide his trembling, but wanting to insult Nathaniel. He slowly sat. "The Jew will be allowed in our school. However, Nathaniel Sterling, his failure will be his own and on your head."

"ENOUGH," Nathaniel shouted. You just accept him. You aren't the sole arbiter here. Remember that too."

Nathaniel started to leave. Before he did, however, Erstwhile told him, "You be the one to say he's accepted."

Turning back to Erstwhile, he told the man, "Some doctor you are. I will tell him when I get home. Before I leave, I have a question. You have heard of the Hippocratic Oath I presume, took it. Would you turn away a sick Jew, a dying Jew?" With that, Sterling left to see Benjamin and his family. He got into his carriage, driving the horses slowly, a smile suddenly appearing until there was a faint laugh as he thought of the confrontation.

At home, he breathed the fresh air from the Bay his house faced, gave the horse and carriage to his stable help, slowly entered the house. "Faith. Constance. Benjamin. I'm here." This was his family. Benjamin, he suddenly realized, was the son Faith and he had lost. God had given him to them in return for Faith's reproductive injuries preventing more children. Nathaniel's faith never failed him. Yet, he must accept that Benjamin was Jewish and his family Christian. He didn't care. "Faith, Constance, Ben," he called again. "I have news."

The three appeared. "What is the hollering for?" Faith wanted to know. "And what's the hurry?" She looked at Ben. She was aware how Nathaniel felt about him, but that he wanted to include him in a family discussion troubled her. Yes, she liked Benjamin, but she doubted she would ever be able ot think of him as anything else but a boy Nathaniel protected from hatred. Yes, she had to support her husband and she would. Yet, when she saw the way Constance looked at him or Benjamin at her daughter, it annoyed and troubled her.

"All of you. I suppose I shouldn't repeat all this, but I won. Benjamin, you are going to be admitted into The Portland School of Medical Instruction, starting in the fall. Now think of that."

Faith and Constance looked from Dr. Sterling to Benjamin. Constance, spoke first, looking with affection at Benjamin. "Ben, I knew my father would prepare you well. And just think, you'll be Dr. Benjamin Blumenthal. And you'll be able to practice in

Portland or anywhere you decide in the state." She was thinking of herself and tried to hide her blush, her heart beat having raced so that she felt it up to her neck. She put her hand to her breast, trying to tell her heart to settle, before her mother noticed her excitement. However, Faith always did see.

"Benjamin. I am very proud if you too," Faith interjected quietly, turning her gaze from her daughter."

Ben stood smiling and excited, his face also flushed. "How? What? I didn't think . . ."

"Stop, Ben. I had a little talk with Dr. Erstwhile. He told me he made a mistake. Read your application a bit too quickly."

Faith looked at her husband, hesitated but began, "Too quickly. What does that mean?" She knew Nathaniel was either lying or had it out with Dr. Erstwhile. As she thought of that, she feared perhaps that Nathaniel might have hurt himself.

"Now, mother, I think I know what's going on inside that beautiful head of yours. It's all arranged."

"That's a funny word."

"Funny, not at all. Ben has been accepted."

Constance reached out to Benjamin, not even caring what her parents thought. Ben, come here."

He shyly did. She kissed him on his cheek. "That's for the future doctor and the congratulations you deserve. Isn't that right, mother and dad?" Suddenly, realizing what she had done, she quickly stepped back, excusing herself. However, before she could leave the room, Faith stepped to Benjamin. "Come here, young man. And from me too." And she placed her hand behind his head, brought it down, also kissing him quickly on the cheek. She had to diminish her daughter's embarrassing, unladylike action. She would talk to her later. Then she thought, *I'll make certain she goes away to college, as much as I want her home where we can watch her, where she'll be a credit to her father and me. She's headstrong, always has been, but she must remember who she is and who she represents.*

"Well, Benjamin," turning to him, "you must be excited. We all are for you. I know you'll be a credit to Dr. Sterling and to your family. You're a lucky boy," as she turned to watch her daughter disappearing.

Nathaniel interrupted. "Ben, congratulations. If Mrs. Sterling doesn't mind, nor your family, I'd like to have you here for dinner with us tonight. How does that suit your plans?"

"Oh, Dr. Sterling what an honor. I doubt my family would mind." Benjamin was even more excited, hardly knew what to think. He had to tell his parents. "May I go home now and tell them?

"Of course," Sterling answered. "You come back about six, all right?"

"Yes, sir." He thought he should leave now but hesitated. "Dr. Sterling, thank you. I'll always be indebted to you. I'll also study hard and try to make you proud of me."

Nathaniel placed an arm about his shoulder. "I know that, Ben. I won't kiss you like the ladies in my family," and he laughed. "You know though how I feel. See you later then."

After he left, Faith wanted to know what happened. She also wanted him to talk to Constance, as would she. She was horrified when she thought about it. "Constance is too taken with that, that, J . . . boy." Faith liked him very much, often forgot his background and religion. Her daughter, however apparently had to be constantly reminded of the boy's, no, young man's heritage.

"Nathaniel, come. I want to know what happened and that you didn't hurt yourself for him."

"Faith, dear, I hurt no one but Erstwhile, not myself. I'm pleased with myself, if you want to know."

"Nathaniel. What happened?"

"I was furious, Faith, when Ben told me what happened. You know I left the house, perhaps not realizing I was in a rage."

She interrupted. "I knew that. It deeply disturbed me. And the way you took the carriage and rode off, Nathaniel."

"Yes, Faith. I know. I could have hurt the horses or myself or others. I couldn't help it. That rotten demagogue Erstwhile. He hates Jews. He rejected Ben because of his religion, nothing else. He also insulted me by doing so. He knows I took in Benjamin. What he did was unforgivable. I wasn't going to allow that to happen. He's the rat in his hole, thinks he can keep this profession only for those of whom he approves."

"Nathaniel. Stop. Listen to me. I know what you think of Benjamin and how. He's like a son to you," her voice dropping, saddening. "I wish I had had that boy." Her eyes teared. Trying to hold them back, she sobbed. "I feel like I failed, Nathaniel. Why? Oh tell me why?" She continued sobbing. "They left me with nothing." She stopped. "Oh, no. I have Constance. You." I should be thankful. But I hate it when I think like this, Nathaniel."

He hugged her to him, seeing Constance come to the door. He waved her away. "Faith, dearest, please. You did nothing wrong. It is a physical thing that happened. Please." She sobbed more, pulled from him, trying to catch her breath, wanting her crying to stop. She wiped at her eyes. "I . . . I'm sorry, dearest one. You've always been so good and kind, loving. But, I can't help it. Yes, I know. It's God's doing, but there are just times I can't accept it.

"And you know what else. I have come to like Benjamin. But Constance. She likes him too much. I see it in both of them."

"Don't you worry about our daughter. She's strong and sensible. We're going to be proud of her. I just know it. Yes, I've seen it too. But you know what, Faith? Whatever happens will. We may not like it, but . . ."

Before he could finish, she interrupted, "I want her to go to one of those colleges she talks about, as much as I don't want her to go so far. They need to be separated. Vassar, Lasalle.

Either one." She cried more. "I'm asking to lose her too. What's wrong with me?" She started crying again. "I'm ruining this for you, Nathaniel. Forgive me. Please."

"There's nothing to apologize for. I admit it. I do think of him as a son. He's worth it, Faith. I believe you may sometimes feel that way."

"Not quite," she answered through her tears. "Yes. I like him, but he can never take the place of what I lost. Oh, look at me. A crying, sobbing woman. You haven't told me the rest."

"Faith, I was so angry. I went into the office, still angry. I confronted Erstwhile, accused him of rejecting Benjamin because he's Jewish. That horrible man told me he should be a peddler like the rest of his people. I could hardly contain myself. I threatened him with going to the rest of the faculty. He finally backed down. So it went. And Benjamin is now accepted. I wasn't about to let that man get away with his prejudices."

He hesitated. "Yes, we were the same way, well almost. But we learned. We know. People are no different because of how they worship, and they are all welcome in our country. Isn't that what George Washington believed? Think of that, Faith."

That evening, Benjamin, dressed in his best suit, nervously pulled the ringer. Dr. Sterling met him.

"Welcome, young man. Tonight is a celebration. You're almost there. Mrs. Sterling has a wonderful meal for us."

They went to the parlor, Benjamin anxious to see Constance. She and her mother rose to greet him. He looked at Constance, and his heart beat faster as did hers as they looked in each other's eyes, seeing to each one's depths, she feeling a heat throughout her body, and he thrilled by a sensation he had never experienced before.

Before speaking to Mrs. Sterling as she greeted him, he held his breath momentarily to gain possession of himself. "I am pleased you could come, Benjamin. We'll just sit for a while until Lucy calls us.

48

She asked about his family, how they took the news. "Oh, Mrs. Sterling, they were so excited. They could not believe I would be a doctor . . . that is if I do well at school and pass my examinations. Truthfully, I'm terribly excited too."

"Well we're excited for you too. We know you'll do well," she hesitated, "like Dr. Sterling. I'm also pleased your family didn't mind that you left them to come her for dinner."

"Absolutely not. They thought you are such wonderful people to be treating me as you do." He looked one to the other of her family, stopping momentarily at Constance, quickly shifting his eyes to Mrs. Sterling once more.

Soon Lucy came and told them the meal was ready. The evening seemed to move quickly for Benjamin. They had chatted about Portland, about other places they had been in Maine, and eventually, Mrs. Sterling telling all, having definitely made up her mind without consulting her husband, that Constance would be going away to college. Constance's face reddened. However, she had just applied and started to say something, looking from her father to Benjamin, back to her father and then her mother. She decided to speak. "Mother, we aren't certain yet. What if they don't accept me?"

"Nonsense," Dr. Sterling interjected. Faith had surprised him, not being the obedient and often silent, accepting wife. He liked that in her, also that when they were alone in bed she enjoyed making love, rarely objecting and telling him what pleased her. Yet, he was a bit surprised by her certainty, even though they had talked about Constance leaving, he having had a time convincing her that Constance should have that college education. She and Benjamin would be separated, just as Faith wanted and was determined should happen.

The fates of the young man and woman had been decided.

* * *

49

Constance received acceptance at The Maine State Seminary in Lewiston, Maine, Mt. Holyoke Women's Seminary in South Hadley, Massachusetts and Vassar College in Poughkeepsie, New York. Faith asked her to accept Maine State Seminary that would become, unknown to them, Bates College in 1859, after she would begin her studies. It was far enough away from Benjamin, at least until vacations. It appealed to her parents because it would be closer for her father to accompany her during those breaks. Its Baptist Church affiliation bothered neither Faith nor Nathaniel, when she received her acceptance. What mattered was a student body enrolled regardless of race, creed, or sex. She would study foreign languages, ancient languages, mathematics, anatomy and physiology, and botany, this latter pleasing Constance as did the study of the human body. She agreed to her parents' wish.

Faith was somewhat concerned that during her holiday breaks she would probably come in contact with Benjamin. Well, that was the chance one takes in life, she thought. She would meet that problem when it arose, so she told herself.

Of course, Constance was excited but also apprehensive about leaving home. After the decision had been made, her mother, in private, took the lead telling her how to behave upon being away and how as a young woman she should conduct herself, assuring that she not bring any disgrace either to herself or her parents, especially at a school where there were also male students.

"Mother. You know I would never cause gossip or concern about myself. You do not have to worry. I have to admit, I wonder what it will be like being with other girls and boys I do not know. However, that will take care of itself. You know I've never been shy. I also am aware you are thinking of the men. I would never allow them to approach or touch me in any unwarranted or loose way." To herself she already, of course, thought about what it would be like to have a male kiss her, vow his love, and then do those shameful things men could if a woman allowed it, even what she thought, were she married, what it would be to lie with a man in bed and have him "make love" to her. After all, she always told herself, she was human and an attractive young woman. She practiced flirtation looks in her mirror, talked to herself as though she were in conversation with one of the other sex. Would it be like when she excited herself? Then she thought of Benjamin. Did she want him for a husband, would she? She did not care that he was Jewish. When it came down to it, she cared deeply for him and doubted there were males who could easily take his place. *Away. I'm going away. Look in that mirror, Constance. You are, well, beautiful. Yes. I am. Why shouldn't someone like Benjamin be attracted to me, want me for a wife? Look at you. You're blushing. You're thinking of him touching your breasts and in those unmentionable places. But oh, it was magnificent that time looking in the mirror at my naked body, how someday it would appear to a man when I'm married. Stop that, Constance Sterling. You're thinking wickedly. Mother had told me some things, like my monthly bleeding; but I could tell by her face it embarrassed her. Yes, my heart beat faster even as she talked, the tingle throughout me. And, oh yes, going beyond, knowing the pleasure my body can give me. Stop that. You are thinking wickedly. Well, now mother will speak again because I'm going away. Away! Think of that! I am a grown woman. Constance Sterling, you will manage yourself well.*

Dr. Sterling arranged his schedule for one of his medical friends to see his patients in case of an emergency and with the Portland School for Medical Instruction. He would accompany Constance, for it was improper for a female to travel alone. It also meant he would miss the first of Benjamin's days at the school. However, his daughter came first. He would assure himself that the dormitory for women would be a proper place for Constance to stay. If not he would find a good home and people where she could live. Certainly there must be someplace nearby the Seminary. They would travel by stage, the first of

Constance's exciting adventures.

Dr. Sterling took care of all arrangements while Faith shopped with Constance for her wardrobe. Knowing she would shock her mother, she asked if they could go also to Benjamin's father's store. Her mother assented without argument, shocking Constance. Faith wanted her to see what a Jewish storeowner was like, what Benjamin's parent was like. He probably had one of those foreign accents.

Uncomfortably they walked to the store location among people who looked mostly Jewish to Faith. Constance reached for her mother's faltering steps. "Oh, mother. I want to see his father and brothers."

"You stop that immediately. It's improper." She pulled away from Constance. "Don't you ever try to drag me like that again. Stop. You are going to ruin this wonderful shopping spree we've had together."

"I'm sorry, mother. I guess we shouldn't go in there. But it looks like a fine shop, and they don't have to know who we are."

Reluctantly, she surrendered, wanting Constance to have a good memory of this spending pleasure. Nathaniel told them to buy whatever they thought suited this new venture. Faith was also aware of her daughter's excitement, that it must overshadow Faith's apprehension.

They entered the shop. Faith hesitantly went toward Amos. "Young man, we are looking for fashionable women's clothes, some for daytime and perhaps something for evening. Can you help us?"

Amos had been watching them looking in the window, saw Constance pull her mother. The girl. She seemed to resemble the one Benjamin mentioned several times. That had to be his imagination.

"Well, young man," Faith impatiently asked again.

"Yes, we do. Come over here to the ladies section." It was

separated from the rest of the store with, of course, its own private fitting rooms. "My sister Arella will help you." Moreover, both Faith and Constance were impressed with the neatness and well-laid-out store, its fine merchandise, and the quiet.

Constance couldn't help herself, despite her mother's silence, looking critically at the dresses and accouterments. She admired Benjamin's sister's dress and her certainty and straight posture as she walked ahead, almost as tall as Constance. Further, watching her, she seemed so self-assured as she led them about the merchandise, speaking softly and with knowledge. It was, actually, unusual to see a female working in a store though she had heard of females working in family stores.

Constance spoke, "We know your brother Benjamin."

Arella looked at her, "How, are you . . ." she hesitated, "Dr. Sterling's daughter and wife?"

"Yes."

"Your father is a wonderful man, and a fine doctor. Benjamin hopes he'll only be half as knowledgeable a doctor."

It was then Constance noticed Arella's questioning blue eyes, their beauty, reminding her of Benjamin. Immediately she liked Arella and wanted to know her better. "Your brother is going to be a very good doctor. My father thinks highly of him."

Arella hesitated, but continued the conversation, noting Faith's watchfulness, yet neither girl uncertain if her nod was about the clothing or their friendly talk.

"Benjamin is very excited about going to the Medical Institute and was thrilled when your father took him under his wing. Perhaps . . ." She stopped, looking at Faith's sternness and then back to Constance, hazel and blue eyes appraising one another, one Jewish, the other Christian. However, taking in each other, knowing, feeling it, startlingly they told themselves they could and would be friends, perhaps confidantes. In the short time left for Constance before college, she would have to do something, probably secretive, to see Arella.

* * *

As the summer progressed, Benjamin began to study more of *Gray's Anatomy*, examined by Nathaniel who was somewhat astounded by Benjamin's memory. He decided that he would have Benjamin talk to one of his patients, a laborer, who worked on the railroad, introducing Benjamin as his apprentice. Benjamin would make a preliminary examination, listening to the man's ailment and then send him into Dr. Sterling's examining room where Ben would listen and watch Nathaniel at work. When Ian O'Neil entered, as planned, Benjamin took him from the waiting room where he asked and heard the man's ailment.

"Well, ah was a liftin' one of them rails wi' anotha' fella, and wrenched me arm."

Benjamin made certain his face was serious. "Well, I think you will have strained the muscles, but after the next patient we'll see Dr. Sterling. When they were in the examining room, Nathaniel had Ian lie on the table. He listened to Benjamin, then to Ian.

"Here, now let me see if you can lift your arm."

O'Neil strained. "It hurt me shoulder, doctor, to do that."

"All right, now let me see if you can bend it."

"That hurts terrible too."

"I'm going to use some hot compresses on these painful spots, then show you what I want you to do at home also. Watch me carefully. Are you married?"

"Oh sure."

"Then I want your wife to hold these to your painful areas. In three day come on back here so I can see how it's progressing. You'll have to miss a few days work, I'm afraid."

54

"Ah, that's bad. But we have a good foreman, another Irishman," and Ian smiled."

"Well, that's good. I'll give you a note for him. Now we understand what we're going to be doing together and at home."

"Ah do, doc."

After the man left, Nathaniel asked Benjamin if he got the idea of patient care and examination, despite this one being somewhat easy for a new student. Of course, now Ben knew just how his summer would go. Most of all, he not only looked forward to being somewhat active in a doctor's office, but he became more excited about his formal schooling.

In such manner the summer passed, but still better there were also days he saw Constance. They would walk together outside into the garden, she looking back to assure their privacy and escape from Faith's watchfulness.

Was she a sneak, she often asked herself? Was she so bad to be seeing Ben talking somewhat intimately and planning with him to meet Arella?

"I don't want to upset your family. Your father has been so good to me. But oh, Constance, being with you is so . . . ." He couldn't finish. He wanted to tell her he loved her. But what was love?

She smiled, felt the warmth of his nearness, reached to touch his hand. As he felt the sensation of her softness, he grasped her hand lightly. Wanting to pull her toward him. He saw the blush in her face.

"Ben, this isn't right. We shouldn't be together. But I want to be near you."

They continued, now twining their fingers through one another's. He felt himself tightening below his waist. "Constance, I don't want ever to lose you," and he did pull her closer, wanting her body touching his. She yielded, feeling the sensation of warmth throughout her body. Softly, almost in a whisper, finding it hard to speak, "I want us like this forever. You feel so good so close." Suddenly she felt the flush growing from her neck to her face, looked into his eyes searching hers. She pulled back. "No, Benjamin. This is wrong. But I like it. Why wrong?"

"Constance, it is wrong. We're different. Yet, would you promise me we can always be close like now. I will promise you. I'll always remember."

She began to turn from him, barely able to speak. "I, I pp . . . promise. I have to go in, Ben," as she slipped her hand slowly from his, the feel of his body still strong within her. It scared her.

"Constance, please let's not stop meeting. We'll just talk the way we had been doing."

Turning back to him, smiling, "Ben. We could never stop feeling the way we do." She surprised herself, blushing again for being so forward, unladylike. "Yes, I want us to be friends and walk together in the garden when we can, talking so softly as if they can hear us in my house."

"Thank you, Constance."

They had forgotten about Arella, how he was going to arrange for his sister to meet her. Then, just before reluctantly leaving her, Benjamin asked what they should do.

"I've decided I'm going to ask my mother if she can come to the house. She may consent. After all, we bought a dress and the things that go with it at your father's store. I believe my mother liked her.

"That's sounds like a good idea." He smiled. "But she can't take my place. All right?"

"Don't be silly. It's different with girls like us being together, Benjamin." she looked again straight into his eyes. "Do you see me?" She forced a laugh. His eyes fascinated her so.

He smiled. "I see you." As they looked at one another, seriously, lovingly, he became joyful, as did she, their eyes holding them together. Impulsively, she put her fingers to her lips, and placed them lightly on his. "That's a seal between us."

He did the same as he watched her walk slowly to her door.

That was the way their summer went until near the time she would be leaving for college. Meanwhile, she spoke to her mother about Arella.

"Mother, I've been thinking. I would like your permission to invite Arella to have tea with us, so we could get to know her better."

Stunned, Faith looked severely at Constance. "She's a shop girl. She's not in your class – ours. And . . ."

"Don't say it, mother. She's a Jew. You said that about Benjamin, but I know you like him now, even though you and father argued about him before he began studying here and being admitted to the medical college. Well, I thought Arella being his sister . . ."

Faith interrupted. "What's that to do with it?"

"I liked her, mother. I believe we could be friends."

Faith's raised her eyebrows, stared at Constance but didn't speak. Perhaps she was thinking, at least Constance thought. Before her mother said anything else, Constance arched her brows also."

"Mother, you look serious as though I were bringing a plague here. I liked her and want to be with her. Please, mother. Say yes. Besides, don't forget I'm going to the Seminary in the fall. Who knows how many different girls will be there?" She thought for a moment. "Perhaps some won't even be of our class. Perhaps even," and she somewhat stumbled, "some may be Jewish.

"You know, sometimes I don't understand why you feel so, well so strongly about Jews. Father is so welcoming." Suddenly she thought that perhaps she shouldn't have said that. But then, surprisingly, her mother smiled.

"Constance Sterling. You are just like your father." Faith

held back a bit of a laugh, thinking of Nathaniel. "All right, Constance. You may invite her."

The following day as Benjamin was leaving her father's office Constance stopped him, assuming her mother would know she was asking about Arella. It then occurred to Constance that a friendship with Arella would also be a cover for times that Benjamin and she would clandestinely meet in the garden. She could tell her mother, if she became suspicious, that she was asking about his sister.

She set a time within the next few days when Arella would visit. Constance could barely hide her excitement when Arella did come. Her brother Daniel walked with her and would return to accompany her home.

"Arella. I'm so happy you could come. Did you have any trouble with your parents?" Constance and she were watching one another's expression, the blue and hazel eyes telling one another of their pleasure. They had already known they would be close. Constance reached for her waist, placed a hand on her back, Arella copying the gesture as they walked to the house.

"Well," and she laughed, "You should have seen the looks on my mother and father's faces and heard the disbelief I would be going to a, well you may as well learn the word, *goyishe* girl's house . . ."

"Constance interrupted, "goy, goyishe," and they both laughed.

"There now you learned my original language. Goyishe, that's it. It is reference to a Christian. So can we make my parents keep quiet about our different religions? Good heavens, Benjamin is an apprentice under your father."

They smiled looking at one another.

"Well you tell your parents we're friends and to accept it. Oh, Arella, I'm so happy."

"So am I"

At that, both squeezed the other's back, sealing a lasting

bond.

Mrs. Sterling somewhat hesitatingly prepared tea and some small cakes for them. If this were to make her daughter happy, then she would relent. Perhaps it was time she started thinking like her husband and accept that Jews and Christians shared a moral and even a religious background.

She took the afternoon fare and set it on a table, watching them, the brightness in their eyes, the smiles. She felt the warmth, surprising herself, pleased Constance did have someone her age in whom she could confide, if she wished and have girl talk.

"Arella, how old are you?" Constance looked toward her bust, her waist, the lovely ballooned-sleeved dress. They were almost clothed alike, wearing their afternoon garments.

"I'm almost eighteen, twin of Ben, and not contemplating marriage. What about you?"

"Me too. That's why I haven't seen you before. You must be finished high school to be working in your father's store."

"Oh yes. I loved school, but everything ends. My mother has tried to pair me with a marriageable man. I haven't met one yet I think I could spend my life with."

Constance laughed. "That's why I haven't seen you in any of my classes. Anyhow, I have no desire to marry now either. I'm going to the seminary college in Lewiston in the fall. Have you ever thought of it?

"Oh, I yes. But my parents think women my age should marry, take care of the home, of course, and have babies. College. I do want to learn more. I love reading and languages."

"Why don't you persuade them to let you go with me? Just tell them you had this idea and see what happens."

Meanwhile they drank tea and nibbled at the cakes, looking at one another happily, smiling a lot. When Constance mentioned college, Arella in surprise hastily placed her fingers on her mouth.

"I think I envy you. But what about religion? Is it a religious school?"

"Oh no. They accept men and women regardless of religion. It was started by the Baptists, but no one need worry about that. My mother and father made certain. Oh, do try to persuade your parents."

"You don't know them. They are very strict. Don't get the wrong idea. I love them both, and," laughing, she continued, "I work my way around my father. Oh, and the store. I know he's becoming rich enough to send me and can get help. Anyhow, you know, I use my eyes and lashes, play nicely up to him. He loves us very much. Besides, you'll meet them. Also I will try to get them to let me apply and if admitted will go with you."

"You could travel with my father and me."

With time, Constance talked confidentially about Benjamin, how she truly liked him, often felt this thrill when he was near her, how strange it was. Then their talk would turn to female feelings, sensations, and anatomy. It was strange having someone to talk to so frankly.

Finally, after still urging Arella to convince her parents about college, one day, after having met her parents earlier and while they were at Arella's home, it happened.

"Constance. I applied. My parents, well somewhat reluctantly allowed it. I have to be accepted."

"You will be." Of course, she was happy, the two friends being ecstatic. Naturally, there was always an escort to one house or the other, either Daniel or even Benjamin. This drew Constance and him closer. Neither would ever tell his or her parents how they felt. Yet Faith worried when she heard that Arella applied to the Seminary. It was possible if she were accepted that although Constance and Benjamin would be separated for a good part of the year, talk between the two girls could come around to him.

Finally, while at the Sterling home, Arella, walking in

slowly, very ladylike, saying her hellos, burst when the girls were alone, "Constance. I'm going with you. They accepted me." The girls reached and held each other, dancing about the room. "Together, friends forever," they danced, their hooped skirts swirling, and sang, kissing one another on the cheek, their faces flushed with joy.

* * *

Fall, 1858, Benjamin had entered his first classroom lecture, Anatomy and Physiology. It would include lectures and recitation. The students started with the skeleton, learning the bone structure of man and woman, the differences between them. They were told at the end of class to read and be prepared for questions, each student perhaps being called upon.

What would follow this class would include among others, for example, Obstetrics, and Diseases of Women and Children, Materia Medica, Ausculation and Percussion, Theory and Practice, and Surgery. These plus other subjects excited the students but made them realize their studies would be demanding.

After their first class in anatomy, the instructor called upon students to answer questions about the structure of the male. A few of the men stumbled and received, "You had better study more young man or you won't last. In fact, look to your right and left. Got it? Now, by the end of the year one of you three will be missing." The instructor stood rigidly before them, a slight smile on his face.

A number of the students decided they would form study groups. They talked excitedly about how they would challenge one another. It never occurred to anyone to invite Benjamin. In fact, they shunned him, especially after one day the instructor called on him for recitation of the bodily structure of the female. His recitation was perfect, despite the doctor professor trying to confuse him by interruptions and further questions. Benjamin, overcoming his nervousness stood and spoke clearly without ever backing down, daring the doctor. It eventually occurred to his instructors and the students that Benjamin had a phenomenal memory.

He often felt lonely. The students, because of jealousy and what he heard walking behind a few, "That damn Yid. He's making all of us look bad." One of the students, looking suddenly behind him and seeing Benjamin, yelled, "Hey Jew Boy, can we borrow your brain? You trying to make all of us look like idiots?"

Benjamin stumbled as he walked, deciding what to answer. His voice rising in anger, answered, "Is that why you never invite me to be in one of your groups? You afraid of we Jews?"

Another student, his face reddened by shame of his friends, even himself, steadied his voice, "We, I don't hate you." He turned to the others. "All of you, shut up. Face it. We're jealous because he is apparently smarter than us. Why don't we act like adults and invite him into our group?"

Stunned, his friends began to walk away until they heard, "Wait a minute. Let's face this. We are prejudiced." He left the others and went to Benjamin who walked slowly so they would get far ahead of him.

"Benjamin," and he placed his arm about Benjamin's shoulder. "I want to apologize for them and me. There's no question we've been jealous of you. Most of us too have never been around Jews so it's, well, although not acceptable, we keep away from the Jewish part of Portland. You're our first experience. We have to learn not to be as bad as we seem. We're not the worst guys in the world, but we sure acted it. Please forgive me, us."

"Well, I thought I had gotten used to anti-Semitism. But, Jerome, you just don't." He then spoke more slowly, "Truthfully, I don't understand it. Here we are in Portland in the United States. We're supposed to all be united, you know, as the name if the country says. What have we done to any of you? You want me to cut out my brain, to talk with an accent? Well I can't do those things. I'm a human being. A good one, and I hate what I just heard and always will. You condemn me without knowing me? How can you? We're supposed to be the best, learning to help and cure people's ills. And what your friends said is not why we're studying medicine. It's an honorable and good way to help people, treat them all alike with compassion." his voice rising as he spoke faster. "You all have met Dr. Sterling. Well let me tell you something," looking Jerome in his eyes, and Jerome his, "You should learn from him about people and how to meet them with courtesy and understanding. That's all I'm asking." He felt tears coming and blinked, looking away, forcing them back, However Jerome noticed.

"Ben. Do you mind if I call you that?"

"Of course not."

"Ben, I'm apologizing as much as I can for them and me for our blindness and unwillingness to take people for what they are. Will you please accept this? I'm going to have a real talk with them. And I want you to join with us. We think we are learning together, but your brain is missing among us. We need you. O.K.?"

"Yes."

Jerome would follow through, but he could not help but watch Benjamin walking slowly away, his head bent but suddenly straightening and walking more quickly with a confidence that some of the others, if not all, would have to emulate in time. *They will have to accept me. They will, if I have to fight every one of them.*

* * *

63

Dr. Sterling went by coach to Lewiston accompanying Constance and Arella. They searched for a boarding house suitable for the young women and found one not far from the college. The woman, Mrs. Stedman, a widow, appeared to be a warm and affectionate person. Showing the girls the room they would have, the two were quite happy. It was large with two canopy beds, two small desks, a wallpaper design with delicate bouquets of pink and blue flowers tied with pink bows, a bay window overlooking the gardens. Mrs. Stedman, of course, served meals and told them she was quite strict about protecting her boarders. In her employ were two cleaning maids, as well as a cook whom she oversaw, perhaps a year or two older than Constance and Arella. Dr. Sterling paid for the year, having received Arella's rent from her father, then taking them to dinner at a restaurant recommended by Mrs. Stedman. The excitement of the day made it difficult for the girls to eat. They talked incessantly while Dr. Sterling merely listened, smiling, and enjoying their company. He would stay in a hotel that night, go to the college in the morning with the girls to make certain everything went well with the enrollment.

Leaving them, Constance noting her father's sadness, started crying, followed by Arella. They were also thinking back to Portland, Hannah being at the Sterlings, and leaving their mothers, the four tightly hugging each as though the mothers would never allow their daughters to go. They left to tears among the four women and difficult stifled sobs from the girls, partly from fear of their new environment and also the loss of their parents' warmth and endearment.

The loneliness, emphasized by nightfall, left the two in despair. They tried to cheer themselves by going through their clothing they had already hung in their individual wardrobes. They decided to dress in blue evening dresses, carefully helping each other with their pantaloons, slips, hoop and over slip, then the evening dress that bared their lower arms. Constance kept her hair as usual with ringlets on either side of her hair and a net holding her neck length chestnut hair in the back. Arella always kept her pomaded hair as usual, parted in the middle with a knot of hair on top and a net for the hair that fell in back. They admired one another, Constance with her hazel eyes and fair skin, Arella with her deep blue eyes and darker unblemished skin. Smiling at and admiring one another, they began to shed some of the loneliness, then went down to dinner.

Mrs. Stedman who had confronted such melancholy before, did her best to comfort her latest boarders, introducing them to the other young women who were also going to be their schoolmates. Suddenly during dinner a constant chatter occurred throughout the meal. Constance looked about, talked to one of the girls at the table, a lovely redhead with green eyes who when she smiled showed one dimple. She seemed rather sophisticated, drawing Constance to her. She gave Arella a slight pinch to get her to make friends and talk. The signal brought her to life and she chatted with someone sitting opposite her. It became obvious they were all appraising one another, who would be friendly, who appeared a bit falsely sophisticated, and who might they trust as genuine.

* * *

That Monday school began with an orientation and choices of courses. Both decided they would take the same courses except that Constance decided to study Latin while Arella chose Greek.

Meanwhile, after orientation and back in the Boarding House one of the young women discovered Arella was Jewish. She chose to go beyond her roommate and whisper to others that they had a Jew in their house. Some gasped and vowed they would never speak to her, raised eyebrows placing hands to their mouths in disbelief, wondering how Constance could live with her. Others merely shrugged and reminded the gossipers they were at a college that admitted all eligible students regardless of their religion. The redhead, Phoebe, Constance liked at the previous night's dinner, asked how it was being in the same room as Arella.

"Why do you ask?"

"I saw you both with that man."

"That man you mention is my father, Dr. Nathaniel Sterling who is also a professor at the Portland School for Medical Instruction," she answered coldly.

"Well, I didn't mean anything bad about him," she said, without telling Constance she was thinking perhaps he was some Jewish peddler of sorts. Thinking this, it had amazed Phoebe that Constance, who she was sure was Christian because of her fair skin, fine upturned nose, and dimpled chin, would come to school with them, and room with Arella. She underestimated Constance.

"You, Phoebe, are a bigot, a hateful person with whom I no longer care to be associated."

"Constance, how can you talk like that? I didn't mean anything. I was just curious."

"You are lying and I'm telling you and any of the others who think like you never to speak to or come near me. I thought you were such a nice person at dinner. I know now I was absolutely wrong." Constance, her face red with anger, her eyes bright with her fury, turned quickly and went back to her room.

The door opened quickly, banging against the wall. Startled, Arella, lying on her bed, felt her heart beat faster. She raised her head, seeing a red-faced Constance. Arella sat up quickly, feeling her heart beat, but now willing it to settle down.

"What is wrong? You look terrible and scared me the way you opened the door."

"I am absolutely furious with Phoebe. She is a terrible person. I hope there aren't many more like her living in this place. If there are we're moving." Suddenly she decided to talk to Mrs. Stedman. At the same time she started thinking of her relationship with Benjamin. . . *I hate it. I hate those dumb people and their hatred, the emptiness in my heart that he fills when we're together, the leap of my heart thinking of him or seeing him. That day I touched his cheek. I'm furious. Settle down before you start* . . . She felt her tears coming and wanted to hide them from Arella, but she couldn't stop them. Tears streamed along her cheeks. Suddenly she sobbed and cried earnestly.

"I can't help it, Arella. I . . ." her voice catching, the sobs louder. Her body shook with anger and helplessness, not knowing what to tell Arella. "I . . . I . . ." More crying, thinking of Arella and Benjamin. "Oh, damn." She had never sworn before. "Stop your crying, Constance," her voice almost hoarse. She turned her head, looking through her tears at Arella. "I want to tell you what happened, but then you'll be miserable. I'm going to talk to Mrs. Stedman." She tried to brush away the tears, wiped at her cheeks. "Arella. I hate this place. If Mrs. Stedman is like all the rest here I don't know what we'll do."

Arella realized what had happened. She went to Constance, sat on her bed, pulled her to herself, hugging her, moving her hands soothingly along Constance's back. She kept moving her hands along her friends back, feeling the shudders growing weaker.

"Constance," she whispered, "Please don't upset yourself because of me."

Constance, surprised, pulled away, staring at the girl she loved as she would a sister. "Because of you? No. It's because..." and she stopped.

"I know what happened. It's nothing new to me, my family, or any of us who are Jews. They hate us just because of our beliefs. Well, I think like Benjamin. The world got its religion from us. We're also a proud people, proud of our heritage." Her voice became louder, tinged with anger. "We know. Oh how we know. My mother and father fled Europe to come here and raise us in safety. They chose Portland because the people seemed to at least accept us as long as we almost kept to ourselves. That can't happen. This is America. We may be shunned, but we'll come and go as we please."

"You sound so brave, Arella."

"Brave," she laughed. "Oh, Constance," and she hugged her with tears streaming. "Constance, dear friend, I get awfully scared. Sometimes when I see a Christian and he looks at me, I think, 'Oh is he going to attack me?' Or the women. 'Is she going to scratch my eyes out?' Those people scare me. I can't help it. You think I don't know the Phoebes in this world? You think we all don't? Please, Constance. Look, if it will make things easier for you, I'll find another place to live. Or maybe, depending on what happens in school, I'll just go home."

"No," she shouted. "We're going to face this together. I'm going to Mrs. Stedman and tell her, ask her what she thinks."

"Is that such a good idea? What if she laughs at you, tells you, us, to leave. Where will we go?"

"Arella. My mind's made up. I'm not listening any longer to this, this hatred, this cheap, unwarranted criticism."

They pulled closer together, both crying. Arella's voice caught, as she started to speak, "I love you, Constance. I don't want you hurt because of me."

"I love you too. Don't you ever forget it. We're seeing this through together." Constance then pulled Arella's face to hers and kissed Arella's cheek, as did Arella to hers. "Come. We'll go to Mrs. Stedman right now."

Arella hesitated. "Are you sure we should do this?"

"I'm my father's daughter. I'm sure. You be too. We're in this together." Constance had no idea what this portended for her. She suddenly thought of Benjamin. *If this is love, then I love him. I'm going to fight for him too. Oh, my goodness. What would my parents think?* She shook herself, rose from the bed, her face tight with certainty. "Come. We're going right now. And if I see that Phoebe, I'll scratch her eyes out." She hesitated. "If you prefer, I'll go to Mrs. Stedman alone."

"It's my problem really. Yes, we'll go together."

"Let me talk. Agreed?

"Agreed."

They found Mrs. Stedman in her drawing room where she usually sat and either sewed or did her needlework when not ordering or talking to the cook and maids. She looked up, watching the girls, their faces, noticing some hesitation, but how lovely they looked in their day dresses, their hair neatly parted and tied.

"Is something troubling you?" she spoke, turning to Constance.

"Yes. There is."

"Is it something to do with your room, the food?" smiling as she spoke.

"No, ma'am. It's much more serious." Now Constance hesitated.

"Tell me. Something is bothering you." She looked from one to the other. "I can see it."

"It's about one of the girls and what she said. It was, it was just terrible. About Arella."

"Ah, yes. Tell me what happened," she spoke softly, reassuringly.

"This girl, and I think her friends, they hate Jews. They, oh she, told me so in the way she referred to Arella. It's horrible, and I think . . ." she stopped, thinking, worried.

"Go on. I'm listening."

"Phoebe." Constance stuttered, not meaning to mention the name. "Oh well. I used her name and didn't want to. Anyhow, she said bad things about Arella. I can't understand that. No. I do. However, Mrs. Stedman, if this is the way people think in this house, we'll have to get in touch with our parents and find someplace that will let us live together in peace."

"You are not going to leave. Don't you realize your father, Constance, spoke to me before he rented space here? I am truly put out by this. I'll call an assembly of the girls and have this out. Now you two settle down. I don't want any of my girls uncomfortable." She hesitated a moment, repeating, her voice somewhat angry, "We'll have this out."

Mrs. Stedman placed a note on the board she used to place notices or announcements. They were *all* to meet the next evening in the living room.

There was chatter and questions among the girls. "What's this all about? Did something happen? Oh, maybe she wants to tell us something about, oh who knows what?" They murmured, whispered, laughed. No one, however, guessed what was to occur. They did see that Constance and Arella were not among them, wondering. "I've got it. Those two don't seem to be the least concerned. Let's go ask them if they know something we don't."

"No!" Phoebe loudly exclaimed. "I know they had something to do with this. Leave them alone." Phoebe was rather frightened but said nothing to the others about what she suspected. She went to her room trembling, her heart beating faster. *Am I right? Why did I say anything to that rotten Constance? No. It has to be something else. Mrs. Stedman probably doesn't like Jews any more than I do. She took that Arella in for the money, getting back at those moneygrubbers.*

So the following evening after dinner, all gathered in the living room, either raising their hooped skirts showing their over petticoats so they could comfortably sit on the floor, others demurely sitting on the available seats showing their ankles and perhaps a touch of their knee length bloomers.

Mrs. Stedman kept them waiting. Her dramatic entrance, her face severe unlike her usual kindly smile, stopped the constant whispering and occasional giggle. Some looked at Arella and

Constance, turning quickly away in an attempt to hide their disapproval.

Mrs. Stedman began in a soft rising voice, showing her dissatisfaction with her house of girls. "I've called you for a serious purpose. You probably are all proud of yourselves for having been admitted to our newly named Bates College. Now let me tell you something in case you are unaware or have forgotten. You are among the small number of female students admitted along with the col . . . those of color, and different religions. This means you are supposed to learn to accept *everyone*. Something has come to my attention. That is, and I believe it is known among you, that someone or some have decided that you are superior to others. **You are not**. Look at yourselves. What do you see? Young women wearing fine clothing, clean, hair groomed, and aware of female hygiene." The girls gasped at this last. "Have I said something terrible? Yes, it is unladylike to call attention to our bodies. However, what I want you to never forget that under that clothing we are all very much alike. *Alike*. We talk about matters perhaps among ourselves. The point is, you ladies, is that aside from your minds you are like I, like all of you. Look at one another. Go ahead. Look. What do you see? Hairdos, complexion, dresses with sleeves that come to your elbows. All dressed in the same layers of clothing. Am I right? You know I am. Now, if I think you are young ladies, if I think you are somewhat exceptional because you are fortunate to be attending college, if I allowed you, yes allowed, forget the money, to live here, I did so because when I met you and your parents, I believed you would be people I can be proud of, just as your parents are of you. However, I am dismayed. I have heard, unfortunately, that some of you have decided you are superior, that you dislike having a girl or two among you you consider different. Now listen to me. You may never shed your prejudices, but one day you will study the great William Shakespeare who in a play wrote the lines, 'If you prick us, do we not bleed? If you tickle us do we laugh? If you poison us do we not die?'" As she spoke the word 'bleed,' there was a titter that continued from one of the girls who had watched a trail of blood from one of her housemates who had started her menstrual period. "Is there something wrong, something funny?" Mrs. Stedman's voice was angry while staring at the girl. She then turned back to the group, her voice harsh. "Isn't this all of us?" she continued, looking about the room. "You remember those lines. In fact, I'll post them on the bulletin board. Read them, think of what William Shakespeare wrote, and without tittering.

Then more softly, "Now, dear ones, let us be a family of friendship and love."

Time passed, the boarding house somewhat settled after Mrs. Stedman's talk. Some even read the board and those words, thinking about them, talking to themselves and realizing how perhaps evil their thinking had been. Some went purposely to Arella to ask her forgiveness for thinking of her as different, bad, apologizing, asking her to forget. Arella could not hold back her tears as she forgave them, wondering how sincere they were but accepting their apparent sincerity.

Classes began to keep all of them busy, some practicing their French to one another, some struggling over mathematics and being helped by roommates or who was excellent at the subject as were both Constance and Arella.

Constance caused a stir in her anatomy class that rippled among the males and females. The professor was hesitant about speaking of the reproductive systems, particularly the female, skipping it. Constance thought of what she had heard from her father about Elizabeth Blackwell, the first female American doctor. She had insisted that her professor in medical school teach about the female reproduction system while she was in the classroom.

"Professor, I must ask that you teach us both male and

female."

"Wha . . .What?" his voice loud, several snickers from the males.

"Yes, sir. I am not being a stubborn or disrespectful female. Dr. Elizabeth Blackwell had to ask her Anatomy professor to do so. He did."

"Well, I never . . ." the professor did not finish. "Yes, Miss Sterling, I understand. But Dr. Blackwell, and, of course, I've heard of her, was in medical school."

"I don't understand the difference, sir. We are studying the human body. I shan't be embarrassed. My father is a doctor. He talks to my mother and me."

"Is that the same, Miss Sterling?"

Some of the girls were aghast at her temerity, their faces turning red with their blushes, as their male classmates looked about the room. One male, however, spoke up. "Professor, I agree with Miss Sterling." He encouraged several of his male classmates. One of the women finally spoke.

"Professor, Constance, I mean Miss Sterling, is right. Please sir, treat us like human beings who are students and learners. Look about the room. We are all different in some way, male and female."

The professor was now embarrassed, his face red both with astonishment and some anger. Yet, he relented, for he had heard of Constance's father and some of his advancements in American medicine, his use of the microscope and the skeleton, his buying these from European doctors. "All right. Let us do what was done for Dr. Blackwell at Geneva Medical College. We'll vote. In favor raise your hands."

All hands rose, male and female.

However, from that day, Constance became known among professors as an eager, somewhat discomforting student. To her classmates she was a heroine, though some male students did wonder whether she was loose, one having the nerve to make advances that she repelled with fervor and fright.

Between classes he was foolish enough to reach for her bare forearm below the sleeve of her day dress and forcefully pull her to a darkened corner.

"You seem like a female I'd like to get to know a little more intimately," his voice low and gravelly.

"Let go of me." She tried to pull away.

He caught her sleeve, holding her. "Oh, come on now. You learned all those things in anatomy and before probably. Try me."

Without thinking, angered, eyes flaring, she slapped him hard. "How dare you touch me or any of the female students. Get away from me. If you ever, ever again assault me or talk to me the way you have, I'll see to it that you are expelled."

He rubbed his cheek while venting an embarrassing laugh, turning away, with attempted threatening. "We'll see. Who would believe you?" he continued in a growled false bravado.

"We'll see all right. Get out of my sight you evil, despicable nothing. And remember what I warned," her heart beating rapidly, her body trembling from the fearful encounter as she quickly walking away, purposely swirling her skirt with disgust.

"That's what it's like to be female, to be coveted for our, never mind the polite busts, but our breasts and the . . . the vagina between our, ohh forget limbs, thighs," she fiercely murmured as tears flowed along her cheeks that she tried to wipe away with her hands, not wanting anyone to see her, particularly Arella.

* * *

By the end of the first year Benjamin was at the top of his class. They had studied chemistry and physiology along with the anatomy. Benjamin enjoyed the laboratory experiments, mixing different chemicals to see the various colors of elements come into being. Yet, there were still students who were jealous and who condemned his Judaism, if not to his face then among themselves.   When he approached and they purposely whispered to one another, it scared him. He could see in their eyes the accusation of an undesirable. He could feel their hatred, perhaps because of his achievements in class, in tests, or in oral examinations.

However he did become more comfortable because of the study group Jerome promised would allow him to join. These students benefited from his presence and knowledge and began to esteem his friendship and help. They came to his defense and would argue loudly with those who refused to accept him.

The studies became more intense with surgery and obstetrics. By their second year they were able to observe their professors as they incised a patient's body, when they treated women or during the surgeries. By that time there was chloroform and ether, used to ease women's childbirth pains and to allow the surgeons to operate more at ease without a patient's screams. Of course, when it came to the women, the doctors would always ask if they minded young male students observing. Many objected from embarrassment, not wanting one of the most intimate moments in her life, including the exposure of her lower body to anyone other than to the doctor and accompanying midwife.

The first time Benjamin, and he imagined others of his group, witnessed the agony it was a terrifying shock. The screams with the increasing pain, and from some, "I wish I were dead," until the doctor used chloroform to ease the suffering. Then there was the sight of the blood, the expelled placenta causing some of the students' nausea. Yet, before, the child crying, brought smiles, extreme sadness if the baby was born dead while the mother profusely bled while the doctor worked often furiously to stop the hemorrhaging.

Thus passed the years of 1859 and '60. Then in their third year, 1861, came their pharmaceutical studies, for example, Materia Medica, Public Hygiene, and Medical Jurisprudence, including further surgery and obstetrics. They were in the hospital seeing patients, being asked questions afterward that they either mumbled unsurely or spoke with certainty. It was a hard but glorious year all of which would continue into their fourth year with more intensity.

Now they studied or would be at the Maine General Hospital, The Maine Eye and Ear Infirmary, the Portland Dispensary, and the United States Marine Hospital.

But before their last year, 1862, in 1861 while they happily did well or some may have failed, most began to feel more and more like physicians. Until . . . it happened.

Headline: SHOTS FIRED AT FORT SUMMTER – CIVIL WAR BREAKS OUT

It was unbelievable that the South would attack a United States Fort. A few of the students decided they would enlist at the end of the year to become assistant surgeons. Benjamin knew that he would go, but he would wait until he finished school and had his diploma. He wondered about Constance and Arella and what they must be thinking. By the next week he did receive a letter from Constance written for both her and his sister. When he saw the envelope, his heart beat faster seeing Constance's writing and thinking of her. He kissed the letter, holding it to his mouth, and then smelling for her scent. To his surprise Constance had placed a touch of her perfume. He pictured her, imagining them walking by and hiding from passersby and kissing. Finally he opened the envelope. A lock of chestnut hair fell into his hand. His heart beat against his chest. Trying to control its beating, he could see her and heard his own voice whispering, "She loves me. Oh, God, I love her, but no one must ever know." His parents and hers would be furious.

"My Dear Benjamin,

I am writing for Arella and me. She said I could. She sends her love and wants so much to see you, especially after the horrible news about the war. You still have a year to go, so please don't think of enlisting. I know you will want to. But please wait. Those horrible Southerners and their desire to kill to keep people slaves. I hate them. Oh, God will punish me for hating. How about if I just tell you I despise them? But PLEASE, Benjamin, don't leave medical school until you are finished. And just think. You'll be a DOCTOR. I'm excited, especially when I heard you're doing so well. My father has told me good things about you. I want to say more to you, dear (this is from Arella, and, well a bit from me) Benjamin. But I am a lady and won't do any such thing that makes me feel loose or you think that way, though I doubt you ever would.

"Arella has told me she wants to be a teacher. I believe with her education here she may be able to do so at the Portland High School where they teach boys and girls. Of course, they do not sit together but have separate classes. She hopes she will be able to help immigrants. That's a fine idea, if they'll employ her. Will they accept a Jewish teacher? But if she marries, she would have to be at her home, of course. Naturally that would solve the problem of being a Jew. She heard from Esther, and is all excited, that a fine young man has proposed. His name is Joshua, a fine name. Your mother and father ~~think~~ believe heaven sent him, that they will have grandchildren. His father also owns as store, but it is in a small town north of Portland. Isn't that wonderful? Imagine. Soon she'll be having children. That sounds exciting. Oh, goodness, you must know all of this. Why didn't you put it in your letters to Arella and me?

"I don't know what I'll do, but frankly I wish I could help during the war. Why don't they allow women to fight? Ben, I'm laughing. Can't you imagine me in a soldier's uniform and trying to carry one of those heavy guns? You know, of course, there were some women who fought in our Revolution. But I suppose, I'll find some young fellow who will propose and my mother will say, "It's time for you to marry. Young ladies of twenty are supposed to be starting families and taking care of their homes." ~~Ben, I'll marry a doctor. How about that?~~

There were then several scratches through that sentence. *Oh well,* she thought, *why not Ben? Wouldn't that throw Portland into uproar, let alone my parents? Oh heavens. Do I really love him? I don't know what love is. But thinking of him, that touch that time. My nipples hardened, and my heart was beating faster. That's terrible thinking like this. Stop it, Constance.*

"Anyhow, you'll be attending a wedding come summer. I wonder being a Christian, if I'll be invited. I don't think I should worry about that. I can imagine what's happening with all the excitement. Write me and tell me about it.

"Your (she hesitated, wanting to write "dear") friend always and love from Arella and your Constance."

* * *

Esther sat in the parlor with Joshua Myer, her mother watching them. She left for the kitchen to make tea, nodding her head at Asa to go and sit. "Oh, Mamma, I'll listen at the door and peek. I don't want to embarrass him."

"It's not right for them to be alone."

Suddenly they heard Esther softly calling, her voice nervous. "Mamma, Papa, Papa, please come here. Forget the tea for just now."

When they appeared, Joshua rose. "Mr. and Mrs. Blumenthal." They could tell by his voice what they were about to hear.

"I have told Esther that I would like to marry her. She said if you approve, then she will tell me, 'Yes.'"

Asa, turning his head slightly toward Hannah who nodded, walked to Joshua, a smile on his face. "Joshua, my boy, if Esther loves you then we will also. God Bless you both. Her mother and I will set the date after you have talked it over."

"Thank you so much Mr. and Mrs. Blumenthal. I am so thankful Esther has agreed to become my wife. My parents will be elated" He then turned to Esther, looking at her face, her blue eyes.

Esther's eyes teared as she tried to hold back a flood of happiness. Joshua smiled broadly, wanting to hold her, but, of course, realizing that just wasn't done. He looked at her, her blonde hair and blue eyes, as she wiped away her tears, shining with love of the tall, muscular, dark- eyed, and black haired man she would wed. Life could be so happy at times, and this was joy she had thought about but found it hard to imagine. Now she knew the reality. After Joshua left, she began to think about her new life and what it would involve, having a man with his hands about her body, and the idea of making babies. She hoped her mother would tell her something.

While thinking she was awakened from her reverie by her mother. "Oh, Gott tsu danken! *Meine scheine tochter!*"

Esther's father was also overjoyed. "Think. His father has a store also. You'll be able to live a good life with a man who loves you."

Later her mother told her they would have to talk.

"Esther, dear, as a woman you should realize that you will be in charge of the home and have to look after your children."

"I know that, mamma. I just wonder what it will be like when he wants to . . . well, you know," her face turning red.

"That's something you will learn. It may hurt you at first. But don't worry. It's like that. We all go through it. Just don't do anything when you have your time of month. All that's enough of that." Now they were both bright red, but her mother was bothered less by the blush than her daughter. This was something she expected. She then continued, "It's more important to run your home the best you can and to be a good mother. That shows your husband you love him. Joshua is such a mensch."

"Oh, he is mamma. I love him so." *I want to know how we'll make love. Will I like it? Will he like me that way? I'm so stupid about things. I'm going to look at myself more closely in the mirror tonight. My breasts are full, good to look at, I'm sure. Oh, don't worry about that. I have used my fingers down there some, but stopped. It's wrong. Anyhow, he'll teach me, and a good wife let's her husband lead, like mamma says. If I have things to say, though, I most certainly will, like mamma does to papa. I'll make him proud. I'm going to be Mrs. Myer!*

"Let's pay attention now to the arrangements," her mother interrupted, having sat watching her daughter's expressions, knowing what her daughter must be thinking, especially as the color in Esther's face changed to a bright blush.

* * *

The wedding would take place about the beginning of June, at their home, the final date depending on the Rabbi's schedule. They also wanted it to occur when it would not interfere with Benjamin's studies and when Arella would be home. They did invite Constance who unfortunately was away that week-end with her family.

The veiling of Esther occurred just prior to the marriage ceremony. Esther watched through her veil as the groom's father and hers escorted him to the bride. Joshua then raised Esther's veil assuring that he was marrying his bridal choice. When the rabbi blessed the marriage, Joshua stepped hard upon the glass, a happy grin on his face. All this followed by drinking of wine, carrying the bride on a chair raised high. Then the dancing of the Hora to singing and clapping, the bride with smiles, listening to laughter and praises echoing throughout the hall. Soon the guests watched as the bride and groom left in a carriage bought by Esther's father as part of bride's dowry. For the occasion, there was a driver in high hat, snapping lightly at the reins to start the horses on their journey to their own apartment of love and a new family.

The party continued. Arella introduced Benjamin to a girl, Rebecca Horowitz, rather new to the community. She was, he guessed, about five foot four, her waist slimmed by the corset beneath her formal dress, her bust pushed upward. She was attractive with brown hair and light grey eyes, a light olive skin. He was attracted to her smile, her soft lilting voice with a slight Eastern European accent. They talked at length, enjoying one another's company, telling stories about themselves.

"What will you be doing?" Benjamin asked, realizing it was a silly question.

"I'll be helping my mother with the chores, the cooking, and the younger children along with my sisters. I have one older sister and one younger than I, my two brothers the youngest."

"Oh. I have two brothers and two sisters, Esther, of course, and Arella, my twin. My brothers are going to enlist in the war, fighting to end slavery. I despise slavery for anyone. Isn't that what it was like living in Europe even though we had our own shtetls? So many of us were confined to them, no?

"As a young boy I heard my father tell of working so hard on the meager farm to assure we all had food. He was very weary when they left the old country. Now, look at him."

"Oh, I agree with you. Tell me about yourself." It pleased her to meet this tall, well-built, blue-eyed young man who spoke so well, aware, unlike her, he had been born in the United States. He made her feel desirable. Perhaps she would in time get to know him better.

"I'm a student at the Portland School for Medical Instruction. Next year, if all goes well, I'll become a doctor. A man, Dr. Sterling, was my preceptor and then helped me to be admitted to the school. He has a wonderful family that has been very kind to me."

Rebecca was further impressed. Of course she was. "Oh, that

must be exciting, but I suppose sometimes it must be sad too. You know, people terribly sick, some dying."

"Yes, that's true. But it's an exciting profession. I'm lucky to be in the school, being a Jew and all that."

"That must be discouraging." She wanted him to keep talking, wanted to impress him. She did not know what to do.

"You mean being Jewish. Well, it was really bad at the beginning. I hated it, the way some the guys talked about me, to me." He looked in her eyes, the sadness and compassion that were there when he told her."

"Oh, that had to be horrible. It sounds like Europe."

"Well, yes. But then there was Dr. Sterling. His kindness helped me think of my studies and that I would win over those hateful guys and their remarks."

"Is it still bad? I do hope it isn't." She kept his gaze, appearing to be self-assured, even if she was fairly new in Portland and felt out of place.

"No. I hardly ever think of it anymore. I'm getting along pretty well."

Rebecca had made her impression. He liked her. Then he thought of Constance, comparing the two young women. Constance was taller, and he imagined sexily slim, despite the dresses of the time. When she kissed his cheek, as she had that time, he remembered the shock he felt that she sent throughout him. He loved her eyes and the way they followed and searched him, their expression when he amused her. He also loved her chestnut hair and the ringlets that fell close to her ears. He was certain he loved her, but perhaps she was untouchable, he being a Jew. Rebecca was within reach. Religion was no problem, and he did like her appearance, her looks, also imagining what she must be like unclothed, convincing himself she'd be just as thrilling to look at as Constance.

She interrupted his thoughts. "You suddenly seem to have drifted miles away. Were you back in Europe?" and she laughed. *Oh, he couldn't have been,* her face turning red.

"Europe. I don't know except for medical discoveries. As I said," reminding her "I was born here," he finished in a proud voice.

"Oh, I think I may have angered you. I'm sorry. I was joking."

He knew he shouldn't answer as he was about to. "It's not a joking matter to me."

"I'm sorry if I hurt your feelings, Benjamin," her answer a subdued anger. "I must go to my parents and also see Arella. I'm pleased to have met you, sir."

"Wait. I was unjust. I had no intention of insulting you." He wanted to see her again.

"I'll accept your apology, but I think you are rude." She turned quickly, her skirt sweeping the floor in a show of anger. With her back to him, she began to smile. *I like him. I hope I didn't push too hard. I like the sound of his voice and certainly his looks and intelligence. Oh, what did I do?*

"Rebecca, please . . ."

She turned slowly, measuring.

"Yes," softly.

"Rebecca, I'd like to see you again, if you will allow it and your parents will permit."

She walked back and stood close, assuring that her skirt would touch his leg. "I'd like that, Benjamin," spoken softly and alluringly.

Constance, I'll still be faithful to . . . and his thoughts faltered. He spoke softly to himself, watching Rebecca as she walked away. "I do want Constance. The lock of hair she sent. I keep it with me all the time. But is it possible? We are perhaps more than friends and can continue to be. Could it be any more than that? Oh, Constance, you're so lovely, so warm. Can Rebecca take your place? At least there would be no talk or question of allowing a closer relationship. Oh, God, Why did you do this to me? Why am I a Jew? Why is Constance a Christian? And, God, did you send Rebecca to me? Are you playing with or testing me? Because I'm not even convinced that you are there."

* * *

Benjamin's brothers, Amos and Daniel, were now in the army, having volunteered soon after the war began. They were with the Army of the Potomac under General Irvin McDowell. They had already experienced battle at Bull Run. They wrote about the people who came out to view the battle, of the men who fell wounded or dead. Amos and Daniel refused to run at first. They tried to stay together throughout the firing of guns, the smoke, the hellish screaming, but then lost one another. Neither started to flee when the first of the Union men ran. They wanted to fight, to show their courage. They kneeled, fired, a Confederate soldier fell, grasping his stomach. They looked at one another, Daniel retching, watching the soldier falling. Was it his bullet? Who may have killed him? But killing to save others from the abomination of slavery was almost like a holy war to Amos, reminiscent of the hatred of the Jews in Europe. They were getting even, although they had been taught revenge is the Lord's. They tried to hold their ground, were soon separated in the smoke and the volleys, noise, the screaming, as Union and Confederates fell, grasping at their legs, arms, stomachs, others shot through the face or head dying immediately or soon after. The howling was more than they had ever heard or what they ever thought of as battle. Now they knew. They rose, jostled by men running past them, losing sight of one another. Daniel screamed for his brother. Had he been killed? He finally started running as the Confederates approached closer, kneeling, firing, or standing in a row and all firing together. General McDowell, called for all to fall back, his orders useless as hundreds ran past him and other officers, some men, including the wounded, being trampled. The rout was undeniable. Finally, as the troops wandered aimlessly back to Washington. Amos and Daniel found one another, falling into one another's arms, sobbing, as they happily hugged that neither had been shot, though saddened by the terrible defeat. They looked at one another through their tears to be certain they were fine, though Daniel did limp after stumbling over a dead soldier, twisted in his dying agony, his mouth open, his eyes clouded.

General McClellan, the man whose arrogance would never allow him to admit his fear of Lee, would soon relieve General McDowell.

When the 20th Maine Regiment was formed a year later, they were transferred to Col. Chamberlain's command to fill the regimental quota. Somehow, both had managed to avoid wounds that would probably have been fatal, either from the wound or some disease to which the army was susceptible from poor sanitation.

No one at home realized that many of the men were dying from dysentery or cholera epidemics that raged because of the poor sanitation.

At home, however, though horrified by the terrible Bull Run stampede, they all loved President Lincoln and often prayed not only for the success of the Union, that nothing bad happened to their soldier sons, but for being American citizens, and wanting the end of the evils of slavery. Although Benjamin and his sisters' mother thought that black people were inferior, his father did not. But they both hated slavery for anyone. The entire family was devoted to the Union cause, of course. By now, too, his father was making more money and was thinking of buying a house. It was almost an unbelievable possibility. It proved that God had been good to them after the terrors of Europe. How happy his parents were to leave behind such hatred. They had seen too much of their friends being beaten and even killed in the old country. Therefore, his father often reminded the family how fortunate they were, that they must never forget it. He usually said something like that when he thought of Abraham Lincoln's Farewell Address to the people of Springfield, repeating that he believed the President was also talking of them.

* * *

I was now in my final year at The Portland School for Medical Instruction. Because we were associated with Maine General Hospital, we were able to watch the surgeons, being taught by them as they performed their operations. Some used chloroform to ensure that patients did not suffer from too much pain. Most had learned that they should wash their hands or use carbolic to hopefully prevent disease. And, yes, I did listen to women as they suffered through the agonies of labor, washed our hands as a doctor watched and I grasped the child from the birth canal, handed to a midwife who washed the crying baby and then handed it to the mother, smiling weakly at her new son or daughter. One of my most thrilling yet horrifying moments was when I delivered twins.

We also helped when children came with perhaps broken bones or deep cuts. It was terrible, that day, one came with her mother, having picked up a kitchen knife and cut herself. The doctor watched as I stopped the bleeding with a clean bandage pressed to the wound. Some days later they returned, the hand and wrist swelling. "Why?" I asked. The doctor looked at me, shaking his head. Obviously, the wound had become infected. There was little he could do. He tried carbolic, then sent them home. Apparently the swelling came down a bit, and the infection has not progressed more. The doctor again used carbolic, but I know he doubted it would stop what was happening to the girl. She might lose her arm, and, if fortunate, she would live afterwards.

"What," I thought was the good. If she lived and grew to a young woman, who would want her? Of what use would she be to a home she could not manage as women were supposed to?"

Perhaps the saddest moments were when we listened to a chest and realized after observing a patient for a while, that the person was suffering from tuberculosis and would eventually be placed in an isolation ward but never recover.

I could tell more stories, some ending happily others ending, obviously, unhappily.

One day, although it wasn't the only time, of course, I thought of Constance and how badly I wanted to see her. I imagined kissing her, feeling the warmth of her lips, telling her I loved her. I did. How could this be? It was against everything she and I had been taught, her religion, mine. At the moment I didn't care. I would defy my parents, and she her mother and father. My eyes teared, knowing the impossibility. I cursed the sadness, all religions. Suddenly I realized there was Rebecca, lovely Rebecca, I like her a lot. I would see her again.

It was a Saturday. I ignored my studies and went to the home-synagogue hoping she would be there. Of course, the men and women sat apart in adjoining rooms, but I looked for her, saw her with her mother. I never heard the service, mouthed the prayers, pretending. When noon came, and the congregation, such as it was, gathered in the dining area, I excused myself from my parents, Esther and Joshua, his folks and walked toward Rebecca. She saw me, followed me, smiling, her grey eyes alight as I came closer. She turned to her parents, whispering something to them. They turned, her father tipping his head toward me, telling me to approach.

"Momma, Papa, this is almost," she faintly laughed, "Dr. Benjamin Blumenthal. We met at his sister's wedding."

"How do you do, Mr. Blumenthal." He introduced me to Rebecca's mother.

"If you don't mind, sir, I would like to talk to Rebecca." I looked at her, she smiled again, urging me on, I imagined. I liked her hair and those grey eyes, her body.

"Of course. You two young people know one another, so you have my permission."

"I'm pleased to see you, Rebecca." I laughed.

"Am I funny, Benjamin?"

"Absolutely not. You're just so attractive."

"Oh, heavens." She blushed, seemed to choke out, "You're serious. Then why did you laugh?"

"I hardly ever come to the home synagogues." I called them that because we had services in homes because there was no synagogue building as yet. Anyhow I felt my face turning red and tried to make my face very serious, as if I were examining a patient. Well, she certainly was no patient. She was that lovely young woman I had hopefully come to see. And here she was. "I was hoping you would be here."

"I'm here. I come every Sabbath morning with my parents and family. Are you usually too busy to attend but somehow got time today?"

"Sometimes I'm at the hospital, others studying, the work is so intensive." I didn't tell her, of course, about my attitude toward religion.

"Come to the table, and we can get a pastry. I don't want to ruin my lunch at home."

I followed her, watching her back, the straightness and confidence with which she walked. I couldn't help myself, although I didn't want anyone in the congregation think I was being obvious. How foolish of me. Why not watch. She was, well, I want to say enchanting; but could it be that both Rebecca and Constance were. Why not? "No," I told myself. "Either you do love Constance or you'll be hurting her. That's not so. I've never declared myself to any girl. But the way she kissed my cheek that day at her home and the feeling I had throughout me. It was just congratulatory, or was it? I wonder what it would be like to kiss her on her mouth. However, I still have not declared myself, and you can think of all kinds of happenings that have thrilled you or would in your imagination; yet, I doubt Constance would ever be mine. Rebecca is Jewish. Come on now, Benjamin. Start thinking of what the Christians think of the Jews. Good heavens. You're thinking like this is the era of the Crusades. Oh, Constance, how I wish . . . what, that she was Rebecca. That's stupid. I'm going to see Rebecca when I can. I have to think about my future and the kind of wife a doctor should have."

I spent the rest of the evening concentrating on my studies, particularly microscopy, because Dr. Sterling had introduced us to it. Also, I had to think about tomorrow, because I was to be on duty at the hospital Sunday. Patients are sick at all times, and weekends made no difference any more than did religion. I'm laughing. I read about George Washington speaking to the Newport, Rhode Island rabbi and telling him that our country accepts all religions, Christians, Jews, and Moslems. So what does that have to do with today, right this minute? My mind's made up. I'm definitely going to call on Rebecca."

On a Sunday, two weeks later, I walked to the Horowitz's. I was nervous when I turned the bell key. Mrs. Horowitz answered. "Well, hello, ah, Benjamin, as I remember." She tried to suppress her smile, knowing, of course, why I was there.

"Hello, Mrs. Horowitz. I am wondering if Rebecca is home and I might say hello to her."

"Yes, she is. Come in and I'll get her. She happens to be dressed for company. You can say hello to Mr. Horowitz first while I get Rebecca. Come to the parlor." She led me to her husband. "Papa. Mr. . . . . Mr."

"It's Blumenthal, Mrs. Horowitz." Her face appeared to turn red a little. "Please. Do not be embarrassed about my last name. I haven't seen you since the synagogue, and there's no reason to remember me."

"Oh yes," she recovered and became more at ease, still smiling. "He's come to see our Rebecca. I'll go call her."

It was a large apartment it seemed. The furniture was very attractive. Mr. Horowitz was smoking a cigar and placed it in an ash tray. "Well, young man. You are the one who is studying to be a doctor, no?"

"Yes, sir. You recall correctly. We didn't get much time to talk. I'm surprised you remember."

"And why not? You made such a good impression on me."

Now I began to blush as my nervousness faded a bit. After all, he knew what I was studying, and I was very proud that medicine was my field. That should help me with Rebecca's parents. I did wonder where her sisters and brothers were, but then I heard giggling, saw shadows. It had to be her sisters. Suddenly that stopped. I saw a peevish expression on Mr. Horowitz's face and heard the softened voice of his wife, shooing them away. I also heard Rebecca angrily tell her sisters to "Get out." Soon, she came in, smoothing her hooped skirt. She was attractive. She wore her hair something like Constance's with the ringlets trailing just to her ears.

"Papa, mamma told me you have talked to Benjamin. Would it be all right if we talked alone for a bit? I thought I'd make some tea in a while."

Mr. Horowitz smiled slightly and excused himself.

"It's so nice of you to visit, Benjamin. What has been happening in your world?"

"I want to know about yours first. You have heard enough from me, or at least something. Like, are you attending the high school?"

"Yes, I am in my third year at Portland High School."

She was apparently catching up and improving her English. She seemed a little older. However, it was understandable she would have much to learn about the world and her home in the United States.

"I have made friends with some of the girls, that is, the Jewish girls. Usually the Christian girls seem to avoid us, but not all. Some are curious as to what we are like, whether we're human beings and not from the moon." She laughed. "People are so funny. Of course, I have heard some comments that hurt."

I didn't know until later that one day she came home crying and told her parents she didn't want to go back to *that* school, that a few of the girls made sad and terrible remarks about her and another girl. However, her parents rightly told her to be proud of who she was and stand up to prejudice or anything that hurt her. She did as they said and seemed to me to be proud of herself, a strong person who could do what is expected of women.

"That happened to me at the Medical Institute. You learn to ignore that ignorance. That's what you have to do to succeed."

"You seem so sure of yourself." She thought, I suppose, that she had to flatter me.

"I like who I am. And when I finish, I'm sure I'll volunteer for the service in this horrible war. I'll join my brothers that way, even if we're not in the same place. I'll become an assistant surgeon, hopefully."

"That sounds very admirable. The war is awful, isn't it? To think that black people have to be slaves and we have a war because of that. I don't know too much about it, but I do read the papers." She stopped, looked at me, and smiled. "I guess you would want a wife who . . . oh, forget that." She blushed.

"No. Tell me what you were going to say."

Before she could answer, her mother came in and asked if we would want some tea. Rebecca rose and told her mother she would take care of that. She left the room quickly.

I like him and have to show him I would make a good wife, that I can take care of a house. Imagine, having children with someone like him. I am good looking, and I could make a doctor proud of me. I'd learn how to be with people he must know or will. But he's going to go in the army. Well, there's plenty of time to impress him. I'll practice more with my smiles and use of my eyes and all that. Oh, my face feels like it's burning. Rebecca you were mean to him at his sister's wedding; you better make up for that. He's here, isn't he? He must like me.

After a little time, she returned holding a tray and smiling. I liked that smile, the way her face brightened, the way she looked at me with those beautiful eyes and long lashes. I do like her. She would make me a good wife, perhaps not as educated as I'd want. Am I becoming a snob? To be honest, I'm comparing her to Constance. Is Constance beyond me? I always carry her lock of hair, look at it often, stroking it lightly, even speaking to myself as though I were addressing Constance. This isn't fair to Rebecca. I'm here, aren't I to get to know her, to find out if she is, well, suitable as a wife? I am really torn, perhaps unfair to both young women. They are young women and of marriageable age. Who am I kidding? I'm not ready for marriage. And with the war, who can think of that now? I can have good times with her, walking, laughing together. See the way she's observing me with those eyes. They're mesmerizing.

"Here we are, Benjamin. Would you like a cupcake? I made them," and she smiled. "While you decide, I'll pour your tea while it's hot. Then we can talk, not that I can't while doing this. I presume you like tea. Name me a Jew that doesn't. It reminds me of my grandfather. He was a fine, learned man," Tears began to form in her eyes.

"You must have loved him very much."

"I did," as she took her hanky and wiped at her eyes. "Forgive me. He was so kind to me, didn't treat me like a lowly female. Oh, you know what I mean. We women are supposed to know our place." Her eyes glared. "I despise that, like we're only good for the kitchen, cleaning the house, and having babies. Oh, don't get me wrong."

I started to laugh.

"Benjamin Blumenthal. Are you laughing at me?"

"Of course not. I think I can imagine how you feel, even though I'm a man. But I would like a wife who could run a home well."

"See. There you go. Just like a man. You are making fun of me. Well let me tell you something you better know right now. I speak my mind. I have opinions."

"Whoa, woman," and I smiled. "I'm not making fun of you. I like a young woman who knows her mind, who has ideas of her own and doesn't mind saying so."

"You're not making fun of me or saying that to make me feel good."

"Rebecca. I do believe you have a temper."

"And that's not ladylike either?" She seemed to be getting angry. You can see that in her eyes that flash. Her face was a little red. I began to wonder how I would like that. Well, she's a human. She has a right to her opinions.

"You're forgetting we were talking about your grandfather."

She settled and smiled more, her full lips turning upward. The redness of them. She's looking at me as though performing an examination. What a doctor she would make.

"By the way, the cupcakes are delicious. You are probably an excellent cook."

"My mother teaches me and my sisters. Anyhow, my grandfather. He used to pick me up, nuzzle me, speak as if I was a grown-up. Of course, he was fooling with me. That's when I was a little older. When we were bigger, of course, he rarely touched us being that we are girls. Oh, the stories he would tell us from the Bible and about people he had met. I forgot to tell you. He was a rabbi, so learned. He could often make us laugh. But, I have to admit, when we got still older and, well, began to look, oh you know." She blushed again.

"Yes, Rebecca, I know," and laughed. "Just look at you now. A young woman. I like you this way."

She smiled, then laughed a bit. "Why Benjamin, I believe you are complimenting me."

I grew serious, watching her eyes. We were sensing one another. "I guess I am. And why not?

"Have I stayed too long? Your parents will be angry."

"No they won't. They . . . they do . . . set limits for gentlemen callers. But I know they like you. That reminds me. You haven't met my sisters and brothers. Some other time."

The way a female tells you she wants to see you again.

"I think I had better leave now. Thank you for everything. I enjoyed visiting with you, Rebecca."

"Me too, Benjamin," *speaking my name softly, thrilling me.*

"Rebecca." How I enjoy saying that name, almost like poetry.

"Yes."

"I'd like to visit with you again. Perhaps your parents would allow us to take a walk."

"I'd like that, Benjamin. Before you leave, I'll get my parents."

They came in to say goodbye. Mrs. Horowitz glanced at her daughter as if receiving a signal. "Do come again, Benjamin when you have time from your studies."

"Thank you."

"Mr. Horowitz shook my hand, glanced at Rebecca, "See Benjamin to the door, dear."

"Of course, father," she spoke as though what did he expect her to do?

I walked to my house a smile on my face, telling myself, "She's all that I expected. I like the way she speaks up. I do want to see her again. Oh God, what about Constance? Why don't you give her to me? Why do you cause me such confusion? Constance. Rebecca. I touched my breast where I kept her lock of hair. I started talking to myself. "Constance. You'll forgive me, please. I know your parents would never allow us to be together . . . to marry. You understand. If I wanted to marry, I would choose Rebecca. Why is life so complicated? Why are there Christians and Jews? Why are they so different? Be honest, Benjamin. You, yes you do, admit it, you love Constance. You're a lie to Rebecca. But if I get to know her better, how do I know? Be honest, Ben, no matter what you do. Anyhow, you're in no way ready to marry. School. The army. The army. This horrible, hateful war. All those men wounded and being killed and how helpful can doctors truly be? I hope I can be like Dr. Sterling and learn new methods so I'll make a good surgeon that the army, my family, Constance, and, yes, you too Rebecca, can be proud."

When I got home, of course my mother and Arella wanted to know how I enjoyed myself. Later, after supper, Arella, came to my room.

"Ben. I hope I'm not disturbing you."

"No, Arella. I am studying, but it's O.K."

"Do you like Rebecca?"

"Yes. She's a fine young woman. Maybe not as wonderful as you," and I laughed.

"Keep quiet," she laughed.

"Come sit beside me on my bed. We can talk." I always like talking to Arella. She was so sensible and intelligent and with a marvelous sense of humor.

"O.K.,' and she dug her elbow into my side. What's the diagnosis, doctor?"

"You mean did I find her sick?"

"Lunatic." She then whispered, although there was no one to hear us. "You like her. But I know something that I doubt mamma and papa don't."

"And what's that?" Suddenly she had a wicked smile. Watching her, I loved her very much, would do anything for her. I started laughing. "Well, what?"

"I saw Constance put that lock of hair in my letter, Ben. I

watched her cut it."

My heart skipped a few beats, came faster.

"You're blushing, brother," and she leaned closer and kissed my cheek. "You two care very much for one another. So don't try to deny it. I wish you could be together. She asked me if I thought it was bad of her to send you that lock. I told her it wasn't. I also promised I would never tell anyone. I love her, Ben, like she were also my sister. We swore to each other we would always be like that. It's sad she never had any brothers or sisters. She told me what happened to her mother after Constance was born. And that's none of your business. Ben, what we women have to suffer. Will you be there to deliver my babies and make sure I'm safe?"

"Arella, dear, you know that without asking. Except, doctors don't take care of their own families. But if you wanted me there, I'd be, if it wouldn't embarrass you."

"That's not what I want to talk about. Constance *is* my sister and, hopefully, always will be. Hey, Ben, your face is turning red. Are you afraid of what I'm going to say, or just anxious to hear?"

"Anxious."

"You are well aware of what she thinks of you. You should by now. I shouldn't tell you this, but we talked about you a lot. I do love her. She's so honest, so sure of herself. Do you love her?"

I was stunned. "Arella!"

"Don't Arella me! I'm your sister, and she was my roommate. You can tell me to mind my own business," she laughed, "but don't."

"Who are you? The matchmaker? Making trouble in the family?"

Again she elbowed me.

"Arella. I think I loved her from the first time I saw her. But what's the use? It will never be."

Arella's eyes teared. "Benjamin," and she buried her head against my shoulder. "Benjamin," and she sobbed, and spoke, her voice shaky from the crying. "I so wish . . . yes, I do. I so wish you two could be together always. And it isn't possible. It just isn't. And it's so unfair. I don't want you to hurt Rebecca or Constance. Oh, what the hell. I hate this damn life and its rules." And she cried more, sobbed loudly, her head still in my shoulder, at least muffling her sounds from our parents. I lifted her head so we looked at one another, she through her tears, her body shaking from crying, the sadness.

"I never knew young women of quality swear like that, Arella."

"Well, they d . . .doo. You should hear the y . . .young l . . . ladies at Mrs. Stedman's. Oh, damn. There! Double damn. You two belong together. You know it and I do. But this whole rotten world says, "Absolutely NO."

"Listen to me." I lifted her head so she could see me, and I wiped at her tears. "You're going to have papa and mamma wondering why your eyes are swollen from tears."

"Oh," and she looked straight at me, "Am I mess? Forget it. Look at you and the sadness I see. What were you going to say anyhow?"

I laughed a little and then became serious. "I started to tell you, I'll have to face life, as will you and what it hands us. Think, though, you're going to finish college this year with Constance, just as I'm getting done and will be a doctor. And you're younger than I by a few minutes. We have our lives ahead of us. You'll hopefully get to teach, and also I bet there's going to be a good man to want you in marriage. Think of that, my dear Arella."

She smiled and wiped at her eyes and cheeks. "You think about it. Having babies and all that suffering through childbirth that I've heard about. Look at what happened to Constance's mother. That's fun? That's life? Oh, you're being dumb and trying to avoid what we've been talking about."

"I admit it. What's to admit? You already know about Constance and me, how we feel about each other. Oh why drag it on? It's a fact, Arella. I do love her. Who knows what will happen after I go to the army and will be away and perhaps for a long time. Maybe she'll find someone and marry. That will end it," my voice saddening thinking of some other man wedding her, holding that curving, shapely body I imagined making love to. The thought of it grabbed my heart.

Our mother called to us to supper.

"We have to quit this, Arella. Let's just not talk about it anymore. It hurts both of us."

"All right. Do I look terrible?"

"No, you're my beautiful sister."

She smiled, rose and smoothed her dress about her hoop, straightened her hair net, her ringlets, and we went downstairs to eat.

Chapter Three

Joy and Incredulity
Hell War

Graduation from Bates College occurred before Constance seriously thought about The Portland School of Medical Instruction or some other medical college. So it was that the Blumenthals and Sterlings traveled together to watch their daughters receive their degrees. They had met when Nathaniel convinced Faith they should get to know Benjamin's parents.

"Why?" Faith asked. "We have nothing in common with, with *them*."

"Faith, try to get over that? You came to like Benjamin. Now don't deny it."

"No, I won't. But I have worried about Constance and him. Haven't you noticed when they've been together how they look at one another?"

"You have a magnificent imagination. And just what do you suppose is going to happen? They like one another, and I'm glad. But I also know nothing will ever go beyond that."

"You're a fool, Nathaniel, but I love you. So we'll invite them."

It was a modest afternoon tea, the conversation stilted. But they managed their way through. And now they travelled together, chatting like old friends, happily anticipating the coming event and feeling sudden warmth between the couples, despite the gossip against Faith and Nathaniel for befriending Jews. The city already knew of his confrontation over Benjamin and getting him admitted to school.

Well, Constance was the valedictorian, chosen over the males to the class's disbelief. She was first in her class, followed by a young man who had continually annoyed her, distastefully asking to be alone with her. Catching her alone while waiting for Arella to walk back to Mrs. Stedman's, he grasped her forearm below her daytime sleeve, trying to get her attention. She stiffened, instantly pulled away, losing her temper. "Don't you ever, ever touch me or come near me. I loathe you. Gentleman." she hissed sarcastically, angrily.

As he watched her reach the podium, he mocked her loudly enough within professors' hearing, and probably hers. Arella who was sitting next to him shoved her elbow hard against his ribs, the audience nearby hearing a fairly loud, "Ouch."

It was a happy day. The females had outdone their classmates. Constance and Arella, third in the class, revealed to stunned males that females not only had intelligence but also self-assurance.

They all happily went to dinner together, a meal at which the parents toasted to the girls. Dressed in their evening best gowns they suddenly saddened their parents, despite their female appeal and accomplishment. They would be finding husbands soon and raising their own families.

However, when the Sterlings eventually arrived home, Constance stunned them. Here it was 1862, with bloody battles occurring after the Bull Run disasters. The Peninsular Campaign under General McClellan was a Union disaster, a result of McClellan's indecision and fear of Johnston's army, then Lee's after Johnston's wound. The lists of Union soldiers wounded or dead were discomforting. Thus Constance had decided she had to help.

Elizabeth Blackwell, the first American female to become a physician, helped form the Central Association for Relief and the U.S. Sanitary Commission. Through the Central Association she began to help train women as nurses, there being no formal nurses training at that time.

Constance, decided she would go to New York for training so she could help with the war effort, wishing also that she would be with Benjamin. She was unaware that he had been seeing Rebecca, Arella never having mentioned it, thinking it was a passing fancy.

"Mother, I must talk to you and father," she anxiously told her several days after arriving home, the flush of accomplishment still with her and her parents.

"What is it?" Faith asked.

"I want to go to New York and meet Dr. Elizabeth Blackwell. She is training women to become nurses to help in the war effort. I want to be part of it."

Faith's face turned red with not only surprise but anger. "You what? Because you did so well in college, now you think you can be independent. Young women marry and keep their homes, have children. Constance, with your education think of what you can do for your children as they grow up."

"Mother," in exasperation, "I know all that. But think of all those poor boys fighting and the help they need. We have to think about our men and country."

"I'm going to see if your father is with a patient. Let him talk to you. You obviously don't want to listen to your mother, a woman who knows a woman's place. That college has, has, I don't know, given you such big ideas about yourself."

"That's not so, mother. Please try to understand," tears forming in Constance's eyes.

"Don't use crying with me, Constance Sterling. I'm going to get your father. Now excuse me." She walked swiftly toward Nathaniel's office, her back straight, her hoop skirt swirling, as she hit it with her hand, trying to stop her own tears. *Doesn't Constance have a right to decide what she will do and be? But she would make such a good mother. Listen to yourself. The thought of her going through what I did. How awful. After all these years, I still can see that day, how I felt holding my dear daughter. Look what she's*

101

done.

She left a note for Nathaniel and asked that he come as soon as he saw his last patient, that they had to have a family discussion.

"Is something wrong?" he asked concerned.

"Come to the drawing room." She called to Lucy and told her to get Constance."

"What now, Faith?"

"Ask your daughter."

"Constance. What did you do to upset your mother?" His face was serious but inside he was amused.

"I told her of my plans."

"And, pray tell, what are they?"

"I have decided to go to New York to Dr. Elizabeth Blackwell and be trained as a nurse who can serve our wounded and helpless servicemen." She also decided to tell them, knowing she could be further upsetting her parents. Perhaps not her father. "I want to wait until Benjamin's graduation and see him become a doctor."

"What has that to do with you?" her mother demanded.

"He's a friend and father's protégé, isn't he father?"

"Yes. Faith, I don't see the harm in that. Of course that's one thing. But New York, a nurse?"

"You don't? That she has set her sights on a Jew?"

"Come now, Faith. They've been friends for some time. But now you tell me what's gotten into you, Constance?" a question asked with admiration for his daughter.

"Would someone tell me what's going on here? Is there some kind of conspiracy between you two?"

"No, Faith. This is the first I've heard this. You do know, Constance," he continued seriously, "good women don't travel alone. Further, you have no idea what horrors you may see. And being alone, what could happen to you, a single female among all those men."

"Father, mother, I've thought of all that. But these are times that demand that all of us who can contribute do so. I proved in college I can do well."

"Studies are one thing, Constance. However, being in a hospital is not college."

"I'm aware of that. I also am aware of all that is required of nice young ladies so they show they're not those, those loose women.

"And you know I'm not one of those. I truly believe I can take care of myself. Please mother and father. I must do this."

Faith started to interrupt, but Nathaniel spoke first. "Faith, I admire her willingness and apparent courage. Let's allow her to do this. I have heard of Dr. Blackwell and the good work she is doing. Constance would, at least I hope, be in good company. Were I younger, I think I'd have gone to be a surgeon.

"This other thing, though. Have you and Benjamin been in touch? Be honest."

Constance's face became somewhat red, thinking of the lock of hair. "No," she fought to sound sincere, never before lying to her parents on such a significant subject. She thought to herself, *I've only been in touch by way of Arella. That doesn't count*, she tried to convince herself. "I just think it would be nice to see him become what he has apparently always dreamed of. So please, dear mother and father, don't be upset. I so want to do this. I must," she ended resolutely, watching her parents' eyes and faces, the near tears of her mother, the admiration of her father. Her mother shook her head, trying to keep from crying, thinking of all the times she tried to protect her beloved daughter, knowing the feeling was always returned. Her father began to feel a sense of emptiness with Constance no longer with them. Yet, what difference would it be if she were to marry?

"Faith, I believe we should allow her to use her mind and skills she'll acquire. I believe she would be an exemplar of female caring." He thought for a moment. "Perhaps I could accompany her."

"Father, please. I want to do this myself. I *will not* allow any undesirable person to touch me, *even dare to.*"

Nathaniel smiled at his unworldly daughter who courageously confronted her parents and had ideas of her own.

"Mother, we should bless her for her desire to help and encourage her. You see that, don't you, Faith?"

Faith was now close to crying, more tears appearing. "Yes, Nathaniel." Turning to Constance, she spoke in a sob, "Darling, I'm concerned, worried, but I understand."

"Oh, mother," Constance, hugging her, and close also to crying, "I'll make father and you proud of me. I promise." She looked at her father through her tears, "I promise."

* * *

I was now studying intensely preparing for my oral presentations and a written examination. I was sleeping less, desiring to do as well as possible, of course. Yet I could not stop thinking of Constance and Rebecca, comparing them in looks and intelligence, at least as I thought of their conversation and interests. I rarely thought of their capabilities, believing that of the two Constance was the better. It was beginning to frustrate me that they sometimes disrupted my concentration. My father was now doing quite well financially and bought a carriage and even hired a driver, Robert. So I decided one late night that I would see Rebecca. I would ask my father to allow me to take the carriage so I could take her for a ride, were my parents to allow it. It was possible that one of her sisters would have to accompany us, limiting our talk. "What matter?" I asked himself. "If her oldest sister, Miriam, the most liberal, would be with us." I knew she would sit behind us and allow us as much privacy as possible. Miriam was being courted and probably would soon marry. The girls, Miriam, Rebecca, and Rose were separated by a year, their brothers, Jason and Immanuel by perhaps two. They were too young for the war. I wondered how the brothers' age difference happened. I thought about the methods of birth control now being used, wondering in my "medical mind," and laughed to myself, whether her parents had learned to use something or thought it against our religion. We weren't Catholic so how could an overly religious Jewish family think? "I don't like such Orthodoxy, but what can I do? I still like her, and that's what matters. Constance. What am I to do? Rebecca is Jewish. That's all there is to it. Her temper though."

The following day after my recitation before Dr. Sterling my Histology professor, the last one before the written examination in Practical Pharmacy, I walked to Rebecca's home. Miriam answered the door.

"Benjamin, this is a nice surprise," as she led me to the parlor, both of us hearing an argument between one of her brothers and Rose, apparently trying to discipline the boys. Miriam tried to ignore the fuss forcing a smile. "You look tired. I guess you've been every busy."

"Yes, we are very busy now finishing up our courses and studying for examinations."

"Please wait a moment. I'll get my mother and Rebecca."

Mrs. Horowitz came followed by Rebecca. "Why hello, Benjamin. How nice to see you." Then turning, "Is it not Rebecca?"

"Yes, Mamma." She started to blush. *I wish I knew what she was feeling and thinking at that moment.*

"Would you like some tea? I'll make some while you two talk," her mother asked, also giving permission for us to be alone as she beckoned to Miriam.

"Benjamin. I'm so happy you're here. I thought you'd be too busy. I imagine you are studying hard right now. You must be excited. You're almost finished and will be a doctor. Think of that. I'm so proud of you." She was smiling with a bit of red showing in her face.

"Well, I have to pass my examinations, Rebecca before you can say that."

"Oh, I have faith in you. The good Lord will see to it that you will become a doctor. I'll pray for you."

"Rebecca, I appreciate that." I didn't want to tell her my religious beliefs. I didn't wait for her to say more. "I love your dress, and you look so fetching in it."

"Thank you, sir." She laughed. "I was just thinking of our first meeting and how we didn't seem to get along too well."

"Time has passed, Rebecca, and now I want to be with you." Suddenly I thought whether I was being too forward. So what? I liked her, her shining grey eyes gazing at me. My heart beat faster.

"I have been wondering whether you would like to go for a ride on Sunday. I could get my father's carriage and we could go to see the ocean or the bay. It would be so nice to be alone with you." I was looking straight in her eyes as she was doing to me. I wanted to reach out and touch her hand, "Why not?" I quickly asked myself and reached for her hand that she gave me. I felt its warmth and smoothness. I loved the feel of her skin. She seemed to be looking adoringly at me. It sent a thrill through me. She *may* be the woman for me.

Miriam came with the tea, seeing us as we quickly pulled our hands apart.

"Don't be apprehensive about me, you two. I know what it's like. Misha and I can hardly keep apart. I'll leave you. But remember, nothing bad between you. I mean it," and she laughed. "I'm going back to mamma and help."

Before she left, Rebecca spoke up. "Miriam, Benjamin wants to take me for a carriage ride Sunday. If mamma and papa approve, would you go with us. It's only proper."

"Of course I will. Now have some tea and continue your conversation. I won't let anyone bother you."

We watched her leave. Rebecca poured tea for us, but neither of us drank. We sat for what seemed long moments before she spoke.

"Benjamin. I'm so happy you came today and that we'll be together Sunday." Her eyes seemed to flash while I thought she was trying to hide a blush.

"So am I. Rebecca, there's one thing we should both be aware of. When I finish school, I intend to enlist as an assistant surgeon, so we won't have much time together."

"That's all right with me." And she ventured, "I'll wait for you unless . . .," but she didn't finish, as she moved a bit closer to me so her skirt touched my leg.

Perhaps she is the one for me. She likes me. Constance. Oh. God, I love Constance and feel so warm toward Rebecca. Am I fooling Rebecca? Constance?"

"You would wait?"

"Yes, Benjamin," her facial expression serious, but her eyes appearing to brighten as she gazed at me.

I took a deep breath. "That's good. Let's make plans for this week-end. I'll come by, say, around 2 p.m. if that's all right with Miriam."

"I'll call her," and she turned to call to her sister who wasn't far from us. Perhaps she was listening. I'll never know, I suppose.

Miriam entered the room, smiling. "What have you two cooked up?"

"We're going for a ride on Sunday, perhaps to see the ocean. Will you accompany us?" Rebecca's face was red.

Miriam laughed, seeing her, the brightness and the color. "Of course I'll be your chaperone. I'd love the ride also."

"Oh wonderful," Rebecca answered loudly, a big smile on her face, the sisters looking at each other as if knowing what they both were thinking.

I stood and unabashedly took Rebecca's hand, feeling its warmth and how her fingers entwined mine, despite Miriam watching.

When I left, I was smiling happily, thinking of the coming ride. I did care for her. I couldn't wait. Studying, thoughts of her interrupted, seeing her in my mind, the way she looked at me, the pleasure she showed. And the way our hands grasped one another. How could I not care about her?

I wrote my last examination that Saturday. Sunday seemed to come suddenly. I would ride to the ocean. It was a sunny spring day in Portland. I was thinking we would go to a beach and walk, perhaps along one of the coves. I went to the door, nervously for some reason. This time, Rebecca met me at the door. She stood in a violet dress, a cape about her shoulders, her ringlets and hair shining. Those eyes. The way she looked at me. My heart skipped and started to beat faster.

"Hi. You look so handsome. Wait a minute and I'll get Miriam."

As she turned, I told her, "And you're beautiful."

She turned back to me, a brightness in her face, took a step toward me, placing her hand in mine. "Benjamin," softly, "I . . . have so looked forward to today."

"I also, Rebecca."

Miriam came, and I helped them to the step of the carriage, held their arms as they got in, Miriam in the back seat. I pulled on the reins as we started for the small beach I had in mind. The water was smooth, sunlit, speckled lights playing from the horizon curving as the gentle waves lapped against some rocks. We heard the cries of sea gulls, watched them glide. I didn't hesitate. "Miriam, would you mind if Rebecca and I walked a little way?"

"I think I can trust you with my sister," she answered with a laugh.

I helped Rebecca down. "Oh, did you wish to . . ."

She interrupted me. "Benjamin," a big smile on her face, "I'm capable of stepping out of the carriage if I wish. Go on. I'll amuse myself with the sea gulls. I even brought something to feed them."

"Thanks, Miriam." I didn't hesitate, holding Rebecca's forearm that she folded for me and leading her to a more secluded part of the beach where there were bushes beginning to bloom. I looked around. Miriam wasn't even paying attention to us.

"Ben, it's so lovely, the water, the warmth of the sun. Thank you for bringing me here."

We walked some more, speaking little, then silent, our breathing touching my ears. A bit secluded now, I pulled her closer to me, turning her to face me. "Rebecca," I breathed quietly to her, placing my hand about her waist, then her shoulders. She stood on her toes to reach my face. "Do you mi..."

"I want this, dear one." I held her head as our lips met. I kissed her harder, the warmth of her lips as she responded, then backed away. I looked in her eyes. "Kiss me again, dear." We did, this time longer. She pulled away then, her breath coming quickly. "I feel different, a thrill throughout me. Your lips taste so good." She took my hand and placed it on her breast. "I want you to love me."

"I do." I moved my hand about her breasts, heard her slight moan, kissed her again, her response sending trills throughout me. I was hard, but she wouldn't know.

She stepped back and spoke softly. "Tell me, dear one."

"I love you, Rebecca. Want you for a wife." *I'm lying.*

"I've loved you for some time now, did you know that?"

"I'm glad, so happy."

"As am I."

We kissed again, longer. I moved to open her mouth,

knowing instinctively what to do. I placed my tongue in her mouth and she met me. She trembled, pressing against me, then moved a bit to take my hand to her breasts again, rubbing them about me with a louder moan, her eyes closed, her head thrown back. I wanted to press my hardness to her and rubbed against her skirt, pressing it inward, feeling her move there also. Breathlessly, she whispered "We best stop. You won't ever tell anyone about this." Her eyes, now open, bright, a becoming blush that rose over her neck to her face.

"I would never tell anyone about us. You're too precious." I hesitated. "But we'll have to wait, Rebecca. I don't want to, but we must. I'm going to war."

She stepped toward me. Brought my head down to her lips as we kissed once more. "I'll wait."

Graduation came. Before, the listing of students who passed was posted. I was number one. I heard it behind me, for it was spoken loudly enough to make me hear. "The goddamn Jew. Wouldn't you know? Sterling probably helped him cheat."

I turned. "You can hate me, call me anything you want." I stared straight at the student who spoke, then angrily answered. "I'm used to your slurs, but don't you ever, ever let me hear you or anyone make a slur regarding Dr. Sterling, one of the most honorable men you'll ever know." Then I walked rapidly away as that stupid man, if that is what he is, mumbled something. To regain his, what, equilibrium? "Benjamin. Wait." It was my friend Jerome from the study group. "Don't ever listen to that crap. He and others like him are ignorant bastards."

"Thank you," I said softly, somewhat still shaken. "I know, and you should know I have always valued our friendship. I'd just like to be alone for a bit."

"I understand. And, hey, don't forget. We're graduating this week-end,"

I smiled. "How could I?" and walked away.

* * *

At the graduation, with students sitting in the front row, the professors called them in alphabetical order. There were now 12 students up from the original three. Of these, Benjamin was second in the class, following Jerome. As Benjamin went to receive his diploma, he glanced at his family seated next to Faith and Constance Sterling. Arella chose to sit with Constance, not with Rebecca and her sister Hannah.

He looked again at Constance and then Rebecca. Already nervous, on seeing them his heart beat faster. He quickly looked away. *I love Constance. How can I desert her? But I told Rebecca I love her and to wait. Oh . . . Good God. Why are you inflicting this pain? I'll be going in the service. Perhaps then I'll be able to make up my mind. Yet, how does one change his heart? Constance I do love you and always will. What is good is that she told me she is going to New York to train as a nurse with Dr. Elizabeth Blackwell.*

A celebration by the Blumenthal-Sterling families was to take place at the Sterling home. During the party, Faith noticed Constance and Benjamin walk toward the library.

"Where are you two off to, leaving your company?"

"I'm going to the library to show Benjamin the new book father bought. I know he'll be interested in it. We won't be too long. Don't worry, mother."

Faith grimaced as Constance turned away, leading Benjamin. "Come on, Ben, before she can say anymore."

They disappeared in a corner of the room, facing one another. She moved toward him, tilting her head until her eyes bright with desire looked in his, her heart beating faster. He reached for her, placing his arm about her waist, gently pulling her closer, pressing against her hoop that gave way. She placed her hand against his head pulling him toward her lips. As they met, they kissed gently then harder. Neither would let go.

Constance felt the kiss throughout her body, felt her increasing desire. She took his hand and placed it on her breast, breathing, "Please, Ben." She felt her nipples harden as he moved about one breast, the other, trying to pull her still closer. They explored one another. Then suddenly but unsteadily, reluctantly, she withdrew, still pressing his hands against her breasts, wanting to prolong their desire. She drew back her head, looking in his eyes, seeing them as never before, the desire in them. He placed a hand on her hair, playing with the ringlets, never wanting to release her. "I don't want to let you go, dearest Constance. I love you." She smiled, her face still warm, "I don't want you to, but . . . oh, Ben, I love you too. I don't ever want to lose you. I . . . I want you for my husband. Promise me, even though we're going to be apart. Promise," tears of happiness forming.

"I promise with my life. It is yours. Marry me, Constance so we'll never be apart. This horrible war. Perhaps we'll try to get leave to see one another." He looked at her intently, laughed, "Wouldn't it be something if we ever served in the same place."

"I hate this war separating us," she murmured. She hesitated. Lean your head down. Kiss me, dearest one," and they did.

"Oh, we must stop." She gazed at him. "I felt your hardness. Did you feel that?" Her face reddened as she asked.

"I did and wanted you to . . . rub it."

"Don't say anymore, dear one." She straightened her skirt, and moved her hands about her hair, assuring the net was correct at the back of her hair, that her ringlets were straight. "Do I look all right?"

"Yes. Constance. You're beautiful."

Constance glanced toward the door, hearing the rustle of a skirt. She watched as her mother appeared, noticing her daughter's reddened face while forcing herself to keep from raising her voice.

"Benjamin. You are the guest of honor," trying to keep her voice gentle.

That night, after the celebration, Faith confronted Nathaniel. "What good can come from this?"

"What good from what, dear?"

"I'm talking about Constance and Benjamin." She was getting angry. "I knew nothing good could come from . . . being so good to . . . a Jew, Nathaniel."

"Stop that now, Faith. You like him as much, or almost as much as I do. I don't want to hear that word again from you or anyone else. Think of the respect that family has brought to this community, even though it may be through their son. But they are decent people. We should accept that, keep our friendship with them."

'And you don't care what people think, how that may affect you and your practice."

"Faith, if people don't want to keep me as their physician, then they can just go to HELL. And I mean it, Faith. You accept that and that young man."

Faith's face reddened. She felt as though she had been slapped. She placed her hand on her cheek. "You have never talked to me like that. I won't have it."

"I'm sorry, Faith. Truly I am, if I hurt you. We so seldom argue. But I won't go back on my feelings or what I believe."

"Nathaniel. That's one of the reasons I love you so. You're so gentle, so good. But I feel as though you have, well, hit me."

"Forgive me." He kissed her.

"But, Nathaniel, they are attracted to one another. You could see it when I found them in the library. You should have seen her face. No good can come from it. It can hurt both Constance and Benjamin . . . and us. Admit it, Nathaniel." She hesitated. "At least they'll be separated."

He smiled. "I believe you've said that before, wife. I'll talk to her, Faith."

Chapter Four

War and Desire

"Mother, I'm going to New York to study nursing for two months with Dr. Blackwell," Constance again seemed to have surprised her.

"And who said we approve? And just who would accompany you? Young ladies do not travel without a family member or somebody close to protect them."

"You knew that I want to do my part. This war is dragging on. Young men are being horribly wounded or dying. I have to help. Other women from good families are serving as nurses. I can travel without getting into trouble. I promise I will not allow anyone to come near me unless I know the person."

"This is absolutely unheard of."

"I understand that. But times are changing."

"They can change without you, young lady. I won't allow it. Your father hasn't the time. So who then?" Faith couldn't help herself. "Who? Benjamin!"

"Mother. That was absolutely unnecessary. And come to think of it. Benjamin is to have his examination to become a regular surgeon in the Union Army.

"Mother, please. I talked to you and father about wanting to be a nurse. Neither of you seemed to be upset. Now that I am ready to study, you object."

"I have heard of young women doing that, but from what kinds of families do they come? And who knows what kind of mischief may befall you?"

"Mother. I am twenty years old, almost twenty-one. I know

how to take care of myself."

"Suddenly you believe you can alter manners."

"I am not even trying. Please listen. I want to do my part. You know I have felt this way, that I believe this is necessary. And may I remind you? You and father never said, 'No.'"

By now Constance was beginning to cry. She tried to hold back her tears, but it was useless. She wiped at her eyes, the tears flowing to her cheeks. "Please, mother. Try to understand. I'm good and will always be the way you raised me."

Watching Constance, Faith also began to feel tears coming. "Constance, dear. I do understand. You are also right that your father and I never objected when you brought it up. I guess I just thought it was a passing fancy." Faith looked at her daughter, wanting to see her eyes, those lovely eyes, this beautiful young lady. "Oh dear. What am I doing? I got angry, dear. Excuse me. Don't cry. Please." Faith took a hanky from under her sleeve and wiped gently at Constance's eyes. "Oh here. You take this. I want you to be happy. We all hate this war and those horrible southerners fighting to keep slaves. Now look at me." Faith was now tearing. She moved closer to Constance, placed her arms about her, hugging her tightly. "I do understand. I want you happy. It's just that you surprised me. I trust you. But it does bother me you travelling alone. It's just not done."

"Mother." Constance was now hugging Faith. They were both crying.

Suddenly Nathaniel appeared. "Why are my two lovely women hugging and crying?"

Faith looked up. "Constance is going to study nursing for two months with Dr. Blackwell and join the service. It's just that it surprised me, and we argued. It's all right."

"We know she wants to. What's the problem? I'd be proud to know my daughter is doing her bit."

They were now both wiping at their tears. "It's just that it surprised me. But she's going to travel alone. That's just not done."

"Well, if you must know, Faith. I have heard that some women have traveled to Washington by themselves. Nothing happened to them. I think Constance can go to New York. Dr. Blackwell is doing some very fine things. Don't forget she's our first female doctor. Nobody wanted her in school, but look what she's done. She helps the poor. For our Grand Army of the Republic she helped form the Woman's Central Relief Association and the United States Sanitary Commission. The Central Association trains nurses. Constance would make a fine nurse, Faith. We know she can do almost anything when she puts her mind to something. Look at what she did in college. I believe we can trust her."

"But traveling . . ."

"Faith, dear. We either trust our daughter or keep her so close to us perhaps we prevent her from doing something outstanding. This is her time, Faith, We have to face it."

"Daddy," Constance almost screamed. "You do believe in me."

"We both do, Constance. We also trust you. You will be a credit to us and to the country."

So it was that in June, 1862, Constance was on a rail car traveling first to Boston and changing there for one to New York. Nathaniel arranged for a friend to meet her and take her to Dr. Blackwell with whom she would be in training for two weeks. The two weeks with Dr. Blackwell passed quickly. Then, still with more excitement, she was on her way to the Armory Square Hospital in Washington.

The travel and learning had Constance in an unusual nervous, yet exciting state. After the training she would be settled in comfortable quarters, a room shared with another nurse. She wore her first black dress lacking a hoop, a white apron and white hat to keep her hair from falling about a patient or her face. This uniform, was less cumbersome than a regular dress. She wore her bloomers to her knees and chemise, and fewer of the petticoats, unneeded because there was no corset. These were each sufficient to protect her legs from showing and keeping her demure and presentable, unless a quick movement might show her ankles.

In her comfortable quarters for the females and dressed properly and admiring herself in a mirror, she was ready for meeting with the nurse Superintendent to learn what was expected of her.

On her ward she learned what she was soon to confront, men horribly wounded, lacking limbs, some with gangrene having settled and spread, others having lost their eyesight, or faces disfigured by bullets or shells. What she expected but was unprepared for was her actual confrontation with these horrors. She also learned about bandages and keeping her hands clean, how to help the men. In other words, she was to be a nurturing female from a middle class family, occasionally asked to write letters for the men. Here she had a somewhat comfortable and private quarter to protect her from the eyes of men. Not only had she learned to wash her hands in diluted chlorinated solution but also the use of bandages soaked in the same solution on gangrenous wounds.

Led to her first patients she abruptly confronted the meaning of war. It was not a romantic manly venture. She was assigned to a ward of dying men, the smells of wounds unhealable, disfigured faces and bodies. The odor and sights made her feel sick. Her face paled and she felt faint. She started to turn away and walk uneasily from the ward when a soldier weakly called out, "Nurse, would you please help me." Constance, aware others saw and watched her, turned toward the bed from which the voice came. There lay a boy from what she could determine. She went to his side, bent, and as though thrust, placed her hand on his forehead. She felt the heat of his fever, leaned closer, softly asking, "Yes, young man." Before he could answer, she reached for a wet cloth from a basin with soap and water with which she was to wash the soldiers. She gently wiped his face.

"Miss, that feels so good. I saw you and thought maybe you could write a letter for me. You see, my right arm . . ." and he pushed aside the blanket covering his infected stump, revealing his lost arm.

Stunned, it being her first patient to wash on the ward, Constance drew back but then forced herself to lean closer again. "What would you like me to write, soldier?" she asked in a soft voice.

"I'd like you to write my mother for me."

Forcing back her tears, she answered, "I'll get a chair, and you'll tell me what you wish to say. I'll do this as soon as I finish my duties with the others. All right? I promise I'll return"

"That's fine nurse."

After that encounter, Constance tried to walk strongly about, stopping at each soldier for the bed bath. Then, it happened again, as she pulled back a blanket, there lay a naked, horribly wounded soldier, shot just above his groin, a wound that hadn't or would not heal. Of course, she had never seen nudity. She felt the shock and her blushing face and again made herself use her soap and water carefully avoiding the wound and washing from his face to his legs. Could she continue this, despite her anatomy course? She then hurried along the ward, finishing, talking soothingly to patients. Some reached for her hand to thank her. She still had to get her dressing tray that contained rollers, plaster, and tins; for the doctor would soon be coming and expecting her help.

Then, remembering, she found a closet she had seen, and closed herself in, weeping quietly. *Do I have the courage to do this? I must find it. Think, Constance what others have suffered and what other doctors, and nurses must, must do. You must also. Think of what Benjamin and your parents would think if you quit, if you hadn't the will to help as you so romantically felt was a woman's war effort.* She wiped at her eyes and cheeks, wishing she had a mirror, not wanting any nurse, anyone seeing her face.

As she opened the door, an older woman moved quickly aside, stopped. Seeing the last of Constance's tears, she told her, "Come here, dear" She placed her arm about Constance's shoulder, leading her from the ward. "I know what you're feeling. We all have gone through this. Don't be ashamed. Just learn and tell yourself there may be many hours or days like yours, mine, and others. You can do it. You'll be proud of yourself and become stronger." She hesitated. "What's your name?" After Constance told her, she introduced herself. "I'm Mrs. Willette. I'm a widow. I lost my husband at Bull Run. I ain't had no children, couldn't have them, so I cried and cried and then decided if I nurse hurt soldiers I would make up for those children I never had and help other mother's sons. I certainly miss my husband, but now I know what he went through, and think of all these men that need the help of a good woman. They like seeing us and having a womanly touch and hearing a woman's voice after the hell they have been through." She patted Constance on the shoulder. "You come with me, and we'll have some tea. That will settle you."

"Oh, I must go back to that soldier who wants me to write a letter for him."

"That's the way to talk. You do that. And remember what I said. These men, and even boys, want to see you, to know a woman's touch, hear a woman's voice, and have awareness of her feminine tranquility. Remember, too, they will always treat you with respect."

On one day, Constance and another nurse were called to come outside in case they were needed. An ambulance pulled up to the door. Male attendants carried the men, some crying others moaning, or even shouting in their delirium. Here, too,

Constance saw her first dead, sheets drawn up to cover their faces. They directed where to take their wounded. One man, in pain, shouted, "What a shaking ride. I need help. I hurt terribly. Help me, please."

Constance went to him, telling the attendants to stop for a moment while she talked to him. His amputation was gangrenous. He felt her soft hand on his forehead. "We'll take care of you." On the ward they would treat him with more nitric acid and opium.

Constance had by now seen the worst. She had been with a doctor who, lacking chloroform which for some reason the hospital had not provided him, watched and helped when asked as he amputated a leg. She had to bear the scream, aid the doctor. He turned to her, and in a gruff voice ordered her, "Nurse, get me some opium." Here it compellingly and terrifyingly struck her about the lessons of war and the need for her nursing skills that she was quickly learning to apply.

She did have one duty night, listening to the reliving in dreams of the battles. One of her saddest moments was when she sat by a drummer boy as he slowly died. She kissed his face then tearfully pulled the sheet gently over his face.

* * *

In July, 1862, while the Union armies were suffering horrendous casualties with more to come, Benjamin went before the examining board for an oral examination to determine his qualifications. He scored high enough to become a surgeon, rather than assistant surgeon that would even have satisfied him. His assignment was to the Army of the Potomac.

By now the army with General Jonathan Letterman, M.D., had discovered the necessity of good nutrition and of cleanliness.

When he reported for duty in December, 1862, the Army of

the Potomac would engage the Rebel Army at the ill-conceived Battle of Fredericksburg. The Union casualties were fearsome, soldiers being left on the other side of the river and having to be evacuated over pontoon bridges.

Once in the ambulances, the wounded were taken to medical tents behind the lines. The casualties suffered not only from their wounds but from the extremely cold weather. The surgeons did their best before sending the somewhat mended to hospital buildings. The shock of those stricken with terror, others with arms or leg blown away, and other ugly wounds angered Benjamin. He worked furiously, sometimes running short of the necessary surgical supplies. Soon a senior medical officer sent him to a rear hospital where he performed his operations more satisfactorily for him. Here he was also confronted with gangrenous arms and legs. He applied nitric acid, made certain the nurses washed their hands thoroughly in a dilute chlorinated solution and did not to use bandages a second time. They were also to look for infections and try to protect these with the same combination. He also went through the wards under him with a nurse attendant to examine how his patients progressed. It was not long before he gained praise from other surgeons but also from the nursing staff.

One night, though needing sleep, he went through a ward with a nurse who reminded him of Rebecca. On returning to his room, he wrote:

"My dearest Rebecca,

"I have thought of you tonight, especially because someone who helped me reminded me I hadn't written for some time. We have been terribly busy with the wounded from the Fredericksburg battle. You probably read about it in the papers. I shan't tell you what I saw or did. However, thinking of you made me realize why we must win this terrible war, despite the times we lose battles. We are fighting for you, my lovely, your family and others and for the end of the evils of slavery.

"I hope you miss me as I do you. I should love to see you, to touch your sweet face with my hand, to watch you as you smile and talk sweetly. I can almost hear you as I write this.

"Take good care of yourself, and remember me to your family.

"I send you a kiss that I hope you will accept. ---- Benjamin."

When he finished the letter and sealed it, he was thinking of Constance. He hadn't heard from her in some time, imagining that she was very busy. What was he to do? He had just written to a young woman who was marriageable and one about whom his family would be happy to call daughter. He was growing sleepy. *Constance, my true love.* He yawned. *I want to write you tonight, but I must sleep some. I think of you in your nurse's uniform, but then I think of the last time we saw one another, you in that beautiful blue dress and the ruffles about your skirt, your shining hair and eyes. Constance, hopelessly, I suppose, I love you. I want to be with you now. I shall write this to you before my duty in the morning. Soon I will also be on night duty. I wish, dearest, that I could attend my wounded with you. It is all so sad. You would understand that. There are times when I hear the screaming in my mind when I do not have chloroform to still the men. We do have alcohol for them to drink. I shall write you this tomorrow. I so love you. But who would accept us in society? I want you for my wife. Will I ever have the nerve to say this to you?* And here I have just written to Rebecca. *Benjamin, what are you going to do? I need you, Constance. I don't like admitting this even to myself, but I cannot help thinking how heavenly it would be to lie with you. Could I ever think so openly and truly with Rebecca? Benjamin, don't lead her on unless you mean to ask for her hand.* He tore up that letter.

He fell upon his cot and dreamed. He was with Constance. Her hazel eyes shone with love. She undid her chestnut hair, and it fell about her shoulders. She raised herself to his lips as they sought out each other. He felt her breasts and himself growing with excitement. Then, she unhooked her dress, pulled it from her, stepped out of her hoop and let it fall to the ground, turned to him to help her undo her corset, then stepped from her slips and finally her pantalets. She stood before him naked.

"You like me?" They kissed, covering one another's bodies with them. He then went below, kissed her there. He rose then to insert himself. He could hear her delight and felt his flow.

He woke. He would have to change his underclothing. "Constance," he dreamily murmured.

The following day he received a brief letter from Constance. Of course, they had been writing to one another. He knew he would never forget her.

"Dearest Ben,

"I am making this short, because we are so busy. I told you how awful it was for me at the beginning. Well, it still is, but I have learned, for I am consoled by those I help and by my part in this war and my contribution to our Union soldiers. I sometimes feel as though I am almost like a mother. The men so look forward to having a woman to talk to, to help them. No one can comfort like a woman. So there. But the men are so appreciative and respectful. This in itself gives me comfort. You must be seeing terrible, terrible things. I wish we could be together and help each other with the wounded. But don't you look at the nurses near you. Oh, Ben, I miss you so much. I see you in my mind and imagine you comforting me, holding me so soothingly. Ben, what is to happen to us? I must stop before I say too much and behave unladylike.

"I *care* for you, dearest Ben, and please watch out for yourself in those terrible battles."

When he received this letter, he was ecstatic. He always looked forward to hearing from her, but the way she ended this one made him realize how much he loved her. He would answer it as soon as he was off duty. This he did.

"My dearest Constance,

"I know that neither of us has much time. Yes, we see horrible wounds and wish we could do more. Like you, I am so pleased I can do something for my country. In between, in moments of some tranquility, I think of you, my very dearest Constance. There is so much I want to say and don't. That may be terribly unfair to you. Now, though, there is no one to condemn us, you being Christian and I being Jewish. I have never said this before, but I want you, dearest one, near me. I want to hold you, to soothe you, to feel you close to me. I can almost feel the warmth of your body next to mine. I also *care* for you, my lovely Constance. Oh how I wish this war would end, the Union winning, of course. I also wish, I want, you and me to be together. Do not be dismayed because I say this, but I send you kisses. Please imagine them so they seal us together."

Chapter Five

Transfer – Dismay
Gettysburg

After the wounded had been evacuated, including those the Confederates allowed to be taken back across the Rappahannock River on the repaired pontoon bridges, the doctors thought perhaps they could get a bit of rest. It would not be for too long, however. They soon found themselves tending to more wounded and performing more amputations. On May 1, 1863, in a conflict that would extend to May 5, the Union and Confederate armies, under Hooker and Lee, were in the battle at Chancellorsville.

Again there were rivers involved, the Rapidan and again the Rappahannock. It was in the area of the Wilderness. Benjamin had been assigned behind the battlefields in a tent to take care of the wounded until ambulances evacuated them.

Then it happened, in a surprise move that caught Hooker off guard. There was gun fire seemingly all about them. Men fell screaming from their wounds, while many mortally wounded lay either silent, eyes staring; or near death. On the ground they were a terrifying chorus of moans until dead.

Benjamin and his attendants had no way of escape as the rebels surrounded them, as well as other doctors and wounded. They were taken prisoners as the Union army retreated across the Rappahannock. The wounded that they could gather before imprisonment were more fortunate than Benjamin's group.

They were held under miserable conditions until May 11, when the Army of the Potomac chief medical officer arranged with his Southern counterpart to take some of the Union wounded and doctors, including Benjamin, back to the retreating Union lines. By now Benjamin was unable to care for the wounded as they should have been. There were moans of pain, odors of gangrenous wounds. Benjamin had no chloroform or ether, alcohol, iodine, clean water, or decent foods for the men to eat or drink. They would have to wait until returned to their own lines and hopefully a rather well supplied hospital.

Benjamin and his doctors required rest but kept working alongside their fellow surgeons. When he was finally able to rest, it was too hard to fully sleep. He dreamed of amputations without anesthetics, heard the screaming as he operated. Unable to sleep, he wanted to write Rebecca and Constance. In the dark, he hated himself, rubbing his arms, wrapping them about his body, pulling at his unshaved face. He would not wear a beard like so many of the others. Thinking of Constance, it reminded him of rabbis. And what had he told Rebecca? *I told her I care for her, that I want her for my wife. I thought I did when I said it. What is going to happen? Oh, dear Lord, I love Constance. I love her with my life. Perhaps I'll be killed and lay among those many dead.*

He went outside and sat by a fire. And wrote Rebecca by the flickering light.

"Dear Rebecca,

"I'm sitting here in the depth of night thinking of you. I want you to know this. I can't tell you what I have been doing. It would be too terrible to mention to you. Are you thinking of me as I am of you? It is somewhat cold now, even though it is May. I believe we'll be moving more northward soon.

"Think of me, my dear Rebecca."

He could not say more. Constance was moving his hand and inside his brain, as he thought of it. He would write to her now. It would not be long before he would have more surgery to perform.

"My dearest Constance,

"It is almost dawn. I'm sitting here by a fire so I can see what I write. Soon I'll be back with my surgical patients. You must know what I am doing. I'm certain you are seeing all the horror of this war. I am so proud of you and what you are doing. The men need a woman's touch, the nearness of one, and their calming influence. Oh, Constance, I may not be wounded. Or perhaps I am. I want to tell you what is deep in my heart, dearest one. Can you hear it talking to you? Why, oh why were you and I born into different worlds?

"To just be able to feel your hands on me, their softness calming me. I would like to be there for you. I miss you so, dearest Constance.

"You must have heard of the defeat we suffered. I do not like General Hooker. General Lee outmaneuvered him, and because of that many of the wounded and I along with other surgeons were caught behind the enemy lines. It was terrible, primarily because I could do so little for the wounded. But finally an agreement was reached and I am back with our army, thank goodness. Now I can practice medicine more surely. I so wish we would come to Washington and we could be with one another when off duty. Constance, I have so many thoughts I want to reveal to you. I LOVE you, dearest Constance, and you will always be in my heart and mind. Don't be upset because I say this. I do hope I am not out of line. How could one such as I not love you? Someday, perhaps I could, if I have the nerve, say this to you in person. Perhaps you would tell me you feel the same way. My love, my dearest and only Constance. Yours, Ben."

Benjamin saw the dawn rising, wondering whether to send this letter. He would, and if she did not answer, that would be the end. He thought he then would feel better about Rebecca and what he said to her. She as his wife would settle everything in his confused mind. But not his heart. The fairness and honesty. Yes, he had told Constance of his love for her.

Later, when he had time, he wrote Arella, wondering whether she had heard from Constance and if she had said anything about him. The answer did not surprise him.

"Oh, yes, Ben, she writes about you and how she misses you. She is very fond of you, Ben. But being her friend and confidante, I don't think I should say more. I must tell you that Rebecca has been to our house to tell mamma and papa how glad she was to hear from you. Since then, we have been friendly but not like Constance. She has had me to her house. Of course, she tells me or asks about you. I believe, Ben, you must not lead her astray. It's liable to cause terrible family problems. I also have to tell you I worry about you and Constance despite the feelings I know exist between you. I so love you both and want you both to find happiness when this war is over and done. Do try to be careful. I worry so about Amos and Daniel. Sometimes I hear mamma crying and papa trying to soothe here. Who can blame her or papa?

"I suppose you have heard that Esther is pregnant again with her third child. They are very happy about it, of course.

"My love my dear brother, Arella."

Other dawns came. He had come to sit by fires if no enemy were present and he was off duty. It gave him a sense of calm, to some extent helping him blot out the screams, the moaning, his helplessness in being unable to prevent men from dying.

Constance did answer his latest letter.

"My dearest Ben,

"You were not out of line, nor was anything you wrote either rash or unacceptable. You see, dear one, though we may be causing ourselves terrible problems, do not forget I am a brave woman. I must tell you also, when I read this latest letter from you, I felt a blush rise through my neck and cover my face. I was so glad my roommate was on duty. Usually we are on at the same time either taking care of patients assigned to us or helping doctors while they work on the men. But you know all this.

"My dear Ben, dearest Ben. I fear writing more. Just always remember that your last not only pleased me but sent happiness throughout me, and I shall always keep it close to my heart. Never forget this. My heart, Ben."

* * *

The Army of the Potomac retreated, Hooker settling on placing his headquarters at Fairfax County, Virginia. He had no idea what Lee would do next. However, General Lee was planning a movement northward. He would move north, skirting Washington.

Many of the wounded had by now been moved to the hospitals in the capitol. Thus, when Constance had received Benjamin's letter, she would be helping those wounded he mentioned and still more that had been sent to the city. Yet, as Lee moved and was nearer Washington, there was some panic. By now, too, the Union lead general was Meade who would meet the outstanding strategist, Lee.

Also about this time the Union doctor, Hinkle, experimented with gangrenous amputees. Others learned from him that they should use permanganate of potassa on the diseased tissue. When Benjamin heard about this, he was ecstatic, as were others. Thus, as Lee moved on to Gettysburg and Meade fell back to meet him, the horrendous battle was about to cause not only thousands of ugly wounded but also the continuation of many amputees. It was necessary during the battle to establish not only field hospitals such as one near Cemetery Hill behind the lines, but also by taking over farms and buildings in Gettysburg. There were also makeshift stations behind hills to afford protection. It was now that more nurses became a necessity. Among those arriving was Constance who was stationed at the Common School in the town. Benjamin had also been transferred there to help take care of the overwhelming casualties that the July days of battle had caused. The horror and the work was intense. Thousands of men lay wounded in the fields and had to be transported by the ambulances from where they lay. All about were dead and wounded, arms and legs blown off. When many came to the school hospital where she worked, suddenly she saw Benjamin bent over a man shot through the face. He did what he could and went to another whose entire leg he knew would have to be amputated. The cries seemed to echo throughout the city and reach to the heavens.

At last, when there was some time, Constance, with tears that she tried to keep from becoming a flood of crying, went toward her room to rest. As she entered, she felt a hand on her arm. "Nurse Sterling . . ." She tried to turn and pull away at the same time. A surgeon would not let her go. He pulled her to force her to face him, as his other hand reached for her breasts and touched them. He pushed her against a wall, moving his body against her, a hand reaching and raising her skirt and petticoats and moving upward to get between her thighs. She started a scream, but his hand muffled her. Suddenly he felt a rough pull at the neck of his shirt. The man choked and moved backward, his other hand grazing her breasts.

"Get the hell out of here, you bastard."

"Ben," she cried out in a trembling voice.

The surgeon attacker turned his face, frightened, red, and angry." Who the . . . O, the Jew wonder man. To hell with both of you," as he tried barging past Benjamin, perspiration on his forehead, and starting to show about his temples.

"You never, ever go near her or any nurse, or I'll kill you myself, if a courts-marshal wouldn't do it."

"Ben . . . B e . . ." she couldn't finish, as she placed her face between her hands, sobbing loudly.

He pushed the senior surgeon out of her room. His face now white, still with fear, he looked at Benjamin. "Who the hell do you, fucking Jew . . ."

"I'm her husband, you goddamn bastard. Now get the hell out of here."

The surgeon faked a laugh, "You two married? You *deserve* each other *in hell.* Married to a Jew?" and still shaken, he quickly left as Benjamin took her in his arms, pressing her against him while she continued sobbing. "He was . . . he would have raped me."

"I know, dearest. I'll report him. Now you cry this out." He ran his hand soothingly along her back.

"Cry it out, dear one."

"R … rape. I . . . I can't . . . go on." And she sobbed more loudly as he shut the door. "If you report him, oh Ben, I could never tell this to anyone. I'm scared of what people will think."

"Don't worry then. I shan't say anything and will always be here to protect you from anything that horrid man says, if he dares."

Constance shook, couldn't stop sobbing, hid her head in Benjamin's chest seeking his comfort. He gently led her to the one chair in the room, seating her on his lap. "Darling, try to relax, if you can. I could kill that man. He won't ever hurt you again. No man will. I promise you, dearest." He stroked his hand through her hair, pulling out a handkerchief to wipe her wet face. Then holding it to her nose, "Blow, sweet, if you wish." She obeyed, smiled slightly, looking at him, kissing his cheek. "Ben, what would I have done if you hadn't . . ." She didn't finish and started weeping. "Oh, Ben, love, I just don't believe this. What if . . ."

"Shhh, dearest. We stopped him. I doubt he'll ever show his face around you. I doubt he'd even allow you to aid him. So don't worry. Would you like to lie down and rest? I'll tell anyone who asks, I made you rest, because we've been so overworked."

"Don't tell Martha my roommate."

"No one. Later perhaps you may want to tell her."

"I doubt it. I don't want anyone thinking I encouraged him. You know the way people are."

"Do you want to lie down?" he softly asked again.

"No. I want to stay here with you." She reached for his hand. Grasping it, she held it against her face. Suddenly the incident startled her. "Ben, you don't think I . . . I couldn't stand that. I'd leave and go home, but what would my parents say?"

"Constance, love, this is never going beyond us and that rotten man." Benjamin suddenly thought, *Would he be stupid enough to say something, to brag, tell people she led him on. I swear I'll throttle him. Constance is right. Who is going to believe a woman's side?* Yet, he had heard that in other hospitals such incidents did occur, perhaps some happening because the nurse was the aggressor. That is *not* going to happen here."

"I wish you would lie down for a bit and try to relax. I'll stay here with you. If Martha appears, I'll tell her you didn't feel well, that you were a bit feverish."

She did as he said, feeling the comfort of the bed and Benjamin sitting beside her holding her hands and occasionally running his fingers through her hair as she finally began to relax. She closed her eyes and eventually fell asleep. Suddenly, however, she woke, raising her head and screaming.

Softly Benjamin kissed her cheek, telling her he was with her. She opened her eyes, her body shaking. "Ben . . ." her voice shaky, "I dreamed I was actually being raped. You won't ever let that happen or think badly of me for what . . ."

"Stop that now, Constance. I will never think badly of you. I'll spend my life protecting you. Constance, sweetheart, I love you and want you for my wife. I'll always be there for you."

"Hold me closer, Ben. Kiss me so I know you mean it."

He held her face between his hands and placed his lips softly on hers, and he felt her press softly back. "I love you, Ben. If we marry, the world could hate us. I don't know that I can talk about this now. I would so love to be your wife. Please let's not talk more about it now."

* * *

After the town of Gettysburg had been cleared of Confederates and the Baltimore Railroad tracks repaired, there were more wounded filling the barn hospitals, as well as buildings in Gettysburg itself. Other men lay on the streets waiting to be taken for treatment. As the battle continued, the 20th Maine Regiment was at Little Round Top under Colonel Chamberlain. Daniel and Amos were with them on what would become a crucial battle in saving the North and routing the Confederates. Southern troops fighting upward toward the 20th suddenly became embroiled in a bayonet attack by Chamberlain's men. Amos lost sight of his brother. He ran as fast as he could, bayoneting a Confederated soldier but suddenly feeling a shot. It penetrated his jaw and neck. It would be a time before he was taken from the field by ambulance, to a tent hospital and eventually by chance to the Common School. He was near death, murmuring, "mamma, mamma, Ben, where's Ben. I need him. Dani . . . Get Ben." His partially open eyes closed.

Either a nurse or a surgeon may have guessed he was Ben's relative. Ben rushed to him.

"Amos. I'm here." Benjamin's eyes filled with tears. "Oh, Amos, what have they done to you?" Having heard about Amos, Constance appeared by Ben's side, grasping his arm.

"Can you do anything?" though she knew he couldn't.

Benjamin shook his head, 'No.' He looked at Constance wishing she could hold him, then turned back to Amos. "Amos, listen to me, I'm going to help you," aware he couldn't.

133

His voice tearful and soft, he asked Constance, "Please, dear, get me a tincture of iodine and also permanganate of potassa. I know it or anything won't help, but if I wash the wound, I'll feel better."

"Yes, Ben. But let me gently wash him, please."

One of the surgeons who heard about Amos, came to Benjamin. "Benjamin, why don't you stay beside him and just let me see if there is anything I could manage."

Benjamin turned toward the voice. "Marshall, thanks, but there's nothing." They walked a little way from Amos whose eyes fluttered. "I appreciate it. Nurse Sterling is getting me some solutions and will also wash him." Benjamin stopped, choking back his tears. "He's going to die soon. I'm just glad I'm here for him."

Marshall rubbed his hand over Benjamin's shoulders. "Ben, we're all here if there's anything." He knew there was nothing now but death and walked slowly away from Benjamin, shaking his head, muttering to himself. "This damn war and to watch your own brother die."

Within hours with Constance beside him, gently wiping away at the feverish brow, Amos suddenly raised his head. "Ben, Ben. Take my hand, tell mamma . . ." Constance took the sheet and raised it over Amos. She turned to Benjamin, the two of them crying, and disregarding what anyone would think, she took him in her arms. "Don't be ashamed, dearest," she whispered. "Cry. I'm here." He buried his head in her breasts as she stroked his hair.

Later, when Daniel heard, he asked permission to go into town. General Meade by now was issuing orders for the army to follow Lee's retreating troops. Daniel would be unable to leave. He hurried a note to Benjamin to let his brother know he had come through with just some scratches the tent hospital behind the lines took care of, that he had stood in the bayonet charge near Corporal Coan. The Battle of Gettysburg was over, except for the wounded and shell shocked, most of these wounded, though, evacuated by the end of August by rail.

Interlude

Constance then told of her and Benjamin's post-Gettysburg experience. I returned to the Armory Hotel to which Benjamin also received transfer, there being so many men to be cared for. We managed to travel to Washington together. When we arrived it was evening. We would have three days of rest to sightsee. Ben was grief stricken. I felt seeing the city would help him.

It was nightfall, the sky showing the last of twilight. As we walked, Benjamin, suddenly spoke softly, telling me, "Dearest, you know I love you with my life. Will you, as I asked before, marry me? I understand the impediments we face, but will you please consider it?" His blue eyes gazed into mine that I am certain now shone. I closed them, then opened widely with perhaps fear, lowered my lashes, covering them with a smile and then looking, my eyes now with tears of happiness.

"Ben, I love you too. I believe I've loved you since that day you appeared at our door. This is almost a terrifying decision. I'm not sure what we'll be doing to ourselves. Will we come to hate one another? I don't ever want to lose your love."

"Constance, we'll never hate. Never. Don't even use that word. After what we've been through and will continue to be, who cares about the world and what it will think? If necessary, when the war is over and we go back to Maine or settle someplace else, we'll be together, have one another."

My smile had faded, but my eyes I know were bright. I wanted to feel him and looked about. There was no one. I took his hand and placed it on my face, covered it with my other hand, feeling tears growing as I looked at him. "Ben, I want to be your wife, to love you and you me, always and forever, in heaven if it will have us. I will be your wife. It is going to hurt our families, Ben. They may never accept what we are about to do. Oh, good Lord," I prayed aloud, "Please accept us, especially after what we've been through. Ben even more because of Amos?"

I turned to face Ben. He put his face close to mine. I felt his lips closing on mine, kissing me softly. My heart beat faster, the emotion filling me with a heat that I felt flowing to between my legs as I kissed him back. We held to one another as he ran his fingers about my hair, placed his arms about me, pulling me close. My breasts pressed against his chest. I felt my nipples growing harder. I wanted him to kiss them, but through my dress that was impossible. But my tongue sought his, and they touched as I moved mine lightly over his lips and then back inside his mouth as he did the same to me. I trembled, feeling a stronger heat throughout my body. Placing my hand on his abdomen, I sought him lower. I could feel him, then pulling back from him. I'm certain my eyes were bright with desire. "You love me?" my breathing increased and my heart beating faster.

"I love you - always," as he pulled me to him again and kissed me more passionately.

"Ben. I want to marry in a Protestant church." I hesitated. "Episcopal. Will you do that for me? But also should we wait? I feel your grief, see your sadness."

"Yes and No. I want this now. I need to be with you forever." *Forever, yes, Amos.*

The next morning, after choosing two rings, he placed one immediately on my finger for our engagement, the other held for the marriage. We sought a minister and asked him to marry us this very day. He asked many questions, our religion, why the hurry, wondering if whether we knew the seriousness of what we were doing, especially with Benjamin being Jewish. Annoyed, I forced myself to listen respectfully. I was aware he was somewhat hesitant because of Ben.

Looking pleadingly at the minister. I couldn't help myself and confronted him. "Sir, there's a war, as you know. We have both been in the worst of it. We have just returned from Gettysburg. We have known and loved each other for years now. We have no idea what will happen to us before this horrid killing is done. We must be together as husband and wife."

Benjamin joined. "Sir, what she says is true. But I have seriously thought of what I am doing, and if it's necessary to take vows in your church, I will do it. Will you do it, sir?

"I love Constance," He stopped as if holding back. "I lost my brother at Gettysburg. My love, though, is undying." Later he told me he was thinking, *I'll raise my children Christian when I don't even believe in religion? If I am to have Constance, I must do this, but I can't believe.* Then, firmly I heard, "This woman sitting beside me must become my wife, no matter what. I love her with my life."

I didn't know then, but he also told himself, I found out years later, *Ben, don't live a lie. Rebecca. That would be the way out. Oh, my God, Rebecca. I don't really love her. Either way it's a lie, Benjamin.*

The minister saw in him and heard the earnestness.

"All right. Come back this afternoon."

We did, and Benjamin submitted to my perhaps unreasonable wishes.

He also later told me, his heart and mind rebelled because of his questioning religion, but he forced himself. He could not lose me. But I did believe marriage this way would protect us both, and God would watch over our love and our children.

Before returning in the afternoon I suddenly thought and told Benjamin. "Sweetheart, I have an idea. When we return to Portland, we'll join the First Parish Unitarian Church. I'm sorry. Forgive me, but I only thought at the time of my parents' church. How unfair. Your parents matter as much as mine." I felt my face growing red as I admitted, "We could have done that here in Washington. I looked it up. There is one here. But I just had to be married in the Episcopal Church to be certain God will join us. You do understand, don't you? Please."

My neck and face were hot, but I forced myself to continue, "Think of it, though. In the Unitarian Church you can be Jewish, Protestant, Catholic, whatever. You don't even have to swear allegiance."

He stopped, turned me toward him. "I didn't know that. We'll do it, all right. And I do understand why we are marrying as you wish."

"It's a deal and promise, my beloved non-believer."

"If it doesn't bother you, we'll join there. Our families will have to accept what we want for each other. But, Constance, you mother and father."

I laughed. "What about yours, darling? Will you be dead to them?" My voice trembled as I spoke, having heard that about Jews marrying non-Jews. I was also thinking of the many dead I had seen, of those dying while I held them. Suddenly I thought of Amos, of Benjamin telling me how he held his brother. *Are we doing the right thing? His parents.* I shook my head to rid myself of the images, taking myself back to the present, forcefully recalling my smile. *If we love as we do then it's right. No matter what anyone thinks.*

He was looking in what he told me were my beautiful, playful hazel eyes. "Constance, how did I ever find you? Speaking of God, of Jesus, of whatever, they led us to one another."

Almost noon and near the church we were looking deeply into one another and about to kiss when I pulled back. "Wait 'til tonight, Ben. They don't allow kissing in the street." I gaily laughed, my face red again thinking about the night, apprehensively, but squeezing his hand holding mine for reassurance.

Benjamin submitted to my church wedding. We listened to the minister again advising us on the proper role of a wife and her obedience to her husband. Benjamin wanted to laugh. Soon, though, he pronounced us man and wife, and we chastely kissed. I whispered in his ear, "I bet you can't wait until tonight." I had to keep from laughing.

We went to the Willard Hotel, anxiously ate our supper, then went to our room. I know I talked nervously, aware he was sad over Amos and the thought of my body being taken. "Think, dearest, we are married. It's the most wonderful feeling I have ever had except for when I realized my love for you. It was hard too, wondering how it could hurt us because . . . our differing religions." I took his hand, perhaps for reassurance, as we walked into the rooms. I turned to him. "Hold me, Ben." He closed the door, hugging me, kissing me softly, then harder as I met his kiss, feeling his lips, then his tongue seeking my mouth. I opened mine as I followed his lead and sought his tongue. I felt it throughout my body, yet apprehensive, when I heard, "I love you, Constance," as I thought of being in bed.

"I know. We'll always be like this, won't we?" I asked, still nervous about lovemaking. "You know we will."

"I'll go change, dearest." I smiled, my eyes challenging him.

"May I watch you?"

"You wait." I changed into a lace nightdress that showed my breasts and barely down to and between my legs. When I appeared, he had already undressed, standing in his underwear. Seeing me he hardened. I saw the bulge, shivered, trying to hide my concern from him. Would I disappoint him? Would it be uncomfortable, hurt like a nurse friend said it would? However, my mother told me I must submit to my husband. But I did not believe that about Benjamin.

"Constance," he spoke softly, "You are so beautiful." He led me to the bed trying to keep his eyes on my breasts. "Would you mind taking off your gown? I want to see all of you."

I reached above and slowly raised the gown over my head. As he watched, I heard his deep breath, as he looked, I believe, at the darkened chestnut hair between my thighs. I smiled, despite my blush. I felt heat again throughout me as he continued to gaze toward my breasts and lower. He moved me gently toward the bed, and I lay down, aware of the mattress giving way to my back.

"Will you undress so I can see you? That's not ladylike, I know, but we're married." I gazed at his growing penis, reached and modestly touched it. "Oh, the cap for birth control you gave me. I struggled with it a bit but had to place it in private," my blush rising through my neck to my face.

We observed one another. He came to me, reached for my breasts, kissed my nipples, ran his lips over them, as they hardened, I shivering in heated feeling to my cleft. He ran his hands over my soft roundness. My desire increased. He looked at my mound and again below at the darker hair. "Part your legs, dear." I responded. He parted them more, then placing his fingers to my opening. He must have heard my gasp and then my shaky voice, "More. Oh yes." I felt a tremor throughout me.

"Ben, I'm ready. Take me."

I watched nervously as he raised himself while I spread my legs still wider.

"You're so lovely," he whispered. He entered me. I gasped as I felt the pain. He moved more into my silkiness. I sensed the movement. I clenched the sheet as I felt him, smiling, thinking, *I hurt, but it won't always be like this. I'm no longer a virgin.* I reached and brought his face to mine and kissed him tenderly then harder. "Can we do that again?"

I felt his weight upon me and heard, "Oh, Constance, that felt so good. Did … did I hurt you."

"Yes. But I want you to do it again. I want you inside me," my mind and body in ecstasy.

He followed my wish. I felt more relaxed and began to tremble throughout as I began to reach my height.

My voice trembling, I told him, "I never knew."

Benjamin and I now felt the bond that strongly held us. Yet the sadness seemed always to hang over us. During the night I heard him speak in troubling voice, "Amos."

Still, in the day we walked about the city, at night, ate later to enjoy supper, then went to our rooms. I had lost my embarrassment as we both shed clothes, enjoyed looking at one another and then experimenting and exploring to find ways to enjoy our bodies that hugged us together.

One morning, he left me alone in our room, although I wanted to be with him. When he returned he held a gift.

"I have something for you, my gorgeous, beautiful wife."

I took the small package. Opening it, I cried out, the excitement, I'm sure, showing in my eyes. "Ben . . ."

"I have purposely saved from my pay." It was a diamond necklace. My eyes teared as I moved close to kiss him, then crying, pleased. "Oh, Ben." I pressed my head against his shoulder. "Darling. I love you so." I sobbed, forced myself to stop, looked at him, then turned. "Fasten it, please"

I went to a mirror. "It's magnificent." Still in tears, I turned, my hand on my mouth. "Ben. We haven't told our parents." I thought for a moment. "I almost don't care. We are in our own little world right now. Away from the war." I hesitated. "And I now feel like a woman. You made me a woman. I love it, knowing what a woman is and can do, oh, and such feeling, if she has the courage. I, Mrs. Benjamin Blumenthal, love you so." Then I stopped, thinking of my married name. *Blumenthal. Let anyone say or do what they want. I'll get them back, if I have to.*

"I'll write to my parents, Ben. Will you do the same to yours?"

"Of course. Constance. Will they disown you?"

I shuddered. "I . . . I'm not certain. I know my mother will be furious. I don't know. I do care, but I'm your wife. That's what truly matters. But you, Ben. I heard that if you marry a Christian your family will believe you dead. Oh, I can't stand that. Promise me, you'll try to stay away from the front line. Don't volunteer. Perhaps your station will remain Washington. My dear love, dearest love. Don't ever leave me. I couldn't bear it." I started to cry. "Ben. Promise me you'll always take care of yourself, of us."

"Don't cry. Please. We have each other. That's the world. Think," he suddenly said, "Someday we'll have children. I want them to look like you, especially girls." His mind went to his parents. "Constance, my parents eventually are going to accept you, me. They have to." He knew, however, his father would shout, "He's dead. And to think, we have lost two sons, one to the rotten Southerners, another to a Christian." Benjamin became silent. *What must they be feeling, Amos, my beloved oldest brother. Dying as I held him.* His eyes teared, as I noticed.

"Ben, you're crying. I said something that hurt you."

"No, my love. It's not you. I just thought of Amos. Constance . . . it was so hard. He died in my arms." His eyes filled.

I pulled him to me, tightly hugging him. "Cry. A man can cry. You should. Here we are. We are so happy, but even in that happiness there is sadness we can't ever forget. I always have wished that I could have been with you then." I rubbed my hands up and down his back. "We have our love," I said softly, repeating, "Our love, undying, even in Heaven.

"We'll tell our parents we are joining the Unitarian Church. That may help some. If it isn't, we'll do what we must. Together, Ben. Together, even it means leaving Portland."

He smiled, then laughed. "You are a brave woman. I've known that, but suddenly just now it hit me how much. Constance, we're on our honeymoon. We are going to enjoy it, revel in one another's company. Yes, we'll write, but it's you and me, as you said, even in Heaven."

We spent the time remaining to us, aside from seeing Washington, even hoping for a glimpse of President Lincoln. Then one day we did see him as he rode out of the city with his wife. Overwhelmed, we grasped one another's hands, squeezing.

In early morning, late afternoon, night, we made love, experimenting how best to please one another. I learned how best to enjoy being on top, guiding him while enjoying the movement within me and our sounds.

* * *

They wrote short letters to their parents, comparing them. Constance told her parents:

"Dear Mother and Father,

"On August 5, after Benjamin and I were transferred to Washington from Gettysburg, we married in the Episcopal Church here in the city. We convinced the minister on that afternoon to perform the ceremony. For us, although it was quick, it was the beginning of our loving lives together. We are deeply in love and hope that you will accept this marriage as something that has and always will make Benjamin and me as happy as possible, being man and wife who, despite what may come, we'll always have one another upon whom to rely. Our love for one another has been over years, dear mother and father. I believe you have known this, although you probably hoped that what I am telling you would never happen. Please, dear parents, try to accept us as your children. I suppose I shouldn't say this this way, but Benjamin will be your son, dear mother and father. I hope I shall be another daughter to his parents.

"My love and Benjamin's for you always, Constance"

She read the letter to Benjamin before sealing it. "Have you written yours?"

"Not yet. I've been thinking about it. Do you mind if I don't say anything about the church?"

She hesitated. "Well, I guess not. No. They'll hear it anyhow."

"I'll tell them we're going to join the Unitarians. O.K.?"

"That's fine." She thought he should tell them everything, but then, they would be furious no matter what. Would they ever accept her or him, for that matter?

"No, dearest. You say what you want. I was also thinking, perhaps I would write to Arella. She and I have always been friends and have told each other intimate things, you know, some female, like when we bleed or wondering," and she blushed . . . "others about what we were thinking, how she knew you and I loved one another . . . and about what . . . well what it would be like to have a man see you and put his thing inside you. We," she laughed, "called it *thing*." Her face still red she went on, "But now I know, and it's a penis. I've known that since anatomy in college and being a nurse. The first time I saw a naked man, it shocked me. I knew it was part of my job to wash them, or seeing them come in, their clothing torn away by wounds. Oh I just don't want to think about it. It's going to start all over again in another day."

She went to Benjamin, moved his face to hers, tightly placing her lips on his. Opening his mouth to hers, pulled back, "Ben, my belly feels like I want to do it. I feel it below too. Ooh, my nipples are hard. Make love to me, Ben. I so enjoy when you hold me, move about me, kiss me all over and I doing the same to you."

"Shall I wait to write," he smiled.

"Yes."

Later, after they rested, holding onto each other, she rose, whispering, "I have to wash."

He waited, then did the same, dressed and sat at the desk;

but before writing, he remembered. "Constance, Arella and I talked or wrote too about you and me and our love. She knew how I felt. Anyhow . . .

"Dear Mamma and Papa,

"I want you to know that Constance Sterling and I married two days ago. As you are aware, we have known each other since high school. I love her more than life itself. We worked together at Gettysburg, and we both were transferred here to Washington and will be at the Armory Hospital. Please try to understand. You will be upset because she is Christian. I hope, however, that someday you will accept both of us and that you will feel as though you have another daughter.

"When we have children, I'm not sure how they'll be raised. We haven't talked about it. We are going to join the Unitarian Church. Before exploding, this church accepts everyone regardless of religion. So don't be concerned about that. I love you bother dearly and want your love toward me to continue always. Try to understand and do think of Constance as another daughter.

"My love always to you both, Ben."

* * *

Faith received the mail. She smiled when she saw Constance's writing, happily noting the Washington postmark, that she was outside the war zone. She quickly opened it, saw one word, 'married.' "NO. They CAN NOT have done this. What has she done?" She began to cry. "That stupid girl. Marrying that Jew. I warned her. How many times? Doesn't she realize she'll be isolated from her good society?"

She was now sobbing, using a handkerchief helping little. "My beautiful daughter." She wanted to rush to her husband but knew he was with patients. "But it's his fault too. Taking to that Jew boy. *His Fault*," and she sobbed more loudly. "He helped do this to his lovely daughter, allowing her so much freedom. It's just not done. Allowing her to travel by herself, to be with God knows what kind of people. To think I was so proud of her serving our country. And this is what she does to us."

She stopped talking to herself, read the letter again and again, wrinkling it. When she looked what she had done to the page, she tried to smooth it to show to her husband. Then he appeared.

"What's the matter, Faith? Why all this awful crying?"

"Look what she'd done, what you helped happen."

Nathaniel took the wrinkled sheet, reading, smiling, but also sad that they married without telling them first.

"Faith. Please dear. She's a grown woman who will have her way. We should love her.'

"But that Jew boy. No one we know will have anything to do with her, with them."

He went to her, hugging her, soothingly moving his hands up and down her back. "Faith. She's our daughter. She did marry a fine man. Yes. You're right. I'm not certain what will happen socially. You may be right. But they did this themselves. We have to accept it and love them. And Faith, I do wish you would stop that 'Jew boy' business. I can't stand it. I hate bigotry."

"No. You just don't care. You never did. Getting him into the medical school. Making him think he's as good as . . . as us."

"Stop that. I won't listen to it. Yes, I'm disappointed. It would have been better to have a husband of our religion. But they made up their minds. They do love one another. It's been noticeable for years, Faith. Please. Try to calm yourself. We have to live with what's happened. We can't give up our daughter to prejudice, other people's or . . . or yours. You *must* get over it."

She pushed away from him, trying to see him clearly through her wet eyes. "Nathaniel. I can't help the way I feel about *those* people."

He quietly answered, "You will learn. When you give yourself a chance, you'll come to love Benjamin. I know you will. Please try."

She sobbed again, shaking, resting her head against his shoulder. "I'll Trrryy. I wiiilll."

"That's better. You just cry yourself out." He hesitated. "Do you want me to write them? Or would you rather?"

"No. You."

Nathaniel sat down that evening. He tried to conceal his concern:

"My dearest Constance and Benjamin,

"I wish we could have been at your wedding, but I know that in these terrible times one must face hardships. You two have been through so much. Just know that your mother and father (in-laws, Ben) and I will always love both of you. You have taken a step that many would not have the courage to have done. There are many people who will not accept your loving marriage. Know that we will always be with you in whatever you do. And do take care of yourselves.

"Love, Mother and Father"

* * *

"Mamma, COME HERE. LOOK AT THIS," Asa Blumenthal was yelling louder than he ever had. Scared, Hannah came running to him.

"What is the matter? Are you all right?"

"NO. I'm NOT all right. *This* . . . this thing, I'm holding, this letter people call it. THIS IS DAMNATION. Our great son, great army surgeon. He's DONE IT NOW. *He's dead to me to you, to his family.*"

"What?" Her heart was beating rapidly. Was another son lost to the war? "Oh, not like our poor Amos," and she started to cry, wailing, "Amos."

"AM . . . o . . . s." His voice caught. "NO, Hannah. It's our son the doctor."

"Tell me already. What's he done that you've scared me so?" She was sobbing now thinking of Amos and Benjamin. She thought, "Has he been wounded?"

Asa's voice suddenly became weak. "He's forever dead to us. HE . . . he MARRIED that Christian woman, that whore."

"YOU STOP USING those words. Tell me. You are giving me a heart attack." Her breathing came harder as her heart beat faster and she began trembling. "Benjamin married who? You have to be wrong. He told us Rebecca."

"REBECCA? NO. That Christian Constance Sterling. He's dead. He'll never enter this house again. No one in the family is to have anything to do with him. I never want to see him again, hear his name again. That whoring Christian. She probably told him she was having his baby."

"ASA, YOU STOP that NOW. He's married? He married that fine Christian woman Constance Sterling? When?"

By now Asa was crying, "My son, my pride. NO MORE. *Dead.*" He choked. "How could he have done this to us? How? *Oi, vai iz mir Gotteniu. Goyeh di.*" Poor Rebecca. He told us she was the one. He lied."

They held together, both crying. Hannah lifted her head, tears flowing, "He's our son, Asa. Our son. I won't let you talk like that. Please do not do this. I love him. You do also. She is a lovely young woman and smart. I hurt like you. But she's a good girl . . . young woman. I WON"T have you talk about her using that word. She's good. Some Christians are. You know that. Remember the old country how some tried to protect us."

"Hannah, my beloved. That's not the point. She's a Christian. Jews don't marry *them.* It's done. He's gone." And he choked more with tears flowing.

"I will not obey you, Asa. I will see her, kiss her, love her as best I can try. And I won't lose my son. I'm proud of what he's done."

"Well, not me. And that's FINAL."

"And I've told you all I have to say."

* * *

Arella felt a thrill when she received a note from Constance. She immediately wrote back telling Benjamin and her how happy she was that they finally decided they should marry, stating also to ignore what some people would say or think or that others would isolate them.

She happened to see Rebecca near her home one day. Arella's heart caught. She questioned whether she should just walk over and say, "Hello" or to tell her the news. Rebecca would hear eventually, Arella kept thinking. Rebecca then waved to her. Arella dreaded talking to her. *I'll have to tell her. Better from me. Maybe.*

Arella looked toward her house, thinking her mother would call her back, if she saw her walking alone. It made no difference. Arella had already convinced the Portland High School to allow her, a young woman, to teach. She would have to walk to the school alone unless her father would allow her to take their carriage. He was so strict and now so hurt and angry about Benjamin. Sometimes his long silences scared her. When she mentioned it to her mother, Hannah told her, "Perhaps when you find a young man to marry, a Jew, of course, he'll be better. You know, Arella, he loves Benjamin, is proud of him. Somehow, I think he's going to realize that sometimes religion is a block to love and even understanding that there can be friendliness of sorts between people of different religions.

"You know," she then whispered, "I don't think he realizes they are going to be attending services at the First Parish Unitarian Church. They accept everyone there. Perhaps those people are happier. Surely they are more understanding. Oy, I shouldn't say that. God will punish me."

"Oh mamma, don't be silly. God doesn't punish people for thinking and talking."

And they both laughed.

Actually, Arella had met a young man to whom Esther and Joshua had introduced her. They both seemed to like each other. He had come to her home to introduce himself and to spend time with Arella. She was also thinking about him at the moment. His name was Ely Levin, tall, handsome, and so well built. He worked in his father's growing lumber business. She loved his black hair and deep brown eyes, his quiet, pleasant voice. In fact, sometimes he sang to her, his voice a beautiful tenor. She had begun to think more seriously about marriage even though they hadn't spoken of it. She could bring him to that. She had learned in college how to flirt and use her eyes and body that she knew would be enticing. Her full breasts, her thin body that flared at the hips and led to her shapely legs. Well, she did look at herself in the mirror. What woman didn't?

Now Arella was almost there with Rebecca who smiled when she saw her friend.

"Hello. We haven't talked for a while. I've missed you. I suppose you're thinking about your new job."

Arella wasn't thinking about that, but managed a stammered, "Hi, Rebecca. You're right. We haven't talked for a bit."

"What's going on in your life? I saw you with that young man. He's handsome."

"He is, isn't he?" She wanted to avoid talking about Ely right now. Or did she? She wouldn't have to mention Benjamin. That was not about to happen.

"Arella, how's Benjamin? I haven't heard from him in a long time. Gettysburg was so bad. He's probably terribly busy taking care of all those poor young men."

"I have something to tell you, Rebecca," she stammered, trying to keep her face from the red she felt rising.

Rebecca noticed and looked at her questioningly. "Is he all right? It would be terrible for something else to happen in your family. This horrid war. All those people who are still enslaved even though the President freed them."

"No. Benjamin is all right." She then spoke quickly. "He wasn't wounded or anything like that. It's . . . well, it's just that he's . . . married. He married a Christian girl that I went to college with. He's known her since he was about 17 or 18."

"Married! He promised me! He told me he cared for me, that I would make a good wife for him. What do you mean?" She was both angry and now in tears. "He can't be! He promised *me*!" She cried and started sobbing, thinking of their kisses and his hand on her breasts, how she had allowed him to touch her so. She now had a difficult time getting out her words and feelings. "That's horrible. He promised *me*!" she sobbed, embarrassed more still thinking about being touched as she was. "I HATE him! He LIED to me! He's NO GOOD. And I don't want to see you ever again either. I hate him doing this to me. Never. You hear." Now she was sobbing loudly, choking as she swallowed, wiping furiously at her face and eyes. "I . . . just don't want to see you or anyone from your family again. I'll make sure the whole world knows what he has done."

Arella tried to calm her but knew she couldn't. She also was now crying. "I can imagine how you feel." She reached for Rebecca to bring in a hug. Rebecca shoved her away. "No. Leave me alone. Your family is . . ." she hesitated. "Your family is no good. Benjamin is not only hateful but a liar," she cried loudly.

Her shoulders bent and sobbing, also embarrassed and hurt, she walked slowly to her house, then running up the stairway, slamming the door.

* * *

Arella decided to write immediately, keeping her letter secret from her parents and Esther, now the mother of four children. She had told Arella she would have no more, that she would use the cup to prevent further pregnancies. Arella had wondered about that when she would eventually marry and decided she had a choice and would use it. She also knew sometimes the cup failed but that did not matter. But all this was not on her mind now. She was the one person in her family who was delighted by the marriage. Of course, she dearly loved Constance and knew she would be just the perfect wife for a doctor. She also knew that Benjamin would not enslave her in the home, that she would choose what she wished to do. How she loved them both.

"My dear, dear Constance and beloved brother,

"May I call you sister, Constance? I know you'll say 'yes.' I can't tell you how thrilled I was to know you two did as you wished and became husband and wife. After all, we are not living in the Middle Ages.

"Ben, I know you are aware how father feels. Please do not let that depress you. Mother loves you still and tried to settle him. But you know that will take time. Mother has always had a way with his stubbornness and, forgive me, but the hell with religion and those narrow beliefs that some people have.

"Oh, how I love you both. I hope I'll always be able to visit with you. I did meet a nice young man, handsome like you Ben, who has finally asked me to marry him. I haven't decided yet. But he will have to accept my new sister and brother as part of the family.

"There isn't much more to tell you. Oh yes, I was actually, note actually, accepted as a young woman to teach at the Portland Public High School. How do you like that? I forgot to tell you that earlier. Now, shall I tell Ely, that's his name, of course, who wants me to be his wife, that he's going to have to allow me to teach and have his children and take care of his home? Imagine me as a mother? I can't say, 'I do,' at least not yet.

"I can't wait until Fall and beginning my teaching, working at something worthwhile, even earning a little money. I guess we nurturing women are good for our society, no Constance? I can imagine that the wounded soldiers enjoy having you care for them. Perhaps I'll buy some new dresses. Or perhaps on vacation, I'll come visit you. I imagine, if the war is still on, and I wish like others it would end, I may have saved enough to come to you.

"I'm stopping, having gone on long enough. Again my love to you both."

* * *

Arella then set about trying to help Benjamin and Constance by trying to reverse Asa's displeasure and disliking that he never talked about Ben. When she talked, he would get angry.

"Father, you are being a stubborn, unruly old man. Ben is your son. Admit it. I know my mother had him, so you have to admit that. Now stop with all this death stuff. Haven't we had enough of that in this family and country? Think of what he's doing down there helping young men recover from the hell they have been through."

"Don't you use that kind of language in this house," and he started to smile.

"Be careful father. You almost smiled. Perhaps I should continue to use that language so there would be more laughter in this house. I know. We are grieving Amos. I still cry at night or other times thinking of him. And I hear mamma. And you trying to console her. I've heard your crying papa. Will we ever recover? Oh, if only Daniel will come through all right.

"So how can you feel like that about your son, that he's . . . he's dead to you. Never. You're wrong, papa. Wrong, wrong, wrong." She felt the tears coming and wiped at her eyes, wanting to stop the tears, but she failed. She cried aloud. "Now, n . . . now see what you've done."

She turned away and started to run to her room, crying loudly, furiously wiping her cheeks.

"Arella," her father shouted."

She stopped. "Wh . . . what?"

Asa went to her. "I don't like you crying like this. Here lean on my shoulder, dear. After all you're the only one we have left in the house. I can't help how I feel. But our religion, all the centuries, and how we have suffered because of the Christians."

She stepped back, her father bleary through her tears. "Papa. Not all Christians are killers. Yes. I know what you're thinking. The old country. Well, we're here in the United States. I was born here. There are people who despise us here too, who discriminate. But papa, the Sterling's aren't like that. Think of how Dr. Sterling helped Benjamin. And I went to Bates College with Constance. She is not only beautiful but a wonderful person. Think of what she is doing." She cried louder, trying to stop the tears.

"What's going on here?" Hannah heard them from the kitchen where she was helping the maid. What did you do to her, Asa, that she's crying like this?"

"I didn't do anything." And when he thought about it, he was lying.

"N . . . nothing, mamma. I just needed a good cry."

"Now you're both lying. You fought. Tell me what it's about."

Hugging Arella again, Asa looked deeply at Hannah. He didn't want to say it, but he had to. "We were talking about Benjamin." He hesitated, wondering how he should continue. Feeling Arella shaking against him, he couldn't help himself.

"We were talking about Ben and Constance."

"Asa, you said her name, and you called our son Ben, like you always have, except when you were mad at him." She smiled. "You said the word. 'Constance.'" She hesitated. "You know, Asa, that woman is doing something God can only look upon as good. We should be proud of her, as if, as if she had come from me. We did meet her. Yes. And Benjamin kept it a bad secret from us. But she's his wife. Think of what they are both doing. I heard from some women what the soldiers think of the nurses. They love having them take care of them, feel better when a woman sits by them, talks to them. Some of those boys are blind, and the women write letters for them.

"Yes. Her name is Constance. Arella has told me how lovely she is. We should love her, Asa, and Ben. I can't hate. I just can't. And if the Christians don't want to accept us, that's their problem. We have a new life here. And think of how well we are living. Who would have believed it?" She laughed. "I even have a maid.

"Asa, I want you to accept this marriage that I believe is going to be good for the world." She went to her husband, trying to put her arms about her daughter and husband. With tears, she spoke firmly, "Good for the world."

He also had tears and nodded a 'yes.'

Arella, his angel, had brought peace to their home.

* * *

In Washington there was no peace. In March, 1864, President Lincoln had appointed Lieutenant General Grant to command the Union Army. He was to lead the Union to its eventual victory. Meanwhile, there were battles to occur, of course, and wounded flowed to the Armory Hotel after the Battle of the Wilderness. With little warning, doctors and nurses heard of many wounded about to arrive in the ambulances after immediate treatment at Fredericksburg. Attendants soon began taking wounded from the two-wheeled wagons. Constance and other nurses started a triage. Some of the men were already gangrenous, the odor and the cries tearing at the women and the doctors.

Doctors, like Benjamin, wondered why those with gangrene hadn't been treated with permanganate of potassa. Immediately Benjamin was applying the medication and then moving to those who would require surgery.

Surgeons called for nurses to aid, to administer chloroform and ether and to take from their trays bandages soaked in the antiseptic.

After hours had passed, there were arms and legs to be discarded. This was left to the attendants, white and black.

Exhausted, Constance went late that night to her room shared with another nurse. She was thinking of Benjamin, wishing she were with him, wondering whether to ask superiors if they could share a room. She knew that would not be allowed.

The other nurse finally appeared. "Constance, you must be as weary as I. You look haggard," she laughed. She looked at Constance's hair the net gone so it draped about her face, her ringlets gone, her face pale with weariness.

"Do I look like you?" Mary wearily asked.

Constance smiled. "Oh, no, you are beautiful. I think we ought not to show ourselves in the city, People will think we're ghosts."

The two laughed, as Mary sank to her bed. "Constance," looking at her wedding ring, "has anyone asked you about your husband?"

"Well, yes. Why?"

"Truthfully," she hesitated, "You know we are friends, but I wondered at first how you could have . . ."

"Stop, Mary, Please. Right now. Yes. I married a Jew. You

asked me about that, remember?"

"I know. Don't get upset. I was just wondering whether anyone has said something to your husband. It's none of my business, but I have thought about it. I couldn't get used to it."

"Enough, Mary," Constance answered in a low, angry voice. "I married a Jew. I love him, have since I first met him years ago. If there's anyone who doesn't like it or doesn't want to have anything to do with me, then to hell with them. NO. A nice girl, excuse me, woman doesn't swear. Well, damn it, if someone doesn't want to be near me, that's their problem, not mine."

Mary, her face red from embarrassment, found it difficult to answer, her voice choked with emotion, tears beginning to appear. "I . . . I didn't mean anything bad, Constance."

Constance breathed deeply, seeing the tears. "Oh, Mary, forgive me. We're both exhausted. It's just that . . . just that, I'm sick of some of the surgeons and nurses I know and imagine thinking but not saying anything about us. I love that Jewish surgeon, Mary. I wouldn't, couldn't have married another man. As I told my mother in a letter, if no one likes it, if people don't want to have anything to do with us, that's their problem, not ours."

"Constance," Mary recovering, but still feeling her face warm, "we've talked about this before. I don't know why I brought it up again. I," she started to weep, "I want you for my friend always, but I could never stand the thought of Jews. I despised them, until I met you, and finally your husband. Oh, we should stop this conversation. I don't want you to hate me. But whoever knew a Jew, met one? I come from a part of the country where no one sees them." She cried harder, fearful of hurting Constance who she had come to love.

Constance rose from her bed and went to sit beside her, placing her hand on hers, wiping at Mary's cheeks upon which tears had rolled. Then, in a sudden rush of love, Constance pulled her to herself. "Mary. I love you. Please. Please. Let's not talk about this anymore, and let's promise friendship 'til whenever."

"You're so dear, Constance." She kissed her on the cheek.

Later that night, Constance who couldn't sleep well and who missed Benjamin terribly, thinking about how weary he must be, walked out to her ward. She listened to the crying of some men, the nightmare of others who called out to fallen comrades or screamed about the shells, others who called to their mothers, wives, sweethearts. She walked among the beds, speaking soothingly soft to a soldier awake, taking another's hand that he held out to her, wiping at the forehead of another, then stopping at one bed. The soldier raised his cold head that she felt, watching his eyes opening and closing, listening to his mumbled words, holding his shoulders as he died. She cried as she lowered his head to his pillow, then pulled the sheet over his face. She trembled, trying to stop her tears. She would never become used to this, "I can't," she told herself, going back to her room and sinking onto her bed, trying to muffle her crying so as not to wake Mary. Under her covers, she shook. *There's so much more to come. They're fighting in Spotsylvania. We keep hearing rumors of all those men suffering, and the battle isn't over.*

That morning Benjamin made certain he saw her. When he approached, she smiled; but as they came closer, she put her hand to her mouth, pained by the weariness in his face. She looked to see whether they were alone. She walked quickly to him.

"Oh love. You look so tired. I have worried about you." She put her arms about him and kissed him lightly, then harder. "I have missed you so."

Moving his tongue about her lips and then kissing her back, he moved away, looking longingly at her..

"Yes. I'm worn through. It's been bad. You know that though." He smiled. "They like my work, have complimented me. Of course, I have done the same to Assistant Surgeons. There's one surgeon who won't work with me. You know why, of course. The fool. And, oh, I submitted some of my microscopy to the Army Medical Museum. Recently I learned how to preserve specimens so they can be sent. I owe my use of the microscope to your father having taught me through his at your home. Do you remember?"

She was smiling, while chewing her lower lip thinking of being with him. He had interrupted her thoughts. "Oh, yes I do."

"You do what?" he laughed.

"Well, I was off somewhere. You mentioned a microscope while I was . . ." She stopped, her face heating red with embarrassment. "Well, what I was thinking was not . . . not ladylike. But yes, I heard, truthfully not all. What did you say?"

He was smiling, starting to laugh again but wanted to spare her. "I said your father had a microscope and taught me about it and how to use it. At your home, dearest. And you needn't be embarrassed. I'm your husband. Remember?"

"Stop." The red of her face fading. "Yes women think about you know what. What's the difference?" She smiled and said almost in a whisper, although they were alone. "I want you to make love to me, Ben. That's . . . Oh horrors. My face is getting red again, isn't it?"

He touched her face lightly, tilted her chin so their lips would meet. He placed his lips on hers, pressed lightly then harder. She met him, feeling warmth throughout her body. She moved her hips so she pressed harder against him, speaking silently to herself, *Damn these slips and dresses women wear. I want to feel him, grind against him. Constance, stop this now.* "That kiss was nice. You still love me."

"I'll always love you. I'll repeat it. I'll always love you. And forget the microscope. Now you did it. I managed to get us a day off starting tomorrow night until the next. I went to your matron. She hrrumphed, looking at me sternly, then smiling, "Oh of course, major. I'll get someone to take her place."

"We better take advantage of the lull. There'll be wounded coming in soon from Spotsylvania. Let's go to the Willard.

"Now we have to get back to work. I'll wait outside the hospital for you, tomorrow around late afternoon."

"I can't wait. It will be so nice to get away from here. Ben, I don't think I'll ever get over what I've seen or heard."

"Neither of us will."

* * *

Before dinner, Constance changed to a dress, disliking the hoop and the many skirts along with the pantalets with its T shape. She made up her hair, assuring that her ringlets were correct. She then applied a light rouge to her cheeks and lips. She would never just be a modest woman, although she would according to custom and depending on the occasion behave that way in public. She knew that Benjamin expected her to be an independent thinker, not that she be, if ever, the retiring, subdued female. Satisfied with her looks, she came to him smiling, knowing later she would assure she was alluring and desirable.

In the evening, she wore the nightgown from her wedding night, except tonight there were no ties. As he watched her come toward him, she dropped the gown. He looked longingly at her shapely hips that led to her thighs and her hair between her legs. He took in her sex as she slightly spread her legs, looked up to her well-formed breasts and the brown about her nipples now hardening. "You look appreciative and satisfied," she smiled, as she slowly turned to show herself, beckoning him with her slender body's curvatures. Seeing him harden, she went to him, "Ben, take me."

160

* * *

General Grant would accept General Lee's surrender at Appomattox, but on April 14, 1865, the North's elation expired as with their martyred President. The disbelief paralleled what Constance and Benjamin and so many others knew before. They would never forget the many sounds of dying men, the soldiers' screaming, mumbled nightmares, the pleading for sweethearts, wives, and mothers, found in the love from soothing relief of female hands while dying, the sights of horrible wounds, the gangrenous odor of war.

Leaving the service in the summer of that year, in a surprise and joyous meeting and hugging, Constance and Benjamin met at the rail station his brother Daniel.

"Is that arm in the sling all right?" Ben asked his brother.

"It was only a slight wound the surgeon told me. The bullet chipped a bit of bone. He said I'd be all right after they treated with some permanganate of something and what seemed constant soaked bandages." He laughed. "Ben, I got the first word right, didn't I? I begged the surgeon to let me keep my arm I was so worried." He laughed and said not to worry. "Ben. I can't, I just can't believe we're together here at the station." He turned to Constance.

"Come here, my sister." She went to him, smiling, both placing their arms about one another. She ran her hand over his cheek and part of his beard, feeling his kiss on her cheek.

"Oh, that deserves a return." She lightly kissed his lips. "Daniel, this is so amazing. Now I do have a brother. No?"

"Constance. I heard what papa said and how he fumed. Mamma told me in a letter. He's an old fool. Look at you. Why he should be happy to have such a beautiful woman in the family. Well, there is Esther and Arella. You went to school with Arella. Now I remember. She always loved you. Let's not talk about bad things now. Papa is a fool."

They traveled happily together.

In Portland Asa was still unwilling to meet Benjamin and Constance. He would not accept their marriage. Hannah began to grow quite angry.

"I'm sick of your stubbornness and stupidity, Asa."

He looked at her in surprise. "You are my wife. You do not talk to me like that."

"Well, let me tell you something. We're now Americans. I speak my mind. I'm no longer that timid girl you married in the old country. You seem to forget what I have learned here. Look how good this country has been to you, to us, to the family." She paused, tears forming, thinking of Amos. "We have already lost one son to this glorious country. I will not accept another. The war is over, Asa, in the country and in our home." She was now crying, "I've already lost one son. I can't stand this, Asa. My heart is so broken," She began shaking and sobbing.

Asa went to her, holding her tightly. She raised her head. "You . . . you don't know it, but Esther and Joshua are planning to meet them."

"What? My whole family is against me? What did I raise?" He was angry again, children and their ages making no difference. "My whole family is against me. It's been that way ever since Arella and that Constance went to school together." He refused to mention Benjamin's name.

Hannah pulled away from him. "I don't want to see you or talk to you. I'll be at that station. I'll love Constance as I do my own daughters and the men. They're not boys and girls any longer, Asa. They're grown men and women. If you can't get that in your head, then I want nothing from you."

Asa looked at her disbelieving she had talked to him as she had. Of course, they had argued during their long lives together, but this? He watched her leave the room, still sobbing. He felt drained, began mumbling to himself, thinking of the war in which his sons had been, the loss of their eldest. He shook his head, sat, his head enclosed in his hands. "What have I done? What am I thinking?"

That night, Hannah slept in what had been Esther's room. He could not believe she had done this.

Arella, arrived home after the argument, surprised no supper was being prepared, that her mother was upstairs. She went to the parlor, saw her father seeming to look out a window. He did not turn to greet her.

"What has happened here?"

He turned. "Ask your mother."

"What?" Arella ran upstairs, found Hannah, still crying. "Your father and I had a terrible argument. I don't want to see him."

"What happened?" She told Arella the entire episode. "You make your own supper. He can get his own. I don't want to see him." She began sobbing again. "We have lost one son, and he acts like a monster from the old country. I just won't have it. When they arrive, you and I, Esther and Joshua will go to the station." She trembled. Arella tried to comfort her, holding her, tears in her eyes. "I'll get supper. I'll talk to him."

"You do whatever you want, dear. Just leave me. I'm not hungry."

Arella went down and confronted her father. "Do you have any idea what is happening here? What is wrong with you, Papa?"

"Oh, my daughter now."

"Yes, your daughter now. You are acting like an old fool. Papa."

"Fool." He glared at her but could not frighten her. She was beyond that now.

"Yes, fool," she shouted. "You are an old fool. This is your family. Your sons are returning tomorrow, one with the most lovely, wonderful, intelligent woman as his wife."

"You cannot talk to your father like that." He was shaking

163

now with anger, feeling his heart beating strongly. His face became pale. He struggled to breathe. He felt for the chair behind him, and slowly sat.

"Papa. What's wrong?" Arella was terribly frightened, her heart now beating more rapidly.

"It's all right," struggling to control himself, catching his breath. He looked at Arella, the one of whom he had been so proud. He was looking in her green eyes now showing fear. "Come here, dear one. I want to hold you. I've lost my temper in a way I never thought I could. I don't like the fear in your eyes, those beautiful bright eyes."

Arella went quickly to him as he reached to hug her, having regained some composure. "Arella, the smartest of us all except for Benjamin. Benjamin my son. And we have lost Amos," His eyes filled with tears. "But . . . your mother and I still have Daniel and Esther. Benjamin. I was consigning him to death." He took a deep breath. "I . . . I am a fool, a growing old fool. This terrible war. We have lost that glorious President and your oldest brother. What am I thinking? Arella, tell your mamma I want her to come down. I have . . . have to make it up to her, to you, to the whole family." He now shook with sadness, sitting with his head bent, crying loudly.

Arella went to him, gently rubbing her hand across his shoulders. "Papa, forgive me. I didn't mean to do this to you. Please papa. Calm yourself. Don't cry." There were now tears flowing down her cheeks at which she wiped. "I love you, papa. But you have to understand. We have always been a family filled with love. We've been so fortunate. You came to America and gave Benjamin and me life here. You've been grand. I just don't want to see that all spoiled now. Believe me, papa. You'll love Constance as another daughter. I just know it."

He looked up at her, her face blurred by his tears. "I want Hannah . . . I mean, please get mamma."

Arella went to her mother, told her about Asa, what she had

said. Hanna shook her head. "My daughter, you'll have to apologize."

"I just about have, mamma. Let's go to him. I think he has thought more about what would be happening to our family."

When they appeared, Asa's eyes were now dry but sad. "Mamma. Arella is right. I have been a fool. I want to make it up to you. Will you forgive me?"

Now they all had tears. Hannah went to him. "You old fool," she smiled through her tears. "Don't you know by now how much I love you, you . . . you old fool."

He stood and gently pulled her to him, hugging her. "You made us all what we are."

She laughed. "We both did. We are a very fortunate family, except for . . ." and her eyes began to fill, thinking of Amos. "Yes, Asa, we are all very lucky, now with grandchildren. Imagine. And, Asa, please remember what you've been told about Constance. She'll be good to us and will love us. I don't know her yet, but from what Arella has told me over all this time, I can't wait to see her, to hug her. Old fool," and she laughed again. "Think about it. Our family is expanding." She hesitated. "You'll come to the station?"

"I will. And I should apologize to God for telling him to take our son because of his marriage. Saturday I'll go and pray for all of us."

The surprise for Benjamin, Constance, and Daniel was that the Blumenthals and the Esther and Joshua Myer family with children and the Sterlings were all there to meet them when they arrived in Portland.

There was still sadness over the loss of Abraham Lincoln, that great President. They talked some about him. Benjamin and Constance having been at Gettysburg, knew of his address at the battlefield. Benjamin had memorized it, would recite it with tears.

But the joys of life were paramount in this family meeting.

Mr. Blumenthal would break some of the tension that may have been there. He would go to Constance. His imagination was so real to him.

'Constance, dear,' he mumbled, then strongly, 'My dearest Constance, my other daughter. I was wrong to think of you as I did.' His eyes teared, as did hers.

'Papa. I'll call you that. Daniel and Ben always refer to you that way. May I?'

I'll kissed her, and tell her, 'I like that, Constance. Nothing should ever again come between us.'

Meanwhile. Faith went to talk to Hannah. This had to be not only a momentary family gathering, but a lasting one of kinfolk. Faith had thought about it for some time after Nathaniel had talked to her. They had, of course, heard their daughter and husband were returning from war. The war had to end also between these two differently believing groups.

When the two women looked at one another, Faith spoke first. "Hannah. I want to get to know you." Faith hesitated. "I have not thought highly of Jews."

Hannah knew she was being sincere and interrupted. "Many people do not like us, shun us. But we think, pray, laugh, and have eyes and cry alike, though our religions may be different. I believe God made it his way. But think of the joy we are now experiencing with that rail arrival. We'll all feel the same way."

Faith agreed. She thought and added, "You sounded something like Shakespeare, Hannah. Have you read him?"

"Arella, came home from school and read parts of *The Merchant of Venice* to us through a whole week, I believe. Something happened at the Boarding House where Arella and Constance were living. Mrs. Stedman read part." Hannah hesitated. "I remember those lines, not perfectly. You know about pricking and crying."

"What happened? Faith asked. "Constance never told me." Faith's face became red, as did Hannah's.

"Well some girl said something about Arella being Jewish."

166

"Mrs. Stedman picked the right play," Faith quickly added to spare Hannah further embarrassment.

Immediately they both smiled. It seemed as though there would be a new friendship between two different women recognizing how much women needed one another.

They were interrupted by the children chasing one another. "They're beautiful, Hannah." Faith laughed. "Look at them."

"Ach, sometimes I can't wait until they grow up and behave. But I love them. Yes, look at them. They're loving children. Our house is a roaring waterfall when they are with us."

Hannah surprised Faith further with that metaphor.

Faith hesitated a moment. "You realize, Hannah, they'll still face problems with this intermarriage."

"Don't we both know?" Yes, here were two intelligent women who could, through desire, find some of life in common to bind them as friends, recognizing the love they both shared and could show the rest of society.

Just before the engine and cars arrived, when they heard it coming, Nathaniel told all that tomorrow there would be a party at their home. Arella and Esther clapped. And then, here were the cars, a loud puffing stop, as the families waited, watched, looking for their loved ones.

When they stepped from their car, Benjamin and Daniel still in uniform, Arella couldn't wait for the other family members and ran to Constance, pulling her face to hers in a kiss, then to her brothers, the same, jumping a bit to reach Ben. As strangers looked on, they watched the families come together, hugging, kissing, crying.

Chapter Six

Physicians Two and . . .

After the partying for the returning veterans, the Sterlings and the Blumenthals quieted everyone. Nathaniel and Faith had agreed that Asa would make the announcement.

"Everyone. Quiet please. We have an announcement to make. All right. Number One: Daniel. Come forward."

He followed his father's wishes. "I have here in my hand an agreement I had drawn up by my lawyer. It states that you are to be a partner in my business as soon as you feel settled and ready to work. Take this my son. It is a reminder of our love and trust in you."

Daniel took the contract his father handed him, his face flushed with surprise and pleasure and tears. He took his father's hand, drawing Asa to him in a hug. He then went to his mother and embraced her, as she also cried in happiness. After the parents, Esther and Joshua went to him, as did Arella, to wish him well.

Asa hesitated. "I have another announcement for the Blumenthal family. Arella has agreed to marriage to Ely Levin. He never gave up." He saw Arella blush. "He lives in Bangor, so Arella will leave us after next June's wedding. We are both happy and sad, because of Arella's coming marriage that means we lose her. What a lucky man he is."

"It's time for me to sit and yield to Dr. Sterling."

Nathaniel rose. "Constance and Ben. First, Ben, you are to become my partner in my medical practice. Second, We have a deed for you to your new home. It is Asa and Hannah's and

Faith's and my gift for you to start your new lives, hopefully in abiding peace. Take this as an everlasting token of our love."

Constance's and Benjamin's faces both flushed in surprise and pleasure. She looked at Benjamin, telling him he should say something.

"Constance told me I should be the one to speak. She has a nicer voice than I. Anyhow, mothers and fathers both, what can anyone say about such a gift? We shall cherish our children and share our love in the home we shall be making. What can we offer you but our love?"

He sat, his face red, placing his hand in Constance's and squeezing, whispering, "I don't believe that our parents will ever have a problem about this mixed marriage that scared them before. I wish I could kiss you here."

"Ben. It's almost unbelievable." She took her hand from Ben's and impulsively rose. "Everyone, I am going to kiss my husband here in front of all of you." She pulled Ben to his feet and raised her face to his lips, kissing and hugging him. She then went to their parents and kissed each on the cheek with a hug. Tears falling down her cheeks at which she wiped, she went to Ben and sat, sniffling, crying, trying to hide her face as she wiped more, took out a hanky and held it to her eyes. Benjamin placed his arm about her, tears in his eyes.

The room was suddenly quiet with the realization they had seen the love that existed not only between these two but in the entire room. Jew and Christian united in understanding and love.

* * *

When they eventually went to their home looking down on Casco Bay beyond the Portland Observatory on the bayside of Munjoy Hill, they found the house entirely furnished with a note in the foyer stating that they could change anything they wished with no cost to them.

Benjamin's and Constance's gift, unknown to all, was located where they could not have foreseen the future but fortunately had their home built where it was. For in the following year on July 4 and 5, 1866, the City of Portland suffered what became known as the Great Fire that destroyed so much of the city.

Their families lost their homes and businesses. Dr. Sterling, after he and Faith recovered from the initial shock, Nathaniel, in discussion with Faith, decided to relocate their home and practice with Benjamin in the West End not far from the Maine General Hospital.

Because the Blumenthals and the Myers had been in business long enough, they had saved sufficient funds that would enable them when rebuilding began to locate not far from where they had been on Middle Street. They also built new homes not too distant from Benjamin and Constance, living among the Irish workers but where other Jews had already settled. Yet Asa expected Jews living where there was a large Catholic population might cause problems. Somehow, Asa told Hannah, they would learn to get along with the Irish and be accepted by them, for all were immigrants, although the Blumenthals came earlier. Asa even had been told by his grandfather that long ago in the Seventeenth Century there had been another intermarriage. His great, great grandfather had come all the way from Ireland during the Flight of the Earls and married eventually into the family. He was known at the time in their usage as doctor, as well as the usual physicus, because of going to college and medical school. They carried with them along with their belongings a faded portrait a woman and him, along with a very worn manuscript written by the physicus (doctor). Asa looked at the painting more closely and even hung it after Benjamin and Constance revealed their marriage.

Now with the fire that had destroyed everything except

what they could carry with them in the carriages, and in their new home, Asa mulled his temper when he heard of the marriage. He began laughing.

"What is it, Asa, this sudden laughing?" Hannah asked.

"I was thinking of my ancestors. The marriage of that Catholic, well, we call them doctors now, to my great great grandmother Ruth. It's a long story."

"You never read all of it to me, or even told me a lot of what you heard."

"Well it never really occurred to me just how important it was to us. I was so angry with Benjamin." Asa's eyes teared.

"You're going to cry, dear."

"I know," he sniffed. "But I love my children and am so proud of Benjamin and also of Amos and Daniel serving in their country's uniform. I miss Amos so. I know you do too."

Now Hannah began to cry and wiped at her tears. They hugged. When he released her, Asa looked at her.

"My dear, dear Hannah. You gave us such wonderful children. Now we can add Constance. I do love her like my own daughters."

She smiled through her tears. "You awful man. How could you not? She's a beauty and so good to us. And such a credit to Benjamin. And after that horrifying fire and the destruction. I have nightmares. But then I think. How lucky we were to be able to come to this country. How we rose from the fire and you have your store again and we this new house. Enough of sadness.

"Now tell me what you never did, and read already."

"The story of my forbears is, as far as I know, true from the beginning. There were actually two intermarriages." Asa laughed. "And that Constance. I don't think I'll ever forgive myself."

"They have. I have. The children too. Now read me more for goodness sake.

"Well sit. It's long and best I know all of it, how it was handed through time . . . like the Bible," she added.

Part II

In the Beginning
Asa Reads

I, Edmond, am no longer in hiding. I am still a prisoner however. I have become a Jew. About me are forests strange and some passably known, but unlike those of my native land. Christ, my former Lord, cannot save me. His Father has damned me to perdition. For, as it is said, "But if I cast out devils by the Spirit of God, then the kingdom of God is come unto you." So spake Matthew. I am certain he was correct. The entire venture was fraught from the start, but we agreed amongst us to the exile, except that I have come farthest than most of the rest. It was the same as though we spoke one to the other, as did Matthew, "He that is not with me is against me, and he who does not gather with me scatters." That is how it was with our leaders, Red Hugh O'Donnell and Hugh O'Neill, Lord of Tyrone, until the year of our Lord 1607 in the month of September. They call it "The Flight of the Earls." O'Donnell and many of the Lords, O'Neill himself for a short while, fled, including myself, the first physician, Skene, to one of those lords whose name better be forgotten. Yet, I am able to call myself Lord still. In a sense we gathered against O'Neill, and as it says, we are scattereth abroad, I with my split Irish and Scots blood having come this far, Lithuania, stopped in Poland where I thought to find succor among my Scot forebears. But I went on to Lithuania, also welcoming a Roman Catholic and those it believed could help it to flourish as have the fields seized by the

English in my native land. They, the English, hast taken the lands, including that lying by the rivers and waters, forcing the peasants to lie on the fallow plains where they have starved.

The English justify themselves by popery against their beliefs. They blamed our beliefs, that it swayed our loyalty and alienated us from our duty to monarch and their country. They called us Papists. If that is what they say, then let it be that we were traitors. Not to our church however. Nor I. Until that day. Hadn't Anthony attempted to destroy the Church creating his own? A blasphemy. And so they be of a mind that we should accept their English Church as rightful but also that we submit to be conquered. They have taken our land and expected not that we shall object or repel them as best we can. Elizabeth, Good Queen Bess, pardon my puke, campaigned against us. Now James continues.

I condemn Anthony, but have I not also blasphemed? Am I not also blasphemer, having embraced the Jewess, my wife, accepting her belief? I may offer the excuse I was bewitched, that I suffered so in my exile and my wandering that I was weak upon meeting her, that I craved her body which she offered but not without acceptance of her faith and name. Lurking in that was marriage. Her face and body. I could not resist. I swear there was fire in her eyes, a heat from her breasts and below, between her legs. Now I am bilious and worry because Judgement cannot be far off, for I have forsaken my land and my faith about which I think more forlornly. I am discontent until there are times my wife believes I have forsaken her also. I cannot do that. The fire that joined is still warm. How can a man, however, destroy his thoughts? Who lives without regret in what could or should have been? We suppress, but it is not lasting. I long to return to the land from whence I came. To the land for which we fought.

We believed we should be victorious. For we had a manner of fighting the English could not understand, coming out of the bogs and strange places unknown, to surprise and defeat them. We hoped they would just give up and return to their own land and leave us to ours.

I lay all that night, and mulled these wild, expectant, and wishful thoughts. To what purpose? For I am reminded of those times as a child, the happiness and freedom of running through the fields, the full growth, the reaping of the harvest. What is our harvest now? Blood and revenge. Hatred of the invaders for us and we for they. Not known to me in my childhood.

My father, from the noble Skene family. Aye, Skene was his name. He, the youngest son, came across the water from Scotland. Though I did not know it then, my father took to the narrow straits to escape what he believed was certain doom. The English again. They wanted to take the rich lands from his family. From what I remember, or what I was told, the English felt they had the right. Many a Scot had crossed those waters to Eire and back again. We did not re-cross. Father settled near Cork. He would have gone to Connacht where it was much more prosperous but feared he would not be accepted. That is what I remember being told.

Then there was my mother. She was a Gael and Catholique, a papist who believed very strongly in her faith and would have none of me father's. Now some may believe that it was no easy thing to cross the marriage and family boundaries, but it was not so strange in this ill-described land that has been compared with that of the Americas and the primitive savages who have unknown religion. And my father coming from good blood and Presbyterian at that. Who can account for the fired blood of attraction, that happens between men and women? Perhaps he saw her the way I saw my Jewess. We Christians, or when I was a Christian, always dreamed of bedding the Jewesses, for if they are God's chosen, then a night with them would be as close to heaven a man could come. And that is the way with Gael women. They have their way with the men, loose, people say.

175

Well, I know my mother was not loose, not for any man's taking, nor would she give for her desire except to my father. It is something I know. In the old times perhaps, from what I heard, the women would take to them any they pleased with their bare breasts firing up the men.

I sometimes want to believe it was my mother and father who influenced me. But that is no excuse, nor am I always sorry I allowed myself to fall to my heart.

My mother, however, was a beautiful woman, at least she is in my mind, though the brood of children, brothers five, sisters four, I the youngest, knew it took its toll. It must be that my father and the eldest of my brothers and sisters saw the changes occur, the lines, the worry. But she was happy, or she never showed her sadness, if it were there. She cared very much for her land, and with time, I believe my father came to feel the same way. How could he not with such a wife as that?

How should I tell you about them? At this time I think of her as a Madonna. Thus, if I sold my soul, had my father? Or have I? Not according to my wife, Ruth, she of peace and pastoral times. But I digress a bit.

Madonna. My mother was not a vision but so real. And when she was happy, the house also. For my father was often angry, and I learned my anger from him, my hatred of the English. I knew that I must grow to fight them, but did not know of any other way except by arms and wile until the time came for me to decide how. She was a fine woman now I think back on it. My mother I mean. I understand her allure for my father. She was never fat even though she bore all those children. Her face was white and set off by her auburn hair and her blue eyes that appeared brighter at times, perhaps because of the paleness of her skin. It was her hands that so fascinated me, so different from a man's, like my father, who farm roughness never left his hands even as time passed and he became more affluent.. Her hands were slender, her fingers long. And when she would gesture it was as though a monument had come to life and she moved them through the aerie spaces as though they were flights of graceful birds. There were times too when she would sing. How we would suddenly, enchanted, all become quiet and listen. But most favored by me, perhaps one of my earliest memories, was at night and she was at my bedside.

When it was the time I was a man, my father told me I must help more about the land. He said, though, I was something special, and my mother did also. They said I would go to Dublin to the college one day, or, if I wished, back to Scotland where my father hadn't been for years, to Edinburgh, or even to one of the great schools of England. I never thought too much about it. Yet, my father by then had been honored by the Queen, though he thought to deny the knighthood, for his good deeds among the people he had chosen and would thereby be submitting to the Queen. Yet this was early on. He would later join Lord Hugh O'Neill. So is the story of my father and my mother and my vision, this last I thought me. But . . .

After they told, though, I would go to university one day, I began to think what I should do. Did they intend I should be a priest? I thought and one day when on a hill, when the sun was bright and when I looked away and could barely see, there was the vision again, leading me toward a thought or a world. It came to me that my calling was that of physicus.

So there were the times when I would see the coastal waters and the ocean, watch the waves spitting white upon the rocks, thinking they could draw me to the horizon and the distances I did not know and wanted to experience so badly. I know now that is when I wondered. How would one stop the blood and the suppuration? How would one restore the breathing and ease the pain within the chest or elsewhere? There was a budding within me, and though now being the son of a nobleman, I would never inherit the title. I never held that against my eldest brother, for I loved him so. Thus, what would I become, and why would my mother and father say they would send me to one of the great universities?

* * *

So it was they sent me off, but already there was the Scots and Irish rebelliousness in me. I did not want to leave, except when I thought of my mountain top and seeing as far as I could toward where eternity lies. For I knew there was more than just the hills and valleys and the ocean waters that were my home.

With time, yes, my mind was set upon being a physicus. That was when I saw my first dead body, the first of many, not only in the laboratory but on the battlefields, in the castles and stick hovels of the starving peasants.

The corpse lay silent, pale white. I wondered what it would be like to be there, naked, unknowing, not feeling the knife that opened my innards, exposing me to the curious enquirers. There was an odor I could not forget. And the thought came to me why should I have desired such a life? And though there was much more to learn, how to palpate the body, what to smell, how to look at the excrements, fluid and solid, to think in terms of the humours and how they might influence what happens to the human body and mind. To study the hysterias, especially in women (in whom there is an abundance of cold and wet humours that influence such states), to learn the manner in which the heart should beat, to see the most intimate details of men's and women's bodies and to listen to their complaints and fears. These often confounded me. Could there be more to the bleeding? Might there be some foreign object? Some claimed there were the worms, those seen through the optic lens, eating within the body, a body the physicus could save were one able to be rid of whatever the devil or evil worm might be? Or, thinking more questioningly, might they be

Leeuwenhock's animalcules?

Our ignorance appalled and depressed me; and yet, I continued until the day I went home a physicus, and my happy parents welcomed me with a gathering of kin and friends, of drink, music, and dance. My father said, "Now you can be my physicus, but I could call you doctor, I learned, for graduation from the university."

"Yes, father, you are right."

Physicus, doctor or whatever. I may have been meant to heal the body, but in the land? By then, though, there was nothing to heal the land or to redirect the battles to come and those that had already taken place, when we would come out of the woods and attack the invader. But they would come with more men and arms, and there was general slaughter all around. The only healing then was bandaging, treating of wounds, I practicing what I heard of the Frenchman Paré, and used his cure of 'digestive of egges, oyle of Roses and Turpentine,' smashed bones either some to straighten or more likely, limbs to be cut, and the flayed bodies buried and prayers said to the moaning of the women.

It was at just such a burial I saw her, the first to catch at my heart. We looked at each other across the lowering body, and just for a moment I had the thought, a bad omen to gaze in love above a dead body. It passed, and I know she recognized me as did I her, how one tells with the eyes that pause on the other being, move quickly in another direction and back again to be certain of what they first saw and attracted and acknowledged in the other's existence and whatever it is that lies behind those eyes.

We seemed to be of the same age at which the virgin young are married. Why was she not? She stood with her family, slightly apart, so it seems now, to distinguish herself and her independence. Her hair was light brown, and when the sun struck upon her in the right direction, I could see the green of her eyes, or so I wanted them to be and what later proved to be. And then she turned, following her father and mother and kin. They went in another direction from us. Her family was unrecognizable and a simple question could settle that. So I asked my parents. My mother smiled. My father showed no expression whatever, though his lips seemed to move ever so slightly.

"They're kin to the O'Neills," my mother told me, "driven from their lands they were. Come from Connacht and now settled here. He's a great fighter, he is, he and his sons. Worthy of the family, but not nearly so important. You want to meet the men?"

"Curious."

"And that is all?"

"Aye."

"Well perhaps they will need a physicus, if you are intending to stay in these parts and not go off and make your fortune in the city."

"We've never talked of that, mother."

"No you haven't," my father finally spoke. "I saw you looking at the young woman. Not married. Peculiar. Marrying age, she is. You got an interest?" and his elbow dug into my ribs, and he laughed, put his arm about me and said, and I shan't forget it, for he was never too affectionate.. 'It's proud we are of you, and glad to have you here. I missed you." That is perhaps my father could ever come to expressing his care for my brothers and sisters and me.

The next time I saw her was in church. It seemed there had been so much peace then. Weeks had passed without notice of the English. Neither had I given much thought to where I should settle, but I thought of her. Short, well shorter by more than a head than I was she, and not quite so full in body as men want in a woman I suspect. Almost starved some would say, but I know that was the way about her and her body. Her bosom, though, was full, her cheeks with color and one dimple, I thought I saw in the church as I watched her. It appeared when she smiled as the priest preached his sermon. Later she told me she knew I was attentive and that she secretly tried to turn to me but feared I would see.

Then my father did something else I never thought possible from him, so rough his hands and hard his muscles, the body of the fighter he had become, besides his farming, to protect his lands. It was after the service, and he deliberately led us toward the O'Neills. Not that I did not know the Lord or his kin, though not she and hers.

"M'Lord," he said, "I think it is time for all to meet my son who's been so long away. A doctor he is, gone to Trinity and then Cambridge for doctor. And my father turned to her and back to Lord O'Neill. "Not all your family was home at the time of the partying, and I would consider it an honor were you to dine with us." Thus it was arranged.

It was a merry night, summer time, when the skies are bright 'til late. The land was so green and peaceful. Many a time I thought of how a bird must see this land, why we call it Emerald. And she was a human emerald freshly discovered, glittering with her jewels and her hair without wig, unadorned. It was the surprise of it that caught me, that she was so natural. You could see the gathering whisper when she entered, especially the women, that she dared to be herself, though she carried her orient fan and fluttered it like all the rest. She sat there among the maidens, and I went to her when the music was at its gayest and asked if she would be my partner. All that time I like to believe she watched me as I did her, when there were others who led her. We danced until another came and took her. As we passed one another, she turned her head, clearly in a low voice saying to me, "I lost my partner." For the rest of the evening we were together. I took her outside. The odors of the land and of her powders made me nervous. I could feel my heart pounding faster when she placed her hand lightly on my arm as we walked.

"You're a physicus, and you're educated not only in your calling but attended university. You must be very intelligent, though I cannot say physicus are the ones a body should see too much for all the damage they do."

Her voice was very serious, and she watched the twitch of my shoulders at the insult, or what I took to be an insult. Though, to be honest, some were not very good. I started to answer, but stopped. And then she laughed. It was a surprising laugh, rippling deep. Without hesitation, which women do, she fluttered her fan, looked at me mischievously, over the top, fluttered some more, waiting for a reaction, her laughter quieter now and softening, fading to the soundlessness of a smile. 'Twas in her eyes, and I knew finally she said it purposely and that she received the reaction she expected.

"You are aware I was joshing, pulling at you," and she smiled broadly, her eyes, shining in their green.

"I know, realized it . . . well after." I admitted, feeling my face redden. Oh she was a poem, intelligent and determined, forcing one to read and interpret her.

"Oh," she exclaimed, brightly smiling, "Edmond, you knew, and I did not doubt it. You should, though, have seen your face at first." She laughed. "Now tell me. What are physicus like?"

"Like others. A different calling. Not soldier or statesman, not for parliament perhaps. Not to say we have one. For our right like all the others. Fighters of another sort. That is what is so frustrating and why you laugh, though I think you ought not."

"Poof. Y're sensitive." She smiled again.

I smiled also, laughed a bit, "I suppose." Then seriously I told her, for she did truly care, "We fight the unknown, and we fight for the people; but they don't see our enemy. We sit there beside the ill and the sickness sneers at us often. I wish there were more we could do. You cannot realize the frustration. So you see it is a double battle, one against illness and the other against the people who do not believe in us."

She closed her fan, dropped her hand to her side, the fan hanging useless and doubtful. "I did not mean to make a joke of you. You must forgive me."

"I am used to it. You must needs be in a hospital and see the terrible toll. But it is not a place for the likes of you, for a lady." I could not imagine her there in her finery, and what struck me most with her odors of healthy womanhood was the contrast, the stink of the sick rooms and each different depending upon the degree of sickness, the sweat and the urine and the excrement. It was no place for a lady.

"Forget this, Aileen. I hope, though, we'll be good friends and see each other again and take walks and for talks. I do enjoy your company and your willingness to speak your mind."

"I'd like that Edmond. I care for you," she answered, her eyes bright as the Emerald Isles, I believed gave her such glow.

"And I too care for you." I reached for her hand that she raised for me to touch.

That is what it was like the first time I met a beautiful virgin lady and to whom I put a hand and felt her warm touch. Such as later with my Jewess wife Ruth.

And then I thought me, only later, of my master teaching me. It was the first time I put my hand to a woman and her veiled bosom rising from beneath her dress. A veil, though, in a healthy woman was temptation.

I was expecting what I had imagined all those years of gazing and wondering when I would feel myself harden and not know what to do until later and older. But I never went to the whores like some of my class mates.

To my surprise, with this patient, at my touch, a spasm of pain crossed her face, and I pressed harder, then ran my fingers about the site and farther and felt another and another. I asked her to loosen her bodice, and her breasts freed themselves, not like those of the dead, pale, flatter, useless, with almost colorless nipples. The lumps pushed at the surface of her skin crowding to become breasts themselves.

"What are they, young doctor?" my mentor asked. "Haven't seen this before, have you?"

I knew, though. "Apostomes, I believe, sir, in a stage of maturation, and it is not only about the breast but on the flesh as well." I touched her again, but as gently as possible, and it was certain the pain was vehement. "We should incise them, then apply the medicinal curatve."

"Good. You do it with me and help the woman. He seemed to leer at her. "You'll be smooth as before in no time and a handful for whatever man you choose." Then my master thought better, as he prepared the woman. Speaking gently, telling her and her Lord husband what he must do. He also said his speech was but fouled wit. It was agreed by all, and the preparation was begun.

She smiled and I wondered whether she agreed or would like to have swatted him, for she colored reaching from her neck and throughout her face. She put her hands about her breasts, though it was still some fashion then for the women to show themselves, to tempt us and draw us in, should they choose. On the other hand, with the Presbyterians and the Catholics, the dress was becoming stricter, but not so close as with Bess, how I hate saying it, our Queen. There was the body of the gown tied at each side and the frame of the woman tightened to the flatness of the board. I did wonder whether the tightness caused the problem. Not allowing the body its natural processes and movements.

I am too far afield perhaps. The incision was made as De Vigo said, in the fashion of the new moon, and as he wrote, that way *the matter whyche hurteth the blayne, maye yssue out by the sayde opened place. Afterwards for the digestion, and mundifycation you shall use the medicines written.*

It was she, with the slight touch of hand and the green eyes, walking with a doctor (I use this term now because Cambridge gave it to us, and I think it interchangeable among many) who led me to this point and this story. You see, I could imagine her with those eyes, sitting before a doctor, questioning and affronted at his touch and mocking him. She could never be sick. The health that was in her face. Yet, someone can suddenly become ill. That is the trouble with doctors. They look at people with practiced eye, and they see what others fail. She had nothing, my beauty Aileen, unless she was hiding it below her gown. Yet, I think I would have seen it in her. Yet, I did think was this the reason for her attraction, the healthiness of her? But I did not agree with myself, and I realized it almost suddenly, when I felt the ache about my heart, thinking about her and seeing her again. I loved her, and I believe she me. It was such happiness when we met again.

We walked. I was quiet, my heart beating a little faster being in her company.

"Why so quiet, Edmond?" she interrupted my thoughts. And as she grasped her fan and raised it coyly, it was as though she knew she had made a conquest or left me speechless.

I reached to touch the edge of the fan, and she closed and allowed it to drop by her side again.

"You have lost the power of your educated words. I like the sound of your voice, Edmond. Do not lose it."

I breathed deeply, smelled her perfumed hair and the blossoms of the trees. My heart again beat faster, for I was not certain what to say. It came though. "I like the sound of you, like it is music, Aileen. And the look of your face, so lovely. I like you best of any I have met." I noticed her face redden and the smile that arose. My heart warmed so when with her or even when thinking about her. "Shall I be allowed to see you again?"

"If you wish. You know I'd like that. You will have to ask my father, I suppose. Come here. We'll sit here. I want to tell you something."

We sat.

"The gardens have the odor of summer. And listen." There was the slightest rustle of leaves. In the lantern light, I saw a petal drop to the ground. It was like an omen, the thought crossed my mind, but of what? It could only be good if I were with her.

"Mr., oops, Doctor Skene," She musically laughed again. "I am not like many of my sex. I like my head in many a thing, and I will not be tied too tightly."

And I thought, *The humours. She, instead of cold for women as we have been taught and now begin to doubt as making the difference between men and women, has an abundance of the hot, and she thinks she will scare me. We doctors know more about them than they think, and yet we cannot. For they are so mysterious.* But then, I was saying to myself about how headstrong I had discovered I too was, that I had so much of my father in me that the others did not. Yet, this was a different experience for me. I knew about women from my studies but not from contact with them. I hadn't searched when in school the way t'others did and found, as I said, the 'unclean or filthy ones in their secret place with malign ulcer, or had the floures lately,' according to the master Joannes De Vigo. Mostly from fear I stayed away, for I had seen the carbuncular pustles, the ooze, and also seen my fellows pained when they pissed. I wanted none of that or the pustule. So when we went to drink and the women sat upon my lap, I pushed them aside, and they would laugh and grab at me between my legs, squeeze or rub. I would let them go no farther.

I looked at Aileen and her cleanliness and again smelled the safe and enchanting odor of her. I was glad for my learning and training, and for the way I lived, despite the writings that say there should be little expectation of joy in married coitus, or should not be, that men should seek their outlets and heights out of marriage with the whores and any one that would let them. I knew I could find my joy in her.

"I think you underestimate me, Mistress O'Neill. You do not scare me."

She laughed. "I did not think so. You have no fear of my humours, or the way we women are. You think you know all about us from your studies? Studies will do no good with me."

"You want to see my anger? You will not." Now I laughed, and suddenly stopped. I wanted to reach out and touch her. Instead, we moved apart and looked closely at one another, I at the softness in her eyes that I am sure she saw in mine, for she said, "I like the look of your eyes. There is a perplexing color in them and a clearness, like somebody I should trust. You must be a good doctor. I would come to you, I would, were it necessary. I hope it will never be so." She was pensive for a moment. "But you will go and fight like the others, will you not? I mean you will be there in the field to help, to do what you can to save. You will be fighting just the same, coming out of the forests, or hiding the sick, the wounded among those trees."

"I will. But I much prefer my place in hospital, and will help the Lords and Ladies when it is necessary. You think the men are foolish to fight. Aileen, though, I'd come back to you, if you'd have me."

"No. The fighting." She smiled though at my words with which I finished, for they were what was in my heart. Her smile faded and she said, "Fight. I'd do it myself could I. I hate killing. I have seen the wounds that never heal, seen the legs and arms that have been cut off. Not when it is done, of course. I imagine it, and I hate the English, the Queen, Essex, all his soldiers. I hate that they took our lands from us and that we must live off the Lord O'Neill, though we are his kinsmen, and no matter how famous he is, and strong. I want to be beholden to no one.

Not even my husband, should there ever be one. I am so headstrong as I told you."

She stopped, almost breathless, and the anger made her face red. It was no blush of the ordinary maiden but feeling she would not hide. I loved her. I can say that. I loved her at the grave and more now and swore she would be my wife.

She looked at me. "I spoiled the moment." She looked down, in sadness, I believe. "I spoiled it, I did. My mouth and me. The flowers, the trees, the bushes, they disappeared in the wave of heat, like that a person sees on a hot day, except that I have made this a hot night. Forgive me, please."

"No. You said what you think. I like that."

She smiled slightly. "You mean that. I can see. Don't ever try to lie, Dr. Skene. It will show throughout you, but most through your eyes." Her smile grew, and her eyes brightened again. She seemed to hesitate. "We ought to go in now. There will be talk, and we barely know one another, but it does not seem so. I do not care to leave you just now, but . . ."

"Nor I you." I somehow managed it. "I love you, Aileen."

She blushed and suddenly reached with her lips and kissed my cheek. "I love you, Edmond, always."

We sat closer. I wrapped my arms about her, pulling her to me and softly kissed her mouth. She yielded and kissed me back. We held that way to each other. Then she sat back, gazing deeply at me. "Yes, I do, Edmond." She leaned in and placed her warm lips on mine. We would not let go. Our mouths opened, our tongues seeking. She pulled back again. "I like that. I never knew . . ." She stopped. "Edmond."

"Yes, my love."

"I don't care to leave you. You'll never tell anyone about . . . about our kisses. I feel so warm throughout me. You won't tell, will you?"

"This is for us only. I would never talk about you to anyone. I hate to leave you. I do, Aileen, love you. We'll be like this forever, please God."

"Yes, please God."

I did not see her again for quite some time. My duties kept me, but I was restless to see her. I had to be at hospital in Dublin, for I had promised my master. Perhaps it was good considering what I learned those lonely and full days.

There were patients of all sorts. There were the poor who might be the only patients unless others had a contagious disease. It was a large room, some parts sectioned by a slight panel, and there were arches that appeared to give the room some semblance of separate areas. There were some palettes by walls, some with windows. All about the room there was activity, shouts, moans. Some might say this was a scene of chaos, and surely it could have been. But that was our business to work in such as described, so as to rid the world of illnesses that caused such ruckus and which tore and ate the body. Instruments lay in heaps on the floor. There were the men and women mixed together. Sometimes a man and a woman lay together, a tent like structure over them, I suppose husband and wyfe sick by the same illness. On low tables sat flasks, some empty, others with urine that had been studied but were as yet to be emptied. On yet another lay an artificial limb to be placed while apart from was a man who lay back upon a chair and a surgeon was ready to saw into and depart his leg. It was about this time we learned not to cut at the diseased part but above it, for some reason unknown to us, for some reason cutting into the diseased portion only helped to spread the disease and to kill the patient. How helpful this could be on a battlefield one can only imagine. I thought on it and wondered how many more lives I might save. By then, too, we had learned much about cautery and ligature and the difference. But my purpose was most to cure the sick, for I had no real desire to just perform surgery unless it was absolutely necessary.

One day, as I worked in the hospital learning about the

various diseases, urgent messages arrived from home and the kin to the O'Neills. My dearest Aileen was very ill requesting that I come home to see to her care. I could not imagine that she could fall to any illness that might cause harm. But then, she is a young woman and subject to all ills that we humans might encounter.

Rather than a carriage, I found me a horse and galloped into the night for a number of days, stopping only at Inns and taking whatever space might be available. I carried with me my medical equipment, of course, and saw to it that no one would touch it. I had medicines and some surgical instruments were these to be a necessity. They explained nothing to me but to hurry.

When I arrived home, my mother cried and all looked very sad, knowing how dear to my heart she was.

"You should hurry to her and see what her trouble is. Perhaps it is something female. We know nothing any more than what her parents told us," my mother weeping told me. "Your father had spoken to hers when he came to us asking for you to come home. They called their own physicus, but he did nothing. He had not the education of you."

"That is what happened, Edmond," my father interjected, taking me by the shoulder. His face sad.

"Mother, if I could rest just a bit and have a bit to eat, I'll ride to her. Oh. I promised I would return the horse I rode to a friend of the man who I paid for the trip here. She is a fast one. And at that, my mother had me rest. I tried to stay awake but could not. Later one of my sisters, Maire, woke me, smiling sadly at me. "Tis time to eat, Edmond." I noticed tears in her eyes. "You love her we know, and she you. She told me once when we met. We had become friends, though she is some miles from us. Come now, brother and eat. You'll cure her."

Thus that night I rode one of my father's horses to Aileen. Her father sadly greeted me, then her very tearful mother.

"She's been like this for at least a week now and cannot even walk or eat much," her father said. "Come, we'll take you to her."

"Edmond," she quietly said. "You've come. I knew you would."

"Of course I would, dearest Aileen." I glanced then at her parents, but they knew what lay between Aileen and me.

"Would you please leave us for now? I'll call you when necessary."

"I hurt terrible, Edmond. My breast, here, and she pointed to her left one. It began after it started lower down about here, in my private place. My nipple sometimes gave something like milk, and even a little blood, like monthly bleeding. It scared me and does. I have never been loose. I'll let you look, if needs be. You won't be embarrassed if I, well, you know, let you examine me in those places. I never let a man see me any place private, or touch me, you are aware," the pale whiteness of her face coming to red. "I have also been irritable, often sleepless, and anxious.

"I know, my dearest. Part of it is also hysteric and from your illness. I'll do something to help this I hope."

"You still love me, do you not?" She weakly smiled.

"You know I do." I wondered then if I could do whatever must be done and prayed to Jesus that He help me.

"I'll call your mother to watch so you'll feel perhaps a bit more comfortable."

"No. Ask Maire, if you must. My mom won't care. But I would rather have it private. Ask my mother to come in and I'll tell her my wish. They have seen me bleed and all that. But this is different. Edmond, my bleeding is not right either."

"As long as you don't mind, we'll be private, but I'll have to let your parents know what I think is wrong."

"Of course."

So I began my examination. "Aileen, I have to see, touch

191

your breasts, and probably below. You'll have to raise your gown. Try not to mind."

I began. When I examined her breast, there were two unusual like pustules, and she gasped at the touch. I had her raise her arm and felt inside. She was swollen there. And then I went below to where her opening was.

"Edmond, I hurt here too." She pointed to her mound and close by her womb.

I did not hesitate. "Aileen. I'm going to put my fingers inside. Try not to mind, though I know you will. I am also going to message you below. You will feel something you never may have unless you have touched yourself. Don't tell me that. That's your privacy. After the entire examination I am also giving you a medicine.

She pulled higher at her gown to her chin, looking at me as she did. "I thought you would not see me until our marriage," she tried to laugh, her face red with embarrassment.

"Well, pretend." I put two fingers inside of her and went deeply feeling toward her womb. She gasped when I did. I felt something warm and wet, and bringing out my fingers they were covered with an unclear vaginal fluid. "When did you bleed last, Aileen?"

"Two months past," she murmured.

"All right. I am going to message. I moved my fingers to her most sensitive places. She moaned as I did so. As I rubbed more she arched her back, threw back her head and let out a muffled scream. As she stopped trembling and settled, she told me softly, "I feel all wet. That felt so good. Edmond. I never knew. I was always told not to touch me and do to meself as did you. May I do it alone when I am scared or hurtful?"

I rose and went to her head, kissed her lips lightly. "Yes, dear one; do that to yourself. It may help at times." I was going against what women were taught, but if it helped her, I knew I was right.

"Edmond, It is bad, is it not?"

"Yes."

"You have tears, dearest," she whispered. "You cannot help me. I know."

I could not speak, only nodded negatively.

"Come hold my hand before you tell my parents. Please, too, put your lips to mine again. I care to kiss you."

And we did lightly, then more warmly. "I want to remember your lips, Edmond. Die with them on me."

It pleased me, and I tried to smile. "I'll get your parents now. Dearest one." I could not hold back my tears.

I called in her parents. Her mother looked at me, saw the paleness of my face, my tears. Some doctor I was. But she was my love. Her father spoke first.

"How bad is she, doctor?"

"Just call me Edmond, sir. Not at all good. I think it will be the year at most. It is terribly hard for me to say to you who love her so." I continued, believing I must. "You are aware of the relationship I have to your daughter. I have sworn myself to her. You should know that. I would have asked you for her hand. I still will, if she will have me. I want to be with her until... This sounds terrible now," my voice soft and sad dramatic, but if you would . . ." I could not finish. I knew I would also have to leave her for others sick.

He nodded, and went to his wife, holding her while she shook and sobbed. He then managed, "We would be proud to have you."

I excused myself and went back to Aileen's room. She smiled seeing me as she grimaced in pain. I would give her some opium powder mixed in wine. But I had to speak first, before she would perhaps sleep.

"Aileen I want you as my wife. Will you have me?"

"Edmond. I am dying. Why? You want to make me feel good."

"I love you, Aileen. You know that. I so want you for my wife, if you will have me. I know. You are thinking about your illness. But I will take care of you."

She smiled again. "It will be a bad choice for you. But I will be as good a wife as may be, God grant me."

We kissed warmly, held to one another. I whispered, "I shan't take advantage of you, only if you wish it."

"I know that, Edmond. I will give you all that is left to me. Hold me. We will have a church wedding and guests. No one must know but those closest to us."

I agreed. All took place as she wished. The gaiety masked the horridness of what was soon to come.

* * *

Thus it was. So, I had my Aileen who died some years, not many, before we fled our country. And it was in my long travels I came to find my Jewess, Ruth, who will always have my heart and me hers, down through the ages of our family growth of children, grandchildren and more. I leave my tale of woe and love to all who will have it and do as they may. God be with you, whether the Jewish or the faith I turned upon, remembering Matthew's words.

* * *

Hannah and Asa looked at one another, the sadness in their eyes. "Well, Hannah, that is the story of my ancestors, and now you know it all. See what it has done to me, taking me, and even you, back to the beginning and our beyond." Then both smiled, sharing their happiness.

———————————

Part III

Chapter One

The Present and Tomorrow
Constance and Benjamin

Benjamin returned home, late as usual from seeing patients in the office and the hospital. Constance had helped their maid, Joyce, prepare a late supper, as was usual. Then, standing somewhat nervously at their front door, watching the darkened waters of the bay in the coolness of early spring, she heard, smiled, as her husband's horses trotted up the drive to the carriage house. She had decided she would talk to him either during dinner or after when they sat by the fire talking about the day, as she listened to tales of the patients. It would be then.

"You're quiet tonight, Constance," Benjamin told her as he sipped at his wine. "That was a fine meal, as usual."

Suddenly, without warning, he said, "Do you ever miss your nursing, listening to me and my stories, especially about the hospital?"

Surprised, she told him, "Let's go to the drawing room. I'll answer your question there," as she bit her lip and smiled beguilingly.

Watching her, he had that feeling she would rouse in him that something was about to happen.

They sat by the fireplace, the logs burning, keeping them warm.

"I think you wanted to tell me something, or answer my question, Constance."

"Well, I've been thinking."

"So I should be prepared," he laughed.

"You may not laugh when I tell you. Ben, I want to go to medical school."

She watched the surprise on his face and then that serious look of his. "You wanted a family. I do also."

"I've thought of that, naturally. We are still young enough for me to have children afterwards. I have to do this, Ben. I just feel it. You wanted to know whether I missed nursing. Well, yes. But society needs female doctors too. I feel I have to be something better and be useful, frankly to women. We're beginning to learn more about female diseases. I could study here at the Portland Institute so I wouldn't have to go away from home. If I need help with my studies, you would be there for me. I need this. Ben. I feel it, as I told you, and I would be so useful. I could learn gynecology and do an important job in Portland and Maine."

Benjamin took a deep breath, then slowly smiled. "I knew when I met you and knew you are intelligent. Enough to be a good doctor. I cannot deny you of this. I could never stand in your way. It does get harder having children when you're older, but we'll wait."

Constance smiled, laughed. "I thought you might be angry. I also knew, though, thinking about it and confronting you made me hesitant and anxious."

"You'll have enough of those days when studying." He rose and went to her, pushing her aside, on the small sofa, pulling her toward him. He put out his arms, hugging her, and kissing her temple and then her cheek, moving down toward her neck. She shivered.

"You agree. I do love you, Ben, just as I always have. Kiss me like that some more. He did as his hand went to her breasts, from one to the other. She pressed into his touch. "Do you want to, Ben?" taking his hand and leading it down to the edge of her skirt that she pulled upward. "Oh, these damn dresses, bloomers, and pantalets." They both laughed.

"Yes. But I also want you to be aware of how much I admire you."

Within the next few days, the year 1865, Constance, went for the application, filled it out, and waited. Like her husband had, she received a rejection letter, despite Benjamin's standing in the profession and his teaching.

Constance trembled, sobbed in anger, telling herself and knowing it. The school rejected her because of her sex. She walked about the house, ran up the stairs to their room, falling on the bed, sobbing, banging her fists into the mattress. "A woman. I'm a woman. Is there something evil about me? Am I only good for a night in bed to satisfy a man? I have no brain? The repulsiveness of these men. They belittle me, laugh at me, deny me the use of my brain for the good of women, yes, and even men. Like I've never seen a naked man or woman." She banged and banged, suddenly rose, tearing off her clothing, staring at herself in the door length mirror. "Look at you, Constance. These breasts, this mound of hair and that vagina between my legs only for babies. No enjoyment. NO BRAIN." She tore at her hair net, pulled at her hair until it hung to her shoulders. She looked again in the mirror, facing herself, turning slowly watching her shapely body, its curves at the hips. "They tell me that's all I'm good for. A bedmate. A cook. A housemaid. And when Benjamin wants his sex, here you are, Constance."

She cried more, walked back to the bed, falling on it naked, lying there, just as Benjamin found her when he came home.

"Constance. What is this? Why are you like this?" The sight scared him, as though perhaps his wife had lost her mind or was having a fit of hysteria.

"I'm lying here obediently, waiting for you to rape me."

"Constance. What . . .?"

"Oh, Ben, they rejected me. Look at me. I'm only a woman. I've been waiting here to do my duty to you." She began crying loudly.

"Constance. Stop this." He went to her, trying to calm her, stroking her hair, her face.

"Ben. They rejected me. Me. I have a degree from Bates. I served in the army. Yet this is all I'm good for." She spread her legs for him to see more of her.

"Constance, dear. Stop this. Remember how they did the same thing to me. Your father went and gave them the devil. Well, either he or I will go to them and tell them it's time they took a woman. Don't forget. There are schools that will take women. If it came to that, I'd support you to go away. But I believe we can manage everything."

"You mean you'd let me go away?" Her face was wet with tears. Now she cried more, but with happiness. "You would support me even if I had to leave you, Ben? I don't want to do that. You have such a good reputation and my father. How could they be so stupid, so discriminatory? I love you so." She reached for him, both sitting on the edge of the bed, hugging, kissing.

"I always knew you are a good man, but that you would make such a sacrifice. I can't let you do that. We should see what we can do and think more on my leaving home, but only as a last measure."

"My wife is an exceptional woman. Listen, Constance. I don't believe in all this belief about a woman in the home. I want children, but as long as you are healthy and still young enough, and you will be, then we'll raise a family. O.K.?"

"I love you, Ben."

"I love you too. You're going to be a wonderful doctor. Think of the women who will be happy to have a female examine them."

Within the following week, Nathaniel Sterling took Benjamin with him and went to the head of the school.

"I've come about my daughter, Constance Blumenthal, along with her husband, Benjamin. I believe you are aware of Benjamin's reputation. The school did not want to accept him. Do you recall hearing about that? Well, this is about the same thing. Isn't it time this school and its men realized that women are becoming medical doctors? How can you reject my daughter, his wife, on the basis of her college degree with honors, her service as a nurse during the war, and Benjamin's wish that she serve our city and state? You seem to think that she should be at home having babies and taking care of the house."

As soon as Nathaniel said this, he watched the doctor's face turn red with embarrassment and some anger. He tried to control himself. "You are trying to get me to retract the letter your daughter received. We did not see her as qualified for our institution. We know her background. But we have never had a woman here. Goodness knows how she would be accepted, how she might endure isolation and dismay among students and faculty. Also . . ."

Nathaniel did not allow him to finish. He was quite angry. Benjamin started to answer, but Nathaniel stopped him, and in a low voice said, "Let me handle this fool.

"I believe it *is time* we allow women. The woman you rejected has sat in classes in anatomy with male students. So what is there to fear? She'll be embarrassed? My daughter, Benjamin's wife, is outstanding. If the male students or even some of the doctors are so prejudiced, they had better learn now to accept the fact that there are medical schools that accept women and even female schools. Are you going to make a fool out of yourself and other faculty by denying a qualified woman entrance and study? Think also what you'll be doing for sick women. You may study gynecology, but have you ever looked a woman in the face when you have had to examine her privacy that she treasures? Think, rather, how a female doctor will be welcome. And, if our practitioners are good enough and the women are comfortable with them, do you believe they'll lose patients? Think, Doctor. Think. The public will cheer. Yes. Some will criticize, yet I believe and you should also, that more will praise. You cannot deny this woman her chance and rightful place."

The doctor who tried to interrupt Nathaniel, surrendered when he realized there was no way to stop him. His face was red, whether in anger or embarrassment as he sat there opening and closing his mouth. When Nathaniel stopped, he started with a tinge of anger but also discomfort. "You, you . . . you," he stuttered, "You are, no we are aware of what we have done. You want us to . . ."

"To what?" Nathaniel interrupted. "You can't even get your words out. Look. Let's stop this right now. Just say you've changed your mind, that the letter was an error."

"Dr. Sterling. You haven't even given me a chance to speak."

"To correct your error?" Nathaniel smiled.

All this time Benjamin sat in wonder at his father-in-law, saw the love and anger of which he was capable. He respected his father-in-law even more.

"My error?"

"How about the school's mistake? The building made the error."

The doctor finally laughed. "All right, Nathaniel. You are right. Your daughter, your wife, Benjamin, will be admitted. However, don't be surprised at the reaction of the students."

Benjamin spoke up. "I know what it is like to be shunned by some of my fellow students, what it is like to endure insults. My wife can confront any of that." He hesitated. "I do appreciate that Constance Blumenthal will be the first female who will earn her degree of Doctor at our institution. I do thank you. You will be proud of her, I assure you."

Nathaniel rose, leaned over the desk and shook hands. Benjamin followed his lead.

"The letter will go out, hopefully today but no later than tomorrow." The red fading from his face, he said, "I appreciate your approach and your belief in your daughter and your wife, Benjamin. I ask your forgiveness."

"There is no need for that," Nathaniel answered. "We merely had a discussion and came to a favorable conclusion regarding our differences."

As they left the building, Nathaniel placed his arm about Benjamin, smiling. "We did well, didn't we Ben?"

"You did, dad." And they both walked away laughing.

Chapter Two

Drs. Benjamin and Constance

June, 1859, was graduation for the medical class. The doctor who had originally rejected Constance led the graduates to the stage. He stood before the admiring audience, searching for Dr. and Mrs. Sterling and Dr. Benjamin Blumenthal. If one looked closely enough, perhaps a person may have noticed a tinge of red in his face when he announced, "The faculty of the Medical Institute take pleasure in announcing that top honors have been received by Dr. Constance Blumenthal, our first female graduate of whom we are all proud. She not only is an honor to the school and herself but to womanhood and the State of Maine.

"We have not rehearsed this," he smiled, "but would Dr. Benjamin Blumenthal please come to the stage and present the certificate of Doctor of Medicine to his wife."

Surprised and happily red-faced, he walked quickly up the short flight of stairs to the hurrahs of the audience and students. The doctor handed the certificate to Benjamin who turned to Constance, both smiling, as he handed it to her while kissing her on the cheek. More cheers from all.

Of course, there was no mention of the harassment, teasing, and rejection by several of the students while she was in classes. It was especially terrible for her in the study of gynecology and anatomy of the female, one male having the temerity to ask what hers was like. He was dismissed from class for a week and forced to make up the work before he would be graduated. This punishment helped to alleviate some of the jeers from the ignorant students.

Constance endured it all. Of, course, Benjamin was aware of the insults and talked to her professors at various times, but for this particular day of graduation, there was nothing but smiles and two happy families.

That night the Blumenthals had a dinner party of for all to honor their daughter-in-law. Before dinner, Asa may have startled Nathaniel a bit when he told how Nathaniel demanded that his daughter be accepted. Of course, it was a magnificent evening for everyone. Arella, having moved to Portland where her husband opened a store for his father, sat next to Constance, holding, grasping her hand and squeezing it.

"I'm so proud of you, Constance. I've loved you all these years and just knew you would do something unusual and good."

"I did what I wanted with Ben's support, but," and looking intently at Arella, "you have your children. I have none. Well..." and she hesitated, thinking back to when she and Ben talked of her going to medical school, "well, I knew they would be impossible," and she whispered in Arella's ear, "unless the birth control failed. Luckily it didn't. But I want them, Arella. I certainly do."

"You take care of your patients, make your mark on this community. You still have periods. As I recall, we had them about the same time. So you will be able to have them when you're ready. In fact, I've decided to be one of your patients. If I need you, of course." She paused. "I'll talk to you later. I want to ask you about sex and how I can better satisfy myself. All I ever hear is that we are supposed to be there for our husbands to have their good time. Ely does things for me but not the best, I believe."

"That's fine. We'll talk more just before Ben and I leave." She looked around the table, whispering quickly. "To start, remember when we were at school and I told you after my

Anatomy class about what we have between our legs? Well, start with your clitoris, showing him how to fondle it with his fingers, tongue, and mouth." She smiled, blushed, turning more toward Arella. "I want to celebrate with Ben alone, even if we do it all night."

They both laughed.

"What are you two laughing about?" Faith asked.

Red-faced, but her hazel eyes bright, she answered her mother. "We were thinking back to college about something that happened where we lived," she obviously lied, while looking back to Arella, both quieting but still smiling radiantly.

When the celebration ended, Constance and Benjamin left as soon as possible without seeming rude. Constance was thinking of her conversation with Arella. On the way home they spoke about the dinner and what their relatives and friends had talked about. She smiled coyly, thinking of what she said to Arella.

"What is behind that look, dearest."

"Wait until we're privately together"

Once home, she immediately went to the bedroom. "You wait until I call you, well, softly enough so neither Paul (their driver) and Joyce won't hear."

"That means I'll have to wait nearby."

"Well, of course, dummy."

She undressed herself, undid her hair, and lay on the bed. "Ben," she whispered loudly. "Come in."

She held her smile. "Dr. Blumenthal, I need an examination."

He lay on top. "Slowly, doctor. Now, Ben, easily, at first."

Constance was true to her words to Arella at dinner. They made love until both were exhausted. She placed her head at his shoulder, kissing him lightly. "I love you, Ben. You make me feel like the woman I believe I should be, can be. I'll love you always."

"I love you too for all our lives. I want you to feel that way, to do and be what you believe. I hope I shall never falter in my support and love. I won't."

* * *

Nathaniel expanded his office enabling space for Constance. Of course, the office became busier than it had been with Nathaniel in general practice while Benjamin had specialized in surgery. Constance had decided in school that her specialty would be diseases of women and children. The three family members made it one of the larger and busier practices. When women discovered they could see a female doctor, Constance became busy rather fast. She not only treated the women and children but found that she was becoming a person to whom unmarried, married, and older women could talk about their private lives. Her reputation for knowledge, compassion, and understanding spread beyond the city.

Meanwhile, Benjamin's practice also grew. Of course, Constance sent him women needing surgery.

At first it was hard on her. A patient came to her about pains in her abdomen.

"Doctor, I have pains here," and she pointed to her the area below her stomach, nearer to her uterus and ovaries.

"Has it been a long time?" Constance gently asked.

"I think it may be a month or so. No more than that. I haven't wanted my husband to come near me. You know, enter me." Her face and neck turned red, and she trembled slightly. "And I don't want him running after some younger woman willing to offer herself. Oh, I'm sorry. My face. I don't want to embarrass you," though obviously Constance was an excuse for Mrs. McIntyre's admission regarding her husband.

"And, doctor, I've always been a good woman, never letting another man touch me, you know how, and I've raised my children, been a good mother, taken care of the house, been obedient the way we expect a woman to be. If I'm terrible sick what then? Who will take care of things?"

"Now don't think that way. I'll talk to your husband. Let me worry for you right now.

"So I do have another question. Have you stopped your monthly bleedings? We women doctors," wanting to make it easier to explain, "call it menopause."

"I have, doctor. Sometimes that bothers me, like making me awfully hot. But I have noticed some blood."

"I'm glad you told me that. Now you just let me take care of what I can, including your husband." Yet, Constance knew there was nothing she could do, except if she had him in during a consultation, if it was as bad as Constance thought.

"I understand." Constance gently moved her fingers, pressed.

"That hurts, right there, doctor." She pointed between her uterus and ovary.

"I'll have to look inside you. Please come to this chair that will tip backward. Make sure you're as comfortable as possible. Don't be scared. I'll be as gentle as possible. You see this instrument. I know. It looks terrible. Well, it may be uncomfortable, but try to be calm and not move, Mrs. McIntyre."

"Will this cure my pain?"

"No. I want to try to find out what is causing your problem. It may have something to do with your female parts."

"Does that mean I won't be able to be like a woman with my husband?" Tears formed and she began to cry slightly. "He . . . won't want me. And the children. I don't want them to know."

"Please try not to worry about that now, Mrs. McIntyre. Let's take a look." Constance handed the patient her hanky. "Here. Use this for your tears." Constance smiled at her, their eyes meeting. The woman began to feel secure listening to her soft voice and watching her gentle hazel eyes.

Mrs. McIntyre forced a smile. "You have beautiful eyes, Dr.

Blumenthal."

"Oh thank you. But let's think about you now."

She moved the chair backward and down, enabling the examination. She washed her hands, then the speculum with diluted phenol. She then moved inward with the speculum."

"Oh. I don't like it."

"Just try to relax." Constance moved in as far as she could, pulling the light closer. She noticed some unusual form of mucus at her cervix. She withdrew the speculum. "There. You were very good about that."

She then went to her lower abdomen, above her mound, and pressed again.

"It still hurts. Sometimes awful. I get sick and, well, throw up."

"I want to call in Dr. Blumenthal." She hesitated. "You may have to have an operation, so we can hopefully get out what may be there."

"All right. Can you call in my husband? You won't tell him what I said."

"Whatever you tell me stays in this room between you and me. All right. I'll see if I can get Dr. Blumenthal as quickly as possible."

"You two are brother and sister or married? You don't look J..." She stopped.

Constance smiled and lied. "Yes, I am Jewish."

"You *are* . . . Well. Oh just forget it."

"If you'd rather have one of your own faith, I can arrange that."

"No. I trust you with those eyes you have."

Constance laughed to herself, thinking, *You're another one who never has anything to do with Jews*. Then speaking, she told her, "Yes, so is my husband. So no, we're not brother and sister. We married during the war when we were at a hospital treating wounded soldiers."

"So patriotic," she said softly and smiled. "Forget what I . . . oh you know."

"Yes. Now you just lie there and be comfortable. I'll be back."

Benjamin came soon, introducing himself, then examining her. She watched his face, could tell. "I don't want an operation. I hear they hurt something fierce."

He turned to Constance who nodded. They moved off a little way, Benjamin speaking softly. "I'd like to look and get a specimen or two for the microscope. If it's extensive, we should just try to treat her medically. I suppose you could give her codeine or morphine."

"Mrs. McIntyre, I'll get your husband."

She got him from the waiting room but talked to him before they entered her office. "Mr. McIntyre, your wife may be rather sick. You will have to be good to her." Thinking of what his wife said she thought, *Master of the house with a sex slave, perhaps no longer.*

"Sick. I know that. Sick with what, doctor?"

"She may have to have an operation."

His face flushed in astonishment. "My loving wife, Bess, sick like that? With some horrible disease?" His eyes teared.

"Let's wait and see what the surgeon says first, all right?" She gently said.

When they were all together in the examining room, Constance spoke, "We are thinking we should take some specimens and look at them under a microscope. Then we can decide what to do. Now, Please, Mrs. McIntyre don't be concerned about pain doing this. Dr. Blumenthal can give you chloroform, so you won't feel what he is doing. If you and Mr. McIntyre agree, then we can do this, say this coming Thursday morning at Maine General Hospital. Then, when we have results, we'll go on from there."

"At the hospital?" Mr. and Mrs. McIntyre, almost in unison,

said loudly and in surprise, "Maine General! The hospital! Why there?"

"Please try not to be excited. I assure you, that's the best place to find out what is inside. It won't hurt, as I said, because Dr. Blumenthal will use something to make you sleep a bit after. We'll give you something for pain that may follow."

Mrs. McIntyre started crying loudly.

Constance went to her, placed her hand on her arm, speaking softly, "Mrs. McIntyre, this will be the best thing for you. You have to have trust that we'll do what is best for you. Yes, there may be the pain I just mentioned, but I'll be there for you. Can you trust me?"

"I think so," she sobbed.

Her husband, watching Constance and listening to his wife crying so, asked angrily, "Is this necessary? Look how you . . . you've made her cry and how you have scared us."

Constance turned to him, speaking as calmly as possible, angry about but understanding his emotion, answered, "It is necessary. If you would like another opinion, I could arrange that."

He stepped toward Constance who backed a step. "You Jews. Do you have any idea what to do with people? The two of you taking twice as much money from us. From your history of causing grief, how can we trust you?"

"Mr. McIntyre. Now you've gone too far. I believe you should go to another doctor. I will not abide your hatred." Her voice was a bit louder.

"Please!" Mrs. McIntyre cried out, wiping tears from her cheeks. "Stop this. I like and trust her. You think I'm going to some man who doesn't know anything about women? You apologize for those terrible things you said. Yes, I've said them too. But not anymore being with her. I'm sick and all you think about is your money and Jew hatred. Nothing about me. I'm just your housekeeper and for" and she didn't hold back, "for your bedroom pleasure. All those years. Do you think I ever enjoyed it? Did you ever try to please me? And now that I no longer bleed monthly and can't have children, I'm there for your pleasure. I wouldn't blame her if she told us never to come back again. I almost made the same mistake." Her face froze with anguish and anger, as she put her hand over her mouth in mortification.

"I . . . I didn't mean . . ."

"Didn't mean what Alex? You insult my doctor and I . . ." She paused. "Oh, I have to throw up. I don't feel so good. Doctor, help me," she cried out.

Constance immediately got a basin. Gently she told, "Here let me hold your head over this. You do what you have to."

As she felt the comfort and softness of Constance's hands on her back and forehead, she leaned over and vomited for several minutes. She raised her head some, "I'm so sorry, Doctor, but I do feel terrible in my stomach." She wretched some more and quickly leaned again to release more.

"I think I feel better but weak."

"You just lie there and try to relax. I'm going to get you something to help you do that." Constance went to a shelf, took a bottle of wine and poured some. "Here, drink this, but slowly. Perhaps it will help."

Mrs. McIntyre lay there, tears in her eyes, then crying. Her husband came to the table. "I'm sorry, Janette. Please. Believe me. I'm so sorry."

She looked at him but said nothing.

"Doctor, if you'll forgive me . . ."

Constance forced a smile, thinking, *The reality of this man has come out. No more tears or sorrow it seems for his wife so it appears. He's thinking more of the money and the Jews cheating him.*

She then spoke aloud, her smile fading. "I shan't forget what you said, but I will let it go. Let's not talk about that but about Mrs. McIntyre. She needs help and your understanding."

His face red in embarrassment, he nodded assent that Constance didn't believe. She couldn't help herself. "I'll send you to another doctor to make you more comfortable."

Mrs. McIntyre raised her head, shouting, "NO."

Constance trembled a bit, but quickly regained her composure. "I'll follow your word, Mrs. McIntyre and try to help you as much as possible."

Mrs. McIntyre, in a loud whisper told her and her husband, "I won't have a man looking at me the way she has. I trust Dr. Blumenthal and her husband. That's it." She thought she would vomit again, and put her head to the basin but nothing came.

Constance held her tenderly. "You just try to relax. I'll make an appointment hopefully by this coming Thursday. All right? And will get a message to you as quickly as possible."

"Thank you, Dr. Blumenthal for your understanding. I want you to be there for me." She looked at her husband. "You tell her you agree," she said as tears came again as she thought of her coming ordeal.

Softly, "Whatever you want, my dear."

After this encounter, Constance who had reluctantly accepted the apology, made an appointment for Mrs. McIntyre for surgery with Benjamin. She appeared at the hospital with her husband, was admitted and given a bed. Constance went to the ward, glanced at her husband, politely said her hello, then started to speak to Bess who interrupted her.

"I'm so nervous, Dr. Blumenthal. I hurt so much last night I hardly slept."

Constance placed her hand on her forehead, speaking softly. "I understand. Now you just trust me. Will you do that?"

She looked in Constance's eyes, seeing her compassion. "I still say you have beautiful eyes, Doctor. They do make me trust you."

Constance smiled. "There. Well, that's a nice compliment. Here's what will happen. Dr. Blumenthal will give you something that will prevent pain. You will sleep. He will look about inside and take some specimens. That is easy enough, isn't it?"

"I'll try to be good."

"I know you will. Just believe you will feel nothing when he does his work. When you are back here in bed, I'll make sure you have something for pain. You will notice bandages and later Dr. Blumenthal will come and look at you. I'll be with him."

Soon, attendants came for her and took her to the operating room. Benjamin bent over her. "Hello, Mrs. McIntyre. I'm going to put you to sleep and do my work. It will take a little while."

Benjamin, opened her between her ovaries and uterus. Immediately he saw abnormality in the tissue and a growth near her ovary. After he had a specimen, he went toward her pancreas. The cancer had spread. He took another specimen, knowing already what he would find. He closed the incision, mumbling, "The poor woman."

He then turned to the nurse. "When you see Doctor Blumenthal, please tell her I'll be with her as soon as I wash up."

A short time later, he saw Constance waiting outside the operating room. "It's bad, dear. It's spread. I know it's a cancer. I hate it. When I think of what women go through, and the demeaning of them by men and even the male physicians, it just infuriates me."

Constance put her hand to his cheek. "I'd like to kiss you, Ben dearest." She looked about, saw a nurse, smiled at her, and turned back to Ben. "Well, I guess you'll have to wait for that kiss.

"I feel so badly for her and her family. What she has to go through. Do you think she won't live long?"

"No. A few months from what I saw. I want to look through the microscope at the specimens, just for certainty.

"I'll see you later. I'll go to the ward and give them instructions for her pain. I think I'll tell them to use morphine. It may help her sleep more."

They touched hands and parted.

When she came to Mrs. McIntyre, she was beginning to waken. "Oh. Hello, Doctor. I feel sleepy."

"Well, why don't you rest for now? I'll tell the nurse to give you some medicine to help you if you should have pain."

"Will the pain be bad? And what about the operation?"

"It may annoy you some, so I want to help you. The operation went well. When you feel more awake we'll talk about it."

"I'd like to talk about it now." She opened her eyes more widely, gazing fearfully at Constance.

"Dr. Blumenthal said you came through with flying colors. He is going to look at some specimens he took in what we call a microscope. I can tell you more then, but you will have to take care of yourself after you leave the hospital and also continue to see me so I can help as much as possible."

"Is it bad?"

"Let me get your husband. He's been walking up and down the corridor worried about you."

She went out and told Mr. McIntyre she wanted him to come in the ward so they could talk together and to try to get him to be with Bess. "You can stay with your wife for as long as you wish. If you need me, please don't hesitate to tell the nurse."

"What's happening?"

Gently she told him, "Before we go to her bed I'll tell you what I know thus far.

"As I told Mrs. McIntyre, Dr. Blumenthal is looking at some specimens. However, we have a pretty good idea what is happening."

"Well what is it? Stop beating around the bush," as he raised his voice.

"Mr. McIntyre. You are in the hospital and there are other patients. Please try to keep your voice lower." She had all she could do to tell him to just 'shut up.'

"Please listen as calmly as possible. Mrs. McIntyre has a disease that will in a matter of months disable her. I can't be absolutely certain, because it depends upon the disease and how fast it will spread. She will not live for too many months later than that."

The entire time she watched his expression, at one point placing a hand on his arm, hoping to avert another of his outrages. "Mr. McIntyre, she has an incurable cancer. We can give her medication to help her with pain. You will have to be very kind and please forego . . . asking for any sexual activity. Unless perhaps she asks you.

"It would be good for you to be calm so your wife will feel your tenderness for her."

They went to her bed. He looked away from Constance and at his wife, finally having the presence to ask, "How are you, Bess dear?"

"I'm sleepy but am beginning to feel a little pain. The doctor told me she would give me some medicine to help."

He looked at Constance as if he were about to ask a question then back to his wife, as if suddenly realizing he mustn't upset her. Yet, this bad tempered, selfish man, started to think of himself. *So now no woman to take care of the house. Sex. She's supposed to be there for me. Damnation. I know. I'll ask our oldest daughter to come home with her husband and child. That takes care of that end of it. That's what I'll do.* He try to hide his wry smile.

He then looked back to his wife. "Don't worry, dear, we'll take care of everything and make sure you're comfortable. We'll do whatever the doctor tells us."

She listened to his comforting words and weakly told him, "I know we'll get through this, Alex. I'll get better as soon as possible."

Constance turned away from them, her face saddened, then forced a smile. "Well, I'll let you two have some time together. Don't tire your wife, Mr. McIntyre. She needs her rest. Stay for a little while and then leave her to the nurses. I'll be back to be sure everything is taken care of to make her comfortable."

Later Ben told Constance that the woman would have perhaps four months. The cancer had spread as he suspected during the operation procedure, showing proof when he looked at all the specimens.

Constance was with her when she died. She had raised her head to say something while her daughter and husband looked on, then fell back on her pillow. The words never came.

With time, Benjamin became well known not only for his surgery but also his use of microscopy, writing about both in journals. Constance was also in demand as a speaker for women and for her contributions to journals about women, their rights, and the necessity of teaching them about their bodies.

About this time, knowing his daughter and son-in-law had gained such recognition, Nathaniel decided to retire. He and Faith had talked and would now take the time to travel in Europe.

Soon after they left, one night, as Constance and Benjamin lay in bed, she placed her hand on his chest, rolled on top of him, looking in his eyes and smiling, "I'm feeling sexy." She kissed him on the mouth. He opened his and they sought each other. She pulled back, "I want a baby, Ben."

"You sure?"

"I'm sure. It's time for us to have a family."

He eagerly agreed. They pleased one another as Constance reached her climax, arching her back, her head thrown back as she loudly moaned while feeling him fill her, as her opening clenched about him.

As they calmed, he heard, "Ah, no birth control. We'll have to do this every night for this week. I've purposely counted. I'm fertile, love. This should do it."

Constance did become pregnant. She went to her office until she grew big, could feel the growing life within her. In the year 1876 their first child was born. They named her Olivia. After her in 1878 she had a boy, they named Joseph, and in 1890 another girl named Millicent.

Constance devoted her time to her children, practiced some, but could not leave them entirely to their governess, Margaret Mosby, a widow. Although the woman took care of and taught the children as they were growing, when old enough, they were sent to the public schools. Benjamin and Constance intended that the children be part of the community and have no airs.

A year after Millicent's birth, Hannah called for Benjamin and Constance to come home. She spoke to Benjamin.

"Ben, come home as soon as possible. Your papa is very sick. His heart is failing rapidly." She cried loudly. "The doctor has been here, and, as you know, Constance has been here when she could. It's important, Ben. Please come as soon as possible."

"I will, mamma, as soon as I see this patient. Is Daniel there?"

"Yes, and your sisters. I wrote Arella earlier in the week because she was visiting in Bangor. Would you talk to . . . Oh, Ben, I can't," and she sobbed without finishing and hung up. Not long after, having lived 82 good and useful years, Asa died of heart failure.

After the funeral, Hannah asked that Joshua take over the family business, wondering whether Ely would help by expanding the store to include lumber. It would expand Ely's father's business, as well as the Blumenthals. A marvelous family enterprise. Ely was certain his father would agree. They had discussed it in the past, as Arella knew. Arella, surprised everyone. "Mother, we have already made up our minds."

Then Hannah astounded everyone. "Daniel and I are going to Palestine. I want to live out the rest of my life in that ancient land of the Jews where our great Temple was built. Yes, I'll miss you all. Heaven forgive me for leaving you, but also please support me in this. It will be hard, but I must do it. I hope you all understand." Her face was quite sad as tears trickled onto her cheeks, thinking of Asa. She managed a slight smile. "But think, Esther and Joshua and their children, as well as Ely and Arella will see to the business. Please agree with me and help me to do this."

When the surprise abated, the children all nodded, telling of their support, despite Benjamin's and Constance's doubts about her health.

Within the year, just after seeing Nathaniel and Faith depart, they watched Hannah and Daniel leave them behind. Benjamin turned to Constance, tears in his eyes.

"Oh, Ben, it is sad." She brushed his cheek to wipe the tears as her own began. They stood on the wharf and held tightly together. He spoke softly "Constance. It's like they are going to become pioneers. Here they are emigrating just as when mother and father came to this country. It will be hard on them, but they're strong. She has Daniel."

"You be strong too, dearest, and so will I. We've lost both sets of parents, well not completely," and she cried harder.

Suddenly he smiled. "Constance, we have our own family to look to. I believe our children will grow strong, be educated, and do us proud."

She nodded through her tears. He placed his arm about her waist as they walked away, the future theirs and his sisters.

* * *

Olivia

When Olivia was 13 years, Constance who was once more pregnant, decided it was time to teach her about womanhood.

Olivia had blue eyes like her father and would have red hair. Constance and Benjamin both thought she would be a very attractive young lady and when she grew into womanhood.

Constance had decided she would talk to all her children about the changes that occur as they reach puberty, including Joseph when his time came. They were both beautiful to their parents, Joseph with green eyes and brown hair. Soon Millicent with whom she was pregnant would eventually have her mother's hazel eyes and chestnut hair.

One day when home from the office, Constance called Olivia to the drawing room.

"Sit, dear, near me."

"Is something wrong, mother?"

"Not at all. But I want to talk to you about something because you are getting older and of an age I know you'll understand me."

Olivia looked concerned that she had done something her mother disliked. "You said I hadn't . . ."

"No, darling. It's nothing you did, as I told you. I just think I have something to tell you about becoming a young woman."

Olivia looked at her questioningly with troubled eyes.

"I'm not going to scold you but tell you things that will change in you. I want you to know about your body. You already know what your body looks like, but I'll explain some things you do not know. As a female you have inside you below your stomach something called a uterus. That is pear shaped. Attached to it are two tubes with the name fallopian, one that goes to either side of your body, ending in what we name the ovaries. Every month they produce ova or eggs. Below these, where you see the crease between your legs is a canal called the vagina. These are very important for it is with these organs that women have babies when they are married. Now, soon, because of your age you may one day, perhaps between now and next year, find that you are bleeding below. It's called menstruation.

There may be a trickle along your leg. I don't want you to be scared. It is perfectly all right and happens when girls like you reach a stage when you start to become a woman like your mother. Your ovaries (the egg producers) send out an egg. Because you are not married, it sends the unhatched egg through your uterus down to your vagina. When that happens, you will bleed because there is no baby. This is your menstrual period. When it comes, tell me, and I'll show you what to do to make yourself comfortable. There will be more blood, but don't worry about it. It's perfectly natural for this to happen. It happens to me, dear and has since I was a little older than you. It will occur every month, perhaps every 28 days. Now please dear. Do not be frightened by what I have told you. It is perfectly natural for women. As I said, you are becoming a woman."

"It doesn't hurt, does it?"

"Heavens no. Well sometimes it may just before you bleed. You may have a backache or headaches. If you do, just tell me. It just is something that we experience and expect. We take care of this monthly occurrence in a certain way, and I'll show you when the time comes. Just remember it's perfectly natural. When we get older our bodies change, and as you grow you'll see yourself come to be the way I am up here, my breasts, dear, and other things you'll notice about which we can talk when you wish. Also you may want to go to college, perhaps where I went with your Aunt Arella. Later, when you meet a young man you love you may have children. That is when the egg comes and is hatched with child by the man sending something named spermatozoa from his body into your canal. It will, what we say, fertilize your ovum. You will feel yourself grow as your uterus keeps the growing baby inside you. Just remember you should be proud to be a woman. I want you when the time comes to think for yourself. I want all my children to do that. We don't have to get into a discussion about all that, but whatever you want to ask me or your father, please, dear, don't ever be afraid to ask us anything. O.K.?"

"Yes, mother. May I go now?"

"Do you understand what I have said, or do you want to ask me anything?"

"No. I understand what you told me. I guess I'll probably think about it and wonder about it."

"That's perfectly all right. Just don't worry. Come here, Olivia."

She moved closer to Constance who hugged her and kissed her on her forehead. "You are my wonderful daughter, and remember. Your father and I are always here for you, as we are for your brother and sister. I want you all to look out for one another. And you being the oldest, sometimes I may count on you a bit more. That's all, Olivia. You go and play."

When Olivia became 14, she was ready to attend a private school, as had her mother. She had experienced what her mother told her and how to take care of herself as a young woman and not to allow any males near her. Constance and Benjamin accompanied her to school with Paul driving the horses. They had not gone far beyond when Constance thought of the past.

"I was just thinking how I felt when my father took Aunt Arella and me to college and we lived at Mrs. Stedman's."

"Mother, were you lonely?" Olivia's eyes filled with tears. "I'm sorry. I can't help it."

"Why are you apologizing, dear? Of course you're going to feel lonely. But you remember what I told you. You can always write or talk to us."

"I don't know why you have me going up here so far from you. Truthfully, I don't like it. I would . . ."

"You would what?" Benjamin softly interrupted.

"I just want to go to Portland High School so I can be near everyone." She cried openly now. "Aunt Arella went there.

220

Look at her. She's a teacher. If she could do it and be near home, why can't I?" she cried openly.

Benjamin and Constance looked at one another, both with sadness and hesitation.

Glancing at Constance, Benjamin called out, "Paul, please stop the horses."

They had gone only a few miles beyond Portland. Constance took over. She put her arms about Olivia. "Dear, I know it's hard. I told you I remember when Grandfather Sterling took your Aunt Arella and me. Your aunt and I . . . I've never told this before, Olivia, even to your father. We were sad going, and when we were in our room and settled by ourselves, we sat with our arms around each other and cried. Oh what tears. You should have seen them. We were lonely, like you now feel. But it is a good school. When that time arrives, you'll meet older girls who may become your friends."

She put her fingers under Olivia's chin, raising her tearful face. "Did you hear what I said?"

"Yes, I did mother. I just can't help it. I don't want to go. College is a long way off. I know you and father want the best for me, but . . . but being away from home. You had Aunt Arella, at least, and you were older."

This stumped Constance. Benjamin, smiling, thinking about Arella and Constance, winked at her. "Olivia. You move to my seat so I can talk to mother." He started to whisper. "Constance, what if we give in? We could tell her a year at home. After that we could see what happens, whether we change our minds or change hers."

"I guess so. It's just that she's got to grow up some time," Constance answered, her face troubled with love for her daughter and wondering what was best for her. She touched Benjamin, nodding, "Yes."

She smiled at Olivia, bringing her back between them. "I'll tell you what. Your mother and father will agree to a year at

Portland. But don't think we still will think in terms of four years there. Do you understand?"

"Oh, yes, mother," wiping at her cheeks and eyes. "Oh, I love you and father."

"Yes. I know. We love you too. But don't think you have completely won." There was a catch at Constance's heart thinking of her children. She hugged Olivia as Benjamin kissed her cheek, telling her, "You will be at home and you will study hard, Olivia. We want you to be proud of yourself." He hesitated. "Olivia, it's all right to be proud but not so you think you're better than other people. Do you understand?"

"I do, father. Oh thank you both for letting me do this." She smiled, still wiping at her eyes. "I love you both so much. I'll study. Don't you worry."

"We won't," Benjamin answered, then spoke to Paul. "I guess you better turn around, Paul. We're going home."

Meanwhile, as they trotted back, though he hadn't said anything, he was thinking of buying a steamer auto. It would be quite a year. Soon, Constance would give birth to their second daughter in January, 1880. Perhaps thinking of that and having felt the movements even now as they talked and decided, her eyes teared, for the wonderful family God had given her. "Here. Put your hand on mommie's tummy. "Feel it, Olivia."

"It moved," she shouted.

"Yes." Both she and Benjamin laughed. They were all going to their home.

So, on the next day they went to Portland High School and registered Olivia. Within weeks, Olivia, an extrovert, met several girls she liked. One Agatha, the other Mary. They were attracted to the tallish blue eyed, red haired Olivia. She also tried to avoid a class with Arella who was teaching algebra but to no avail. It was a requirement. Meeting with her aunt, Arella told her niece, "Olivia, I know you won't be upset. But I must tell you, if you need help I'm here for all the students. But I shan't show any favoritism."

"I'm aware of that Aunt Arella. I'll call you Mrs. Levin. Just don't think I'd try to take advantage."

"I know you won't, darling." Arella kissed her on the cheek, and they separated.

The three girls had all their classes together. Besides Algebra there was Latin, English, and Western Civilization, Physical Education.

Mary and Agatha sat one in front and the other in back of Olivia, the better performing students on the right side of the Latin class. However, Olivia began to outperform her friends in the other classes and occasionally could be seen, by her aunt, especially, looking toward the two girls, wishing she were sitting by them. However, she could not bring herself to do poorer in her examinations or to cause a problem that may have brought them closer in the other classes. There was no question that Olivia would have caused her parents to wonder. Perhaps, too, they would have heard from Arella. As it was, trouble came to Olivia, because she was the first in all her classes. A poorer student, Prudence, who tried to join Olivia's friends did not really want to have anything to do with Olivia. She always seemed to have a sour look, pursing her lips, chewing on them when she couldn't answer a question. Then, one day, in the girl's restroom, she realized Olivia was having her period when she saw a bit of blood on the stall floor when Olivia's hands slipped going to her pantalets.

"What's the matter, doctors' daughter? Can't your doctor mother and doctor father see to it that you don't dirty our floor? You're just like the rest of us, ain't you, snobby?"

Embarrassed and angry, Olivia began to lose her temper. She started to go toward Prudence, her hands in fists. When they faced one another, Olivia spurt, "What are you so jealous about?" I'd like to scratch your eyes out. Is it my fault my parents are doctors and your father is a store keeper?"

Prudence grabbed for a lock of Olivia's hair and pulled.

"Ouch. Don't do that." Olivia's eyes began to tear. "I'll get you for that." She moved closer to Prudence, the two in anger staring at one another.

"Oh, look at the doctors' daughter. She's beginning to cry."

At that point a teacher walked in. "What's going on? We don't tolerate fighting."

Prudence answered first. "She was going to hit me."

"That's not true."

Knowing of Olivia's excellence, the teacher asked her, "Is that true?"

"No. It is not." She made fun of me and pulled at my hair.

The teacher had separated them and told Olivia, "Please come with me."

As they opened the door, the teacher and Olivia heard, "Yeah, your aunt gives you good grades in algebra. You gotta help family out, don't ya."

The teacher turned back angrily, staring at Agatha. "Don't you say another word, young lady." Then she thought. "You are to act like a lady." This time they made it through the door, Prudence sticking out her tongue.

"Olivia, tell me what happened."

Olivia blushed. "Well . . . Mrs. Thompson. It's my time. You know."

"I understand."

"She made fun of me and my mother and father for being doctors. That's not my fault I'm lucky enough to have parents like mine. It also isn't my fault that my algebra teacher is my aunt."

She smiled. "I know, Olivia." She noticed tears. "Don't you cry. You did nothing wrong. Don't be angry with Prudence. She has a harder time with her studies. You might try to help her."

"Well, I'll think about it."

"I'd appreciate it if you would. She could use the help."

"I'll try then."

Olivia told her friends what happened and that she was going to talk to Prudence.

"Olivia! You aren't! She's such a troublemaker. We can't believe you're going to try to help her."

"I am. I promised Mrs. Thompson. If she doesn't want it, well, that's her problem."

Mary mockingly wiped her brow. "Good luck, Olivia."

Olivia laughed. She hugged Mary and then Agatha. "I'm so lucky to have two friends like you. Sometimes I have the feeling a lot of girls look at me like I'm a freak."

"That's silly," Agatha told her. "You're smart. So what? Sometimes I wish I had as good a brain as you do."

The girls looked at one another smiling. Mary suddenly said, "Well, I guess it must be, having two parents who are doctors and an algebra teacher aunt."

"Oh, cut it out," as Olivia lightly hit her on the arm. The three then walked away from school, arm in arm, all waiting for their carriage rides.

At home, Joyce opened the door to Olivia. "You look somewhat sad, dear one."

"It's nothing, Joyce. Just something that happened at school today. I guess my parents aren't home yet."

"Nope. Why don't you see Mrs. Mosby? Maybe you could talk to her."

"No. I'll wait for my mother and father. But I will go see her. She'll want to hear about my day and whether I need any help with my studies."

Later, rather unusually, Constance and Benjamin arrived home the same time. Olivia and Joseph heard the door and ran down the stairs to greet them.

"Mamma. Daddy." Joseph shouted. Benjamin, raised him. "Tell your mother and father whether you were good today at school and when you got home."

"Of course I was. Oh, I did get in a little trouble. I was fooling around with one of the boys and the teacher kept me after. Do you know what she did? After everyone left the room, she called me to her desk. "Joseph. Can you promise me you are going to behave from now on so I don't have to keep you?"

"And what did you answer?" Constance asked

Joseph had a mischievous look. "I was honest, mother."

"Ah, Oh. What does that mean?"

"I told her I'd try, but I couldn't promise."

They both laughed, then asked Olivia about her day.

"It turned bad. That horrible Prudence caused me trouble, made fun of you and father, Aunt Arella, and me. She pulled my hair even. Mrs. Thompson asked me to try to help her. I told her I would."

"Good for you. We're sorry you had a bad time," Constance answered, but do try to help her." Later Olivia told Constance what started it. Constance ran her hand soothingly along her daughter's hair. "Well, those things happen, sweet. You know I understand. We can talk about it. There are some things I ought to talk to you about that I haven't. We'll do that soon."

"It's all right with myself, mother. But I am curious about growing up to be like you."

Constance smiled. "There are a number of happenings in a young woman's life. Some you'll learn all by yourself. Others I can tell you when you have questions. But remember. You always be yourself. Don't let men or anyone else tell you you are not a man's equal. Look at your father and me. If some foolish girl makes fun of what you can do or who you are, let it go, if you can. You know better."

"I perfectly understand, mother. I'm lucky to have you and father and Joseph, and Millicent." She laughed. "Thanks for the good brain." With that they both laughed.

Sometime after, at school, the friends learned that Prudence was to have a party.

"Did she say anything to you, Olivia?"

"No, Agatha."

"That's mean."

Mary interjected, "Why should we care?"

While this conversation was taking place, Prudence appeared.

"There you are, the three stuck-ups. Well I'm having a big party. I thought of inviting you, but you're not worth it to be with all my friends. Look at you, the three outcasts."

"Prudence, where did you learn such a big word?" Agatha asked.

Mary lightly punched her in the back, then replied about the party. "I don't think we'll feel too bad about being left out. Whatever made you so mean and jealous?"

"Me jealous of you three? That'll be the day," as she pranced off.

The three friends laughed loudly. "I just love her," Olivia told them. "She's such a fool."

The first year of school had such problems, becoming accustomed to different kinds of people. Sometimes she saw girls with more ragged clothes, black people she had hardly ever seen before.

In the sophomore year she became friendly with a girl, Edwina, who came from a poor family. She was quite shy and hardly ever spoke to anyone, struggling through her schooling. Watching her in some of her classes, Olivia felt terribly sorry for her. Hearing her stammer when called upon about a question, occasionally she would be able to answer, others her nervousness forced her to falter or to make mistakes. One day when called upon, she was so nervous, Olivia noticed tears forming. Edwina looked down, a small puddle forming at her feet, and she hurried from the class.

"Oh, I just don't know," Olivia heard the teacher mutter. She called on one of the pupils to get a janitor to clean the floor.

Some girls giggled, holding their hands to their mouths. Olivia, disgusted by the behavior and smiles, asked if she might go and help Edwina. Given permission, she went to the girls' room and found Edwina weeping.

"Edwina."

She looked up, crying harder. "I hate it here. I don't want to come anymore. You're so smart. Everyone says you are. Well, this place is for girls like you. Not me."

"Edwina, let me help you get cleaned up."

"You'll laugh at me."

"I'm not going to laugh. Have you seen me do that?"

"Look at your nice clothes. I don't want to dirty you."

"You won't. Come on." Olivia took a nice handkerchief from below her sleeve. "Here, Edwina, take this and dry your eyes."

"Why are you helping me? No one hardly ever pays any attention to me."

"Well, I am. Now come on. We'll go in one of the stalls and take off your wet pantalets."

"Well, All right. You won't laugh at me?" She hesitated. "I've been a good girl. No one has ever seen me down there before. I've heard some say they've let boys . . ."

"Forget that," Olivia interrupted, her face turning a bit red. "Now, come on. Let me help. I promise I won't look at your private place. We'll just raise you skirts, take off your wet things, and then you can clean yourself. I'll wait until you are ready. Here now. Let me help you with your dress near the floor. I'll raise the skirt, and you do the rest."

Edwina did as Olivia told her, smiling slightly. She hesitated. "I don't have many clothes and nothing as nice as yours."

"Don't think about that. I'm just fortunate, that's all. We're all alike in many ways. Some are smarter than others. Some more mean." She was thinking of Prudence.

After Edwina had cleaned herself, she told Olivia, "I have no place to put this wet stuff," as her eyes teared again.

"I'll take care of that. I have something you can carry them in and take home to clean."

Suddenly, trusting Olivia, she blurted, "I have a sick mom. My daddy can't afford a doctor. Sometimes it seems as if . . . as if she may die."

Stunned, Olivia without thinking, told her, "You take your mom to see my mother. She's a woman's doctor."

"But we couldn't pay."

"I'll tell my mother that." Olivia took a piece of paper from her purse and wrote Constance's address.

Later that day, Olivia suddenly thought, *Maybe my mother and father were right about Kents Hill Or Berwick Academy. I like it here, though, being near home.* Then when Paul came for her it occurred to her. *I like meeting and helping all kinds of people. After Bates, Med school!*

Part IV

Auld Lang Sine

1901, the year of the new 20th Century. The family gathered
to celebrate Benjamin's and Arella's 60th birthdays one year
before Olivia will be graduated from medical school. Nor had
Hannah forgotten her twins, nor did Daniel. Birthday presents
arrived from a Palestine where Hannah had purchased land for
a home in Jerusalem. It was also where Daniel learned and
started a wine business and met a diamond merchant who was
willing to teach him the art of cutting. They had managed to do
this under one of the Ottoman Empire's open policy to Jews
until it again closed. In Europe Theodore Herzl was starting a
campaign to open the Holy Land to all Jews who wished to
emigrate, particularly those from Russia who were suffering
under pogroms. When they heard the news, they joined many
of their fellows arguing for Jewish emigration. Despite their
desire for more of their people to join them in this new-ancient
land, it could be dangerous should Arabs or Ottoman Turks
crack down which the Ottoman Empire unsuccessfully did.

At home, meanwhile, Nathaniel and Faith landed in New
York anxious to see their daughter and grandchildren, Millicent
having been born a few years before their arrival home. Yet,
when in Portland when Benjamin and Constance looked at
Nathaniel, they both noticed his thinner face and dullness in his
eyes.

Constance said nothing. She had Millicent go to Faith who
took her with smiles a kiss, and hug. As Nathaniel watched and

touched the girl, Constance looked to Benjamin, asking silently whether she should wait to say something about her father. He motioned to her to wait, placing a finger on his lips.

They waited a day to celebrate the homecoming. Before going to her parents' home, late that afternoon, Constance and Benjamin decided they would talk to Nathaniel.

It was a gay time, that neither Constance nor Benjamin wished to dampen or interfere with Nathaniel's happiness. He seemed to be himself, smiling, talking, asking questions about the practice.

"How I wished I could join you both again. But I suppose age is catching up with me."

"Yes, Dad," Constance answered. "You can continue your vacation here at home, be with your friends and family." She thought of asking him what was happening, that he looked thin, his face now appearing haggard, because he was tiring. She wanted to lead him to the drawing room, thinking also of the times they sat together when she was younger and he would read to her or tell her stories about what it was like going to college and learning to be a doctor, how he told her she was so intelligent and would do well at college. In this room, too, she told him she would be a doctor, remembering how he had looked at her astounded but telling her he would be proud of her.

"Father, you don't look too good. What is bothering you? Now don't fib."

He hesitated. "What brought this up? You've taken me away from our guests."

"I'm a doctor, remember? You also must remember how you looked at me when I told you I would go to med school."

Nathaniel laughed, hesitated, then told her with a forced smile, "I am ill, Constance. Your mother has worried about me since we were in France before coming home. It was quite a circle, or almost one we made going through those countries and coming back to Cherbourg. Well, by the time we got there," he faltered, "I knew. You can see it in my face and the weight I've lost, good doctor that you are."

"You've got a cancer, father. It's almost obvious. Don't lie."

"I do."

"Would you allow Ben and me to both examine you?"

"Yes. But I know what you'll find. I doubt that surgery would do any good." He now had tears. "I am so worried about your mother."

"Before we talk about her, and don't worry about that, because Ben and I will look after her. I'd like to know where it is."

"It started in my stomach." He sobbed. "How I hate leaving you and your mother."

Both were now crying. "This is not what we should be talking about now, Constance. We can't go back to the guests looking the way we do."

They sat, each wiping eyes, one with a silk handkerchief, the other men's linen. Constance took out a small brush with a bit of black, slipped it along her lashes, and used a little lip cosmetic.

"You look beautiful, Constance."

"Thank you, father. I may believe you."

"You'd best. You may be older, but you've never lost that lovely face."

She smiled. "Listen, Nathaniel, you're my father."

He laughed. "I just wonder what Benjamin says."

"You'll have to guess."

They both laughed and went back to the company.

Faith, seeing them, walked toward the two, taking Nathaniel's arm, looking seriously and sadly at Constance. Benjamin lingered with some of the doctors until Constance joined him, and when far enough away softly told him, tears in her eyes she tried to hide, "It's as bad as we thought."

"Well, we have to put on a show for now."

The following evening, Faith and Nathaniel visited with Constance and Benjamin. Of course, Faith insisted that she be allowed to hear everything said about Nathaniel.

Benjamin had already talked to Constance about him being the one to start the conversation after dinner. The talk was pleasantries, some regarding the European trip, others about Olivia and her studies. Constance told them of Olivia's plans and how they came about.

* * *

In 1894, Olivia was in her senior year at Portland High School. Now, as tall as her mother, her blue eyes shone with perception and understanding and along with her red hair, caused men to glance. By then she had had experiences she thought could never have happened had she gone to a private academy.

Her parents having been delayed at Maine General, Joyce served them a late supper. As they ate, Olivia decided she would tell them more of what she thought about rather often, her experiences at the high school. They had talked before, but now the consequences had helped her decide her future.

"Mother, father, I've been thinking."

"About what?" Constance and Benjamin asked simultaneously, all three laughing.

"Just hold on a minute, huh?" Olivia stopped them. "Anyhow, mother, you remember you took care of Edwina's mom?"

"Yes. She was a lovely woman."

"I told you Edwina was scared because she thought you would charge more than they could afford. They were so happy that you looked after her. Anyhow, you know we became good friends. What bothered me was that Agatha and Mary were not too pleased, but they did come around so we became a foursome. Well, since meeting Edwina, she introduced me to other girls who don't have as much as we do. I never realized how lucky I am to have parents like you and to be able to live in a house like ours.

"You know, they have such ragged clothes. Oh, and a couple of them were Irish." Olivia laughed, "When they heard my last name they looked at me as if they had met a peculiar creature."

Her parents laughed. "We knew," Benjamin told her, "When we looked at you, we knew you had come from the moon." He then added, "Does it bother you to have the last name I gave your mother, you, and your brother and sister?"

"It does not," she huffily objected. "I am who I am. If people can't accept that, then that's their problem.

"That's beside the point. What I want to tell you is that I met all kinds of people being at the high school, poor and otherwise. I also even talked to some black girls, although they were hard to get to know."

"You already told us some of this, Olivia," Constance interrupted.

"Yes, but that's not my point. I did not mean that. I never told you I once had Paul take Edwina and me to her house. It wasn't in the best part of Portland, of course. But. Mother, father, Edwina was hesitant about getting in the carriage and afraid of what her friends would say, that she was getting puffed up riding about with a doctors' daughter. Somehow, I managed to calm her."

"So what is the point you're leading to?" her parents asked.

"You know I'm going to Bates. But . . ."

"Oh, we knew there was a but," Benjamin said, smiling at her."

"Mother. Father. I want to go to medical school. I feel it here," she said pointing to her heart. "I also think if I return to Portland, I want to help poor people."

Constance and Benjamin smiled across the table. Joseph and Millicent who had been sitting there restlessly, finally brought some notice to themselves, when Joseph said loudly, "Olivia's goin' to be a doctor." Millicent giggled. "Are you, Olivia?"

"Oh, you two cut it out. This is serious. Anyhow, why aren't they in bed? It's so late."

"They wanted to wait up for their mother and father and 'old sister.' Did you know Joseph called you that one day?" Constance laughed.

"Well, since I'm so old and going to college next year, you listen to me give the orders around this house." Her smile faded as she thought. "I wanted to tell you more about Edwina. Anyhow, after I got her into the carriage and we came near her house her face turned red. I couldn't imagine why. But I found out,

"'Please, Olivia, let me get out here and walk the rest of the way. I . . . I don't want the neighbors or my family to see me. They'll think I'm gettin' uppity.'

"Well, I was embarrassed and felt so sorry for her. I hate seeing people poor or with so little.

"But you know what I like," she smiled again. "When both of you have the week-end off and we all go for a ride in father's auto. I have to admit it's fun to see people look when we ride by. That time you took us to Scarborough Beach too was the best. I hope we can do it again." Constance and Benjamin nodded 'yes.'

"Aside from that, I hope you both agree with my plans."

"We do," Benjamin answered, wondering to himself how much, if at all, she would change her mind. "You know we are both proud of you and your accomplishments. Of course, Aunt Arella told us a little."

So it was that graduation came, with Olivia as Valedictorian. Come the fall, they both happily and sadly took her to Bates for her new experience, one that she also loved. She never changed her mind about medical school. That did not surprise either of them, aware of her ability and that once her mind settled on something useful, she rarely changed it.

When she arrived home after having visited with Agatha and Mary, she found her handsome brother now 20 and lovely Millicent, 18, discussing with their parents their schooling, as well as Olivia's.

Olivia's face showed a little chagrin, that her younger brother and sister would be part of a conversation regarding her future.

As her parents, brother and sister greeted her, she wanted to know, "Why are you discussing my plans without me?"

Constance answered. "Dear one, don't come into the house with that look on your face. Yes, we were talking about you, because Joseph just now told us what his plans are, as well as his experiences at Harvard, Millicent talking about her happiness attending the University of Maine."

"I chose it because it's in Orono and closer to home. I don't want to be far away," Millicent interrupted, smiling brightly. She was now just a little shorter than Olivia. A lovely young woman, slim, shapely like her sister and mother, her red hair and observant blue eyes captivating those who either looked at her or knew her. Because of her friendliness, she was popular among the girls while in high school. Like Olivia, however, she met two girls with whom she and they could confide in one another.

"Did you have any idea that Joseph has decided he wants to go to med school?" Constance asked.

"No, I didn't. That's exciting. How come I never heard about it?"

"You never heard of it, Olivia," Benjamin answered, "because he just a while ago told us. How could he have said anything to you? I know he writes you, but this is the first we've heard of it."

Olivia smiled and told all of them, "I apologize if I sounded angry or a bit out of joint. I guess you already know I have to discuss with mother and father what they think of my choice of medical schools."

She had heard Joseph asking, "What medical school do you think Olivia will attend?" It interested him, for he had made up his mind while in Cambridge.

"Well, I'm fortunate that the two schools I'm interested in accepted me. I like the idea of the Pennsylvania Women's Medical College. But now I'm thinking I should attend Vermont Medical College, because Vermont is closer to home or even Tufts University School of Medicine. But I want most of all Vermont."

Millicent laughed.

"You sound like me."

"I guess I do, Millicent." Despite the age difference, the two were very close, and they adored Joseph who despite his teasing, of course, they knew it was in fun. However, he was critical of the way they dressed, often asking why they wore this or that. Of course, though older there were arguments and noise when they were together. Alice or Mrs. Mosby, who the parents kept on for her intelligence and wisdom, often interfered. When either one entered the fray, brother and sisters would separate, laughing at the beloved woman.

The conversation continued with Olivia's eyes tearing. She had been away from her home for so many years and now would leave again.

"What's wrong, Olivia?" Constance quietly asked, knowing what was bothering her, for she had felt the same way talking of distance from home.

"Oh, I'm just thinking. Did you feel the same why as I, mother when you thought of leaving everyone?"

She started to answer when Joseph interrupted. "Olivia, I even feel that way sometimes. We love our parents and each other and miss our home. Why shouldn't we feel lonely occasionally?"

"But I was thinking if I go to Pennsylvania, I'll never see you all. I know what med school's like by listening to mother and father."

"So you think being in Burlington will get you closer because we have a new auto?" Benjamin laughed as did the whole family.

"Father, you love that machine of yours, especially now that it has gasoline. So do I. Will you let me drive it this summer?" Joseph interrupted. "Not only that. What about Olivia and Millicent? I know, you could buy another one, have two, one for us and one for you and mother."

"I don't think I'd trust you, Joseph," he mocked, pausing, rubbing his chin, looking at Constance, who knew immediately what he was thinking. "On the other hand, maybe we ought to have two. But how will Paul drive two autos and a carriage? But think of it, what a picture that would make for Portland to talk about, the Drs. Blumenthal being such rich Jewish doctors. Hmmm. Do they realize that you're only half Jewish, all of you. I'm outnumbered."

Everyone laughed. Yet, Constance uneasily at first looked at Benjamin, biting her lower lip, then smiling coyly, her eyes brightening as she looked at her husband, thinking, *If he gets serious it will be all right. Hmm. Cars and the women's laughter as the wind sweeps at their bonnets whisking their hair. She thought of the time Ben drove to a deserted wood. Oh, I'm beginning to feel sexy.* She felt her nipples harden and heat reach to her center. Then, looking at her children, she pulled herself short. "Were we talking about cars?"

"Well where have you been, mother?" the children asked laughingly.

"Oh. Daydreaming, I guess."

Benjamin smiled, "Olivia, you have to make up your mind.

Or do you want us to do that? You know no matter where you go, we'll see that you are financially taken care of."

"O.K. I know you'll see to that, father. I'm going to tell Vermont I'm coming."

"Hurray," Joseph and Millicent shouted in chorus. "Olivia's going to Vermont. Hip Hip Hooray."

"Oh, shut up, the two of you," she yelled as the entire family laughed. Constance and Benjamin both hugged her, Joseph kissing her cheek and Millicent waiting her turn to hug her sister.

Supper that night was somewhat noisy. Yet, some stranger entering would feel the love among them.

Later, in their room, Constance went into the bathroom as Ben showered. "I want to get in with you."

"Come on."'

As the water wet them both and they moved their hands about each other's bodies, she told him, "Let's dry and get in bed.

"You have no idea why I seemed to drift away when we were with the children. I was thinking of you and that day in the auto. Remember?"

"Of course I do. You want more of that, more than an auto can offer?" He took her hand, led her to the bed and fell gently on top of her, but she slipped out and placed herself above, then leaned over him.

"I'll take care of you and me, dear lover. You know what I like, and I know what you enjoy. To start," she smiled down at him, "do put your tongue to my nipples and then . . . ," she whispered.

Finally, she lay back, allowing him to enter.

Later, after more, and resting, catching their breath, she told him, "This is how we made such wonderful children, how I enjoyed it, and oh how I love you."

"I love you also, always will."

"And our children," she whispered.

"And our children," he repeated.

"How fortunate we are, Ben. They are so good and intelligent. Sometimes it frightens me that God has been so good to us." She laughed. "See what happens when you marry in an Episcopal church?"

Suddenly she felt tears coming. "Ben. Our children's vacations will end soon, and they'll be gone. Children. They are grown young women and a man. It will be so lonely. Look at me. I'm crying. The beauty of love for you and them."

By the end of summer, each child left for his or her destinies.

* * *

Not too long after, a call came from Faith. Benjamin answered. "Ben, can you and Constance come here a soon as possible. It's Nathaniel. He's been vomiting and is so weak. He looks wretched. Please come soon."

"We will, mother. I'll call Constance at the office, or, if you wish, you could, and tell her to come straight to you. I'll be on my way as quickly as I can get on my coat."

He phoned Constance to be certain she had the message. As soon after she saw her last patient, she walked into the house where a tearful Maud met her at the door. "Your mother, Dr. Constance, is with your father. Dr. Ben should be here very soon." She smiled slightly. "He'll get here fast in that auto he loves so."

"Thanks Maud," she called over her shoulder as she went quickly up the stairs. In the room, she went to her mother who turned slightly toward her, her face tear stained. When Constance kissed her cheek, Faith began to sob. "He looks so pale. Constance, look at him."

Nathaniel weakly smiled at his daughter, speaking through his pain. "My daughter has come to doctor me. Have you ever imagined that?" He forced a laugh. "I remember how I used to take care of you when you were such a little girl. When you grew up I sent you to other doctors. Now look at us." His voice faltered. He closed his eyes, grimacing with pain.

"Father, let me examine you."

As she began to remove the covers, Benjamin entered, stopped, not wishing to interfere as he watched Constance. He brought a chair to sit beside Faith.

"Ben, come over here," Constance told him. She could not hold back the tears, started crying, whispering to her husband, "You look."

Benjamin was watching Nathaniel, looked in his eyes, felt his hot face, his pulse. Shaking his head. "Father, can you hear me?"

Nathaniel nodded, weakly pulled Benjamin toward him, telling him in his ear, "I'm dying, Benjamin. There's nothing anyone can do now. You've been so good to us. You'll look after Faith."

"I will, father. Don't worry about her. Constance and I will take care of her."

Nathaniel then asked Faith to move closer. "You've been the finest wife any man could have."

Faith could not hold back the sobs. "How I have loved and admired you all through our marriage, Nathaniel. I . . . ," and she whispered, "Don't leave me."

She felt his hand slip from hers, wailed, looking toward Constance. "Daughter, he's gone, isn't he?" And she sobbed still more loudly.

Constance placed her arms about her mother, both women crying, as Faith hid her head in Constance's shoulder. "My Nathaniel is gone from us." She leaned toward his face, kissed his cheek and then his lips, "You're gone. How can I live without you?"

Nathaniel died in December of that year, just before the

beginning of the new century. The funeral brought many people to the cemetery, doctors, close friends, even patients. Benjamin walked slowly from the service, his arms about Constance and Faith.

When they arrived at the Sterling home, Lucy, Maud, and Ambrose had set the house for the many people who would come to help and encourage Faith in her grief. Eventually Constance and Benjamin broached Faith about the house and living.

In the quiet of the drawing room, Constance spoke softly, "Come sit with me, mother. Ben and I want to talk to you."

Faith obeyed and sat between them, as Constance hugged her, drawing her mother closer. "You know how much I love you, mother." Constance's eyes teared. "All that you and father have done for me. I can never forget or even repay you for all that love and caring." She laughed a bit. "Except when you first heard about Ben and me marrying."

"Oh, Constance. Stop that. You know your father and I accepted your marriage and were happy for both of you, even though it did take a little time." She smiled slightly.

"Well, mother," as Constance looked at Benjamin, "We want you to come live with us."

"I couldn't do that to you. Besides it would mean giving up my home after so many years and memories. I have Maud and Lucy. Ambrose will continue to drive me. Of course, they are all getting older. Have you notice how Ambrose stoops when he walks. I don't know how much longer he can continue. But I'll take care of him." She laughed. "And Lucy and Maud. Have you noticed their greying hair? But together we'll manage."

"We know that. But I think we have a better solution. We would like you to come and live with us. Maud, Lucy, and Ambrose would come also. He would have Paul's company, and you'd have the women, as well as Ben and me there for you in whatever you may need. There's lots of room. When the children manage to come home, you'd be so happy to be with them. You and father certainly made certain we had plenty of space when you gave us the house. Also, I know you like the bay. Please, mother. It would delight us."

Benjamin interrupted. "Mother, we need one another now more than ever."

Faith placed her hand on Benjamin's face. "Ben, I look on you as the son I never had."

"If that's the case," he answered smiling, "we'd sell this home. I know it will be hard, but we want you with us. Please say you'll do this. Now look at me. I'm begging," he laughed.

"It will be hard," Faith answered. She tried to hold back her tears, wiped at her eyes. "I love you both so dearly. Yes. It will be hard, but I know I must do this. I'll talk to Lucy, Maud, and Ambrose so they can also prepare."

So it was that at the beginning of 1901, the house on the West side of Portland was sold, and Faith came to live with her daughter and son-in-law.

———————————

Part V

Encounters and Unsuspected

Chapter One

Palestine

Hanna and Daniel had now been in Palestine for a little over 10 years. Daniel was well settled in his wine business. They had a larger house in Jerusalem. Hannah was now in her nineties, amazed she was still living. They kept in touch with Benjamin and Constance, of course. They wrote about more Jews being allowed to come to the Holy Land.

Two years after arriving in Palestine, Daniel met a woman, Riva Kaplan. She was in her early forties, perhaps about five foot four with black hair and dark brown eyes, a sadness about her rounded face that caused him to question what he observed.

* * *

"Daniel," his friend, Abraham, he met one day in the hills outside the city where his family farmed, "Don't you think it's time you settled down with a woman? What are you? A bachelor for life, none of your blood to leave?"

"All right. What's up? You come to the city to sell your food and diagnose me. So tell me what's bothering you?"

"I've met a woman whose family migrated from Russia. They have farmland here also and nearby me. Oddly enough she can speak your language. She told me she insisted on learning English, pestered her father, who, of course, thinks women have their place in the home. Somehow she persuaded her family to allow her to go to a male friend of mine who knows the language. Of course she'd have to be accompanied by one of her sisters or brothers. She has two younger sisters, Katya and Tamar and two brothers, the oldest of the children, Efram and Emanuel. Anyhow, I think she drove her family crazy but insisted she had a brain and that English, not German, was the most important language to learn, no matter that the family had decided to settle where they are. She's probably no more religious than you. In case you're wondering, they were thinking of America, but her father obviously decided upon the Aliyah, our Palestine. She's smart, and I think you should meet her How about meeting her? I think you'll get along fine. What do you say?"

"If I say 'No' you'll never leave me alone. O.K."

When Riva said she wanted to see more of the city and received permission to accompany two of her oldest brothers, Abraham made certain Daniel would be available and that Abraham would arrive in Jerusalem before they would. Abraham, however, was unaware of the argument in Riva's family about her accompanying her brothers.

Her father argued, yelled, "You are a woman. What is this? You learn your place. Look at you, so much older, no longer thought of as marriageable. You're a disgrace."

Mrs. Kaplan shrank when she heard her husband and Riva who shouted back. "Yes. I'm a woman. Look at me. I have everything any woman has. You treat me like a servant, and I won't have it any longer."

"You will not talk to me like that. It's that talk of yours and the way you shun people by being so direct. What kind of woman is that?"

"A brain, Pappa. A BRAIN!"

Her father stepped toward her, his hand raised. Riva's face revealed her fright, as she raised her arm across her face, tears already beginning to form.

"Akiva. Stop this. Stop now. She's your oldest daughter. Not your slave," her mother, Naomi, screamed.

Akiva dropped his hand, staring at Naomi and back to Riva. *Go then, brainy.*

The argument set the appearance of Riva in the city and her introduction to Daniel.

Abraham behaved as if he were the man meeting a marriageable woman. His wife had told him to settle down. "Perhaps you want to be a matchmaker?"

"Riva will just meet him. She'll be with her brothers."

"Oh, I thought you could get money on the side. And don't forget, Abraham, I am your wife, and there are to be no other women in your life except for your daughter."

"All right already. He's my friend and he needs to marry. O.K.?"

His wife laughed. "Oh, get out of here. You've done your duty by Daniel. Frankly, I agree with you. He needs a woman, not just his mother."

After Daniel met Riva, he thought about her frequently. He wrote Benjamin and Constance:

"I was attracted to her because of a weariness I saw in her that I wanted to erase. Well, you know me. I always have to help people. Not like you and Constance as a doctor but as a man who wants people around me to feel some of the joy we can experience. Perhaps it's a left over from the war and the family we have lost. Oh has she a beautiful smile and the darkest, beautiful brown eyes. You should see her. I wish you could meet Riva. By the way, she's older. We have made plans to marry. She wants to have children before it's too late, and you know I like that. I would love to have children like yours. You must be so proud.

"I didn't tell you a friend of mine introduced her to me. He thought we would get along well together. Well, you know me. She and her family fled Russia after those rotten Cossacks attacked their village. In the ensuing hysteria, a most terrible thing happened. A horse trampled one of her brothers to death. Of course, you and I have seen the worst; but she and I became friendly."

He omitted what he was thinking, of his proposal: *The second time I met her, I couldn't help myself. She walked away from her sister to be by my side. The way her sister held back, she must have known how I felt. But later we managed to meet secretly. I'm sure I wasn't her first man. She was not young as women go, but I didn't care what she had done, whether she was virgin or not. I loved her.*

We walked some way from people and the city. I looked at her, imagining she was full breasted, that her legs would be slim like her waist. Oh my imagination ran away with me. It was quiet where we were. I looked at her, lifted her chin and leaned down to kiss her. She stood on her toes to meet me. We kissed deeply. I sought out her tongue, and she met mine. We quickly parted, holding on to one another, unable to let go. We kissed more and deeply. I could wait no longer. I stood back so I could see her.

"Riva, I know it is soon," gazing in her eyes, kissing once more the warm fullness of her lips. "Will you be my wife?" And the surprise the way she looked back, blushing, taking my hand to her breast, "Daniel, I love you too. I would be honored to be your wife." The excitement. We kept touching one another, kissing, our hands searching out one another through our clothing. I was so hard. Oh well, on with the letter.

"Mamma likes her. They seem to get along so well. Perhaps she sees the peace in mamma's eyes that mamma has found here in the Holy Land. No, I'm still no more religious than I ever was but enough to get along when we go to the synagogue. Mamma wants to go every week, so we do. She tells me she prays for papa a lot. She still talks about him with such love. Sometimes she has tears when doing so.

"Well, now that Riva has met mamma, I'll be meeting her family soon.

"But we get on pretty well. Mamma is getting old as you know. I don't know how much longer she'll be with us. You know her. Always as strong as a man, at least she thought and still does.

"All my love to you and the children. You'll hear more from me, of course."

Soon after writing this letter, Daniel went to Riva's home to meet her father and mother, as well as whoever of the family was present.

Riva met him outside the family farmhouse. She had been attracted by his height, blue eyes and light brown hair, a man who could not only take care of himself but also her, a man who would allow her to be herself. She would not even have to pretend submissiveness. They would be a pair.

Being a self-assured woman, she tried to appear more compliant, the way her father thought women should be, obedient, always recognizing that women are inferior to men. However, when they first met, Daniel already had his impression; this was no meek woman but one with strength who could help him, take control of a home, and someone with a sense of humor, a woman who would be his equal, and one of whom he would be proud.

"Hello, Daniel," she softly said, reaching and touching his hand. Daniel felt the softness and the thrill of her. No woman had ever excited him before. Here he was in his 50s, and she was willing to be with him, be his wife. How fortunate.

"Hello, Riva. I guess I'm ready to meet your father and mother," he smiled self-assuredly.

"Then welcome to my home." She looked at him intently.

Their eyes met, holding one another. She broke this intimacy with, "My parents are waiting to meet you. My sisters and brothers are in the field." She laughed. "I wanted them there. You can meet them another time.

"Papa, Mamma, this is Daniel Blumenthal."

Akiva spoke for Naomi. "We welcome you to our house."

"Thank you, sir. I believe you know why I am here."

He merely nodded, looking seriously at Daniel.

"I wish you and your wife's permission to marry Riva."

Riva had stepped back, watching her mother smiling and who saw her daughter's redness rise from her neck to her face.

"Tell, me sir," Akiva started. "Are you a religious man, a good Jew?"

"I am an American Jew, a believer in Zionism and the Aliyah and am going to help all I can. That's all I can tell you. I don't want to get into a discussion of religion. I just want your permission and blessing to marry Riva."

As she listened to Daniel, Riva stepped to his side, wanting to hold his hand.

"I want her to marry a good man, a good Jew who wants a home and a fine woman to look after it." he hesitated, looking at both Daniel and Riva, thinking of their ages. He decided not to mention children.

"Sir, I love Riva. I do well in my business and am certain she will have a good home in which she can live with warmth and love."

Riva stepped a bit forward. "Papa, Mamma. I love Daniel." She looked at him as she said it.

Naomi went to Akiva's side, giving him a hard touch. He knew Riva took after Naomi.

"You have our permission. May I call you Daniel?"

"Absolutely. I will make you a good son. You can count on me if you need help. I thank you both so much."

Naomi went to Daniel and hugged him. "I believe Riva has found a good man. I can see you love one another. Be together with our blessing. *Gott tsu danken.*"

"I want you both to know that if you have need for anything, I'll be there for you," Daniel repeated.

Akiva went to him, grasping his hand. "I trust you, Daniel, to take good care of my daughter. We also know what a good family you come from, because Riva told us what you and she had talked about. Your family in America. Do you think they would come to the wedding? It would be a pleasure to meet them."

"I can't promise that. You know my brother and sister-in-law are both doctors, and their children are in schools. We'll see what I can do."

Naomi then said, "Riva and I will talk about the wedding day. Do you have any preference for a month?"

Daniel laughed. "I'm not laughing at you, Mrs. Kaplan. I wish it could be as soon as possible."

"Oh you men," as she hit his forearm, also laughing. "We'll see what we can do."

"I best go now."

Riva, smiling, took his hand. "I'll see you out, dear one." She now cared little about being direct in front of her parents. As she watched him leave, she thought, *I have been with other men, but no one like him. The way he excites me. But I have never allowed them to be inside me, though we played about. I know how to satisfy myself even though they say that's bad. I don't care. Somehow, I just do not believe he'll be demanding and will let me tell him what pleases me. I can't wait. He excites me so. Thinking of him the other night, the way I used my hands. Stop this. Just think of the wedding. What will he be like? He'll be gentle. I know it, and he'll listen to me. How I do love him.*

When Daniel came home, Hannah waited excitedly.

"Mamma. There was no trouble at all. They accepted me and will set the date." He then told her the conversation, adding, "I think they are more religious than I. However, they seemed to overlook that. I told them exactly what I think."

"Daniel, I am so happy for you." She smiled, laughed a bit. 'I thought you'd always remain a bachelor. You know I like her and will grow to love her, I believe. I do wish your sisters and husbands, your brother and his wife and children could be here. We should have the wedding after the children are out of school so they could come, if Benjamin and Constance can arrange their schedules. They should see Palestine. Think of having them in our home."

"Well try not to be sad if they can't come, mamma."

"Yes. I know. But look at me, Daniel, Your mother is growing so old, but I'll live to see you married, hopefully have children," as she thought of Riva being older.

He kissed his mother's cheek. "You and I haven't talked about this, but Riva and I have. You'll live with us where we can take care of you. If necessary, I'll expand the house, but we'll see. That's so much farther away. You won't mind, I hope."

"No. I appreciate it." She hugged Daniel while thinking of Amos. Tears formed that she tried to hide, wiping at her face.

"What's wrong, mamma?"

She couldn't lie. "I was thinking of Amos. That terrible war to free people. Ach. Slavery. I am proud my sons served their country. But I do miss him."

"I understand. I think about him too. Come here." He hugged her, holding on, as she cried into his shoulder.

"You are a wonderful son, always have been. I am a very fortunate woman."

And at a distance, Riva was thinking how fortunate she was.

* * *

Daniel by now was building his business that enabled him to support Hannah and himself quite well. He had also opened his own diamond business and hired help for the wine store. He wanted a wife with whom he could share his success and his love. When they had children they would live well. He would also teach them that they were part of the Zionist dream. Now that he had met Riva, he finally knew what love was. She may be older, but the thrill that both felt in each other's company, the common desires, and the comfort told them they were meant to be husband and wife. Both anxiously awaited the wedding date that would be in July to give time for Daniel to contact Benjamin and Constance. He had decided he would offer to pay the ship fair for Olivia, Joseph, and Millicent, if they could all come.

When Riva knew that she had finally found love and a man who wanted her as wife, there were times she could not believe her fortune. Talking to Katya, selected as the Maid of Honor and Tamar who would be her bridesmaid, she told them one day, "I can't believe this." They were looking at bridal gowns and dresses for Riva's sisters.

"Riva," Katya told her, "you are beautiful. Wait until he sees you. I cannot wait for the expression on his face." Later when they sat in a park together after settling on the dresses, they talked breathlessly about the wedding and Riva leaving them for her own home. Tamar, giggling, suddenly exclaimed, "You will no longer be a virgin. You are one aren't you? Of course, at your age . . ."

Riva laughed. "It's none of your business what I am and what I have done, but . . ." She hesitated, blushing, "I have done things with men that if you ever tell mamma or papa, I'll scalp you both." She laughed. "Now wouldn't you both be lovely without any hair?"

"Have you done it?" Katya wanted to know.

"Stop right now," Riva pretended anger. She then whispered, "I am a virgin. I have wanted to do it, find out what it's like, but even at my age and what our religion teaches us, I could not do that."

Katya and Tamar started to giggle again. "You'll tell us what it's like won't you, so we can be prepared?"

"That's enough." Riva's face was red again. "You know very well I couldn't talk about that," although she knew she would, because the sisters were so close and loved one another.

They rose and walked home with their arms about one another, the three with their own thoughts but exuberant with happiness.

Later, Riva arranged that Daniel and she could meet alone. They rode in Daniel's wagon until they were beyond the farmlands the Jews were cultivating. He stopped at a field.

Taking her to him, he leaned and kissed her deeply as she responded. He heard her moan as their tongues reached deeply. As they breathlessly separated, her hand went low on his pants feeling his hardness, as he pressed his hands against to her breasts. She continued to wear European clothing and wore a dress with several buttons in the front that she helped him unbutton so his hand could seek her more. He caressed against her slip to reach her nipples, listened to her moan more loudly. "Don't stop." She took his hand and led him lower. "Oh, these dresses and underclothes we wear." She then reached to the buttons of his pants, opening them to massage him.

"Riva," he could barely whisper, "I want to be inside you. I have protection."

"I want to feel you entering me. There's no helping this." She too was breathless. "I do want you so." She laughed slightly. "I don't think I can undress wearing these clothes. Let's just do what we can with our hands." She took one of his as she raised her skirts to her waist. "Come, reach. With both touching in their most sensitive places, they spent themselves, as she felt him emit, her hips moving, then arching into him, throwing back her head as she loudly moaned reaching her climax.

After a while, as they rested, she lay back pulling him on top of her. "We can move against each other," she told him softly. "When we're married. I can't wait."

"Neither can I. I love you so."

"And you have my love for always, Daniel.

* * *

Daniel wrote Benjamin and Constance, as well as Esther and Arella, about the wedding, hoping, of course, that the women and they could take that much time from their practices to attend. "I am willing to help pay for the children, if you can bring them. They are older now and could appreciate the trip. Imagine. You all would be in the Holy Land and in Jerusalem. Please do try. Think of our aging mother too, the thrill of seeing both of you and her grandchildren.

"I realize it is a long trip, but how many such will you ever take? I believe Constance would enjoy Riva's company. Imagine, too, the explorations the children could take under guidance, of course. I'm laughing at the word children. You have one in medical school, your son at Harvard who will soon be graduating. And your youngest daughter in college also. I can't believe it. I suppose neither can you.

"Please do think about it and try to come. It's been so long. My love to you both and to the children."

* * *

It would take some time for the letter to arrive in Maine. While awaiting a reply, Riva and Daniel met as frequently as possible. His business kept him very busy, his days occasionally long.

When possible, in the evenings he would go to Riva's home. The family allowed them privacy. Her father and mother became accustomed to the two walking out alone. At Riva's age, they finally felt that she was mature enough to take care of herself. So it was that they walked in the quiet night, the wondrous sky, the hills about them.

"Riva. I am so hoping that Ben and Constance will come and Arella and Esther with their families. It would be something if they all brought your new nieces and nephews. I can't wait to hear. The travel will be long, but I believe they can afford it. I told them I would help."

"I agree with you and think it was lovely to offer financial help. But I doubt they would need it. Now let's just talk about us, or better still, talk silently, tenderly." She reached up and brought his face to hers. She kissed him warmly, feeling the softness of his lips and his return kiss that sought out her mouth. She felt him reach inside as she followed and felt the warmth spread throughout her, feeling desire growing and wishing. He led her to a hillside where he gently pulled her down as they hugged one another tightly, she feeling a streaking though her body.

Daniel reached for her skirt, pulling it up, reaching below to her bloomers that he moved down to feel her sex as she moaned loudly. "More, Daniel. He obeyed. He followed her desire, until she screamed at the orgasmic shuddering throughout her body. As her breathing came more regularly, she reached inside his pants that he had unbuttoned. They spent more time satisfying one another.

She then straightened her underwear and skirt as he buttoned up.

"I can't wait. I so want you inside me. We should do it."

"Do you want to now?"

She hesitated. "No. I want you to take me as new on our wedding night. I hate waiting. But I want to. Do you mind?"

He felt frustration, but would follow her wish. "It's all right, my dearest."

They waited until they were both calm before slowly walking back to her home. At the door, she kissed him, and spoke, softly, "My parents want you and your mother to come to Friday night dinner."

"We'll be there. I hate leaving you, I love you so."

"Me too. Goodnight, dear one."

* * *

A letter arrived from the United States addressed inside to Daniel and Riva.

"Dear Daniel and Riva,

"I am taking this opportunity to address you, Riva, as our sister-in-law to be. Your wedding will mean that we shall have to take a month or two off from our practice. We are happy to do this so we can be with you, Riva's family, and mamma. Olivia is finishing her third year of Medical School at the University of Vermont Medical School. Therefore, she can't make it. I can tell you, she's a beauty and has a marvelous brain, like her mother. She reminds me so much of Constance. Now that Joseph has graduated Harvard, he is finishing his first year of medical school at Tufts University College of Medicine. He says he wants to join the family practice. We'll see. The Harvard graduation was beautiful with its music and the graduates receiving their degrees. We're very proud of him. He will accompany us to your wedding. Millicent, another beauty. If you think I'm bragging, well I guess I am, but wait to see for yourselves. Mamma will love Joseph and Millicent. She just wants a man. I know Constance had talks with the girls when they were quite close to puberty. Millicent will be graduated next year. So you will see her also. She met a fine young fellow at the University in Orono. I think, though, she's young and hope she'll wait, perhaps a year after graduation so she can find her footing. She needs an extra year to decide whether she wants to go further with her schooling. I know they are in love and want to marry after they are graduated. His father is a large merchant in Bangor, and Ely will be joining the business. His brothers have gone elsewhere. I know one is farming north of the city.

Millicent brought Ely home for the Christmas holiday. You know, of course, we have a tree. Constance loves that and has taught the family how to decorate the tree and the house. We have her mother staying with us, and she was so happy but sad at the same time thinking of Nathaniel, Dr. Sterling. Constance and I miss him too. But you see how religious we are. We are all inclusive.

"Yes. Now you know we are taking Millicent and Joseph to the wedding. I'm sorry Olivia will miss out, but she is, as you know, a very busy woman. We can't wait to come to you. We've made reservations on a liner and will travel down from France to you. The trip will take a while, but it's worth it. See you before the wedding so we can all spend time together and get either reacquainted or acquainted.

"All our love. Please tell mamma I never forget her. Dan, you make sure you take good care of her until the doctors arrive to examine her. ----- Love to you all, Ben, Constance, and the girls and Joseph. Olivia is unhappy she won't be with us, but, of course, they know you from your letters and their mother's and my stories."

* * *

When they did arrive in Jerusalem, there was such joy and celebrating. When Hannah saw Millicent and Joseph, she cried, thinking of the time she had missed seeing them grow. She took them to her arms, as the children kissed her on either cheek. Here it was late June, 1901 to renew love and meet new family.

They also wanted to travel as much as possible in Palestine and to discover Jerusalem. They climbed the hills, rested from occasional weariness of the climbs, visited the farmlands that the Jews had bought and had enriched the soil. They viewed the

Holy Mount, Benjamin wishing he could visit the Wailing Wall with the entire family.

Beyond the exciting explorations there was, of course, the coming wedding that would occur after their second week in Palestine.

There was also other news Daniel had for his visitors. "I have been invited to meet Theodore Herzl," Daniel excitedly told his family. "I have become quite the Zionist. You must know we should have our ancient lands. I managed to meet Herzl as our representative when he was in Jerusalem with the Kaiser. There has also been money that has flowed from wealthy Jews as in England from the Rothschilds. It helps rebuild Jerusalem and farmlands outside Jerusalem, of course. I will do all I can to ensure that the land thrives under us despite the Ottomans and the Arabs who do not want us here. But we are. I give what I can and have meetings about our settlements. There has been talk of giving land for the Jews in Uganda. I hate it. So does my committee. Then there's been talk of El Arish in the west in the Sinai, but both fell through. So we will do all we can where we are. Besides, Herzel has said all Israel is going to be ours.

"Daniel," Benjamin interrupted, "Don't you think you're going overboard. You're an American, a veteran of the Civil War."

Raising his voice in anger he answered, "Yes I'm a veteran of a war. You don't get it, do you? I am an Israeli. Do you hear me? An Israeli. We are in a war. They kill Jews in Russia and the Germans hate us, call us the vermin money stealers of the world. It's up to people like me to make this land ours."

"Daniel, you call yourself a diplomat. Listen to you. That's not the voice of a diplomat."

"I'm not a diplomat. I told you," he yelled. "I am a Zionist. This is our land I told you, from thousands of years. You hear. Yes. I'm repeating myself. But you must understand."

Constance, horrified, grasped Benjamin's arm. "Daniel. Please calm down. I meant no insult to what you are doing. There's your wedding to think about. That's why we're here, almost the entire family together." He thought of Olivia missing, a tear forming in the corner of his eye.

"Do you or don't you understand where I'm coming from, Benjamin?"

"Yes, Daniel. I do. Please forgive me. I do understand how you feel, but you're going to be married tomorrow. Please calm down."

"Well, just remember. Riva and I will be leaving to meet again with Herzl in Europe. Some of the proposals have split the movement, and it's important to talk to him. Why? Frankly I wonder. Maybe he won't see me? Right now I don't care because of the split in Zionism.

"But, aside from my feelings and all my talk about Zionism, Europe will be our honeymoon. I can't wait for Sunday and the wedding."

Benjamin answered, "What about mamma?"

"I have taken care of that. She is to stay with my friend Abraham who introduced Riva and me," he answered, squeezing Riva's hand. He turned to her. It was impossible for Benjamin and Constance not to see the love between them.

"Are you going to be there long?' Constance asked.

"Well, long enough to convince everyone that this is not just a junk heap of buildings that some have called Jerusalem."

By now, Daniel's face was again growing red with anger. He started repeating himself. "Everyone, everywhere must learn that Zionism is exceedingly important, that this is a Jewish land and that as many Jews as want or need to come here should be able to do so. We must always proclaim our right to live in the land of our forebears."

"Dan, you're angry. We're talking about your wedding and your honeymoon. We like hearing about what is happening here. But, brother mine, tomorrow is your wedding day."

"Don't worry. This will be a honeymoon. We'll travel about Europe as I said. We also hope to go to England."

"You seem to have gone overboard, Dan," Ben said.

"Listen, who has lived here for 11 years and knows something of what it's like here? Anyhow, let's not get into this anymore for now. Riva and I have to think about Sunday, our marriage day," he now jubilantly spoke.

"Daniel, dear, while you calm down, I'm going to take a walk with Constance and have our own talk."

He looked at her, calming still more, seeing the love in her eyes. He hadn't cared who heard him or listened. Benjamin was right though. He took a deep breath, allowing himself to fully calm and think only of Riva and their marriage. "Yes, dearest Riva. Forgive me everyone. I ran away with myself."

"Did you hear what I said, Daniel?" Riva laughingly asked. "Constance and I are leaving for a walk."

Red-faced he apologized again to everyone. "Yes, dear. I heard. Go. Enjoy."

Riva led Constance with a smile. She had been charmed by Constance's personality and ease, a woman that one would want for a close friend, someone in whom she could always confide. They walked from the house along the street, speaking softly to one another.

"Constance. I feel so comfortable with you and want to ask you something."

"I feel the same way, Riva. Let's be friends for life," she smiled, her eyes wide, looking into Riva's. "I love the way you look and the way you conduct yourself. From this moment on, anything we say to one another is between us." Constance took her hand and squeezed.

Feeling her hand, Riva's heart beat faster from happiness as she repeated the gesture, holding Constance's hand.

"Constance, you know I'm older. I have been with other

men, of course, but I never allowed them to enter me, despite everything else we did. I feel that's sacred. Of course, I have read the Bible, and that influenced me. But everything else, I guess I thought that was up to me."

They both laughed. "So what are you telling me? You're a terrible woman. Good Heavens, Riva."

"No, no. That's not what I mean. I have no guilty conscience. I suppose I had some sexual intimacy, the other things, but a man entering my vagina, I never allowed."

"Riva, I never had any experiences until Benjamin. You want me to be a doctor and tell you what it's like?" she smiled, and pressed Riva's arm.

Riva's felt the blush move up her neck. "Oh, my goodness. My face is hot."

Constance laughed. "I can see that. Riva I know what you are going to ask me."

"You do. I don't want to hide it from you. I do want to know what it will be like. I've heard it hurts."

"It does, Riva, with some women like hell. I was sore even the morning after, sometimes even the next day after that. Do you get wet enough now, do you think? That helps some."

Still embarrassed talking like this, Riva answered, "Yes. I can get very wet when aroused. So it will hurt. I'll accept that. But should I do anything when he's inside me."

"That will depend on how excited you become. We all react in different ways. You are worrying too much, Riva."

"And an older woman like I am. I know. It's stupid."

"Now there I disagree. Some men are terrible and . . ." She stopped, thinking of some of the tears in the vaginal walls she had found when examining some of her patients. "Riva, please try not to worry about anything. Daniel is a wonderful man. I believe he'll be tender and take care of you. Anyone watching him, sees how much he loves you."

"Constance, I hope you don't mind I asked you such

intimate questions or talked to you the way I did."

"Of course not. Now let's just enjoy our walk."

"One more thing. I want you to know I'll take good care of your mother-in-law. She's a love."

"She is. I have my mother at home you probably know. Ben is so good to her. At their ages it's our responsibility to take care of them."

There was silence for a while as they sauntered arm in arm, talking, laughing. Riva finally said as they turned toward Daniel's home, "I love his mother. And your children are such a wonderful man and woman. They are so accomplished. I hope my children will be the same. If I have any, that is. I'm not too old."

"I had mine later than usual. Some women may think that's funny or that you should have had them when younger. Pay no attention. These days, women are learning to be a bit more independent. In the United States there are women arguing about suffrage. I have been to some of the meetings and will be out there, I assure you. It may hurt my practice. If it hurts Benjamin, I guess I'll have to stop."

"I hope not."

When they arrived home, before they went in, they looked at one another, moved together and hugged with much affection.

* * *

The wedding took place at Riva's home in a flowered garden. Akiva insisted on this rather than a synagogue, because he knew of Benjamin's mixed marriage and that their children had not been raised in any religion; for Benjamin and Constance had decided the children would choose when they were older and could decide for themselves.

It started solemnly, of course, but when Daniel stepped hard on the glass under the canopy, Benjamin's son and daughter started to clap. Then, realizing the presence of a Rabbi, whose smile they couldn't see, red-faced, they stopped when Benjamin reached across Constance to them.

The Rabbi, and somehow this had escaped Akiva, was reformed. Daniel and Riva had purposely chosen him behind her father's back, realizing that if he discovered this before the wedding there would be a terrible argument. The Rabbi looked about at him at this garden congregation, a smile on his face, he told them, "Clap. I do not object. This is a happy occasion."

Listening, they all clapped except for Akiva who though pleased his oldest daughter had finally found a husband, still regretted that the Rabbi was not Orthodox. Naomi hit his arm. "Rejoice, you fool. This is one of our happiest days that I began to think would never happen."

They went to the couple, kissing and hugging. Hannah, somewhat disabled, sat, carefully rose as they came to her. She looked at her son and new daughter. "God protect you both. *Geh gezunterheyt* (Go in good health).

All that was left for now was the sadness of soon seeing Benjamin and his family leave and the joy of Daniel and Riva going on their honeymoon.

Riva went to her mother and father and brothers and sisters, thanking them for all they did. Her happiness was evident in her eyes that filled with tears as she hugged her mother and father. "Thank you both for making this such a beautiful and memorable day." Naomi also started to cry, as Akiva placed his arm about her. "We won't see her as much, Akiva. She is going to her own home. I am so happy and yet so sad." She then cried into his shoulder to try to hide her tears from everyone.

Riva then went to Katya and Tamar. Tamar smiled, then giggled a bit. "You will find out tonight, Riva."

"Stop that you little fool," as Riva's face reddened. "Please tell us what it's like so we'll know what to expect when that day comes." Now she laughed seeing Riva's blush.

"Stop it, Tamar. That's none of your business. As she spoke, Katya went to her, tears in her eyes, "I am going to miss you so not being in the house. All the fun we had."

"Yes," interjected Tamar. Now all three were crying.

Her brothers, Efram and Emanuel waited, then stepped in. "Riva, don't forget us."

She moved toward them, pulling both to her in a hug. "I can never forget any of you. I'll count on you if I need help."

The four looked at her, "Happiness forever," they almost spoke in unison.

Daniel and Riva, after helping Hannah into the wagon, drove Riva to her new home. He had arranged another room farther away from his mother, next to the guest rooms. *It is such a grand home*, Riva thought when they arrived and when she saw their room.

It had running water that Daniel had installed himself, a toilet, shower, sink, and cabinet, and all Riva would need for comfort. There was a large closet for her clothes and another for him. When she looked at the double bed, her face shone; but as she thought about the night, she felt a blush rising to her face. She began wondering what it would be like, if he would be gentle with her. She also thought of her conversation with Constance. Daniel had left her alone so she could become accustomed to their room and unpack her clothing. She had purchased a new nightgown that showed off her body's curves and the fullness of her breasts.

That night, after the entire two families had their wedding dinner, Daniel led Riva upstairs. She felt her neck and face becoming red again when she was leaving the company. Once in their room, she told him, "You wait here." She changed, went to the bedroom, her head slightly bent, then raising it, to look at her husband. He had already undressed except for his underwear.

"Riva, you are beautiful." Again she blushed but with love

and pride.

"You do like me."

"Of course, silly. I love you."

"And I love you." She wasn't quite certain what she should do next but then walked toward the bed.

He went to her. "May I take off your lovely gown?" She nodded, as he lifted the hem, and more quickly lifted it until she raised her arms and it fell to the floor. "Oh you are so lovely." He was looking at her breasts and then down to the hair between her thighs. She felt his stare. As they stood there, he took off the remainder of his clothing and took her hand, leading her to the bed. She was gazing at his penis, as he placed her gently on the mattress.

"Spread your legs, dear."

She obeyed. "Be gentle, Daniel."

He lay on her, kissing her, his mouth finding her nipples. She felt it to her center, moaning. He then went below and placed his mouth on her bud. She moaned more loudly, moving upward to him. He then raised himself to enter her. She lay quite still, hearing, "Am I hurting you? "Uh, yes," she mumbled. It hurt as Constance had told her. She tried not to cry out, lay still, but then, suddenly began to move with him. She thought, *Now I am a woman and a wife*.

The following morning when Riva woke she lay cuddled to Daniel, her head nuzzling his chin. She tried not to wake him, but when she moved he wakened. "Hello, my lovely. I love you so, Riva."

"I love you just as much, my lover." She threw back the sheet to go to the bathroom, seeing herself naked, she started to find a shirt to cover herself, then thought, *I have a beautiful body. He's already seen it, and I want him to see me in daytime.*

Daniel, fully awake, watched her, admiring her slim legs, the curve of her hips, and her full breasts. "Are you all right?" he asked thinking of their sex.

She blushed. "I hurt in here," pointing between her legs. Well, Constance had told her what to expect. "I must go to the bathroom."

He laughed. "Well, go." He watched her, admiring her backside, wanting to go to her. Perhaps they could shower together. *No. The shower's too small. I'll have to get a larger one.*

Later, when ready they went down. Constance was helping the maid get breakfast, listening and smiling as Hannah gave directions.

"Mother. I have done this before."

Hannah laughed. "You're sweet, Constance. To think I never wanted him to marry you because you're a Christian."

Soon Joseph and Millicent came down with their father, as did Arella's and Esther's families. "Good morning all." As they sat for coffee, Daniel and Riva appeared, both with smiles. "Oh, it's so good to have all the family," Daniel stated. Riva punched him lightly in the ribs. "Olivia. How wonderful it would have been if she had been able to come."

"Well, a doctor's life," Constance answered, unable to hold back a tear. She wiped at it. "Yes," she softly spoke again, "A doctor's life," thinking of Olivia telling her she wanted to study Ob/Gyn." She looked at Riva, their eyes finding one another. Riva slightly nodded. Constance smiled. They would talk later. Constance was thinking she must tell her how to truly enjoy this newfound inner world of the woman.

The Blumenthal and Kaplan families spent several days, picnicking, sightseeing, all the women with tears, as well as the men who didn't try to hide them, as Benjamin, Constance, and the children departed.

Perhaps three or four months after they arrived home, a letter came, written by Riva but signed by Daniel and her.

"The news everyone. I am pregnant with our first child. Except for the mornings I am so excited, can't wait to feel the boy or girl moving inside me. Daniel and I are terribly happy. I hoped this would happen but did wonder whether I was too old. Well, of course I'm not. I'll let you know how I progress. I'm sure Daniel will write also. I do wish Constance could be my doctor."

A month later sadness greeted them. "Mother passed away just two weeks ago. I couldn't write," Daniel told them, "until now. It was her heart. You were aware it was weak. I am happy she lived long enough to see all of us. She mentioned Olivia just the other day, sad she could not have seen her oldest grandchild. She also would have been so happy to see what is in store for Riva and me when the child comes. Riva is just fine, getting bigger. It is so exciting knowing you will be a parent."

His tears fell on the paper. He tried to blot them. "Well, I guess you can see how we feel by the paper. I loved mother so. She said Riva became like a daughter to her. She wanted so to live and see her next grandchild. That makes it sadder. But of one thing I am very happy. She died in Jerusalem, in the Holy Land where she wanted to live out her life. I intend to have a nice monument for her. Riva's and my love to you all in this sadness."

After the news arrived, Benjamin, asked Constance to attend the synagogue with him. He had never been there but asked if kaddish could be said for Hannah. Benjamin went to the holy place of worship to say the mourner's payer. He gave funds to ensure the prayer would occur for the entire year.

Constance wondered how long Faith would be with them. She hoped her mother would live to see the children in their glory. Yet, it was not to be.

Chapter Two

Ending and New Beginnings

Along with the sadness in Palestine, not too long after their arrival home, Faith weakened. She had lived the longest of their parents. Now in her late nineties, she could no longer take care of herself. One morning, Constance went to her room to ask her whether she would like to go sit in the garden. There was no answer.

"Mother," Constance spoke softly, shaking her gently.

Faith finally opened her eyes. "Constance, dear. I just feel so weak I believe I am going to God."

"Mother," Constance told her, trying to hide her tears, wiping her cheeks, hoping to hide them from her mother.

"Dearest. Don't weep for me. I feel quite satisfied that I had the best life has to offer. When I am with our Lord, I'll look down on you all and know you are protected." She smiled. "Constance. Do you remember," she paused to catch her breath. "Oh, now I . . . I forgot what I wanted to tell you. Do you remember how I objected to Benjamin? Of course you do."

Constance nodded, and whispered, "Yes, mother. How could I forget? But you and father were so good to him and to us when you got to know him."

"Well, I could not have had a better son, if he had been my very own." She was thinking back to when she lost her son in childbirth and could no longer have children. "Constance, you both and the children have made these last years so very happy for me."

"Yes, mother. I'm going to call Ben and get one of our

friends to come see you." She knew, of course, it could make no difference.

Faith weakly laughed. "Dearest, you know it will do no good. But do call Ben. I wish the children were here."

When Benjamin came to the room, he looked at Faith, then Constance, shaking his head while placing his arm about Constance.

"Benjamin."

"Yes, mother."

"You were such a good son." Her eyes were now filled with tears. "Oh, this is silly of me. It's just that I hate leaving you both and the children. But I will look down on all of you, and our Lord will protect you. Always remember I love all of you."

She closed her eyes. Benjamin bent over her with his stethoscope, shaking his head, tears in his eyes.

Constance sobbed and rested her head on her mother's chest. "Oh mother. How I have loved you." She sobbed loudly. Benjamin gently raised her, hugging her, both crying.

The church service occurred in St. Luke's. They buried her next to Nathaniel.

For a few months Constance worked long hours to lighten her grief. Finally she told herself, "Enough. You have your family to think of."

That evening when she came home, she asked Benjamin to sit with her, pulling him into her arms, tears in her eyes. "Ben. I guess it's been hard on you the way I have grieved and worked. It's time to realize I have you and the children."

He hugged and lightly kissed her. "I know what you have been going through. We'll go from here and carry on with our lives.

"I have also been thinking, if you wouldn't mind, if you would allow me to go to the synagogue and ask if they would say kaddish for your mother."

"I think that would be lovely, Ben."

The following day he went and talked to the rabbi who knew he had never come to pray.

"I would appreciate it, Rabbi, if you would allow me to say kaddish for my mother-in-law. I realize this is asking quite a lot, especially because I am not religious, and she was Episcopal, but such a magnificent human being. I'd be glad to contribute."

The rabbi hesitated, but seeing Benjamin's sincerity, he agreed.

Faith now had her final rest with her Lord.

* * *

After Millicent's graduation in May, 1902, from The University of Maine in Orono, Benjamin and Constance now had Olivia, Joseph and Millicent to think about. Olivia was in her final year of school, Joseph in his second. Millicent, now graduated had frequent visits from Ely. He would drive down to Portland. On one of these rides with Ely, he finally proposed and both entered the house, their faces bright.

They had stopped by the ocean.

"Millicent, you know I love you very much."

"I love you also, Ely."

"I want you for my wife."

"Ely. Of course. I want to be your wife. I want that very much. But you know that my mother is Christian. Therefore your parents may not like that I cannot have a baby that will born Jewish." She felt as though she would cry and forced the tears back, closing her eyes tightly.

"Hold out your left hand." Nothing she said could stop him. Nervously he went to his pocket, and brought out a small velvet box, opened it to a shining diamond. Millicent's heart beat fast. She could hardly speak when he placed it on her finger. They kissed, hugged. Millicent's eyes filled with tears.

Ely ran his fingers through her chestnut hair, looking deeply into her hazel eyes.

"I love you so." He laughed. "I'm repeating myself. And I don't care if your mother is Christian. Don't you know I am aware of that? I already told my parents who at first objected, but they knew I was determined. Just this is important. Translation: I love you with all my heart, Millicent."

"I like it. Always tell me you love me, because I know I'll tell you."

They hugged and kissed again.

"I just can't wait to tell my parents."

"Can we just sit here for a while? I want to hold you, to be sure you're to be mine."

"Ely, you've known since Orono that I was falling in love with you. I just didn't know how long it would take you to ask. But I'm pleased you waited until we could both tell my parents."

"Well, before I came down this time I told them in no uncertain terms what I'm telling you now. I'm weary of riding that distance to see you. Now we'll live in Bangor and always be together. I have a house I picked out. I hope you'll like it. It is to be a present from my parents, if you accepted me and like it and after we got over the argument of your mother being Christian."

"You did that already? Of course I'll like the house. At least I'm pretty sure. If I don't?" she laughed. She then became serious. "Was the argument bad? Why fight about something like that? My father isn't religious, doesn't believe in it. My mother once in a while goes to church to pray for her parents, mostly, she tells us. Enough of religion. Let's think about the house. And as I said, I believe I'll like it, and if not. Seriously. What if . . .?"

"Then I'll find another."

He looked about. There were some people on the beach, but there was a place where there were bushes. He took her hand and led her, while taking a blanket from the back seat.

"Here. We'll have some privacy."

As she stood above him, gazing in his eyes, she allowed him to gently bring her to him. He kissed her softly, then harder, his tongue moving along her lips, then forcing them open. She followed his lead, feeling the heat throughout her. She pulled back from him, for the sensation flowing through her to between her thighs. "That's enough. We can't do anymore. Just hug me." As he did, she placed her arms about his neck, pulling him closer, kissing again.

"Oh. Enough. You wait until we are married," her heart beating rapidly, wanting him to touch her all over. She did take his hand to her breasts to feel him as much as she dared.

He laughed. "I had no other idea but to wait, believe me, dearest," despite being hard and wanting to enter her.

She rose, straightening her skirt and brushing back her hair, placing her bonnet on her head. "Come. We'll go to my parents."

Then she excitedly came home, while he stood back, wondering what might happen.

"Mother. Father. I'm to be married. Isn't it magnificent? Wonderful?" She told them of the proposal, showing her finger. "Look at my gorgeous ring." She hesitated. "You won't object will you?" Of course, she left out the details of being by the ocean. Yet her face was red with blushing and happiness, thinking of the life to come and all that her mother had told her when she was younger.

Standing before her parents, she gently pulled Ely forward, wanting him to speak. He was beginning to recognize that she was a rather fearless young woman.

Benjamin stood and took Ely's hand, "We are very happy for both of you. Welcome, Ely, to our family," while, at the same time, Constance, watching her younger daughter, thought back to telling her parents about her marriage. She also was smiling not only because of Millicent but because of her boldness before

Nathaniel and Faith. She knew both her daughters inherited her confidence and self-assurance.

Benjamin brought Ely to Constance who was smiling about the past. Looking then at the handsome young man, she stood beside Benjamin. "Yes, Ely, welcome to our family. We are so pleased for both of you."

"Mother. Father. Ely has already picked out a house for us. Of course, it's in Bangor." She hesitated for a moment. "Oh think. We'll be in our own home." Suddenly she thought of losing the safety of her parents, but she told herself, *I'm strong. I am a woman like my mother, and I'll be like her even though I'm not a doctor.*

"Do your parents know that you were proposing?' Benjamin asked.

"Yes, sir. They are well aware, and they do love Millicent."

Benjamin laughed. "Why who could not love my daughter? I am glad they approve also. Mrs. Dr. Blumenthal and I will invite your family for a dinner when it can be conveniently arranged."

"That would be wonderful, sir. You realize I do work with my father. I also imagine, when my younger brother is older, he may come in the business unless he decides on something else, such as a profession. He has said he wants to be a lawyer. We'll see."

"And you sisters?" Constance asked.

"Well, Rachel says she wants to be a teacher."

Benjamin interrupted. "One of my sisters taught school here in Portland. Anyhow, who else?"

"I have one more sister, Isabel. She's just starting high school."

Constance interrupted. "Your family sounds lovely. We look forward to meeting your parents, your whole family. She felt some tears forming but blinked them back, thinking of Olivia and Joseph being away from home.

"Millicent, have you thought of a wedding date?"

"Yes, mother. But I want to talk to you first and then let Ely and his family know. I also want to be sure Olivia and Joseph and my aunts are there."

"Well, we'll settle that together, O.K.?"

"Of course. Ely you talk to your family so we can make sure all the arrangement are satisfactory."

"I will, Dr. Blumenthal."

"Listen. Call me Constance or mother and the same with Dr. Blumenthal, Millicent's father," she said smiling at Ben. "Oh, call him old man. Seriously, we both, I'm sure will be happy with mother and father."

"Settled," Ely answered. Constance moved to him. Pulling him close in a hug. "Welcome to our family."

"I can't wait until it's formal. By the way, I would like Millicent to come to Bangor and see the house."

"That sounds lovely, doesn't it Millicent?" Constance asked.

By now it was getting toward night.

"Ely, I believe it would be good if you stay with us tonight so you aren't driving in the night," Benjamin told him. "You can call your parents and tell them we invited you."

"Thank you. If you don't mind, I will take Millicent out for a while. I promise I'll get her home before too late."

"That's fine. Perhaps your new mother and we can talk about the date. I want to be sure our oldest daughter, Olivia and our son Joseph can be present."

"I've heard all about them from Millicent."

"Well, Constance, why don't you let Joyce know we are having company tonight so she can prepare a nice meal. Oh, you know I'm on call tonight. Here's hoping."

"Don't worry. It seems I am able to help prepare meals as I have done in the past. Oof. What a man. You still think I'm worthless?" Constance laughed. "However, I do hope you'll make it through the entire evening with the company."

The following day, Millicent and Ely left for Bangor to see his parents and the house. First they went to see his parents who had Millicent stay for lunch with them. The conversation was light, and Ely's parents nodded when he mentioned the house as their gift. Then, however, his father, Efram, looked at Millicent. "I understand your mother is Christian, that you're from a mixed marriage."

His wife, Madalyn, surprised, glared at him. "That's enough. We already had this discussion."

"I just want to know what Millicent, well, what it's like in a family like hers."

"I don't think that's any of our business. Don't you ruin the day and their happiness." Madalyn then looked to Millicent, seeing the tears forming.

"Ignore him. He didn't mean anything bad. Let's give him the benefit of the doubt, that he is curious about a mixed marriage. If you care to answer him, that's up to you, Millicent."

Millicent loved her future mother-in-law and went to her and hugged her, burying her tears in her shoulder."

She stood back, wiping at her cheeks. Efram watching her, told her he apologized.

"No. That's all right. You must know I have talked to Ely about this. I'll tell you what I told him. I have gone to church with my mother, especially when she went to pray for her dead mother. I used to go with them, as did my older sister and brother when they were home. I did not attend the synagogue, because my father does not believe in religion. And as I said to Ely, our children will not be Jewish, because Judaism believes I am Christian. I'll tell you this. I have been in Palestine to visit my grandmother and uncle. He and my father are veterans of the Civil War. But Uncle Daniel, a confirmed Zionist, went with my grandmother when she insisted on moving to Palestine. Now that's all I have to say," she politely told Efram, wiping at her cheeks.

"Now, if you don't think Ely and I should marry, then I will understand your reasons. But I can tell you you will hurt not only me who loves Ely but also your son. And that house I haven't seen yet, you can sell." She ended beginning to feel anger toward Efram but not caring.

At that point, Ely stepped to her and placed his arm about her. "Father, I love this woman, and I intend to marry her. She's brave, intelligent, and knows what she wants or expects from me and for herself."

Madalyn looked at her husband and the couple. "Are you satisfied, Efram? Do we have to have a family argument before they are even married? I'm embarrassed. I love Millicent. I thought you do also."

Efram, now red faced from what Millicent said and the manner in which Madalyn seemed to protect her, stumbled a bit, "I . . . I did say I apologize. I have no intention of hurting Millicent or Ely." He went to Millicent. "Will you allow me to hug you?"

She smiled. "Of course. You are going to be my new father." Looking at Madalyn, "And you will be my new mother. I love you both and hope I always will. I suppose it was best to get all of this out before the wedding so we all know where we stand."

"A family, dearest Millicent," Ely interjected. "Yours and mine combined.

* * *

They decided they would wait for the wedding until after Olivia's graduation from medical school. The family would, of course, attend. Joseph would be free, and they would also include Ely. So the couple chose Sunday, June 21, as their date.

The graduation from the University of Vermont Medical School was a grand day, not only for Olivia but for the family as well. Constance and Benjamin were overjoyed to see another doctor in their family. Watching her on the stage, Constance through her tears, not only saw her tall, beautiful daughter make the family a trio of doctors, but also the past, her heart filled with joy, pride, and love. *I remember your birth, Olivia, how joyful to have held you to my breast the first time. Watching you grow into womanhood, and the excitement when you received you medical school entrance. And I always wondered what man you would find also and still do. But you be yourself as you have always been.*

Benjamin noticed the tears and placed his arms about her. His eyes also were teary. They all waited together as the class stood for its photograph. Ely, watching his future father-in-law whispered, "Dr. Blumenthal. You're a softy."

Benjamin looked at him.

"I see the way you are looking at her and your eyes with those tears. Your pride is so apparent. You can't hide it. I also saw Mrs. Dr. Blumenthal. I want so much to be a member of such a loving family." He them went and talked to Joseph and Millicent, taking Millicent's hand, and squeezing it, feeling her grasp his fingers. They both looked at Joseph. Millicent spoke.

"It won't be too long for you now, Joseph. I am so proud of you and Olivia."

Joseph kissed her cheek. "Isn't Olivia lovely? She'll be so good in what I hope I can call our profession. I still have two years to get through, you know."

Millicent laughed. "As if you won't. Wow. What a family we have. I'll just be what I chose, a good wife and a mother."

Later, they all gathered for lunch and prepared for the trip back to Portland. While packing, Olivia told her parents, "Mother. I want to specialize in Ob/Gyn like you."

"Come here, dear." Constance hugged her. "You'll be excellent. I know it."

"I have been accepted at the Mary Fletcher Hospital here and Maine General Hospital for my internship, as well as The Women's Hospital in Philadelphia. I also applied to Deaconess in Boston. I like the idea they pay a lot of attention to the poor. I must answer soon, but I want to know what you and dad think."

"Let's go to your rooms and talk," Constance answered. "Olivia, dear, if you are going to specialize in Ob/Gyn, then I think you ought to go to Philadelphia. I know it's a long way off. But that school was particularly founded for women. They also have much knowledge regarding the female body. When I went to school, I had to beg to have the professor discuss the female intimate parts. Of course, there were all those men in the class. But why should we be ashamed of saying labia, vagina, clitoris, or uterus, ovaries, fallopian tubes, let alone our breasts? They happen to be a fact of our life. And as doctors, we should be able to study this without embarrassment or being told it's unladylike. Therefore, I think you should go there. Why male doctors still have a problem about us, is far beyond me and reason. This nonsense about female hysteria. That's a great one," Constance laughed. "As doctors women are just as capable of being objective as the best males practicing, even if most won't admit it. It infuriates me. And you should do what you wish, specialize in what you desire and also help the poor. There will be poor patients there too. Of course your father and I will miss having you closer, but if we can arrange our practice as we did to go to Palestine, we'll visit somehow."

"Olivia, darling of whom we are so proud. Everything your mother said I agree with. Don't ever forget that. We will always be here for you," Benjamin interjected. "We both had difficult times when it came to school and specializing, I because I'm a Jew and your mother because she's a woman. Good heavens," and he sat closer to Olivia, placing his arm, about her, kissing her cheek, "You look so much like your mother, that you're almost twins. And you both are not only impressive with such inspiring minds but in your self-assurance and know who you are and what you want out of life."

Olivia tried but could not hold back her tears of happiness.

"I love you both. I've always known I could count on you for help or advice. We all feel the same way, Millicent, Joseph, and I. I'll tell you a secret. The three of us have many times spoken of this." She started to sob, and through her emotion, she managed, "I so love you both, and I know you'll be there not only for me but for my brother and sister." She leaned her head into her father's shoulder and grasped her mother's hand as Constance reached to hold hers.

Olivia later wrote letters to the hospitals, accepting Philadelphia. The thought of being so far from the family frightened her. However, she was now 26 and a young woman on her own, knowing she had a family upon which she could rely were it necessary. A number of times she had been approached by men, especially when they saw this tall, slender woman with her blue eyes and red hair that she carefully coiffed. She wore fashionable dresses, occasionally showing her shoulders and breasts but these only when there was an affair at which some of the other women were present. She, like most of her female classmates, would not wear a tight corset because of the troubles they could cause to a woman's abdomen and pelvic area. She would eventually wear a softer corset or a girdle with a brassiere. Several of the men at medical school to whom she was attracted had taken her to dinner or to the dances.

When she was learning in the hospital during her final year in medical school, one of the students in her class, fascinated by her, wanted to take her to dinner, while wondering about after, if she accepted. "Olivia. I would like to see you sometime when you are available." While saying this he thought, *You are a very attractive young woman, and who knows how far she would go. She would be something.* He was taller than Olivia and had what seemed to her to be gentle green eyes off-set by his dark brown hair.

Listening and watching, she thought, *He's such a handsome man. Perhaps he would be an enjoyable evening.* "Well, when

Henry? We do have a lot more studying to do, but if the time is right I think I would like that." There was nothing about him that set her heart beating any faster or that she felt particularly more than a nice evening with a good looking guy. Of course, she had been out with others over the years of schooling, but her studies always came first.

However, she had also allowed out of curiosity being with a female student who had been her roommate for most of the year. The roommate, Alicia, came to her one night, sat on the edge of her bed, daring to touch her hand, then reaching to kiss her lightly. At first, Olivia drew back but then went to her and placed her own lips firmly on Alicia's. Olivia drew back again. This wasn't she. Recovering, she told Alicia to find another room and roommate but that they could continue to be friends. *I did like the kiss. But that isn't me. Would she tell anyone they started to? She wouldn't want to expose herself. She answered my question when she came to me soon after and told me, as I had her, she wanted to remain friends. Thank goodness, I've never heard any more about it.*

He interrupted her thought. "I was thinking about that restaurant they have by the lake."

"That sounds fine. What time?"

"I'll pick you up at seven."

"O.K." She then thought, "I have to make this dinner only, no fooling around, if he tries. I'll take care of that, always have. Olivia, you are so suspicious."

They ordered their meal, talking constantly about classes, about themselves, what they liked or didn't. He asked about her family.

"My mother and father are doctors, my dad a surgeon, my mother an Ob/Gyn specialist."

"Oh. Is that why you are in med school?"

"Partly, yes. But I also had a strong inclination. I believe we need more female physicians."

He chuckled. "We do?"

"Are you making fun out of what I believe?" She began to

grow angry.

His face colored. "I'm sorry. No. I am not. I believe you are quite serious."

"Oh bother. The hell you do. Come on. I want to get out of here."

"Olivia! I meant nothing. I know how serious you are, also that you're one of the top students in our class."

Still angry but trying to muffle it, she continued, "I suppose you think it's silly of me to want to follow my mother in Ob/Gyn." She wanted to tell him more, but it was her privacy she valued, wanting to help scared young women when they came to see her for examination and advice.

"Henry, I thought you were more understanding. Did I make a mistake?"

"Olivia. Please. I am not making fun of you. I am aware how men dominate the profession and what many of them think. I believe that you are right," he lied. He didn't want this date to end in disaster, not at this point. "Please. Let's have some dessert and then perhaps we could ride by the lake, watch the sky, the moonlight on the water."

Olivia softened. "Perhaps I was hasty. Anyhow, let's finish our meal." *Have I been wrong about him?*

They did have dessert, as he said, "Your mother and father must be very busy."

"They are. But they always had time for us."

"Who are the 'us'?"

"My sister and brother. My brother is in med school, his second year. My sister, the youngest, is now married." She smiled, thinking of Millicent, wondering whether she would ever marry and be happy like her mother and father.

"What about your family? I've been doing all the talking. Tell me about you."

"We're nothing like your family. Well on another scale. "I have two brothers who are older than I. I also have two younger sisters. Anyhow, my brothers are engineers, have their own business. My sister next to me is in college and the youngest starting. We live in New Hampshire. My father is businessman, has a fairly large store where they sell machinery and also manufacture small items."

"Wow. That's impressive." She suddenly wanted to make him feel good but was still smoldering about his chuckle, as she took the last bite of her cake.

"I guess it is."

"How did you decide on med school?" she asked as she rose for him to help her with her coat.

His arms went about her. She pulled away.

"I liked science in college and that decided me," as he grasped her arm.

She started to move his hand away but waited until they left to walk to his car, allowing him to hold her hand. He opened her door, watching closely as she moved her skirt more comfortably, showing her ankles and the lower part of her legs.

That's for me. What a body she must have. I'm going to try to discover more of it, if I have the nerve. Jewesses are supposed to have hot bodies.

He drove to a spot by Lake Champlain where it was quiet, the sky clear with its many stars. As the full moon shone on the water, they could see the ripples of water and even the darkened sand of a small beach.

"Would you like to walk to the beach? And if you like, we could sit on a blanket I keep in the auto. It's such a beautiful night."

"That would be nice." *But watch this fellow. He may be up to something. Why have I been so suspicious? He does come from a nice family. Big deal, Olivia. But to be here is so lovely.*

He took her arm that she raised for him to guide her and prevent her from tripping on the uneven ground. As it became softer, he stopped.

"This seems like s good spot." He haphazardly threw the

blanket to the ground. "How about this?" Looking at her, her narrow waist, the long skirt, her breasts apparent in the upper portion of her evening gown that showed her bare skin at the neck to above her bosom. Taking her arm he told her, "Let me help you."

She let him guide her as she felt herself struggling somewhat to sit in the cumbersome dress. *What was I thinking? I hate this clothing. I feel so awkward. Why do we have to be dressed like this?*

As she sat, she felt more comfortable. He went down close to her enabling him to feel her body as much as possible in her formal dress, gazing at her bare neck, imagining what her breasts looked like. Olivia pulled her skirt closer to her to enable her to move from his body.

"Well, isn't this comfy, Olivia? Or maybe not so much for you in the dresses you women have to wear. But they do make you look beautiful, just like you actually are. And your eyes. They reflect the moonlight. I want to kiss you," and he turned so his lips would meet hers, but she pulled back. "Please. You're so lovely. And I want to be near you not just tonight, but on other nights, not wondering what you are like when I see you in class or lab."

"You seem to be easy with your compliments, Henry." She forced a smile.

"Not easy. I mean what I say."

She wondered whether he just might be sincere and felt her heart beat a bit faster, for he made her feel like a desirable woman.

"May I kiss you?"

She moved her head so their lips would meet. She liked the warmth she felt, the softness of his mouth. He moved his tongue about her lips, then tried to open her mouth. She felt the heat through her body, sought his open mouth as their tongues met. Her heart beat faster as he hugged her, bringing her as close as possible, turning her, placing his hands on her breasts.

Abruptly she realized this was wrong despite her desire. She did not know him well enough. She took his hands from her breasts, moved back her head.

Suddenly she felt his hand at the hem of her skirt working to raise it while his other moved up along her leg.

"Stop. Now."

"Please. I want you. You'll enjoy yourself."

"And what makes you think so? Are you so experienced?" She could not see the blush increase in his face.

"Experienced? How could I be?" he lied. He had been with other females and prostitutes. "I believe I'm falling in love with you. Please. I just want you to feel good." He hesitated. "I have protection."

"Save your condom for some female who falls for your false charms. Now help me up and take me back to my rooms."

"I'm sincere about you," continuing to beg, thinking, *This goddamn Jewish bitch thinks she's so special. I'll get her now.* He pushed her to the ground, pulling up her skirts and grabbing at the waist of her underclothing, rubbing against her.

She struggled away from him, hit him with her hands as hard as she could, punched at his body. He pushed so she fell backward. Wrenching her body, she reached toward his face, scratching his cheek.

"You Jew bitch," as he put his hand to his face, feeling a slight trickle of blood.

"Let me up, you bastard," she shouted.

"Yeah. I'll let you up, but you help yourself. She was now crying, began to sob as she turned, wrenching at her long skirt, hearing it tear some. She struggled to her knee, grasping at the edge of the blanket and feeling the sand. She pushed, despite her tears and sobs, her loss of breath, pushed her body more so she could rise and stand. She pulled up her skirt, freeing her lower legs and feet, kicked at him, catching him in his leg as he stumbled.

"You fucking Jew bitch," his voice gravelly

"You bastard. You tried to rape me. Take me home. And if you try any more, be sure I'll report you," she managed loudly through her sobs, wishing she could walk to her rooming house. It was impossible.

"Get in the auto, bitch. Report me, and I'll see you're taken care of."

She felt her fright and the hard beating of her heart. She could not stop crying, her face completely wet with her tears. "Just take me home," she gravelly whispered. "Hear me. Take me home. And don't you ever, ever let me hear another thing about tonight, or your lies. I have enough clout, you better believe," her voice a bit clearer, wavering, cracking, as she continued crying. She looked through tears at her torn skirt, saw a wet spot, felt a bit of moistness on her pantalet. Semen?

Now he was scared. He believed she did have influence, probably at school through her parents. He again put his hand to his face where she had scratched him. How would he explain it?

"Don't worry, Jew bitch. I'll take you home."

"And stop using that word, and my heritage. I'm sick of hearing that disgusting insult, even if you believe it. I . . . I . . . can't even stand being near you. In class and lab keep your distance."

On the ride to her rooms, through her sobbing, trembling, she kept her face in her hands.

By now Henry was scared by what she might say or do. But how could she prove anything? Could he be dismissed from school? Who would believe her? A man's word against a woman's. He put his hand to his face, feeling the deep scratch. Explain that? He could lie that he fell."

Finally, at her rooming house, he went to her side to help her out. She pulled away from him. Holding her skirt tightly to her, she put a hand to the auto's edge to stabilize herself, stepping down while holding to the auto, managing to leave and slowly walking to the door, realizing her hair was in disarray. She also realized her bonnet was missing. She unsteadily walked while her hands tried to form her hair.

He watched, shaking his head, still frightened, then drove to his living quarters.

When she entered the living home, the housemother happened to see her. Olivia hoped she could have got to her room to talk to her roommate with whom the two exchanged confidences.

"Olivia." Mrs. Hopkins exclaimed, "You look horrible. You're crying, your hair is in disarray, and I think there is a tear in your skirt." At the same time she went to place her arm about Olivia's shoulders. Olivia just shed more tears and twisted to free herself from Mrs. Hopkins.

Mrs. Hopkins held her more tightly. "Olivia. Please tell me what happened to you."

"Mrs. Hopkins," she sobbed, her voice unsteady. "Please, let me go to my room. It's just . . ." She hesitated. "It's just too horrible," her voice quavering. "I don't care to talk about it. I want to go to my room. I need to lie down."

"Dear girl. You are my responsibility. Please let me help you."

Olivia looked at her, listening to the motherly tone of her voice. She just sobbed more and then managed," I was . . . I was attacked."

"What do you mean?"

"Assaulted, Mrs. Hopkins. I thought he was a nice person."

"Who was he? Did he, you know . . .?

Olivia managed to form the words. "Rape me? I . . . I struggled and stopped him. Please let me go. Oh, I want to talk to my parents. Please." Her crying became louder. "Please. I want to talk to my parents. They'll pay you for the phone call. Please."

"Who was it, Olivia? Someone you know? Another medical student?'

She wanted to get away from Mrs. Hopkins, to see her roommate Edna, talk to her mother and father.

She finally sat in a chair close by, her face in her hands, crying uncontrollably. Mrs. Hopkins thought she should call the police. "I'll let you use my phone. Don't worry about that. Let me call the police."

She looked up, Mrs. Hopkins a bleary face through her tears. "I'll call my parents, please. I don't care . . . no. I want to talk to them privately. Mrs. Hopkins helped her from the chair and led her, Olivia's shoulders stooped, to the table phone in one of Mrs. Hopkins's rooms.

Lucy answered the phone. "Lucy."

"Miss Olivia. Or should I call you doctor."

"Not yet," Olivia forcing a smile. "Is either my mother or father home yet?"

"Your voice sounds strange, Miss Olivia."

"Pease Lucy, get my parents. My mother first. Please hurry."

Lucy suddenly realized there was something wrong, aware of Olivia's tear choked voice. "I'll get your mother right away. Please wait."

"Olivia. What's wrong? Lucy sounded terrible telling me to hurry."

"Mother. Oh mother. The most horrible thing happened to me. It's the worst experience I've ever had." She started crying, sobbing. "Mother. It's . . . it's horrible."

"Olivia, dear. Try to calm a little and tell me everything. I'm sorry I can't be with you." Constance was now trying to hold back tears that she felt forming.

"He was a terrible man."

"What man?"

"He's in my class. He asked me to dinner. I . . . I was flattered. He is so handsome. But he's a monster," she sobbed.

"We . . . we went to a small beach by Lake Champlain. It was so beautiful. But it became so ugly. I can't stand it. I . . . I. He tried to rape me, mother. I think some of his semen may have gotten on my gown and an undergarment, I don't know. My gown is a wreck. It tore when we fought. I know I scratched his face hard. Oh, mother, I never expected . . . Wait." She let the phone drop, wiping furiously at her eyes, trying to compose herself.

"Do you want me to come see you, Olivia?" She was unaware, of course, Olivia was standing by the phone, wiping at her face, crying about Henry and her gown, what he tried to do."

"Olivia," Constance shouted, "Talk to me."

She finally heard her mother, grabbed at the phone. "Mother. I dropped the phone. What. I'm trying to stop crying. I didn't think I could have so many tears."

"Shall I come to you? I'll rearrange my schedule."

By now, Benjamin had arrived home and heard Constance shout. He placed his hand on Constance's arm. "It's Olivia. A man in her class tried to rape her. Oh, God, Benjamin. It reminds me of that horrible doctor from whom you saved me during the war. But this is worse. I want to go to her. The police won't do anything. Who will believe her? I'd like to report the man to the school."

"Mother. Your voice isn't loud enough to hear clearly."

Constance realized, heard Olivia. "Your father is here. Olivia. I'm going to come to you."

"Oh mother. I feel horrible. I don't know if I can face anyone. He's probably telling all kinds of stories about me."

"Olivia. This is your father."

"Hello father. Did mother tell you?"

"Well, the most she could right now. I'm going to see what we can do."

"Father. I don't want to be dismissed because of that horrible man."

"You are not going to be. Your mother and I will see to that."

By now, Benjamin was quite sure of himself and angry. He had already become well known for his surgery, particularly those on cancer. He had also written many papers and was invited to medical schools as a guest lecturer.

"Father. If he finds out you are going to do something, or mother, he may do all he can to discredit me. I could be dismissed from school, and I'm in my last year. Oh, I've already said that. I don't know what I'm saying anymore." She began to sob loudly.

"Here, Constance, you talk to her, try to calm her." He whispered.

"Olivia, it's mother. Please try to calm a little. I know how hard it is. I am coming as soon as possible. I'll have Andrew, our new driver, take me. If it's absolutely necessary, your father will come. Please, dear, go to your room and try to rest. I'll see you as soon as possible."

When she finished speaking to her mother and father, Olivia thought to thank Mrs. Hopkins. She wanted to get to her room and Edna. She wiped furiously at her eyes and reddened cheeks.

"If you need anything at all, Olivia, you tell me, all right?" Mrs. Hopkins was almost in tears. She tried not to listen to the conversation but heard part, placed her arm about Olivia's shoulders, moved her hand lightly about her back to soothe her.

"I'll go to my room now. My mother will be here as soon as she can. May I have her stay here?"

"Of course."

* * *

Within a few days Constance arrived. She made certain Olivia attended her rounds and lectures. More importantly, she went to the dean's office. She told the secretary that she would like to see the doctor.

"Your name, please."

"Dr. Constance Blumenthal."

The dean heard her name from his open door and rose and went to her. "Dr. Blumenthal, how are you? It's a pleasure to see you again. Do come in."

She followed him and took the seat he offered.

"It's such a pleasure to see you again. You know your daughter is almost number one of our graduates to be. What may I do for you?"

Constance explained why she was there, going into as much of the detail as she wished.

"Do you know this student?"

"No."

"What would you have me do?"

"I should like you to talk personally to him. I'm not asking for punishment. However, if he is to be an honorable physician, I believe even if you scare him, that if he is to be accepted for his knowledge in his community, he must apologize to you and to my daughter, if she wishes to see him again. If she does not, I expect that you will sternly confront him. Incidentally, I am requesting that you allow me to be present, even if my daughter is not."

"Well, your presence is a bit irregular, but being that you and your husband are, well, let's say so well known, perhaps that will be good. When I hold a discipline hearing, I usually do this in private. However . . ."

"There is no 'however' in this situation, doctor."

His face flushed, showing his discomfort that pleased Constance.

He, to settle himself, suddenly referred to Benjamin. You know when your husband was here for a lecture on surgery and in the amphitheater, the students were enthralled." He cleared his throat, his face still flushed in his discomfort regarding

Constance's insistence that she be present. He had no choice.

The following day he sent for Henry Anderson to face Olivia and Constance, although he had not told him her mother would be present. He laughed to himself as he walked to the Dean's Office thinking how he would call Olivia a liar and a typical woman with imagination and hysteria. However, when he entered the office and saw Constance, he began to tremble and tried to compose himself.

"I suppose you know, Henry why I've asked you to see me."

"Well not exactly. My grades are quite good, and I have been praised for my diagnostic skills." Suddenly, however, he could not prevent himself. "Who is this woman and why is Olivia here?"

"This is Dr. Constance Blumenthal, a well-known specialist in diseases of women. And, of course, you know your fellow student, Olivia Blumenthal."

He stuttered. "Certainly . . . certainly I know Olivia. We, all the men in our class do." He forced a smile at his implication that all the men were aware of her sexual proclivities.

"Why don't you take a seat, Henry, while we discuss why Dr. Blumenthal and Olivia are here also."

"Oh yes. I hadn't thought. But why am I here? I don't understand," attempting bravado.

"I called you in because I have a very serious problem that you may be able to help solve." It seemed to Constance the Dean tried too hard to be diplomatic.

"If I can help . . . help . . . in any way," he stammered, looking at Olivia, "I'll be happy to oblige."

"Dean, may I say something," Constance interrupted.

"Of course, Dr. Blumenthal." His face was becoming a deep red thinking of what she might say.

"Henry. I am glad to meet you."

"And I also. I have heard about you and your husband."

"Well you are about to hear a bit more. I hope you will

understand why we are here, why I traveled this far to meet you. Olivia, my daughter . . ."

At this point Olivia's heart was beating rapidly. "Mother, please. Let's get on with this and all of us stop beating about to be nice."

"Olivia, dear. I'm coming to this."

"Dr. Blumenthal, may I interrupt?" the Dean asked.

Constance let out a deep breath. "Yes. If you wish." She was becoming angry about the forced politeness in the room. Her eyes took in Henry, gazed intently at him, studying him.

"Henry. These women are here to ask you questions."

"Oh, hell," Constance muttered to herself. "Please, sir. Let's get on with this."

"Henry, I am going to let Dr. Blumenthal and Olivia ask some questions. I have heard a story that disturbs me."

Now, Constance, no longer patient, interrupted again. "Henry. You attempted to rape my daughter."

The room suddenly seemed as though a shell had exploded.

"I attempted to rape . . . to rape your daughter? I did not. She encouraged me."

Olivia now spoke. "You did and I expected that you would deny what happened. You probably told all your friends about what happened between us. They have shunned me."

"Olivia. I kissed you. You kissed me back. I could tell by the way you were breathing you wanted more. You urged me."

"I urged you! I urged you to go to my slips, to try to raise them, and you tore my gown to have a sexual intimacy with me that I rejected! Your hand moved up my thigh! You have a scar on your face, Henry. Do you want to show it clearly to the Dean? Do I have to show this gathering my torn gown, the stain on it . . . on my," She stopped unable to talk of her pantelet.

"This is a lie," he shouted. "You encouraged me to make love to you."

"You liar!"

The Dean again interrupted. "Please. Do settle down. This was to be a polite discussion of certain events." His desire to help Henry, infuriated Constance, but she forced herself to remain calm. "Dean. Let us have this discussion in a calm manner." She looked at Olivia, then Henry while softly placing her hand on Olivia's arm.

"Henry," she continued, not allowing the Dean to speak. "You are studying to become a doctor. It is an honorable profession that you are entering, one that demands respect for others, one that does not lie but tries to help those in pain and various illnesses. Do you understand that? Do you understand the Hippocratic Oath?" Constance stopped to regain her composure, forcing back the tears burning at the back of her eyes.

"Mother," Olivia spoke, knowing her mother was about to cry. "Mother. Please let Henry and me talk, and you and the Dean listen. Is that all right with you, sir?"

He swallowed phlegm, speaking softly. "Yes."

"Henry, please come here." He held back. "Please come near me, Henry." She put out her hand as he finally reached her. She touched his face, forcing him to show the facial scar her nails had caused. "Now quietly. Please explain this," she softly demanded, looking at the Dean.

There was a long hesitation, suddenly a very quiet room.

"You don't want to answer, Henry?"

"Who are you to touch me, to try to intimidate me, to even question my . . . HONOR?" he finally shouted.

Now the Dean spoke again. "I believe we have to settle this as amicably as possible. I do believe Olivia, Henry. But I can do nothing without your cooperation. I have no desire to dismiss you in your senior year or to destroy your professional honor that you are about to assume. I want the truth, and I want it now." He surprised Constance who now looked at him, he also turning to her, realizing he had to regain his own honor and not to demean his position.

"Henry. Do you understand me?" He then turned to Olivia. "You also, Olivia." He would not admit he had no desire to believe Olivia. *Women are hysterical. It's difficult to know when they are speaking the truth or to know what they are hiding behind their looks and hidden female ways of seeing life, unlike men who see it clearly.* He believed.

"Yes, sir. I didn't mean to hurt Olivia. We went to dinner, then I drove my auto to Lake Champlain. We sat on the beach. Yes. We kissed." He stopped. He did not wish to go further, to condemn himself, rather, hoping his silence would damn Olivia.

"Is that all you have to say, Henry?" the Dean asked.

"Yes, sir," he answered quietly, trying to hide his shaking voice and fearful discomfort.

"Dr. Blumenthal, Olivia, Henry, I just want to have this, as I stated, settled amicably. Are you satisfied with the discussion with Henry, Olivia, Dr. Blumenthal?"

Although Constance wanted the man dismissed, she again placed her hand on Olivia's arm, speaking for both, "We are satisfied, Dean. I just hope that Henry has learned from this experience. If he hasn't, he will find himself in trouble when he enters our profession." She noticed Olivia's eyes tearing. *Olivia merely wants an apology and no further harassment from his friends."*

"Henry?" the Dean asked.

His face quite red, knowing he had no other choice, he uttered, "Olivia, I apologize."

"I accept your apology." She wanted to tell him not to treat other women as he did her.

The session ended. The Dean dismissed Henry. "Thank you, Dr. Blumenthal for coming here for this unpleasant situation. And Olivia, you have handled yourself both like a lady and a doctor."

Constance wanted to scoff. *Yes, like you mean it, helping to demean women and keeping them in their place.*

They left the office and Constance walked with Olivia to her rooms. "Mother. I can't believe this. That man did nothing to help me. Suppose another woman is actually raped? Will that dean also excuse the man with an apology to the woman he has scarred for life?

"I just can't help myself. I'm crying mother. Look at me," as she shook with her tears.

Constance looked about. There being no one visible, she took her daughter in her arms. "Shh, dear. You did all you could. I am proud of you." Olivia buried her head in her mother's shoulder, feeling her warmth and love.

"Mother. He made me out to be a liar. I want to leave this place as soon as graduation is over. It won't come too soon," she sobbed. "You don't suppose they will lower my standing in my class?"

"They wouldn't dare do that. You are one of their top students. No one can take that away from you. You showed your spirit and courage. Although it was extremely unpleasant, I am proud of you." She lifted Olivia's face, kissing her on the cheek. "Let's just go on from here. Remember, Olivia, this is supposed to be a man's world. But women like you and I and others are going to show them who we are. That we can think and do what we want. There's a time coming when we will take our place along with those people like the dean and that awful Henry."

Olivia smiled through her tears. "Mother. You are so sure of yourself. I have always admired you for that. And I do love you so and thank you for coming here."

"I love you too, Olivia. Don't ever forget it. Your father also feels like I do. I wish he could have been with us. But always remember. We love you and are proud of you, not only because you will be a doctor quite soon but that you have the willpower to go to Philadelphia." She laughed a bit. "Think of it. Joseph will be graduating in two years. I think about my children and love being a mother to all of you. Millicent is happy, and has given us grandchildren. What more could a mother and father ask for?

"Do you have an appetite?"

"Some, mother."

"Then take me to a good restaurant. I'll buy us dinner."

They walked for a while, often silent.

"Here, mother. I have been here on dates." She laughed. "With a couple of nice young men who were not grabbing for my body."

"That's enough now, Olivia."

When seated, Constance ordered a glass of wine. "How about you dear? It will relax you."

"All right." She sipped, unaccustomed to drinking much. It did, however, remind her of home. The thought made her sad. Tears formed.

"Come now. To us and to the newest doctor in our family."

Olivia smiled but could not hold back the tears. "Mother, I'm so embarrassed, even ashamed. Why should I feel like this?"

Constance took her hand. "Darling. Let me tell you about a young patient of mine who was actually raped. The family blamed her. I had to talk and talk to convince them that there are men who have no respect for women, that their daughter was the victim, not a loose young woman. Finally they believed me. That may have convinced the family, but they also had to accept the horror their daughter endured and love her. Her mother and father thought and then went and hugged her, telling her they would do whatever was in their power to protect her, that they loved her. Fortunately she did not become pregnant and her secret remained.

"I purposely told you this because of your experience and what you endured in the Dean's office. More important, however, is that you always hold dear your self-esteem.

"Remember, Olivia, who you are and what you are, that no one, I mean no one, can ever debase us, no matter how hard they try. We are women, strong and able."

Part VI

Tranquility and Turmoil

Chapter One

Emergence

It was late spring, May, 1904. Benjamin and Constance made arrangements to travel to Tufts Medical College. Millicent, Aunts Arella, Esther and their husbands, and, of course Olivia would also be with them. It was not only a family gathering but a gala event.

Olivia began to think back to her graduation now that she was a resident physician at the Women's Hospital and progressing well in her OB/Gyn studies. Not all in the family attended her graduation but to be with everyone at Joseph's emergence as a M.D. excited her. It had never bothered her who attended her graduation because her mother and father were there, the two people most important in her life thus far. Millicent also came, the sisters still confidantes.

While a resident, Olivia met a young doctor, Alexander Levine, about her age who would be graduated from Temple University College of Medicine the same date as Joseph.

She met Alexander because of the resident with whom she shared an apartment.

"Olivia, I have known a fellow I believe you would like,"

Gail, her roommate with whom she shared a small apartment told her. "My date the other night introduced him to me before dropping him off at an affair he was invited to. He seemed very nice, spoke in a lovely soft voice. He's tall, has amazing sky-bright blue eyes and blonde hair."

"You make him sound like he's a god, in a way. I'm not particularly looking for an evening out right now, Gail. I have so much work to do. I'm on duty every night this week. Who knows about the next?" For some reason she thought of her traumatic night with Henry Anderson. *Olivia. Stop this. Not every male is like he is. You have found this out. Listen to Gail.* "Let me think about it, Gail."

She had been to dinner engagements with young men who suited her fancy. If she liked her admirer she might allow an occasional kiss to tempt him, if she desired to see him again. However she never went beyond this. Other times she flirtatiously used her eyes, facial expressions or for further enticement perhaps slowly swing her hips. Conceivably, if Gail were right, despite the Anderson event that she could not forget no matter how hard she tried to rid herself of that burden, she might enjoy meeting this 'god,' laughing silently at her vision.

"I'm telling you, you'll like him. Of course, I only got to talk to him for a little while, but so pleasant. Immediately I thought of you."

"I'll let you know."

After several days, thinking of the dates she had had and using temptations, she told her perhaps it would be a pleasant night. Gail told the physician she knew that Olivia would like to meet Alexander and gave him their phone number.

They did meet, the attraction between the two immediate. Despite herself, this was no flirtation but perhaps something serious. He was a gentleman and treated her with respect. Then one night he walked to her door and slowly moved toward her. She did not move, waiting.

"Olivia." He hesitated, moved a step closer noticing she did not back away. "Olivia."

"Yes, Alex," smiling.

He gently placed his arms about her shoulders, drew her close, bent and kissed her. The warmth of his lips sped through her as she took his mouth to her and kissed harder. She felt a thrill that had never happened before.

They separated, gazing at one another. He broke the silence.

"Olivia, I know we have only been together a few times, but when I look at you . . . Olivia I'm falling in love with you."

She reached up, smiling, bringing his lips to hers again. "Alex, I feel very warmly toward you. I'm not going to use 'love.' We need more time, more . . . oh, that's not what I mean. I want you near me. I miss you when we're not together."

He smiled. "You mean you accept what I just told you."

"I think I do. But let's spend more time together when I have free nights. You also have to be sure not to allow your final studies to slip. Goodness. I sound like a mother."

"If that's so, I want you to be the mother of our children."

"Just a minute. Come here." She raised her head, put her lips to his. Feeling his tongue now seeking out her mouth, she allowing him, opening herself to him, their tongues playing against each other. She felt streaking heat throughout her body. She drew back, breathing harder, her heart beating fast as he began rubbing against her. "Alex, no more. Please. I don't mean to shun or frustrate you."

"I know," he murmured. "I do love you, Olivia."

"Shhh. Give us time, as she gently kissed him. "Goodnight, dear one."

Without telling anyone, he went shopping for an engagement ring, finding exactly what he wanted, small with a ruby in the middle surrounded by diamonds. *I'll give her this at the right time, if she'll take it7. I know she cares, but how much?*

There were other times. Eventually she acknowledged to

herself she loved him, thinking often of him, what life together might be. On one particular night, Gail being at the hospital, Olivia having the apartment to herself, she invited Alexander to come for dinner, telling him, "Alex, dress informally, no tie, no jacket. If you wish, wear a sweater over your shirt."

"That's great, Olivia. Shall I bring take-out food? Tell me what you would like."

"No. I'm cooking for us." She prepared a beef stew, baked bread as Joyce had taught her, remembering her saying Olivia had to know these important ways to keep a home, never imagining she would become a doctor. She also baked a cake.

When he sat at the table, he watched her walk to the kitchen, unable to keep his eyes from her swaying hips. She had allowed her red hair fall to its natural length, had dressed in scant, comfortable clothing, a blouse, pants almost like pajamas that she wore when Gail and she were together. The pants did show off her hips and backside. When she turned, taking the dinner to the table, her breasts pressing against her waist length top obviously fascinated him. How he wished he could see her, all of her.

"Here you are. Alex."

"You did all this?"

"Of course," she laughed. "Come, sit." She reached out and touched his hand, running her fingers across. "You look hungry," she laughed while thinking, *But what kind of hunger?* Watching his eyes move about her, feeling the warmth from his eyes flow throughout her.

After a bit, eating, "This is good."

"Taste the bread."

"Wonderful."

When they finished, she went back to the kitchen and brought out the cake. "Here you go, doctor."

He helped her clear the table and wash the dishes. "You could be handy, Alex, a real helpmate."

"Oh, yeah. I'm showing off. I didn't grow up with a maid," he laughed. "I'm lying. We did have two, one who cleans and the other whom my mother taught to cook Jewish dishes."

"Ha, so your family isn't poor. You told me they were not the richest Jews in Philadelphia."

"No we aren't. What I didn't tell you, and don't ask me why, my father started another Jewish newspaper in the city. Yes, it is prosperous. He prints it in English in case Christians might want to read it. It contains the usual news of the day and what is happening in the Jewish community. Oh well. But . . . we aren't a family of doctors. That amazes me."

"So now we know about each other's families."

She looked at him lovingly, took his hand and led him to the sofa. She moved closer, leaned in, taking his lips to hers. They kissed passionately, pulling their bodies against each other, yet so soft and yielding.

Olivia felt warmth throughout her body, desiring more of him. He moved his hand under her loose top, feeling her breasts, gently caressing her stiffened nipples. She pulled up her blouse so he could see her. He gasped at the firm upright pointing breasts, as she lay back pulling him between her thighs, feeling him against her. She felt him rub. She pulled him higher so he would touch her sensitive places, moving her thighs to meet him, throwing back her head as she moaned, arching as she heard his groan and she reached her edge. Breathless they lay holding to one another until he moved off and to her side.

"I love you, Olivia, always will. You are part of my soul."

"I love you also. It has taken me so long to tell you. But I do. I love you the way you do me."

He rose from the long sofa, then kneeled before her. She bent to kiss him, laughing. Why are you kneeling? Am I the queen?" Of course she knew what was to come except . . . .

"You are my queen." He placed his hand in his pocket, took

out the small package. "Dearest, put out your hands." He went to her left, held it. "Please accept this offering, oh queen." He opened the packet and drew out the ring, placing it on her left ring finger.

"Alexander. It's so beautiful. I love it."

"Will you marry me, Olivia? I do love you so and want you for my forever wife."

"I will marry you, Alexander and pledge my love to you, all of me." She felt her heart beating faster, the blush of happiness rising to her face. "Come here, dearest." She pulled him beside her, held his face, closing on his lips as they passionately sought out one another's mouths, their tongues playing." He pulled back. "I'm so happy."

"I too."

"When shall we wed?"

"I'll talk to my parents. It will be in Maine, of course." She was thinking of Joseph's graduation day and the family gathering. It would be after he had his celebration. She would not have anything interfere with that. "You realize we must wait until after Joseph's day. And you will be there too, as we will be at your graduation."

Alex still had to be admitted for an internship, as, of course, would her brother. She convinced Alex to apply to a hospital in Philadelphia for his first year internship. After she finished in 1905, she persuaded him to apply to Deaconess. She saw this as her opportunity also to serve the poor.

After the eventful evening, thinking of their love making, looking intently at the ring, feeling her heart full with love and happiness, she called home.

Margaret Mosby answered, the now rather old governess but who still remained with the family. Olivia, hearing the weakened voice, thought back to the love, patience, and learning this woman had given her, Joseph and Millicent. "Hello, Mrs. Mosby."

"Yes." Suddenly she knew it was Olivia, thinking back, seeing a young, lively girl who so resembled her mother. "Olivia?"

"Yes, Mrs. Mosby. It is Olivia. How are you?"

"I'm getting past my time, Olivia." She shouted.

"Don't you tell me that. I won't accept it." Yet Olivia did feel sadness, aware this magnificent woman was well into her eighties and might possibly die soon. "Mrs. Mosby, are my parents home by chance?"

"Well, you being a doctor," she hesitated, "and your brother so soon now. . ." She sounded as though she was filled with tears. She sniffled, then answered, "Your father is not home yet. That's so unusual, of course," she forced a laugh. "But your mother just walked in. Why are you calling so late? Oh, she is with your father. Did something happen to you?"

"Yes, dear Mrs. Mosby. Something wonderful. I'd like to talk to my parents first. They'll tell you."

She handed the phone to Constance. "It's Olivia."

"Ben. Olivia is on the phone. Come here. Yes, darling. It's so late for you to call."

"I have something magnificent, so wonderful to tell you and father. I'm getting married." Now Olivia was crying. "Mother, I'm so happy, and he's so, well just everything I have wished for in a husband."

"Who is this man who has captivated you?"

"He goes to med school at Temple. My roommate introduced him to me. His name is Alexander Levine, tall, blue eyed and blonde hair. And mother, he's such a gentleman. Not like that horror in medical school. He treats me with respect and honor. Wait til you see my ring."

"What about his family?"

"His father is a newspaper publisher in Philadelphia. I have to laugh. He thinks we're so far above him with you and father, now Joseph and me being in the same profession. I bet his family has more than we ever dreamed of. But I don't care about that. I persuaded him to apply to Deaconess because that way I can help with the poor who come to the hospital."

"Well, I'm overwhelmed and so happy for you, dearest. Here is your father."

"Olivia, when are we going to meet this young man? I must tell you, too, that you should see the smile on your mother's face. Mine too. I have been listening on the other phone but did not want to interrupt."

"You're a sneak, father. But I knew you would be there. Father, I just can't believe this, that I met someone I can trust and love as I do."

"So, darling, you can see not all men are beasts. I wanted to go after that fellow in med school who frightened you so. Your mother held me back. Anyhow, that's the past."

"Mother, Father, I'm going to invite him to Joseph's graduation so you can meet him. That way too we'll all be together. I hope he can make it, because his graduation is the end of May." She was so excited she was running her thoughts together, she felt, not at all like her. "I guess we could invite his parents to Portland. What do you both think?

"I'm not being very logical now, I have so much on my mind and want you to love him as a son. Of course, not like I love him. Mother and Father . . . We will settle the date and everything, including a honeymoon."

They simultaneously answered that would be just fine. Constance then interrupted.

"Olivia, how about if we set the wedding for July and have his parents come here the last week of June. You'll have another year to your residency. If you are to be married, I suppose Alexander will start his internship in Philadelphia. The next year you both can go to Boston, if Alexander is accepted. He perhaps could report the second week in July. Well, when you come home we can work all that out. No. Maybe we should make it the last week of June. That would be best for you and Alexander."

"We've already decided on Alex being in Philadelphia. Then we'll go to Boston. He's too good for Deaconess to turn him down. Anyhow, I'd like the last week of June. That sounds more feasible. You could have his folks there for several days before the wedding. I also have to get a dress. Mother. I am so excited. We'll shop for a dress and be together. We have to have Millicent with us. I have talked to her about Alexander."

"All right. We'll manage everything, and it will be so grand to have you home."

"It will," Benjamin interrupted. "I'm just wondering about a honeymoon. You may not be able just now. I suppose you could ask for leave the beginning of June. Perhaps they'll allow you time."

"I like that. Joseph's graduation is this month. So that gives June to deal with the wedding. I just can't stop thinking about it. Were you and mother as exuberant as I feel?"

"We were, Olivia," Constance answered.

"Well, I'll hang up now. We can talk again. All right. I love you both and appreciate your support over all these years."

"We love you, Olivia and will always be there for you. Remember that." They almost said it simultaneously.

When the conversation ended, Olivia thought back to talking with Millicent:

Millicent. I met the most lovely, sincere man and fell in love. I haven't told him yet. I think he loves me. He intimates it. Mill tell me, 'You know how to make him do what you want him to. Use those female wiles of yours. We all do, even after marriage.' Then after we made love, telling how we loved, and the ring. I told her all that and how I showed myself. She told me, 'I was never as brave as you. You didn't actually do it, did you?' No, but I sure wanted to. What's it like? 'OH, my first time wasn't what I guess I expected, but when he went inside, I expected the pain, but he was gentle. Don't you ever tell anyone about our conversation.' Mill, you know me better. 'I know. It did get better. I did as mother had told me and let him know what I wanted and, well, how. It became better. Olivia. Don't be afraid to speak up.' You know I won't. I just can't wait. But. Mill, I did, that night have the big one. I sort of screamed and trembled all over. Was it something like that for you? Millicent laughed. 'I know what you felt. I have. But I had to teach him how to excite me to that stage. Men. They think only of themselves sometimes. So don't be surprised. But don't lie there like you're there just for his satisfaction. I've heard stories about the way men do things and women forget that they have bodies too that belong to them, that they just don't have to be a receptacle. Women are so . . . so . . . many times submissive. This is the 20th Century, Olivia. We have to speak up for ourselves. Oh yeah. I know. Men will want to make us outcasts.' Take it easy, Millicent. I'm with you. I let him know how I feel and what I want and how he should satisfy me in bed.

Olivia, smiled thinking back and then laughed. It was so wonderful having a sister like hers. *I had never imagined her as so assertive.*

The rest of the night she thought of the wedding preparation and of Alexander and that night. She became heated, reached down to her cleft, imagining she was with Alex, and satisfied herself.

* * *

Alexander received permission to go to Medford and Portland with the proviso that he would take his exams upon his return. Or course he agreed. There were one or two others who had asked the same as he. His parents gave him enough not only for fare but for enjoying himself with Olivia and her family.

An auto, he hired, drove up to the hotel in Medford. Alexander wanted so to reach for Olivia but restrained himself for his introduction to her mother and father, Joseph, and Millicent. He then went to hug Olivia. She placed her arms about him, stood on her toes and kissed him on his lips that he returned. It surprised him and wondered what her parents would think.

"Alex, your face is red. Don't be embarrassed because we kissed. They know we are engaged. Besides," she giggled, "I've seen my parents do the same, oh, and Millicent too. It's too bad her husband couldn't be here. He had so much to do to take care of his business."

His introduction to the family rather overwhelmed him, though he knew he would be marrying into a medical family.

"Mother, Father, here he is."

On graduation day, they watched Joseph as they had Olivia, tears in his parents' eyes. He would be staying in the Boston area for his internship and residency.

That evening there was a grand celebration. The Blumenthal medical family was complete.

* * *

Constance and Benjamin, and Joseph accompanied Olivia for Alexander's graduation. Of course, this gave both families the opportunity to meet.

They had dinner the night before graduation. David, his father, and Ora, his mother were delightful hosts. They talked throughout the meal of the coming graduation and the wedding. They were delightful hosts.

"We love Olivia," Ora told them. Olivia smiled with a blush. "To think, she's a doctor and Alexander is about to become one. I cannot get over it."

Constance also smiled, wondering, however, if Ora was a bit old fashioned and thought of women only as house wives. She decided, "Well our world is changing, isn't it. Here I am and there's Olivia. Female doctors are beginning to make their mark. We love Alexander and believe they will make a wonderful doctor couple."

"Well, look at you and Benjamin," David interjected. "I hope they will be as good as you two. I've heard such marvelous stories about both of you."

"You have?" Benjamin asked.

"Good heavens," David laughed. "Don't forget I'm a newspaper man and have connections in Portland," he smiled, "an editor there."

"That sounds like our Military Information Bureau during the past war, well the war between the states."

"You served? I missed that one. I'll have to get after the man I know up there. It must have been horrible."

Constance answered, "It was. I try not to think about it."

Ora looked at her unbelieving. "Were you already a doctor?"

"No. I was a nurse and then decided on medicine. Benjamin was a surgeon. In fact, I learned nursing from our nation's first female doctor, Elizabeth Blackwell."

"That's fascinating." Ora looked at her with admiration so visible in her face and eyes. *What a family. All those doctors. I wonder how she got to marry a Jew. The children don't seem to practice any religion. I wonder whether Olivia will lead Alexander away from our people. I can't worry about that now. She's considered Christian. Their children? There's too much excitement and happiness to try to put that in the picture. But how did she manage to marry a Jew?*

The conversation continued. "One thing I know, after the wedding, we'll still have Alexander . . . and Olivia here for another year." Ora told the group.

"Yes, you will," answered Benjamin.

Soon David and Benjamin went in the drawing room to talk while Ora showed Constance through the house. Alex and Olivia were already outside walking in a starlit sky, light sprinkling on them through the trees from full moon and cloudless sky. Alexander stopped. Holding her hand he pulled her gently to him.

"I love you," and he bent to her mouth, kissing her softly then harder as she responded, her mouth opening to him, their tongues licking at one another's. She moaned softly, taking his hand and placing it on her breasts, urging him, feeling his hand reaching inside her evening dress that came to her bare shoulders, her moaning louder as he played about her nipples. She wanted him, wished, then pulled gently away. "How I want you, Alex, in all ways." She panted, wishing his hand could seek between her thighs. "I love you too, Alex."

He pressed against her thigh, frustrated by the skirt of her gown. She reached down as he guided her hand along his hardness. They could not see the redness that had risen in both their faces. They paused, both allowing their breath to return to normal. Soon she spoke.

"Alex, how frustrating. And to think, I'm marrying a man younger than I," she laughed. "But, youngster, you certainly know how to please me. We'll always be like this, won't we?"

"I promise we will. And younger. Well. That's the first time you've mentioned that. Next you'll be telling me I'm older for a graduate of med school."

She laughed again. "Foolish one. I know you started to become a newspaperman, but I'm happy you became a med student." Her voice became excited. "Alex, just think. You are about to graduate, and we're going to marry. I do love you and want you so."

"I can't wait for both." *I'll see her naked. I'll be able to enter her, feel everything about her. Some of the fellows who have been with those loose women told me what it's like, how it feels. Stop now. Olivia is not a whore like those stupid men went to.*

"I think we better go back to the house, Alex. They'll be wondering about us." She smiled, "What do you suppose they're thinking."

Now he laughed. "You know quite well what they're saying or thinking? Let them. You know. I can't believe I'm going to be a doctor and start my internship. We will go to Boston, if they'll have me. And marriage, a married couple in medicine together." He thought suddenly. "We'll be like your parents."

How I hope we will. They love one another so much and have given that to we, their children.

* * *

The graduation at the School of Medicine of the University of Pennsylvania was exciting for both families. Alexander was being graduated from the oldest medical school in the United States. After the ceremony, Ora, Olivia, and Constance watched through tears. The same could be said for David and Benjamin, David, Ora, and Olivia with pride, Benjamin and Constance thinking back to Olivia's and their own times.

After the celebration of two days, the Blumenthals returned to Portland, both to the necessities of their practices and Constance continually thinking of preparations for the wedding and the thrill it would be to shop with Olivia.

Before leaving for home, Olivia talked to Millicent. "Hello Mill."

"Who is this? Oh, Olivia, my heart's delight," Millicent giggled.

"Cut that out," Olivia laughed. "This is serious."

"Well, at least you'll always know when I'm kidding." She took a breath to keep herself from giggling more. "You know it's wonderful to hear your voice. What's happening? I know you went to the graduation and are getting married. But what else is happening, as if anything can?"

"Mill, dear, I wanted to talk to you about the wedding. I'm so filled my heart may burst. Did you feel like that?"

"Pretty much," she laughed. "I think it's funny. You sound like I did and how I bothered you and mother. I must have driven you to the insane asylum."

Olivia also laughed. "Mill, I want you to be my Matron of Honor."

"Olivia! That's an honor. I mean it. Thank you so much. I love you dear Olivia and will be so pleased. I am excited about your wedding."

"Mother and I are taking the railroad to Boston to shop for a wedding dress. Perhaps you can get away from the children and Ely," she laughed again, then became as serious as she had been. "You could come with us so you can get your dress at the same time."

"That sounds great. The maid and Ely will just have to put them to bed and get them off to school etc. When are you going?"

"Well, mother told me she would take off Friday and Monday of this week. I believe she's thinking of retiring. Well why not? She's still young enough to enjoy some freedom. Anyhow, how's those days for you?"

"Fine. I'll come down Thursday night. See you then."

"That sounds fine. Mother will enjoy that. We can sleep together in my room and stay up all night talking. I love you, Mill."

"Love you too, Olivia."

In Boston, the three visited several stores, sometimes arm in arm when there was not a crowded street. The nearness of the women to one another thrilled them, particularly Constance having her daughters with her.

Eventually they came to a dress shop where the wedding and Matron of Honor gowns caused excitement. Olivia eventually chose one that had lace covering her upper chest, closing just above her breasts, the skirt straight in front, the back a long satin train trimmed with pearls. Millicent's dress was something of a copy. After a fitting they went to lunch, having been promised the gowns would be ready by Monday late morning.

The evenings were spent with fine dinners and much talk. Constance and Olivia had made an agreement there would be no medical talk, not wanting Millicent to feel like the odd one out.

"Children, my grown daughters. Look at you, both so beautiful. I want to get up from the table and give you another hug. She reached across and both gave her their hands, squeezing, softly, withdrawing, feeling the loving caress, all with tears of love and happiness forming. They had rarely seen their mother so emotional, although thinking back to their growing years they remembered the time their mother spent with them, teaching them about womanhood and making certain they felt secure.

"Olivia. You'll be married soon and having your own home." Constance forced herself to keep from crying. "You and Alexander could come to Portland and be part of the family practice, after Alexander finishes his training. Perhaps Joseph would join too. He says he's most interested in cardiology. Think of it. We could have a clinic and be close to Maine General Hospital. Your father and I have talked about this many times. Oh, I'm sorry, Millicent. We had agreed not to talk about medicine."

"Mother. I don't feel left out and never have. I chose my life and love it and am so proud of all the accomplishments in the family."

"I appreciate that, dear. Now, while we're on it, I'm thinking of retiring next year."

"You are!" Olivia and Millicent spoke in unison, then laughed. "Mother," Millicent said, "Olivia and I talked about that. We think you should and enjoy life. Perhaps father could take some months off. I know he has young, promising doctors work with him. Then the two of you could go on a long trip through Europe, perhaps even visit Uncle Daniel and Aunt Riva."

"You two have always been ahead of me." Her eyes filled again, but she made no effort to hold back the tears. Do you realize how much I love you both? Don't worry. I feel the same about Joseph. But the additional happiness to be with you now, the three of us together on such a happy occasion to look forward to."

The day of the wedding, Constance and Millicent helped Olivia prepare. "Look at yourself in the mirror, Olivia," Millicent told her. "You're beautiful. Alexander will be stunned."

"She's right," Constance said, as she stepped forward and brought her daughter to her in a tight hug.

Benjamin came to the door and told them all was ready. He watched Olivia, could see her happiness and nervousness. "My gorgeous daughter. Be happy and have a good life together." He kissed her cheek, then led her down the stairs to the waiting guests as the wedding march played.

She walked toward the canopy, smiling at Alexander, barely hearing the whispers of beauty.

Alexander broke the glass, sealing their bond, neither really thinking about religion but about one another.

After the wedding meal and the cake, they left for the Lafayette Hotel in Portland. Olivia was tearful looking at her parents and Millicent and Joseph, thinking of the night to come, nervous and anxious to please Alexander.

He asked that he watch her undress, but she demurred. "You wait, Alexander." She put on a light lace nightgown that allowed the protruding of her breasts. She then walked from the bedroom, finding him already undressing. She then twirled, smiling at his obvious desire for more. Then she beckoned for him to follow her into the bedroom. She faced him, blushing as she slowly drew up her gown as she showed between her thighs. then quickly up to her breasts and hardened nipples, over her head until the gown fell to the floor. Naked and feeling the redness in her neck and face, remembering the night she showed her breasts and the following climax. Would it happen this night?

Quickly he shed his underwear, showing himself. Gazing at him, he came closer and led her to the bed, gently laid her on the mattress and lay atop as she spread her legs for him to enter. As he did, she grimaced at the pain that she tried to ignore so as to feel his movement within her. She raised her legs to wrap about him, arching her back and moving with him. She felt his release, listening to him, smiling, despite the painful persistence. As he rested beside her she drew him to her, taking his hand, raising it to her breasts, urging him to gently massage her nipples. She felt the heat surge through her and quickly took his hand below. As he followed her lead, she reached her peak.

As they both learned one another's desires, they finally lay exhausted, content. In the morning, snuggled against him, smiling, she seductively murmured, "I hurt down there. It needs intimacy."

He laughed. "Now?"

"But I lead."

* * *

Alexander's parents helped them find a home in Philadelphia so they would be as close as possible to the hospital but in a good neighborhood.

When he finished his internship and she her residency, they would now go to Boston.

———————————

Chapter Two

Displacement

Constance and Benjamin lay in bed reading, he the daily newspaper and she a novel.

"Ben, you know I'm going to retire, probably in May. The spring will be here, and I want to enjoy it."

"Mmm. How will I replace you?" he smiled. "Not as my wife." He turned toward her, moving her face to his and kissing her. "How about it?" He moved her lips with his tongue, slipping it inside as she responded. Their lips pressed harder against one another's. She hugged him tightly, but then pulled back. "Not now. Later," she told him reluctantly. "We have to talk. We've been putting this off."

"Oh well, if you insist. But later. No outs."

"All right, sex fiend." She wanted to have sex as much as he did. "You know we've had a letter from Olivia."

"Say, is she ever going to have children?"

"Listen Ben. This is serious. You know she wants to return to Portland and take my place. She isn't that happy in Boston. But she's having trouble with Alexander. He likes it there."

"Well, I imagine his residency is good, and he doesn't want to leave it. They also get to see Joseph and his new girlfriend, Marie Lewis. He said when he has a bit of time he'll bring her to meet us. Constance, she's a Christian. You'll have company."

"I'm looking forward to that. And you keep quiet," she laughed, "my wonderful Jewish husband. It does sound like she's a keeper. And she's a lawyer. Maybe . . ."

"Maybe what."

"I was just thinking, if he would come here, we'd have a cardiologist in the practice," she said wistfully, a tear forming, thinking of how much she wanted her son to have a fine wife.

"You know, if they all came to Portland, we could start a clinic. And with the Maine General close by, think of that set-up."

"Hmmm. That . . ." her eyes now fully tearing." "It . . . would be so wonderful, all of us together. Except for Millicent. But she said maybe Ely was planning on expanding to Portland. Imagine."

Soon after they did hear from Joseph that he would be arriving in Portland on the following week-end.

In the meantime, in Boston, where Alexander and Olivia managed to be together at their Brookline home that Benjamin and Alexander's father had agreed together to buy, they were eating dinner that their maid-cook, Ellen, had prepared.

"This is so good, Ellen," Olivia told her, as she placed the meal before them. Olivia was quite tired from long days seeing patients and also being at the hospital. Her usually bright blue eyes showed weariness. This was one of those rare times they were together when he also had time off.

"Alex, I realize you still have more time for your residency, but I want to move back to Portland and take my mother's place in the family practice. You could finish your residency in Maine. I know that's quite a disruption, but another surgeon in the practice would be a magnificent addition. You could even study under my father; and when he retires, you'd be taking his place.

She paused. "And now I'm thinking I want a child, in fact more than one. We have talked about this, and you said you'd love that. I'm thinking, my mother has retired . . ." She stopped. She had given him too much to think about, and she wanted to wait until she assured her mother's continuing practice before having children that she would so much like to have."

"Wait just a minute. Just what are you talking about? I

should quit here and go to that hick city of yours?" He had been growing weary of hearing about Portland and Maine, although he admitted to himself that it would be nice to be near the sea again, to fish, and swim. But practice there. No! He had to live in a large city.

"Hick? Just what the hell are you taking about? I'm a hick? My parents and brother and sister too? Have you thought of the places my family has been? And just where did I meet you? And Joseph has been here for how long, Alex?" She had raised her voice and was becoming very angry. "Joseph's girl friend is from where, Alex? Do you recall where Harvard is? Do you know where my brother went to college? He and Marie are coming to see us. Do you think she'll sound like she's from the hills?"

"Calm down."

"Calm down, hell. You apologize for your ignorant remark. Do you have any idea about my mother and father marrying in Washington during the War Between the States, about their service there and my father and she being at Gettysburg during that horrendous battle, about one of my uncles being killed there? The hell . . ." She could not go on, being about to cry, swallowing her words, coughing, and slamming her fork and knife on the table to run upstairs. She turned back, furiously telling him as she reached the stairs, "Everything I've done for you, Alexander. Shit. You can go back to . . ." And sobbing, she ran up the stairs, went toward their bedroom, thought of going to one of the guest rooms, telling herself, *What the hell. He can come in here and apologize.*

Sitting at the table, Alexander stared at what was left of the meal, talking to himself, "What the hell do I want to go there for? Damn. The meal is ruined." Should he wait for desert? "Ellen must have heard the whole thing." His face colored from embarrassment and from watching Olivia run from him. He called to Ellen. "Forget the desert tonight, Ellen. And we won't be eating anymore."

She looked at him, deciding whether to say anything, then did. "You know, Dr. Levine, I did hear you both fighting. It's none of my business. I like you both so much, but I have to tell you," and she smiled, "I never told you all where I come from. I'm one of those hicks from North Anson, Maine but knew I could do better down here. My family was so hurt. They own a gas station and do O.K. Now . . ." She began to think she had said too much. She touched his shoulder. "Why don't you go up and talk to Mrs. Levine? Listen, thinking about it, I'm old enough to be mother to both of you. So you listen to me."

Alexander laughed. "Ellen, you know we both love and trust you and want you with us. O.K., 'mother.' I'll go upstairs now."

While walking up the stairs to appease Olivia, he started whispering to himself. "Just what has she done for me that's so outstanding? The nerve, 'all that I've done for you.' I should apologize? For what? Well, she did help me when I was at school and some stuff was tough for me to understand or to get at. She did help me studying for exams. And she did get me to Boston. But now? She wants me to go live in that city. I didn't like it that much when I was there visiting her parents. They are great. And brilliant. But . . ." He came to the bedroom door that was ajar. He slowly opened it, seeing Olivia turned away, her head almost buried in her pillow in an almost inaudible crying. "Her shoulders are shaking. Still crying?" He went to her and tapped her shoulder. She shrugged him away but then turned, her eyes filled with tears, her face red.

"Olivia. Please. I'm sorry," his voice low with forced sincerity. "I don't want to see you like this."

She wiped at her eyes and cheeks, thinking how terrible she must look, thinking how she would like to slap him for what he had said. *Portland is Hicksville. My family is nothing to him. Philadelphia. Yeah. He signed the Declaration of Independence by not following his father, the king newspaper man . . . for struggling through med school. He's never talked to me like that.*

"What?"

"I'm sorry. I will consider it. I know how important it is to you."

"Then consider it and let me know your decision. We could go our separate ways, you down here and me up there." She suddenly thought of what she had said. Was she asking for a separation? *We've had arguments but nothing like tonight. Insulting my family. Me. And here I am giving him an opportunity he would never get elsewhere. I love him but . . . but love is something above all else. Don't do this. He could leave me.*

"Well, you consider it. Now please. I'm just very tired from seeing patients today and also helping in a cancer operation. The poor woman. Cancer of her ovaries. She isn't going to make it," she spoke sadly. "We women, the awful things that can happen to our bodies and how we try to make them so lovely, so presentable. Alex. Please. I appreciate you came to me. I just want to think and sleep."

"All right. I'm going to stay up for a while and do some reading." He ran his hand softly over her shoulders. "I'll let you sleep. Don't forget, though. Joseph is coming with Marie for dinner tomorrow. I'm not on night duty."

She already knew his schedule and had purposely invited her brother for tomorrow. She was getting to like Marie, a beautiful blonde with intelligent hazel eyes, about five foot five, a slim, attractive body, breasts that seemed to Olivia to be more full than hers. She wasn't shy and talked freely to Olivia, having taken to her also. Olivia felt they would be friends, and if Joseph married her, believed she would be a good addition to the family. She was sure her mother and father would like her. They would be meeting her in two weeks. She thought of calling her mother but hesitated, wanting her parents to make their own judgments without her interference. Sometimes, however, she felt that Joseph was not too pleased with Alexander. She thought of asking her brother but hesitated, probably wouldn't, just allow circumstances to take their course.

* * *

Joseph arrived at Marie's home for dinner. She lived not too far from the Harvard campus. On arrival he was greeted by her parents, who long ago now had insisted he call them by their first names, Caleb and Deborah. It was the week before they would be traveling to Portland.

They had at first objected to Joseph after first hearing about him, a Jew with the name of Blumenthal. They could not imagine how their eldest daughter could have allowed herself to become friendly with him and seemed to see him secretly, which it was. They would manage to see each other for tea or coffee, occasionally lunch. Eventually they were openly together for dates in the evening, for now she had been graduated from Radcliffe, and Boston University School of Law. They had met on the Harvard campus, and here he was, now a doctor, she a lawyer.

* * *

It was the same old story retold as when Ely wanted to marry Millicent, the daughter of a Christian.

Marie, in what now seemed ages ago, had told Joseph about her argument with her parents. Her mother was particularly upset imagining her daughter being with him, listening to the criticism of her friends.

"What is it with you? So you met him at Harvard while you were at Radcliffe, my oldest daughter. I don't care if you talk to him but to become so friendly that you begin seeing one another, and we don't even know about it. That's more than I can allow, and you have to think of our position. Your father is a well-known lawyer."

"Mother, I'm not marrying him, and his family is medical. Isn't that important?" but she was thinking, *It sounds good, and if I can attract and get him, perhaps that will happen. She hasn't even met him yet.* "He's a nice man. I know you would like him. Besides, his mother is Episcopalian. Shouldn't that please you and father? He's only half of what you object to. Please, mother. I want you and father to at least meet him."

When Mrs. Lewis told her husband Caleb, he asked Marie to come to the parlor. She was, of course, apprehensive.

"I understand you are seeing a Jewish young man. You argued with your mother." He tried to be stern, but he loved his eldest daughter as his favorite. Of course he loved her two brothers and two sisters, but Marie, so intelligent and she had gone to a fine women's college and was now in his law firm.

"Now you tell me what is going on."

Marie was apprehensive but still started to break into a smile, watching him and the lack of sternness on his face and his eyes.

"Father, I met Joseph before he went to medical school. Now he is a resident. He's studying cardiology. Think of that."

"No, you just tell me what's going on. He's a Jew. Your mother won't have it. You know I have to support her."

She laughed. "Is this a court of law, father? I'm going to have to argue my case before the stern judge that you are."

He started to laugh also, but caught himself. "Well?"

"Father, I know how you and mother feel about religion, that you take it very seriously. But as I have said, he's only part Jewish."

Her father wanted to ask which part, imagining Marie seeing his circumcised part, hopefully he not having seen her between her thighs, or that they had not engaged in anything so intimate.

"We have talked about religion, but it has never stopped, well, my attraction to him or him to me. Father, mother must have told you his mother's beliefs. I don't know whether she still goes to church or not and don't care. You know very well that two people attracted to one another . . ." She wanted to tell him 'strongly attracted' and that she intended to try her hardest to make him wish for her forever. "Will continue to see one another and perhaps, who knows, marry. I expect that you will find he respects me for who I am. And don't forget, judge," she smiled unaware her father would soon be named a judge, "I am a lawyer who was graduated near the top of her class at Boston University. Imagine, father, a doctor and a lawyer."

Caleb watched Marie's eyes, saw tears forming. "I only wish mother would not be so prejudiced. I want you both to meet him. I'm willing to say you will like and care for him, that you will appreciate his intelligence; and I know you admire the profession in which he will soon take his place. We have talked about that. Mother pooh-poohs it, because of his religion. I FEEL it. Wouldn't you please talk to her and try to persuade her to at least meet Joseph. Please father," she ended, now fully crying. Mr. Lewis went to her bringing her into his arms.

"Shh, my lovely child, young woman, my oldest daughter."

Wiping at her eyes and her face with her father's pocket handkerchief, she looked up at him, "I can't help it, father. I just can't." She started to say, "I love him."

Of what they were both unaware was that toward the end of their discussion, her mother came into the room and heard.

"Marie, Caleb. I have some idea of what's been going on here. She looked at them also with tears. She wanted to apologize to Marie, partially did. "Marie, darling. I hate to see you cry." She gently, soothingly passed her hand across Marie's shoulders. "We'll invite him to dinner. All right? Let's meet this young man. Your youngest sister, Marilyn will be here."

"Oh mother. Thank you. You'll like him, I know it."

Upon meeting him, Deborah tried to hide her surprise seeing this young, handsome doctor, tall with observant green eyes, soft-spoken and so well mannered. Caleb shook his hand, welcoming him to their home.

It was Joseph who managed the meeting without awkwardness. As they ate and the conversation became one of what he and Marie did and politics that Caleb surprisingly brought up, each admiring President Theodore Roosevelt and his challenges to the monopolistic oil and railway companies, his brilliance and lack of fear evidenced in his desire to see that the government achieves the freedom of free enterprise.

There was no doubt that Joseph had made a good impression. As he thanked them for the lovely meal and exhilarating talk, Caleb and Deborah, practically in unison told him to come again. They watched as he chastely kissed Marie on the cheek and then walked to the auto his parents had bought for him and in which he had taken Marie for rides.

Caleb placed his arm about Marie's shoulders as they watched him depart. Marie then faced her parents after they closed the door, "Well, wasn't he all that I said?" she hoped, feeling her heart beat faster as she watched their expressions while awaiting their reply.

"Yes. He's a fine young man I have to admit," her mother hesitantly told her.

"Well he is," her father firmly said. "I like him. He isn't afraid to say what he thinks. He would make a fine lawyer." They all laughed.

"Where did he get the money for an auto?" her mother questioned, as they walked out.

"Moth . . .ther. Why do you ask that?" *She's thinking of him as a Jew with bags of money.*

"I'm just curious. Does he make a lot of money as a resident?"

"Certainly not!" Marie was trying not to show her anger. "Mother, his parents gave it to him as present when he started at the hospital."

"That's nice of them," she said as they walked to the

drawing room. She continued. "You really like this young man, don't you?"

"It's obvious. Mother. And don't deny it. You liked him." She laughed. "He'd be such an attentive son-in-law."

"Has he already asked you, you devilishly, scheming young lady. You are a lady and a lawyer. And don't you ever forget it. And don't you ever forget our place in society."

"Don't you think I know all that? What do you suppose their place is in their society and profession? I've heard about them from Joseph, of course."

Caleb interrupted. "Deborah, I said I like him. He would not be a blot on our standing, or my practice, even if he is half Jewish."

"Well," she blushed, "I wish he had a different last name."

"What, mother? Moses?"

Her father laughed. "Listen. Before we get all excited. Marie likes him, and I know now you do, dear. I could see it as we ate dinner. We'll just wait and see what happens."

"Thank you, daddy. Mommy, if he did propose to me, I'd accept him." Her face began to flush.

"Caleb, our daughter is in love."

Marie did not answer and asked if she could be excused. As she walked up to her room, Marilyn, stopped her. "Marie, I like him. He treated me like I was a grown young lady."

"You're a sweetie, Marilyn."

In her room, she lay on her bed, seeing Joseph, her breasts heaving as she breathed more quickly imagining him close to her, remembering their first kiss and how she enjoyed it. She felt it in her imagination and the way it warmed her to her core.

* * *

The night before they were to take the train to Portland, Joseph and Marie went to dinner. After, despite it being fairly early, he took her home.

"Joseph, would you like to come in for a while."

"Yes. I would. But before we go in, come closer. He placed his arm about her, leaning into her face, kissing her firmly, she responding, their tongues seeking.

"No more, sweet. Come in."

The family had heard his car stop. As the door opened, they disappeared upon seeing her with Joseph. Quietly she took him to the drawing room, having him sit close to her on the settee.

"Now you come here," she told him. She kissed him, hugging him tightly. "Ooh, that feels so good."

He slipped from his seat and fell to his knees. "Marie, I love you."

"I love you too, Joseph, have for a long time."

"Hold out your hand. No, your left." He was nervous. "Marie, I want you to be my wife."

"I would love that."

He pulled from his pocket the small package, knowing she was aware of what he was about to do. He showed her a ring with an emerald surrounded by small diamonds and placed it on her finger.

In her excitement, she at first held her breath, then felt her heart beating faster. "Joseph, it is so lovely." Her eyes filled with tears.

"I love you dearly, Marie. I can't wait until we marry."

She pulled him up to her, hugging and kissing him. "I'll be so proud to be your wife. I love you now and for always.

"Oh, Joseph, can I get my parents?"

"Of course."

She ran up the stairs to her parents' room, knocked. "Mother. Father. It's me, Marie."

The door opened. Deborah, saw her tear stained face. Wha..."

"Look." She held out her hand."

"Oh, my darling daughter. The ring is beautiful." She hugged Marie and started to call to Caleb, but he was already beside them.

"We're so happy for you, Marie," Caleb told her while also hugging her. "Is Joseph here?"

"Yes, He's downstairs."

They went to the drawing room. Joseph stood, watching them. Caleb shook his hand and Deborah asked, "May I hug you?" Her voice had a bit of coldness she could not hide as she asked, for she thought, *Her name will be Blumenthal. What will happen to her law practice? All her clients will be Jews. What Christians would have anything to do with her?* She was forgetting that his mother was a Christian, ignorant of the fact that Constance's patients were all types, white, black, Jew, Christian.

"Of course."

Caleb, listening, gave her a nudge. Realizing why, Deborah forced a softening. "Joseph, I had doubts about you two, but I don't any longer. We'll love you like another son."

The family that was still at home, Marilyn and their second oldest son Angus, ran to them, having heard the excitement.

"Look everyone." She held out her hand. "Joseph and I are to be married."

After the congratulations, Caleb told his family to leave the couple to enjoy each other's company.

* * *

The following day, late morning, they were on their way to Portland.

Millicent was at the station to meet them, enthralled by Marie's beauty, thinking a perfect match in looks for her handsome brother. She hugged him; and as soon as Joseph introduced Marie, Millicent hugged her, kissing her on the cheek. "Welcome to Portland and our family. I'm the ambassador," she told her smiling. "Mother is at home and father is at the hospital. She wanted to be certain all was ready. Ely will be home as soon as he gets free from the store. Aunt Esther and Joshua will come tomorrow, and Olivia and Alexander are going to try to be here by Saturday. Please don't be overwhelmed, Marie. We have heard so much about you that the whole family wants to meet you. Try not to be nervous." She hugged Marie again. "The family will love you. I know it."

Marie was nervous and held tightly to Joseph's hand, thinking of the new family she would be meeting, wondering how they would react to her. She was sure of herself but still could not help wondering about her pending mother and father in-law.

"Don't worry about a thing, Marie," he whispered to her. "We are a loving family who by circumstance have a few doctors but also someone in business."

Arriving at home, Constance met them, with a welcoming hug for Marie and Joseph as she kissed him on the cheek. Watching Marie, Constance not only beamed at the beautiful young woman but also knew she must be anxious.

"Marie, Joseph, come with me to the drawing room, Millicent following. Marie looking about when she first saw the home and then the entrance and now the well-appointed drawing room, was thinking how lovely and larger this home was than her own. She could feel the warmth.

They sat and talked, Constance taking the lead. As they watched one another, Benjamin suddenly entered, looking weary but pleased to see his son and Marie.

"So this is Marie." He too was taken by her looks, her smiling hazel eyes that caught his attention. "Joseph has written about you and your family. You are a lawyer. I think this city needs a female lawyer. Have you thought about it? At least I'm hoping you and Joseph have settled on where you will live and practice. Joseph has mentioned it to me."

"Yes, sir. I have and I know."

"Please. Call me father, for that is what I intend I'll soon be to you. If you wish you can say father Benjamin. But that seems awkward to me, almost like a priest. Oh," he laughed, "Are you Catholic?"

"No." She felt slightly hesitant answering this question. "I'm a Congregationalist. I hope . . ." She thought of him being Jewish. "I hope this is all right with you. I mean, my religion." She blushed thinking about Constance.

"Well, you see Mrs. Dr. Blumenthal. She's Episcopal. So you have something in common regarding Christianity. Marie, in this family we don't think about religion. It just is."

Marie managed a smile.

"Why don't I leave you with Constance, Joseph's mother, and you two can talk without me and the rest of us. I am truly pleased to meet you Marie and look forward to having you in the family."

After they had been left alone, Constance smiled. "Don't let him bother you at all, Marie. He is gentle and warm. In fact, I feel that way about all the family, hoping Ben and I have raised the children this way. I want you to be comfortable while you are here. Goodness, you haven't seen your room yet. Well you will. If you need anything or want to go shopping, either Millicent or Esther will take you to the stores. We have some good ones here." Constance laughed and Marie reacted happily to it, seeing in this woman a lack of pretense and a certainty about herself. She didn't know it yet, but Constance was beginning to think the same about her and liked it.

"You come from Cambridge and here I am talking about shopping. Would you mind telling me what you would enjoy while here?"

"Dr. Blumenthal . . . No. I mean mother." Both laughed. "I want you to know I feel quite welcome. I know now what it feels to be in a family of mixed religion and that there can be such evident love.

"I love Joseph dearly. I never thought I would meet someone like him. I suppose that sounds foolish, but it seemed to me that all the young men to whom my family introduced me were, well, not only Christian but just so dull by comparison. You know how we met." Marie now felt that she could tell Constance almost anything. "I'm sure Joseph has written about me, but truthfully, we began to meet secretly because of my parents. Oh, we never did anything, well wrong." She felt herself blush.

Constance reached for her hand. "You have not struck me that you would do anything untoward to catch any male, let alone Joseph. But we women," she gaily smiled, "have to watch these men. Marie, I believe you do love Joseph and also am aware of what you must have gone through with your family. I have some idea. His father and I, if he hasn't told you, married in Washington during the war, away from our families and secure in ourselves. You should feel that way, Marie. I know you will."

She rose and Marie followed. Constance reached to Marie and brought her into a warm hug, kissing her on the cheek. "Now it's time for you to have some relief for yourself. I'll have Millicent show you your room. Marie, I believe you and she will be close one day. She's very warm, truthfully more so than Esther who is also lovely. Don't get me wrong."

"I won't, mother. Thank you so much for talking with me."

Constance found Millicent in the parlor, her hands wrapped about herself, half asleep in the plush sofa, waiting for her mother and Marie. "Millicent, are you awake?"

She opened her eyes. "I'm not asleep, mother, just relaxing."

"Would you take Marie to her room so she can relax? She probably also wants to put away her clothes."

"Of course." Marie followed Millicent up the stairs, Millicent every so often turning to talk to her. "You'll like your room. It used to be mine, but my parents have done things to it to bring it more up to date."

Entering, Marie noticed first the double bed and went to it and sat. "It's so soft. And what beautiful covers." She noticed some pictures on the walls that Millicent had left. She rose and went to the large, carved armoire. "Oh that will be plenty of space."

Millicent touched her shoulder. "Now let me show you how they changed it. Once upon a time there were only three bathrooms, one for my sister and me, one for my brother, and, of course, my parents had one. But look now. Here's your own. It also has a shower."

"Millicent, it's so lovely. I'd love to have a shower and then lie down for a while. It's been a bit trying meeting everyone. I was nervous."

"Marie. You seem like you're over that." Millicent reached for her and kissed her lightly on the lips, and Marie, surprised, responded. "Thank you, Millicent. Everyone is so good to me."

"Well, why not? We liked you almost immediately. I do hope you will come to Portland to live. I know it's not Boston, but we have lots of sites, and, of course, the beaches, and," she softly said, smiling, "some secret coves where you can go to be almost alone."

"Hmm. That sounds like you've been there and snuggled," she laughed."

Millicent joined her in her own laughter. "Well, why not? You're wicked, Marie. I bet Joseph will take you. Or," and she was laughing, "if he doesn't, tell him you want to go. You deserve time to yourselves." She thought of Olivia. "Marie, you are going to love my sister. She's still my best friend, and I think," and she looked intently into Marie's bright hazel eyes, "I believe the three of us will get along like loving sisters. I can see that in you."

Marie's voice was almost a whisper, feeling tears coming to

the backs of her eyes until Millicent noticed them appear, Marie blinking to hold them back, then wiping slightly. "I love it here and the family. Your mother and father are so dear. So are you." Her tears were now quite visible.

Millicent drew her close, hugging her. "I'm not going to wait until your wedding to call you sister. You already are." Now they were both crying and hugging. Millicent backed away, wiping at her face. "You go have a shower and a good rest until dinner.

"Pamela, the maid and cook, you met her, may come to get you. But knowing mother, she may want to. Joyce used to be our maid. She was a wonder. She lives in the small house behind us that mother and father had built for her. My, we sound like we have scads of money. We're just normal people."

"I know, Millicent. Anyone should be able to see that. Well, I am a bit sleepy and do want to shower. Thank you, Millicent for being so good to me."

"It's easy with you, Marie. Now make the room your own."

Marie lay in the bed, closing her eyes thinking, *How fortunate I am to soon be part of this family. They are all so loving, so kind, so easy to be with and to talk to.* After a bit, she rose and went to the shower, relaxing under the warm spray.

On Saturday, Olivia and Alexander arrived. Marie waited upstairs until the family greeted one another. Constance looked around. "Where's Marie?"

"Mother, I think she's waiting, doesn't feel as though she should interrupt us yet," Millicent told her.

Constance turned to Olivia. "You go and get her. Tell her we expect her for family gatherings. Please bring her down. She's in yours and Millicent's old room."

"Olivia," Millicent interrupted. "It's not old. See how mother and father changed it, well after you meet Marie and before bringing her down."

"I'll get her mother," Joseph interrupted. "After all, she's my fiancée."

"Well, go get her," Benjamin told him.

Joseph ran up the stairs. He gently knocked on the door. "Marie."

As she opened the door, he pulled her toward him, warmly kissing her. "Darling, mother and father want you downstairs to meet Olivia and Alexander. You are part of the family now, and don't forget it," he smiled. He looked more intently at her. "You are beautiful, Marie. Your hair looks lovely, and I love your dress. Come now. Don't be shy."

"I thought I might be interfering. And Joseph, I am definitely not shy."

"Come on. Everyone's waiting for you."

As they entered the parlor, Benjamin stood and hugged her before introducing her to Olivia and Alex. On seeing her he was stunned by her beauty, comparing her to Olivia, thinking, though exaggerating, *She's more beautiful. What a girl. That's what you find in Boston, and Olivia wants me to move.*

Olivia went to her, also hugging her. The two women stood close, appraising one another, blue eyes intently looking into hazel, both aware they could be friends. Olivia whispered to her, "We have to get away by ourselves so we can talk and get to know one another. Wait just a bit. I have to make a date with my husband to show him the city. Have you seen it?"

"Well, Joseph has shown me some and wants to take me to a beach."

"That can wait until later. Do you mind? I do want to know you."

"Me too." She was smiling and soon talkative to Benjamin and Constance and everyone else. She brought the family into her heart and they into theirs.

On Sunday, she asked Constance, "Would you mind if I went to Church?"

"Of course not. Which one?"

"Congregational. And mother, I won't ever force Joseph to go. That's up to him. I'm not particularly religious, but today, it just seems I should. I have so much to be thankful for. I do believe in God and want to thank him for the way I feel."

"Come here, Marie." As she moved to her, Constance took her in her arms, kissed her lightly on her lips, telling her, "Darling. You are free in this family to do what you wish. I just know you will be a wonderful wife. Joseph is very fortunate. He's like his father in many ways and will make certain, I know, that you are happy." Both women now had tears.

Olivia happened into the room. Seeing them she asked, of course, what was happening. When told, she spoke to Marie, "Would you mind if I went with you? I'm not a church goer, don't even know yet what religion I would follow, if any. I'd just like to accompany you. We can go either to Cape Elizabeth or South Portland. And, believe it or not, being modern, I drive. Of course, we could ask Andrew and be ladies of class."

"I would love to have you with me."

"Shall I ask Millicent?"

"If you wish."

She went to find Millicent. "Mill, Marie and I are going to church. Want to come?"

"I'd like to go with you, but I don't know how Ely would take it. Oh bother. That's his problem." She paused. "He may be angry when he finds out. It won't be the first time," she laughed. "The three of us will go. I'll get dressed properly and we'll be off."

Watching Marie, the sisters both crossed themselves, then sat in the pew praying with the congregation, listened to the sermon after which they decided they would have lunch. Olivia called home and told Constance who was pleased that they were all becoming friends.

Upon coming home, Alexander took Olivia aside. "What's going on?"

"Going on?" She laughed. "We were looking for men who wanted a good time."

"Be serious, Olivia. You may be the practicing doctor, but you're still my wife."

"Alex. Calm down. We went to church with Marie and then had lunch."

"You went without telling me?"

"Was it necessary? Mother or father could let you know. Or didn't you think to ask?"

"Ask, you say? You leave without telling me. And you go to a church with ... because Marie forced you to."

"Alex, you apologize. I won't stand for this nonsense. We are three women who enjoy one another's company."

"Church? What the hell do you call that? Now you're into Christianity."

"You hold your mouth. My mother is a Christian. Don't you ever forget it."

"She doesn't flaunt it"

"Flaunt? No one in my family flaunts anything." Angrily, she turned from him and ran upstairs to their room, locking the door.

After he was able to get Olivia to open the door, still angry, her face wet with tears, she hoarsely asked, "What?"

Softly he told her, "I want to apologize. I shouldn't have lost my temper. I love your family, Olivia. Please forgive me. I'll try not to lose my temper like that. You already know I have one. But I've never turned it on you, have I?"

"No you haven't, but you did a damn good example of it downstairs. I refuse to forgive an insult to my family and me." She started to push him out the door.

"Olivia. Please," he seemed to beg. "I love you. I don't want us to fight like this."

Wiping at her face, she stepped back a bit as he put out his arms.

"Please, Olivia. We won't fight like this again. I was wrong."

"You most certainly were," as she weakened a little.

He reached for her, kissing her, trying to lead her to the bed. She allowed him to do so. As they sat, he placed his arms about her. "I was wrong. Forgive me."

She managed a smile. "All right. We shouldn't fight, but we probably should expect to," her voice low, but suddenly suspicious, thinking of the way he looked at Marie. *I am not a jealous woman, but the way he stared at Marie, my future sister-in-law. Olivia, get hold of yourself. Forgive him.*

The following day, after Joseph and Marie left to tears of happiness, Olivia told Alexander she wanted to show him the city. He said he would drive, that they shouldn't bother Andrew who was working in the garden.

"No. Please let's ask him. I want to show you the sights."

"All right."

Andrew drove through the main part of the city where she pointed out Esther's and Millicent's husbands' store expansions and other city stores, telling him about the Great Fire and stories about the Revolution as they saw the Observation Tower. Andrew then drove them to Cape Elizabeth and the Fort William Head Lighthouse where they watched the rising wind blowing white crests beating against the rocks. As Alexander had looked about and even was affected by the ocean's angry seas, he saw little that could ever be like either Boston or Philadelphia. Even after he had been to the hospital with Benjamin, he wondered whether he could get the same kind of training. He wanted to be the best of surgeons, and Boston was the place for that kind of training, if it wasn't to be Philadelphia.

He barely said anything as Olivia talked, making only occasional remarks such as, "That's nice" or "That's interesting." *It is a hick town. She talks about the Revolution. I come from Philadelphia. I wonder if I can get her to change her mind and live in Boston as a compromise.*

Arriving home, but alone and before they entered the house,

the wind rising, she asked, "Well, wasn't that a nice tour? You've seen our history and how the city is growing." Then, thinking back to the fight over attending church, she told him, "You can attend the synagogue, join, if you wish." However, noticing a sour look on his face, she paused, then not wanting another quarrel, she pleasantly asked, "What's wrong. Alex?"

"Well, now don't get angry, but couldn't we settle in Boston? It would be good for both of us. You have started a practice and I'm almost finished. We could practice together like your mother and father."

She felt distress, aware of his disdain. She hesitated before saying anything. "Alex, we agreed that we would come here where you would finish your training, and I would take my mother's place. And" . . . hesitating, "Where we could raise our children."

"Well, is that so important to take your mother's place, or for that matter, for me to be there when your father retires?"

"Don't you have any feeling for what I believe we should do? I love it here, as you well know. I'm repeating myself, but this is a good, safe and beautiful place to raise our children."

He laughed. "How many are you counting on having?"

She glared at him, her eyes burning with scorn, "A dozen, you bastard. Fuck you, Alex, for breaking your promise to me, for complaining about everything from my family to where we said we'd practice. There are so many poor here that need help. Just fuck you, Boston, Philadelphia, and your ego. And yes," she hadn't told him yet, "I'm already pregnant. I hope my son or daughter doesn't grow up to be a beguiler."

"Are you accusing me?"

"I married you because I saw in you not only that handsome face but a fair minded, honest man." She thought, becoming furious, but forcing herself to hold back some, "You don't even think about what I just said. I'm having a baby, Alex. A baby. I want it to grow up loving and trustworthy, male or female, not deceitful." She was thinking back to some of the females she had met in school who could never be trusted, who used their looks and their figures, their bodies even, to gain who and what they desired.

"Now I am a liar, deceitful, and just plain rotten. You go to hell, Olivia. And don't think that child inside you is just yours."

By now her face red with fury and disappointment, she sobbed. "I never . . . never thought our marriage would come to this. I have loved you with all my being. I still love you. Damn I love you, Alexander. Do you hear me? This is not a marriage carrying on like this. This is a living hell." She sobbed more loudly, her eyes burning, her face streaked with tears.

He tried to calm her. "I do love you, Olivia. Believe me I do. I want this child as much as you. You certainly did surprise me."

She had taken off her hat at Fort Williams. Now she brushed at her hair, some of which had fallen to her eyes. She looked up at him, "I am so pleased to be pregnant and wanted the telling to you to be such a happy occasion. But how you heard, now it's ruined. I meant it to be a surprise of happiness." She cried more, bending her head again, unable to look at him, hurt not only by their fight but how in anger she had announced her pregnancy, using it as a tool against his lies and selfishness.

"Olivia, I can't stand seeing you like this. I want us to be happy and loving as we have been." He sighed, "We will settle here. I'll be fine. Please believe me. I understand how you have wanted to follow your mother. I will be a good son to your father and learn from him."

"Are you sure?" she muttered.

Uncomfortably, he forced an impressive, "Yes."

Although Olivia was still uncertain, she turned and reached to kiss him, holding tightly to him. "I don't want to argue so hurtfully for both of us. We'll be happy here. I just know it, Alex. Please believe me. And our child. Think of it. The wonder of our own child."

"Now don't keep anything secret about how you feel during your pregnancy."

"I won't. We have to tell the family."

When they entered the house, she called to Constance and Benjamin. "Mother and father, I am pregnant. I'm so happy."

"My love," Constance said while hugging her. Turning to Benjamin, "Ben, we're going to be grandparents again." Benjamin hugged Olivia and reached out his hand to Alexander. "What a happy occasion this will be. When, Olivia?"

"January I think. It should be about then."

Constance looked at her. "I thought you were hiding it. I heard you in the bathroom once as I walked by."

"Well, I have had my mornings and have tried to hide it until I was ready to let you all know. I told Alex today," looking at him with his slight smile, "and then knew I would tell father and you at dinner."

"We'll have a celebratory dinner tonight for you and Joseph and Marie."

"Mother, please let me tell everyone, all right?"

"Of course, darling. Millicent will be ecstatic, as I believe will your aunts. The family is growing so. I am so pleased. Look at your father. See the pride in his face?"

"You said it. And I'll have the father working with me in the not too distant future."

"Yes, father," he answered unemotionally.

Olivia apprehensively glanced at him but said nothing. Her thoughts now were on the child growing within her and the happiness she felt. Nothing would interfere with her desire eventually to hold her newborn child, alone, if necessary, without Alexander. She hid her uneasiness, forced back her smile for everyone. At dinner, she was more herself. There was uninterrupted talk around the table, Benjamin talking to Alexander about his coming eventually to practice with him,

Constance and Olivia smiling as Constance told her she wanted to be with her when the child came. They also, of course, talked about the coming wedding.

* * *

In late June, the wedding between Marie and Joseph occurred. Her gown was white, her shoulders bare, her full breasts apparent, the train long flowing held by her young cousins while Marilyn was her Maid Of Honor. Her parents decided they would hold the reception in Cambridge where the bride and groom would be staying. It had also been settled by Marie and Joseph that she would continue practice with her father until Joseph finished his training as a cardiologist in 1908, after which they would move to Portland where Benjamin had talked to several lawyers who wanted Marie to practice with them. She had her choice, for they were anxious to have a woman who would attract female clients.

———————————————

Chapter Three

Apprehension and Transition

Near the beginning of January, 1908, Olivia went into a difficult labor. Constance was reminded of what her mother had said and why she never again could have another child. Frightened by her thoughts, she asked Olivia and the doctor if it would be all right for her to be with her daughter during the labor.

"Of course, mother," Olivia weakly answered, her face revealing the last of the previous pain. Constance wiped her sweaty forehead.

"Mother, it's wretched."

"I know dear. Try to relax a bit now and take deep breaths."

The labor went on for about eight hours, the pain wracking her body. Finally her cervix expanded sufficiently to show the head. The doctor decided she would have to use forceps, because she could not reach the baby with her hands. The birth canal was sufficiently wide for such a delivery. After hearing what seemed an eternity of "Push," finally Olivia gave one with the doctor reaching with her forceps. The baby emerged at six pounds. After being slapped, Olivia heard the cry. She had given birth, a slight smile on her perspiring face.

"You have a boy," Dr. Levine. She had changed her name on marriage, knowing she would be known at home as either Blumenthal or Levine.

Weakly she looked as the nurse handed her the child. "Look, mother. It's mine. I did it."

"Yes dear you did. He's going to be handsome like his father and grandfather."

Olivia tried to laugh while watching her mother's hands trembling, perspiration on her forehead.

Alexander finally saw the child, asking Olivia what they should name him. 'I'd like to name him after my great grandfathers: Nathaniel Asa. I know Nathaniel doesn't sound Jewish, but Alex, dear, this *is* the 20th Century." She smiled.

"That's fine, Olivia. That is his name. Nathaniel Asa Levine."

* * *

A year after their wedding, Marie and Joseph prepared to leave for Portland. Marie was tearful for a day thinking of leaving her parents behind even though she had lived separately with Joseph for the year. It was a happy marriage the way he was always considerate of her feelings and her desire to excel at law. She did. In fact a client with a business that she had helped, told her he would follow her to Portland, for she was keeping her Massachusetts license and already had passed the bar in Maine. As a matter of fact Joseph had already taken his license examination for Maine. However, he had been in the Boston area for so many years now, he was tempted to stay. They had a home for which she had insisted that her father allow her to pay a large portion, although her mother and father wanted them to have it as part of their wedding gift along with the Blumenthals. Homes seem to have become a habit as a gift by Benjamin and Constance. This aside, with her salary, Marie and Joseph had been able to employ a maid, Mary Ann. They insisted that she come with them.

"I can't do that, Mrs. Blumenthal. It's my mother. My brothers give money but now have their own families, so I promised to help also. So, you see, I have to do my share so she can get by. You remember my dad died when I was 13, hit by a train where he worked. And how would it be if I leave her alone. I can't even bear to think of it. My sister went away with her man."

"First of all, Mary Ann, I told you could call me Marie." She laughed. "Even Ma'am. Think of all the Ms that we can have. We make a poem. Anyhow, we could take your mother."

Mary Ann smiled. "Would you really take my mom with us? If that happened . . . of course, I don't know if she would leave here. She came over with my dad and three of my brothers, as you know, from Liverpool, where they worked the docks. My dad hated it, even though my mom and he grew up there. Now my brothers work for the railroad. My poor dad was killed when that train hit him," she repeated, tears forming at which she wiped with the back of her hand. "I guess there is enough money for my mom without me." She laughed. "And then they had me over here in Boston, and then another sister. Was I happy." Tears again appeared, but she had a harder time wiping at them thinking of her sister. "Well, I'll talk to my mom and ask if she would leave here." She thought some more. *It would be an adventure to stay with the Blumenthals and live in Maine.* "I'll go," she blurted.

"Wonderful. You tell your mother what we talked about. Just think. A new home." Marie was now happier about leaving, she, too, thinking of the challenge of Portland. But she had a loving husband and one to whom she had given her heart unwaveringly.

One day, after finishing his rotation and having been taken to be mentored by one of the senior cardiologists, he came home, perplexed. What was he to tell Dr. Kendall after his friendliness and help? Perhaps he may have been able to join his practice later. So?

"Joseph, you look perplexed," Marie told him as she greeted him with a hug and kiss, smiling, because she wanted to tell him about Mary Ann.

"I was thinking. I am so anxious to go back to Portland, but

Dr. Kendall has been so kind to me."

"It's not a problem, dear. He has been a friend and a teacher. You are a better doctor for it. But we have decided. Don't tell me you're hesitating. You sound like Mary Ann. Joseph, she's coming with us. I persuaded her. I also told she could take her mother to work for us, if her mother will leave. I am so happy. Now look at your face. Poor child. We are going to Portland. I have already three choices of a position, thanks to your dad, as you know. And imagine. So do you have it made there?"

He now laughed. "My father will be overjoyed, as will mother. And they'll have you as a legal advisor. I do have to tell Dr. Kendall I'm going home to practice with my father, Olivia, and Alexander. You know, I talked to him on the phone, and his voice sounded sort of strange, like a hesitation when I said, "Think, we'll all be together." And he answered rather faintly, 'Hmm, yes.' What's bothering him? You know. Sometimes I think he has superiority complex. Like Portland isn't good enough for his skills. Bull shit."

"Listen. Come into the drawing room where we can be comfortable and close. I've wanted to be near you all day. Come on." She put out her hand and grasped his tightly pulling him gently along. She then closed the door and kissed him firmly, her tongue seeking his. He answered with his, listening to her slight, loving moan. Moving undesirably back, she looked at him. "You swore," as she pulled him to the settee. "Do you know what I'd like right now?"

He smiled. "I think I do."

"But tell me. Are you certain of his reaction?"

"Yes. You know, he may be a nice fellow, but, Marie, he bothers me. Olivia and he seem happy together, but the way he talked."

"Stop, Joseph."

"I know. But has Olivia said anything to you?"

"No. I believe if there were anything she would tell me. You know how close she, Millicent, and I have become. We're friends who confide in one another. They make me feel so comfortable and welcome."

They moved soon after the conversation and settled near Constance and Benjamin. Now the entire family was in Portland. Benjamin came home for dinner one evening, and when greeted by Constance he was laughing.

"Now what happened that is so funny?"

"I was told this afternoon by a patient that our family not only was taking over the medical profession but that now we have started on law. Not only that, he told me we had a compound, having heard we live fairly close to one another."

Constance smiled. "A curious fellow, isn't he? Does he need a lawyer? If he does, be sure to refer him to Marie."

"You know, poor fellow, he has a pancreatic cancer. I thought I would refer him to Alexander because I'll be retiring soon. I want to lay back and just work as a consultant."

"That's not a bad idea. Why are we standing in the hall? Go get ready for dinner."

Thinking of the growing family. Constance thought back to their marriage during the Civil War. *The hell, the wounded, the dead, all those limbs amputated and thrown about like so much garbage, though it wasn't meant that way. The noise of Gettysburg. My goodness, how we ever got through that.* She laughed. *That day Ben came to our home wanting to paint. I fell in love with him that day. My parents would have been horrified at what I was thinking. And my mother's prejudice. Now look at us. Christians and Jews in one family. Marie. What a beauty. Her practice is going to grow not because of her looks but because of her brain. She may prove to be smarter than any of the males with whom she chooses to work.*

Benjamin, after a shower and change of clothes came down ready for dinner. Joyce started to serve as soon as they sat.

"As I started to say before dinner, I'm going to retire next year. I'll be 68. As I also said, I referred the patient to Alexander. He has a good manner about him and seems to be a competent surgeon. I just hope he gets along with Joseph. Joseph seems to have a problem with him but doesn't say anything."

"Perhaps you're imagining that, dear. Let's forget the clinic and hospital and enjoy this meal and the evening."

The following day, Marie chose the lawyers with whom she would work. They were happy to have her, although they knew there still was prejudice among men especially but also women being appalled that a woman would practice law.

She waited for Joseph to tell him she would be in downtown Portland. It meant that they might need another auto or Andrew could drive her. It was a minor problem except for the cost. However, she had her own money that she earned practicing with her father who also had put aside funds for her in a trust. Although Joseph had changed to Buick, she would buy a Ford. They both tried not to bother Andrew who cared for three gardens, those of Benjamin and Constance, the others of Olivia and Joseph when he had time. Marie loved working in the garden and gave as much time as possible to it.

In her law practice she specialized in Tort cases. Now with automobiles and lacking the best of roads, a woman, Marie's first case, hobbled in one day asking if she could have an appointment with Marie. Her friends had told her not to use a woman who should be taking care of her home and not working among men. The woman, Mrs. Dorothy Able, a suffragette, told them to mind their own business and to learn that women had brains that should be used. She often wondered that many of her neighbors even talked to her because of her views.

She received an almost prompt appointment. The secretary led Mrs. Able to Marie. She was immediately impressed by the tall, blonde, hazel-eyed woman dressed in a black suit and white blouse who came from behind her desk to greet her with a thin attractive hand she held out in greeting. Dorothy grasped her hand, then took an offered seat.

"Mrs. Blumenthal," she thought. She's not Jewish looking, "I

346

had an accident as you can see from the way I walk, and my young son is still in the hospital with a broken leg. I am wondering what I can do to get expenses for what happened that was not my fault."

In a soft, encouraging voice, Marie answered, "Tell me exactly what happened and where this mishap took place."

"I was crossing Munjoy Hill, my son sitting beside me in our horse and wagon. Well, you know the tracks there and the hilly road. Well, an automobile came rushing down the hill as though the driver could not stop it and crashed into us. He wrecked my carriage and killed my horse, beside the injuries to my son and me."

"Mrs. Able, when did this happen?"

"Two weeks ago. It was just horrible, my son screaming in pain, the fright, and my poor horse. And my carriage is just a wreck. My husband is not the richest man in the world, but he has provided well for us. He has a store in Middle Street."

"Did you get the name and address of the driver?"

"I did. He was angry about his car. I wondered if he cared more for that automobile than what happened to us. I'm weary of these men who think they are so superior and that nothing is ever their fault."

"Now, Mrs. Able," Marie softly told her, "I know about your work on Women's Suffrage and admire it, but tell me anything else about the accident. Then I will ask some questions."

"Well, he seemed to be coming down very fast. I was going to ride up Congress Street but never got there. Instead he wrecked us. I tried to get information from him, his name, for example, that he gave me. George Fuller. He was yelling at me, telling me it was my fault, my carelessness. "And what's your name?" he demanded. I told him as I shook and cried about my son who was screaming in pain. He's a child, just 6 years old. You should have seen the expression on his face . . .' She hesitated, thinking of her son and his scream when he saw the auto coming at them and then crying in pain. Tearfully she continued, "Being a Saturday, he had no school. He wanted to go for the ride. Some ride. Now he's in the hospital. I go to see him all the time."

"Where does this George Fuller live? Did you get his address?"

"All he told me was that he lived in Cape Elizabeth. He must be rich."

"Then what?"

"I screamed for an ambulance. That man. He tried to back up his car and get away. Finally he was able to disengage the car from the wreckage and drove off. I hate him. I got someone to call for an ambulance that came and took my son to the Maine General Hospital."

Marie listened politely, interrupting only when necessary.

"Is there anything else I should know, for example, what happened in the ambulance? What about your limp? Tell me about your son."

"Will all this help me?"

"I hope so. I have to determine if there is a case. Right now it seems so. Then we'll have to find this man Fuller."

"Well, they put a splint on my son's leg. They looked at me and told me I had a serious sprain. But they would make certain at the hospital. They took X-Rays of my son and me. That is when they were certain he broke his leg and that I did not. But the money, Mrs. Blumenthal. It costs so much. It's hard on us." She tried to hold back but began to cry.

Marie put out her hand and ran hers soothingly over the back of Mrs. Able's, having moved her chair to be closer to her client.

"Now, Mrs. Able, there. Try not to get too upset." Having said that, Marie felt foolish. "Mrs. Able," she spoke softly and soothingly, feeling terrible for the woman, wondering how she would react if it were a child of hers. "Mrs. Able, do you have a telephone?"

She nodded her head up and down, trying to stifle her tears. She sniffed. "Yes, Mrs. Blumenthal, we do."

"Now I'll tell you what we are going to do. I am going to locate Mr. Fuller and try to speak to him. Perhaps he'll come see me. I will want your hospital bills."

"Then what will happen?"

"I'll ask Mr. Fuller to pay your bills and perhaps ask for more for damages to your carriage, and for my fee." She would take a small percentage of the damages, if there were any. Otherwise she decided she would ask for nothing. She thought now of Olivia with her poor patients. "You leave your address and phone number with my secretary. All right? Then I'll be in touch with you."

"Thank you so much. I am so glad you are a woman. You understand the way a man can't."

Marie smiled. "Well, let's see what happens. I won't promise. I'll do my best and be in touch." She helped Mrs. Able from the chair and went with her to the secretary. "As I said, we'll be in touch."

Within a few days, Marie with the help of her secretary, Agnes, located Mr. Fuller. Marie talked to him.

"Yes." He was polite answering."

"Mr. Fuller, I am Marie Blumenthal representing Mrs. Able, the woman with whom you had the accident on Congress Street."

My God. A damn Jew. Wouldn't you know it? "What do you think you want from me?" his voice now gruff.

"Mr. Fuller, would you be willing to come to my office and talk to me, or would you rather speak on the phone."

"It was her fault," he practically hollered. "That damn woman should have watched where she was going."

Forcing her patience, Marie said, "Mr. Fuller, please do not swear. I would like to settle this amicably."

"I don't care to see you. We can talk now and get it over with."

Is this what Cape Elizabeth does to people? They think they are special. "I'll be happy to talk to you now."

"NO. I am very busy. You called my business number."

Telling herself, patience and quiet, Marie answered. "I can wait until you are at home, if you won't come to see me."

"Forget it. I want nothing to do with this."

"Mr. Fuller. Being a businessman, I'm sure you don't want anything unpleasant. Neither do I. I just want you to understand Mrs. Able's side."

"Yeah. And how much money does she want?"

Marie was losing her patience with this hateful man. "Mr. Fuller, If we can't talk amicably and settle Mrs. Able's claim, then it will be in court."

"Then take me to court. That woman was at fault. That's all I have to say. You women think you're so big these days. You all belong at home."

"Mr. Fuller." Marie raised her voice. "Please do not talk to me that way. From what I know of your business, you have women coming into your store to purchase your upscale clothing."

"So you think I will pay an absurd amount. Take me to court." He slammed down his phone.

"That fool," Marie told herself. She called in Agnes who came in with a smile until she saw Marie's angry face. "Mrs. Blumenthal, I believe there's trouble."

"Agnes, I told you. Call me Marie. Anyhow, we have trouble. We're going to court and will be getting a subpoena to force him to face us. Let's see what happens. We'll also need the X-Rays. I presume Mr. and Mrs. Able will both be in court, if they care to."

"This isn't your first court case, Marie," Agnes said with a smile.

"No. I've been in court in Massachusetts when I was with my father's firm. I'll ask my husband to recommend a doctor, in case we need one. The way Fuller talked, it would probably be a good idea."

Several weeks passed until a court date came. Agnes called and spoke to Mrs. Able and asked her to come to the office to see Mrs. Blumenthal. If her husband was available it would be good to have him accompany her. Also, she should bring her son, for Mrs. Blumenthal wants to meet him.

When they did appear in the District Court, Mr. Fuller sent his lawyer. After some discussion by both sides, Marie had the doctor present the X-Rays, telling the judge that it was a fractured leg.

"May I see that, Doctor?" the judge asked. "Now tell me, in your opinion, how bad this fracture is."

"The boy was in hospital, in the Children's Section, of course. He was in extreme pain until we splinted the fracture and gave him some medication. After a week, his physician felt it was time for him to go home."

"Thank you, doctor, you may leave the stand." He hesitated, then continued. "After listening to all of the evidence, I find that Mr. Fuller was at fault, that he should pay for the boy's treatment and hospitalization, that he further pay for Mrs. Able's injury and her treatment, and further still, that the plaintiff be reimbursed for her carriage destruction and all damages."

"Your Honor, sir," the defending lawyer rose. 'I believe that we never actually determined who caused the accident."

"Mrs. Blumenthal laid out what occurred and the result being the accident for which I found Mr. Fuller at fault. The objection is overruled."

There were smiles on the faces of the Able family, as well as on those of Marie and Agnes.

Following the trial, the newspaper, of course, ran an article that reflected well not only on Marie but on her firm. At home there was a celebration of Marie's victory.

Her practice then spread throughout Southern Maine and, of course, reflected well upon the firm of which she was a member.

* * *

Coming toward the end of 1908, Marie told Joseph she was finally pregnant. "I believe the child will be born in July by my count. I didn't want to say anything except that my morning sickness is starting. I felt sick this morning and tried to get out of bed without waking you. Joseph, I hope you're as happy as I."

"You know I am. I am so pleased for us." He hugged and kissed her.

"Well, wait until the men at the office know. They'll probably want me to leave."

"It seems to me they have seen pregnant women before. Why should that interfere with your work?'

"You know how prejudiced people are about women in professions, especially when they are pregnant." She laughed. "I think they better keep me now. Think of the business I've brought the firm."

"You'll be all right." He laughed also. "Ask them if they want a note from the doctor?"

"Joseph, I'm so happy."

After this conversation, within a few weeks, Marie invited Olivia and Alexander, as well as Benjamin and Constance, to dinner. She knew that Olivia would not look after her but wanted her to suggest a colleague. Before dinner, she told them. The excitement in the room among the women hardly ever stopped.

"Think of it. We're producing cousins," Olivia told

everyone.

Constance's concern was that she and Benjamin knew, so she asked. "Have you told your parents?"

"Of course, I phoned. They were so excited and happy. They'll be here for the birth. I also promised I'd keep in touch during the pregnancy."

Joseph at some point, and then at others, watched Alexander, wondering whether he should be so suspicious of him. After all, they practiced together along with Olivia. He was a good surgeon who pleased almost everyone. *I think I'm being paranoid.*

So the happy meal went. Then in 1909, Marie had her child, a girl, 5 pounds. It was a rather easy birth. They named her Sandra May. As her eyes changed they became grey and her hair red. She was lovely like her mother.

The following year, 1910, Olivia was pregnant again and would have her second child by November. As she grew larger, she began to think perhaps she would take off some time and enjoy herself and the thought of another child. Meanwhile she noticed that Alexander was coming home later and later.

"Alex, are you that busy now that you are home so late every night?"

"Of course, Olivia. You know my practice has grown," he smiled. "I've become one of the most popular general surgeons in the state, no less."

"Stop that bragging. You mean there are no other surgeons in the state?"

"Of course there are. But I told you a long time ago I would be good, that I'd make myself that way by study, observation, and my own work."

"I still think you're becoming a braggart."

Angry, his voice louder, "I am not. You ought to be proud of me. I told you I would need" . . . "well, that we should be in Boston, but now I wonder."

"Oh, you've become a Mainer. You poor boy. Damn you, come here and kiss me and stop feeling sorry for yourself for not being in Boston or Philadelphia. You have a good life and practice here."

He bent over her and lightly kissed her lips. At the same time, Olivia smelled an odor, thinking, *a perfumed soap? Perfume definitely.* She shook her head.

Noticing the look on her face, he suddenly told her, "I'm going up and take a shower. I left the hospital in a hurry. I do need one. Would you have Ellen get me something to eat, though I'm not too hungry."

"Alex, it's 10 p.m. You've had nothing, no supper?"

"No, dear, well, just something I grabbed earlier in the cafeteria." he shouted back as he ran up the stairs. "I'll have Ellen put these smelly clothes in the wash."

"His smelly clothes. I guess." She cringed, felt tears forming and forced them back. *That odor was perfume. He's been seeing someone. The larger I get, the less I see him. I'll call Marie.* She rose from her chair, looked toward the stairway and went to the phone. Joseph answered.

"Joseph . . ."

"Olivia, it's getting late. Why aren't you resting?"

"Joseph, don't worry about me resting. I know I've been told to, but I also know a few things, remember?" she laughed.

"I guess you do. What's up?"

"Is Marie available?"

"I'll get her."

"Please do," as she glanced toward the door of the library.

"Is there something wrong?"

"Joseph, please. Just get her."

Soon Marie was on the phone. "Olivia, hi."

"Marie." Her tears started. "Marie," as she wiped at her cheeks, "I think Alex is having an affair."

"Olivia," surprise in her voice. "What makes you so sure?"

"Marie, I can't stand this. I'm certain I smelled perfume on him, and it isn't mine."

"Do you want me to come over?"

"Well, not now. It's getting late. Tomorrow?"

"I'll be there, say about 11, and we'll have lunch together. O.K?"

"That would be fine."

"You'll be all right tonight?"

"Yes. See you tomorrow. Goodnight. I love you, Marie."

"I love you too. Try to sleep. The doctor told you to rest."

"Yes, Joseph told me that too, before he got you." She forced a laugh. "I better hang up. I think I hear Alex."

"Hi dear. Were you on the phone?"

He looked at her suspiciously. "Who were you talking to?"

"Marie. Now that's enough questions."

"Well, you know you ought to be in bed by now. The doctor said you have to rest."

"Everyone is telling me that. I'm weary of hearing it." She rasped, hiding her anger and suspicion. "I do know a little bit about babies. Remember?"

He forced a laugh. "Oh, you're your own ob/gyn now."

"Keep quiet. You do look better now that you took your shower, a little more rested. You ought to take it easy," unable at last to avoid her sarcasm.

"Well, perhaps. I'll try."

"Try harder." She felt her face growing red, thinking of another woman. "I think you're right. I'm going up to bed."

She couldn't help herself. "I did a bit of shopping today, bought a new perfume," she lied. "It did tire me. You do whatever. I may be asleep when you come up."

She walked slowly up the stairs, her eyes tearing again. *He's having an affair. I just know it. Goddamn. I won't stand for it if I find out I'm right.* When she got to the bed, she put her face to her pillow, suddenly crying, her pillow becoming wet. She threw it on the floor, deciding she would sleep with the one she usually kept below her head. Finally she fell asleep. It was a restless night. She rose early to make sure Nathaniel was all right. She smiled. He was growing, now two years old. She ran her hand softly over his hair not wanting to wake him, "I love you so, Nathaniel." Instead of returning to bed, she went downstairs and made herself coffee.

Alexander rose early as he usually did and went to the kitchen, surprised to see Olivia.

"Didn't you sleep well?"

"No." she was curt.

"What's bothering you?"

"Nothing."

He sat beside her waiting for Ellen to get his breakfast. "Why don't you try to get some more sleep?"

"I'll sit with you. Besides, Nathaniel will be up soon."

"That will be nice."

They talked very little. Suddenly Nathaniel came running to them, throwing his arms about Olivia. "Mommy, were you in my room? I thought I saw you."

"Yes, sweetheart. I tried not to wake you."

"You didn't really."

She pulled him close, burying her head in his hair. "Mommy. You are holding me tight. I want to see daddy."

"You do that." She smiled watching him.

Finally Alexander left. She looked at herself in a mirror. *It won't be long now, Olivia.*

Marie had told Agnes she would be late at the office. She had an important lunch. She then walked to Olivia's house. They kissed on the cheek and hugged as Marie entered.

"It's so good to have you. I hope they won't say anything about you being late."

"Don't be silly. You know I have those men wrapped around my fingers. Count them, all five."

"I guess it's too early to eat. Would you like your tea?"

"Yes, please."

Olivia got it and they sat in the drawing room across from each other.

"Tell me, Olivia."

"He came home last night . . . late, trying to tell me he had an operation that lasted a while. When he hugged me, I smelled another woman on him Her perfume."

"You're sure?"

"I am, Marie. If it happens again, I'll throw him out." She had tears again that she had no desire to hide.

Marie started to rise and go to her. "Come here," She put out her hand, grasped Olivia's and led her to the settee.

"I have a question. I've always thought Joseph doesn't like him too much, the way they look at one another, or Joseph when he thinks no one sees him. I do. Has he said anything to you?"

"Well . . ."

"Please, Marie. We're like sisters."

"Joseph doesn't like him. He did at first, enjoyed his sense of humor and his ease. But then . . . well he left the office early when it was close to evening, telling Joseph he was going home. For some reason, Joseph got up and watched, saw him drive in another direction from home. Now don't get upset. Oh, that's a stupid remark." She watched Olivia's face growing very red. "Please, Olivia."

Suddenly Olivia felt pains. *It's only October.* The pain increased. "Marie, walk me to the bathroom."

Frightened, Marie quickly rose and led her. As they got there, Olivia's water burst. "Oh this damn mess," Olivia shouted. Nathaniel heard and came running. Olivia turned. "Mommy. You all wet."

Gasping, Olivia told him to go to Ellen. Marie knew they had to get to the hospital. After cleaning up, Olivia softly told Marie to take her. "Please, make sure Alexander knows."

Later that day, Olivia gave birth to a daughter. She had already decided her name would be Kathryn Anne. As she became older her eyes were green and her hair blonde.

Alexander did not appear until early the next morning. "Darling, I'm sorry. I had an emergency last night and didn't want to bother you. We have a daughter. She'll be as beautiful as you. I already saw her."

Olivia smiled as he took her hand and leaned to kiss her lips. "I fooled you. Me too. Marie looked terrible. Luckily she was with me." *Like hell you had an emergency. Joseph was here. I remember asking him. I fooled you. Too bad you got her soap and perfume off you.*

The nurse appeared with Kathryn Anne and placed her in Olivia's arms who bared her breast for her daughter to eat. She was thinking, *Another lovely child and a poor, stupid husband. I hurt. Oh how I hurt.*

"Are you all right, Olivia? You look terrible," Alexander told her.

"I'm fine. You must have to get to the office or the hospital. We'll see each other later," She forced a smile.

"Love you." And he left.

When she was home and stronger, Joseph came with Marie when certain Alexander would not be there. "Olivia. Be strong. I hate being like this. I saw Alexander with a woman."

Olivia allowed her tears to flow. "Well, you only confirmed what I suspected."

"I hate being the one to tell you this. I didn't want to, but Marie said I must."

Sobbing, thinking of her children, the new child, she hid her face. Marie rose, went to her, rubbing her hand across her shoulders. "Olivia, remember we are always here for you, as is Millicent."

She raised her tear stained face to Marie. "Can . . . can you get me a good divorce lawyer?"

"Yes. But talk to Alexander first. Perhaps it's been innocent." She did not believe this herself.

"Innocent," her voice rising. "Innocent? He's as innocent as a criminal who has just stolen from a bank. Yes. I'll talk to him. What I didn't tell either of you is that I had Ellen briefly look after the children and went to one of the women's stores, putting the perfumed soaps and perfumes to my nose. Yes, he came home with one of them on him, certainly not mine. Innocent? I'll confront him."

That night when Alexander arrived home, Olivia called him to her. "I'm in the library." As he approached here, she put up her arms. "Come here for a hug."

It was there again. The same odor. "Alex, I want you out of this house. Get away from me. You smell of that woman you've been fucking."

"What are you talking about?"

"You fool. Go take a shower and get that fucking woman's odor off of you. You shower wherever she lives. Is she one of your patients?"

He started to answer, but she cut him off. "Get out of my sight. I despise you. My loving husband. Don't you ever appear in this house again. I'm getting a lawyer."

"Have you lost your mind? Too much staying at home, taking care of a baby and Nathaniel? What woman? There is none." His face was now red. "Another woman?" He protested, feeling the heat of his face and the perspiration trickling down his neck and into his shirt. "I'm going up and take a shower."

"Oh, you son of a bitch. Washing her off. I thought you'd be smarter than that. Using her soap and smelling of her perfume. You don't need a shower. You need a hotel. Get the hell out of this house," she shouted, "and don't ever enter it again. Go to your whore and fuck her until you both drop."

"You're crazy." He couldn't tell his wife the woman was

pregnant by him.

"Get out of my house. Get out of here. Now."

He grabbed his coat, perspiring, trembling, and ran for the door, slamming it as he left.

Not long after, at his office he received divorce papers from a lawyer in Marie's office, naming him as the correspondent. He was to appear at the District Court on January 3, 1911.

As he sat with his lawyer and listened, he stopped his attorney from either objecting or protesting. "Let it go. She can have anything she wants just so I can get out of this city and back to Philadelphia." *We'll marry just as soon as this over. I promised her.*

"But . . ."

"No but. I don't want the other woman," his face now red in embarrassment, "dragged through this." She was a divorcee with her own apartment where the assignations had generally taken place. It was settled. He was giving Olivia the children, money if she wanted, although he knew she would take nothing, didn't need it.

Olivia had his clothing and all his personal possessions sent to his hotel. It was settled. She lay on their bed, sobbing, for her loss, for her folly, as she saw it, being taken in by his manly, muscular body, handsome face, and manners. All was a fake, and she had fallen for it. She felt shame and hatred. *My poor children. She would never know her father while Nathaniel Asa would never see the man again as he grew.*

The following day, Nathaniel came to her. "Mommy, I didn't see daddy 'fore he left for work."

She hugged him to her, tears falling along her cheeks. "Mommy. You crying."

"It's nothing, darling. It's just . . . just that your daddy has gone away and won't be home again."

"Why?"

"It's what he wanted, darling. Just remember, I'm always

here for you and your sister. We'll all grow together. All right?"
She hesitated. "When you're older I'll explain it. You'll
understand. Now please, Nathaniel, go play. It's Kathryn
Anne's feeding time." She went upstairs to the nursery, raising
her baby from the crib and giving her breast. Feeling her
suckling, Olivia cried more, "My poor child. But you'll always
have me, your grandparents and aunts and uncle. Poor child.
We're alone." Olivia cried loudly now, shook, but forced herself
to calm as much as possible as the baby suckled from a breast.
Both children would only be hers now.

———————————————

Part VII

Contending Worlds

Chapter One

Family Evolution

1914: Archduke Ferdinand and his morganatic wife Sophie Assassinated. In August of that year The Great War started among the Austro-Hungarian Empire, Germany, Russia, England, France, and Italy, ending the 100 years of peace artfully created by the Congress of Vienna. The United States, a neutral, tried to ignore the slaughter in Europe. Life continued on its merry way. With the sinking of the *Lusitania* in 1915 with the loss of 128 American lives, apparently some people did worry, but for the most part, life continued without war concerns.

Meanwhile, when the children were older and now in grammar school, Olivia who had occasionally done some work, gave more time to her practice at the office and hospital. At first, it disturbed her, because she did not believe she was as well prepared as she should have been, despite her studying. Being who she was, however, she became a female doctor whom women once again sought out.

Her divorce, though, like a peace also ended, left her depressed with a feeling that she had failed and that she was not satisfactory as a woman. There were men who sought her. She did occasionally accept invitations to dinner. However, there was no one who attracted her. Moreover, with her remembrance of the attempted rape in medical school, and then her marriage to a man to whom she had given herself and her love and who she was sure would always be faithful, she refused offers of marriage, made up her mind that she would remain single and devote her life to her children and her practice.

However, Marie and Millicent tried to get her to look seriously at another man. On one evening, when Marie, Millicent and Olivia, went together for dinner, Marie raised the issue of loneliness, for she and Millicent had talked about it, distressed that Olivia did not seem to be herself.

They were on the phone. Millicent brought up the subject with Marie. "Marie, Olivia seems depressed. She has the children, loves them dearly, but she needs more. Yes, she has her practice, but that is not enough. Should we push a little more?"

"I don't think so, Millicent. She'll become resentful of our interference in her life."

"I suppose you're right."

What they didn't know is how Olivia tried to overcome her loneliness. There were times at night when in bed, certain the children were asleep, she would use her hands to wander about her body, satisfying herself, imagining a man until at last she threw back her head, as her fingers went to her clitoris, those of the other hand thrusting, moaning loudly as she climaxed. Satisfied and tired as her body relaxed, she would sleep, partially waken, then sleep restlessly.

With the years passing, she knew she had to allow the past to recede and that she must encourage herself to remember she was a mother with children who adored her and that she was a successful doctor.

She knew she could always count upon Marie and Millicent, that despite her now occasional depression, she could intimately talk to them. She would, however, have to be the courageous woman. She eventually decided that she would take up with the Suffragettes. It hurt her practice, but she believed that women must now depend upon themselves, show their strength, and take their place among the men no matter how long it would take.

Eventually, with the war in Europe having become slaughter fields, with the Germans having made a mistake by flirting with Mexico by promising that government if it went to war with the United States, Mexico would get New Mexico, Arizona, and Texas. Woodrow Wilson having learned this asked for a Declaration of War in 1917.

That year Joseph told Marie he would like to become an army doctor. Morosely, she agreed. She had Sandra May, now 8 years old and in school with her cousins Nathaniel and Kathryn Anne. She, Olivia, and Millicent would prove their strength and come to rely more upon one another even at a distance as Joseph, now 39, joined but kept in the United States at Fort Bliss. Settled, he sent for Marie and Sandra May. They enjoyed the multi-lingual environment and the desert, the beauty of the mountains, especially at night when above the dark shadowed ranges the sky appeared enveloped in stars.

Friends told them to visit Las Cruces and to see in Old Mesilla where Billy the Kid had been jailed, that they should drive the narrow roads to Santa Fe for the art and to see the Indian traders sitting in the shade of the Old Governor's Palace. Then there was Taos as they drove that narrow road. In a hotel by the small square, they looked out in the morning at the Indians sitting wrapped in their blankets. They also visited the pueblo, fascinated but feeling as though they were intruding. However, they drove about, suddenly arrested by the beautiful young woman standing as if to catch the sun in her adobe doorway, a photographic symbol they would hold in their minds and hearts for the stillness and beauty in the present but also of the past glory, its contrast to the fury in which the country was now engaged.

Soon after this tranquility Joseph received orders for overseas. With Marie and Sandra May packed and sent off to Maine, he bordered a ship in Boston eventually to be stationed near the front in hospital tents.

He and the other doctors and nurses constantly heard the sounds of battle, especially when they moved to the Battle of Château-Thierry. Suddenly, shells exploded near them, one close to Joseph's tent. A fragment struck his leg. He fell, feeling the heavy weight of a wounded soldier thrown upon him. Despite the pain and the blood he managed to raise himself, pushing the body from him. He looked. The man was dead. He had been hit between his eyes by other fragments. Two scared nurses ran to Joseph and pulled him toward a vacant cot, taking care of his wound. An orderly moved the dead man outside. From then on Joseph had a slight limp.

Hearing of his wound from Marie caused Olivia to think of serving. *How though can I leave the children? I'll ask if wounded come to the United States here in Maine. I'll volunteer but still be with the children.*

Because there were Forts in the Portland Area, there would be some men in need of medical attention. Despite there being Medical Officers who had no use for female doctors, Olivia volunteered through the Red Cross and was able to choose her hours, enabling her to be home after school.

Then suddenly, though the hour and the day known to the soldiers on both sides who continued to shoot at one another, the horror ceased, November 11, 1918, when an incredulous silence descended as the guns no longer slaughtered. The Armistice had been agreed by all the combatant nations. Yet, despite the unimaginable destruction and deaths of a generation, The League of Nations created to counteract aggression failed, for President Wilson was unable to convince the United States Congress of the necessity of such a body to preserve peace.

And at home, Olivia had not only been proud to have aided the war effort, but also her pride extended to her children. Nathaniel had skipped two grades and Kathryn Ann the same when they attended grade school. It astonished teachers that a brother and sister separated by two years were so intelligent. Each of their teachers believed they were bound for accomplishment that other students might or might not achieve what they expected from Nathaniel and Kathryn Anne. As they advanced they became even closer.

One day, while in high school Kathryn Anne finally said to her brother, "Let's take bets on who becomes the better known in whatever field we choose."

"O.K., Kathryn Anne. What's the bet?"

She laughed. "Are you thinking of money?"

"I suppose."

"Yeah, but we don't know how much we'll be making. Oh, I know what you'll be doing. You'll be a doctor like mother and Uncle Joseph. Oh, and Grandfather and Grandmother. All right, if it's money, I guess I will follow Aunt Marie into law school. I have to keep up with you somehow." She laughed again. "I know one thing. I can have the children and you have to count on a wife. How about who has the most children?"

Now Nathaniel laughed. "You're daft. I know you don't want a lot of kids. You've already said so."

Before answering, she thought of what their mother had told her about puberty and becoming a woman, even what it was like having a baby. That is why she wondered whether having several children would be something she did not want. "Anyhow, if you bet me, I could change my mind."

"Why did you say 'anyhow'?"

"That's private women stuff."

"You think I don't know about that stuff? Mother talked to me too. So you may change your mind, but I think that's not a fair bet. Let's make it who will pay for a trip to see out West, like visiting Yosemite or something like that."

"I like that. It's a bet. But if we're married, we have to take our families."

"Shake, silly-face."

They shook hands, then hugged tightly and kissed one another on the cheek. Kathryn Anne had a warm feeling in her. She loved her brother and knew they would always be friends." Suddenly she felt a glow when she heard . . .

"I truly care for you, Kathryn Anne. We must always be friends and be close. That's a better bet."

"And I truly care for you too. We must never allow anything or anyone to separate us."

While they were in high school, they came home one day, finding their mother crying.

They ran to her, "Mother, what's wrong? What happened?"

"It's your grandfather. I was at the hospital. They called me in to see him. Children, he's very sick."

"Won't he get better?" Kathryn Anne asked.

"It depends. He must have an operation." Kathryn Anne and Nathaniel sat beside her on the sofa, trying to soothe her. Looking at her son and daughter through her tears she told them, "We'll just have to see."

In Millicent's and Joseph's homes it was the same. Joseph had also been at the hospital and visited with Benjamin. He looked at his father's face, read his chart, stunned, he could feel tears. He pulled up a chair to sit by him, "Father, I'm here." Benjamin did not answer, he was too sleepy from the morphine the nurse had given. He did turn to Joseph and forced a weak smile.

Joseph went home and told Marie who knew from calls she

had from Olivia and Millicent. Sadness permeated the family.

At about the same time they received a call from Constance, asking her children and their spouses to come to her.

When they arrived she told them, "I need your strength with your father in the hospital. I'm aware Joseph and Olivia already know from being in the hospital."

"We know what's wrong, mother." Olivia and Millicent said in about the same way.

"Yes. But I need you here. They believe the cancer has spread. I'm certain it has. He is so weak and in so much pain. The radium treatment has helped some. Perhaps it will prolong his life. Here we are in 1921, and what more have we learned in medicine? Why haven't we progressed more?"

Despite her grief, Constance, though older, still showed her beauty. But now, this woman of so much strength, needed that from of all her children when speaking about Benjamin. They had been married 57 years. She could not believe it was ending.

"Thank you children for coming. I know you all have visited your father."

"Mother," Joseph insisted, "I know father is ill. I saw him in the hospital. I read his chart. I also told Marie."

Olivia broke in. "Mother, I was there too and read the chart. I thought I should wait for you to call. I did, though, tell Millicent. I suppose I shouldn't have waited for your call."

"I don't mind that. I had to get myself together before calling you." She could not, though, hold back the sobs. "We're going to lose him. I know that, but it's so hard after all these years. He's been a good husband and father. And now it makes me angry when I think back about how some people hated him because he's Jewish. He triumphed over them all through his excellent surgery and in keeping up with the latest advances in medicine. It killed some of these people that he succeeded so." Now she was angry thinking back to the past and what they endured. "But we made it, just like you all did." She could not stop her tears.

Joseph went to her. "Mother you both made our lives better, allowing us to express ourselves, to be what we chose."

They now sat, all in tears thinking about husband and father. Finally Constance spoke up. "All I want from each of you is that you continue to be examples for our society as you are already."

After the gathering, weeks followed until the colorectal cancer took Benjamin. The funeral was large, attended by doctors, nurses, former patients, all paying tribute to the man some thought could never succeed in Portland.

* * *

Nathaniel Asa, in 1923, followed his uncle to Harvard. He knew he would become a physician. While there he met a young Radcliffe woman. She reminded him of his mother in some ways with her self-assurance, her attractiveness. He was tall like much of his family, she about 5'6", blue eyed, red hair, a face and figure that made men turn, some to flirt and be ignored. She was a year older than Nathaniel, but they would be graduated at the same time. They met in the Square one day in a coffee shop, introduced by a student friend who had invited him to meet them.

"Nathaniel Levine, meet Evelyn Doris Blake. Her father is also a doctor, like your mother. She lives in Brookline." Nathaniel never talked about his father although he had met him several times in Philadelphia as did his sister when they traveled there together. Neither liked him, repelled by his self-satisfaction and disliking the woman he had married who talked deprecatingly to them. They would leave wondering how their mother could have fallen for him. The only good part of their visit was when their half-brothers, Albert and Edward, years older than they, took them to the sites of the city. They became rather friendly and kept in touch while he was in medical school. Yet, Nathaniel and Kathryn Anne could not find in their hearts any love for their father or his wife.

* * *

Not long after, in 1924, while in his medical Residency, Olivia called Nathaniel.

"Nathaniel. Your grandmother is quite ill."

"Grandma. What's happened, mother?"

Olivia started to cry. "Darling, she's had a bad heart attack. Uncle Joseph looked in on her and said she has little chance of survival. I know you need to be at the hospital. But I want you to know."

As her children sat about the bed, they did not know Constance, though weak, thought back, her eyes open, speaking in a dream: *Look at the family we spawned, Ben. The mixture of religions. Please, just look at the family we spawned. What would our forebears think? Well, I'll see you soon, Ben, my love.* She closed her eyes, a smile on her face, her hands holding each of her children's, slipping from them.

"What was she thinking?" Olivia managed, as all three allowed their tears to flow.

This independent, strong willed woman who had defied her parents marrying Benjamin, who had shown the way for others like her after Elizabeth Blackwell, to go to medical school, died. Like Benjamin, the funeral had many people who followed them to the cemetery. A generation that had served and seen the horrendous deaths of the Civil War lost another. It would be Kathryn Anne who would tell her brother most of what he learned. This death embittered him even more against his father, thinking of the time his mother would grow old and leave them. He forced himself to stop thinking this way. The family still lived.

* * *

As Nathaniel, who never talked of his father, sat across from Evelyn, he knew he would have to see her again. She felt the same way, gazing into his blue eyes. They almost ignored her companion.

Occasionally they met in the library and studied together. One night they walked together and in the shadows of her apartment she shared with two other students, they kissed passionately. His hands wandered to her breasts. She did not stop him. They kissed more fervently. She felt the heat flow throughout her. Drawing momentarily apart, both with faster beating hearts, he then pulled her to him again. They pressed their bodies together, until both realized they must part. Sighing, reluctantly she drew back from him. However, she then reached to hug him tightly, until she softly whispered, "No more."

Regaining their composure, she reached to kiss him softly, listening to, "I love you so, Evelyn."

"I love you too, Nathaniel."

"Let's marry."

"We should meet one another's families."

"Agreed. Do you think your parents would allow you to travel to Portland to meet my mother?"

"Well, after mine meet you, I think they'll agree. You'll also meet my brother and sister. He's two years older than I and my sister a year younger. My brother is an engineer but still at home."

"I don't mind. But before we take care of all the meetings, please let's get engaged."

"Yes," she answered without hesitation.

He gave her a sapphire ring surrounded by diamonds. She proudly wore it, showing it to her family and friends, gazing at it in private, smiling happily, aware they would not marry at least until he was in medical school.

When she took him home, her family balked, not knowing her suitor. However, after meeting Nathaniel, they approved of him and allowed her to travel to Portland, accompanied by her mother. When Mrs. Miller, Natalie, and Olivia met, they immediately liked one another, as did Olivia and Kathryn Anne take to Evelyn. The two young women would become close friends over time. During the visit, Olivia took them all to dinner. The women seemed never to stop talking until Nathaniel, laughingly interrupted, "I'm here you know."

The laughter at the table endeared everyone as they came already to feel like family.

* * *

One night, coming from the library, Evelyn stopped him. "I wish we could marry soon. Perhaps we could elope."

"Hmm." He was thinking of making love to her, seeing all of her magnificent body. "We will."

They did so during Christmas vacation, 1927, the middle of his first year of medical school. She had followed him to Vermont for graduate work in Chemistry. As an engagement present, Olivia had given him new a car. They drove to Cape Cod. After the ceremony, she looked at him after their kiss, "I am now Mrs. Levine," she spoke softly and smiling. They went to Boston and spent several days in the Copley Plaza Hotel. When the families heard, there was anger that eventually became acceptance and love for both. After their parents' commotion, that became pleasurable acceptance, Nathaniel and Evelyn found an apartment near the university. Eventually, they decided they would not have children until the end of their studies when Evelyn would receive her doctorate and he his M.D. They agreed he would become another family surgeon and join his uncle in Portland.

In March, 1927, Evelyn believed she was pregnant. It happened on a night they were in such a hurry to make love, they did not use birth control. When she told Nathaniel, he was excited, kissing and hugging her, asking if she were certain. "I believe so. I've missed two periods and have made an appointment with a woman doctor." The doctor confirmed her pregnancy, telling her she should have the child in November. Pleased with herself, suddenly she had conflicting feelings. They hadn't yet been graduated. Nathaniel was to finish medical school, and she suddenly thought about studying law, influenced by Marie and Kathryn Anne. But to have a baby she and Nathaniel would love did excite her.

In November, 1927, Evelyn went into labor. It lasted a long while. Finally, when the female obstetrician examined Evelyn, she found it to be a breech birth. Discussing the alternatives with Nathaniel and Evelyn, she suggested a Caesarean Section. Evelyn, trembling, nodded. Nathaniel, holding her hand, running his fingers soothingly over hers, agreed.

With operating room prepared, the operation went forward. The child was a healthy boy. The doctor spoke to Nathaniel before Evelyn woke from the anesthesia.

"I expect she will recover well. She's strong. I believe your wife will be healthy and pleased to see and hold her son."

"Thank you, doctor."

"Congratulations to you Nathaniel. I now look forward to telling Evelyn. When she woke and found she had a son, she smiled at both the doctor and her husband. "Nathaniel, we have a healthy son." The doctor had the nurse present the child for Evelyn to hold and feed. "Look at him. May we name him Matthew Robert Benjamin? That way we include both our families."

"That's fine dear. You just take care of yourself. Now sleep. When you wake you can feed him again, our little Matthew Robert Benjamin."

When Evelyn recovered from her surgery, she told Nathaniel when Matthew was older perhaps she would go to law school and join the family practice started by Marie. *Perhaps. I'm not certain. We'll see. I think I would rather have another child and be a mother but not bound to the house when the children are in school. Perhaps that's best.*

The child growing older, with his black hair and green eyes, fascinated both parents. He was now three, talking and lighting their apartment with his probing intelligence and his playfulness. Evelyn decided she would have another. So it was that in January, 1931, a daughter was born and named Samantha Eleanor. Samantha would grow to have bright blue eyes and reddish blonde hair. When she was a four years old, Nathaniel would begin to save sufficient funds for a nanny. Evelyn, who did get her Ph.D., found part time teaching in her field at Westbrook Junior College. She and Nathaniel employed Mrs. Goddard, a widow with grown children. She was just the wonder they would like for their children. She had a natural sense of humor and a knowledge of such subjects as the sciences, mathematics, and history with which she would help and also influence the children. Not only this, she would often give Evelyn advice on raising the children when Evelyn seemed stumped.

"Mrs. Levine, I think there are times you lose yourself in your work and apparently ignore the children, although I know this isn't so. You read to them and show your love by hugs and kisses. Just trust me and listen, and do, even it means you won't always be the top teacher of chemistry. Give more time to Matthew and Samantha."

"Well, I enjoy my chemistry."

"Enjoy is one thing, but how about paying more attention to the children? I know you love them. They adore you. So you may or may not be the best chemist in the world, but think of being the best of mothers."

Evelyn listened and made certain she would be able to spend more time with Samantha and Matthew. Thus the family grew with Evelyn having taken Mrs. Goddard's advice. She was happier than she thought she would be.

The family, long after the immigration of Asa and Hannah had come to the city, was one of the outstanding in medicine and law. They managed through the Depression, never losing sight of their service to people of lesser means, whether it be law or medicine.

Soon, Nathaniel started a clinic for the poor that grew beyond anything he imagined. He began to devote most of his time to this, gathering doctors from Portland and as far away as Brunswick and Saco and towns in between. Maine had never seen anything like this. He followed a model started in Boston in 1927.

Like many Americans they paid little attention to the events in Europe, the growing power of Hitler and his band of Nazi thugs. By 1938, however, and Kristallnacht, they now understood about the killing and imprisonment of the Jews, would learn about the concentration camps. And this family of Asa and Hannah, now of mixed blood, felt it could not just stand by.

Chapter Two

World Dismay

In 1933, after having waited with indecision, Kathryn Anne finished her law studies at Harvard and passed her bar examination. She was striking with her inquisitive piercing green eyes and blonde hair that she wore to her shoulders, curled toward the bottom. She wore little make-up, although she did use lip rouge, tinted her long lashes, and lightly rouged her somewhat narrowed face. At five foot six, she was tall like the females in the greater family. She met a young man at school, Bryan Wilson, tall, slim, and muscular. He always seemed interested in world affairs.

When they both passed the Bar Examination and although they had known each other from some classes, one day he found the courage to ask her for a date before the examinations.

He stopped her outside class. "Kathryn Anne."

"Yes?" She smiled, knowing what he was about to ask.

"Could we get together one evening on this coming week-end? I'd like to take you to dinner." He sounded somewhat nervous.

She felt warmth looking at him and pleased by his finally asking to see her out of class.

"Well," she appeared to be hesitant, not caring to seem anxious that she had been waiting for him to approach her. They had both sat in class occasionally looking at one another, the appeal apparent. "I imagine you have much studying to do as I. But, I would like that, Bryan."

The soft sound of his name, thrilled him as, of course, did her acceptance.

* * *

His friends had talked about her, watched her walk and the way her dresses showed off the curves of her body. One fellow told him he'd like to get her in bed. Bryan, angry, looked at him. "You go to hell. I know that's not the kind of woman she is. I resent you talking about her that way."

"Crap. It's obvious you like her and want to get in her pants."

"You son-of-a-bitch. Don't you ever talk to me like that again or about her. As far as I'm concerned, you can also get the hell out of our study group."

The student walked menacingly toward him. "You shit. Who do you think you are?"

"Who do you think you are? And step back or I'll beat the crap out of you. Kathryn Anne is not that kind. And if you come any closer to me . . ."

His antagonist was suddenly frightened, knowing how muscular and certain of himself Bryan was. Stepping away and looking back, "Oh, you use her name and don't even know her. I'll get out of the study group," his voice shaking, "I don't want anything to do with you or any of the fairies in that gang."

"Don't you ever again use that word or anything derogatory about her anywhere near me." As Bryan stepped forward, his antagonist hurried away.

* * *

Looking now at Kathryn Anne, and briefly remembering the argument, he felt as though she entered his heart. "I'll pick you up about 7 Friday night. Is that O.K.?"

"That's fine. Do you have any place in mind?"

"Do you like Italian food?"

"Absolutely."

"There's a good one near the music hall."

"I know it. It is good," she smiled brightly. "I'll look forward to it."

"Great." He almost seemed to be dancing from her, looking back over his shoulder to be sure he wasn't dreaming.

As she watched him, she laughed, waved and thought *I like him. I want to know more about him too. There's something about him that I feel the warmth flow throughout my body. Be careful Kathryn Anne.*

Yes, she was careful. When they sat across from one another at the restaurant, they began to talk about their families. "Mine," she told him after he asked, "is medical and legal, oh and one chemist, my sister-in-law. My mother is a doctor, my brother, and my grandparents were. My grandmother was exceptional for being a woman and becoming one in the 19th Century. And my grandfather broke the Jewish barrier with help from my great grandfather. Of course, I'm part Jewish with mixed blood, quite proud. Anyhow, my aunt is a lawyer, a good one, as is a cousin. What about you?"

He smiled. I was supposed to go to West Point and refused. My father is a colonel. It's almost like it's hush-hush. Sometime we don't know what he's doing. Anyhow, when I said I wanted to just be lawyer, my mother and father were sad but got over it." He wondered how she would fit in his family if it ever came to that. He continued. "We're just solid Christian. Does that make a difference to you?"

"That's foolish. I just told you my family is mixed. Like my aunt Marie, I rarely think about religion, let other people worry about it. But yes, sometimes it's hard when people hear you're a Jew, the way they look at you and whatever. I don't want to talk about that."

"Me neither, Kathryn Anne. We are who we are."

When their dinner was finished, he asked if she would mind going for a drive. She agreed and they went through the countryside toward Walden Pond. He slowed, driving into the rest area. He looked at her and placed his arm about her. She allowed herself to move toward him. He felt her round soft breast against him, and started to reach for her with his other hand.

"No. Bryan." As much as she wanted him to touch her, to feel his hands wander over her body.

"A kiss?"

"Don't be silly. Don't ask and see what happens." They did, then more firmly. She pulled back, looking penetratingly at him. "I think we should go back to our rooms."

He did as she asked. After that they saw each other fairly often. He would drive to a quiet, somewhat hidden site. She only allowed him to feel her breasts.

Eventually, Bryan asked to see her soon. *I will.*

When they met, he questioned if they could go to either his rooms or hers.

"Mine." She answered.

Once there he did not hesitate. "Kathryn Anne, "I love you."

"I love you too, Bryan."

As they kissed, he drew back. "I want you to be my wife."

"And I do want you for my husband."

He took a small package from his pocket. "Open it, darling one." He whispered.

She pulled off the ribbon, trembling, knowing the content. She withdrew the diamond. "It's so lovely. Here. You place it on my finger." She gave it to him, holding out her left hand, then raising her finger, looking at the ring, thinking of the wonder of being a wife. *If only we can be like my grandparents, not end like my mother.*

Their families met in Boston, his flying from Washington, Olivia, Joseph and Marie, Nathaniel and Evelyn, coming from Portland.

* * *

The wedding occurred in Portland before summer's end, 1933, as Kathryn Anne wished. She wore a gown of silk that twirled at her feet, her shoulders somewhat bare, long sleeves, and showing her bust.

After the service held with a Rabbi and a Minister, with Bryan breaking the glass, they had their wedding, and then came dancing. Soon Kathryn Anne and Bryan left for their honeymoon in Bar Harbor.

In their room, shyly she looked at Bryan. "I want to go into the bedroom and change. Do you mind?"

"Yes," he smiled, "but I'll wait to see you." He did wonder whether she would accept him without anxiety.

Then she appeared. She wore her gown showing her breasts through lace, beckoning him to her, as he gasped, seeing what he had always wanted and still imagining below. They went to the bedroom, and she lay down to watch him undress. He then approached her as she pulled her nightgown above her breasts. He saw the curves of her body, her slimness, then moved onto her as they firmly kissed as his hands felt the softness of her skin as they wandered from her breasts and nipples to her thighs. He raised himself, whispering, "All right, dearest?"

"Yes," in a whisper, as he entered and she tried to remain silent from the pain. She lay quietly, then moved some with him until she heard his quiet groan.

That morning, as they ordered breakfast in the room and sat to eat, she smiled, telling him, "I hurt below."

"I'm sorry. I wanted to be gentle."

"Sorry is foolish. I expected it." She hesitated. "Bryan, do men want their wives to be virgins?"

"Well . . . yes. They don't want them to have been with others." He felt his face turning red.

"Did you ever?"

"No. I waited for you."

"I never did either. I wanted to be pure for you. Oh, this is a funny conversation. Forget it."

They ate then went to watch the ocean, the clear blue sky and the gentle waves against the shore, as they held tightly to one another.

He waited until afternoon and after they had been in bed again, to tell her. "Kathryn Anne. My father has asked if we would come to Washington. He was vague, but he told me there may be work for me, perhaps you."

"I would like to be in Washington. My mother may be disappointed, but she will understand. But I'm not sure I want to work. Do you mind? I'd like to wait." She looked deeply at him, then shyly said, "I'd like to have children first.

"Would you want that?"

"Absolutely. Especially if they are girls and look like you."

Once back in Portland, Kathryn Anne told Olivia about their plans. She looked at her daughter, fighting to hold back tears, forcing a smile, "If that is what you two want that is what you should do. Of course, you've traveled some. But Washington, think of it. You may even get to see President Roosevelt. Kathryn Anne, wait 'til you see the cherry blossoms. The monument to Abraham Lincoln is overwhelming. What a great man he was."

"Yes, mother. He's my favorite. I can't wait to go there. I do hope Bryan's parents will like seeing me more." She then whispered, "Mother, what is it like having children?"

"It's nice making them. But when they start coming, it hurts, darling. You know that. But wait until you hold your child for the first time and hold it to your breast."

"I read about it, and despite all you told me, I don't think you ever told me about what it was like having me and Nathaniel, except to tell us how much you love us. Anyhow." She laughed, "Mother. I like being married, you know all that you do with another." She felt the heat of her blush.

Olivia tried to hide her laugh, but couldn't. "It's wonderful being a woman, isn't it? Sometimes I think we have it better than the men imagine. Anyhow, enough of this.

"You move to Washington and enjoy your life with Bryan."

Bryan's parents lived in Alexandria. When Kathryn Anne saw the house, she gasped. It was large and magnificent. *What does his father do to have such a house?* Before she could finish thinking, Bryan's mother, Margaret took Kathryn Anne to her and hugged her lovingly and kissed her cheek.

"Welcome, my daughter. It is so nice to have a daughter and full grown." She never had more children, being unable to. "If you like, while you stay with us, you and I can look for a home for you and Bryan."

"Just a minute, mother, what about me?"

"You house hunting? Now I've heard it all. My spoiled son. Don't worry. I'll step back when you want."

They did settle in a home not too far from his parents. Within a year he began to disappear for days at a time.

* * *

Eventually, Kathryn Anne confronted Bryan. "Have you found another woman? If you have, I'll leave immediately. I don't want to go through what my mother did, but if I have to I will."

"Please, Kathryn Anne. I promise, assure you there's no other woman for me. I pledged my life and love to you."

"I want to believe you." She tried to hold back her tears but couldn't. "What has happened to us? What I have done?"

"Please believe me, dearest. There is no one else." He went to her, hugging her tightly. He tried to figure out a way to tell her he was now doing classified work for the Division of Investigation. He had to tell her.

"Kathryn Anne. I am doing secret work. My father asked me to join the Division of Investigation. I couldn't refuse him as I did with West Point."

She looked at him, her face red with fear. "I'm your wife. Why couldn't you have told me so I wouldn't have suffered all this time? Are you in danger? Is it so secret?"

"I . . . I am investigating undercover. I have to be certain no one knows what I'm doing. You can never tell anyone, not your friends, just your mother and brother. But they must keep quiet. You can also talk to my mother, but please, dearest. Do not be upset if she won't talk much about it."

"I'm already upset. I'm scared, Bryan."

"I should have told you sooner. It had nothing to do with not trusting you. Let's just sit and hold each other. I swear I will always be faithful to you. Shall I get you some tea? We could both have something."

"Yes." She sat, starting to tremble a bit. *He must be in danger. And it's so secret. What if whoever or whatever he's investigating discovers who he is? Why did I never ask him about the gun he has?*

Bryan came back with the tea. They sipped until she asked, "You are in danger, aren't you?"

He didn't want to answer but felt he must tell her. "I could be at times. But please do not worry."

"I'm always going to worry. Yet, suddenly I feel pride that you are helping our country. Can you ever tell me more?"

"I'll talk to my father. All right?"

"Yes."

Later Bryan did as he promised Kathryn Anne and talked to his father.

"Father, I told my wife something about what I'm doing. Not, however, about my undercover work in the German American Bund. She wants to know more. Is it all right if I tell her the organization we are investigating?"

Andrew glared at Bryan. "You shouldn't have told her

anything," he answered in a gruff voice.

"She had to know. You must have told mother what you do."

He hesitated. "Yes. She knows. But I'm not in danger like you. You must be very careful, Bryan."

"I understand that. I'm not a child." He was exasperated. "Neither is my wife."

His father started to smile as if suddenly an idea came to him. "You know, there will be a time we'll need some women. With her law degree, my superiors may want her."

"I have thought of that. But I know she wants children."

"Well, let's see what happens. But I'm sure we could use her, perhaps a bit later."

They were talking about the German American Bund that had started in the United States in 1933 with the advent of Adolph Hitler and his storm trooper brown shirts and SS. The Bund's head was a man Fritz Kuhn. He commanded a fiery anti-Semitic organization such as in Germany. Here, close to 1936, those opposed to what was happening in Germany became more concerned as Hitler began to build his armed forces. The Bund was also helped by the radio broadcasts of Father Coughlin, a rabid anti-Semite. It was the Bund that Bryan was watching and had secretly joined.

It then occurred to Bryan. "Father, Kathryn Anne, as you know, is Jewish, well, mixed blood. If she tried to become involved in what we are doing, she could die."

"Let's not worry about that now. The point is, they'll be using those men to spy." His expression suddenly showed more warmth. "Make me a grandfather first, perhaps. Your mother would love it."

After Bryan left his father's office, he began to worry, about Kathryn Anne becoming involved, being primarily Jewish, and about himself. She needed him as much as he did her. He had to decide how to approach her.

He let himself into the house, hearing nothing. Perhaps Kathryn Anne was out shopping. He went upstairs to their bedroom. She lay in bed, her hand over her eyes. Hearing him, she brightened, but her face was pale.

"Kathryn Anne. What's wrong?"

"I was going to shop, as I told you, but suddenly I didn't feel too good. My stomach was upset this morning and this afternoon."

"Have you been like this all day?"

"No. Well, it's time you know. I'm pregnant. I talked to your mother who sent me to her doctor. I also called my mother. Bryan, you're going to become a father," she smiled. "I guessed, as I imagine you did, when I missed my periods. That's why I wasn't so anxious to have sex, but we'll make up for it very soon. Goodness, you must have a lot on your mind. I'll be fine. Aren't women usually? These upset stomachs oughtn't to last more than 12 weeks. I'm so happy, Bryan."

"Kathryn Anne." He went to her and raised her into his arms. "Darling." He thought of his father and laughed.

"Why are you laughing? Are you that happy?"

"Very. But I have to tell you about my dad. He must have known. Mental telepathy. He wants to be a grandfather."

They were both laughing now. Suddenly he thought of his undercover work and the idea of her becoming a member of the Division of Investigation. She obviously would not be part of the team because of the coming child, but he worried about himself and his undercover work being exposed. His happiness was mixed with this anxiety.

He would be going to a Bund camp not too far from Washington. That would mean more time away. Somehow he must be home for the arrival of their child. They would also be moving to Baltimore, and he must tell her it was necessary for their protection.

* * *

In July, 1936, while Bryan was helping create a Bund camp for young people of German descent, Kathryn Anne went into labor. Bryan's mother, Margaret, was at the hospital and contacted Olivia who would come to her grandchild.

Kathryn Anne was in a room by herself, the delivery room nearby. The head nurse was not too far from her. She listened to Kathryn Anne's cries of pain. "No. It's so bad." The nurse went to her.

"Now do as I told you. Take deep breaths."

"Ugh, Oh. It's worse."

"Breathe deeply. Stay with it, dear. I'm going to call the doctor."

"Tell him to hurry," she gasped. "I think it's going to come soon. It has to." She screamed.

The nurse grimaced, remembering her own deliveries. Kathryn Anne had been so good, considering. "Breathe, Kathryn Anne," as she screamed loudly.

"It's so bad. It has to stop." She then forced a smile. *It will stop when I deliver. I'll have my child.*

The doctor arrived. "Get her to the delivery room."

"You'll be fine," he told her after he looked. Her cervix was now dilated sufficiently for the birth. It was a normal birth with Kathryn Anne feeling pleased but weary. "Mrs. Wilson," the doctor pleasantly told her after slapping the baby and Kathryn Anne listening to the cry, "You are the mother of a baby girl."

Wearily, she asked if she could have her child. The nurse cleaned the baby and handed her to Kathryn Anne, smiling happily. Suddenly it occurred to her that Bryan would not see their child yet. Tears formed. Looking at the child she quietly said, "We're naming you Andrea Louise Wilson and every year come July 1, your birth date, we'll celebrate as a family together."

* * *

Kathryn Anne should be delivering any day now. I have to get out of here without appearing weak. Tell the truth. It ought to work with even these monsters.

"Herr leader. My wife is about to have our first child. I want to be there to welcome a brand new German into the fold of the Party."

"You have been a loyal Bund Teilhaberschaft. You may go. Return when it is most convenient."

"Thank you. I'll get the first train." He pretended to live in Maryland, the Division of Investigation name having been changed to FBI that provided him with an address kept for his family and him.

While packing, it occurred to him that someone could follow him. He must tell Kathryn Anne where he would be taking her and their child in Baltimore to a completely furnished and protected home in a middle class district. His mother also assured him she would be with Kathryn Anne, move in for days at a time with his father and he being often absent.

Thus time passed. They would move again as Andrea grew older and was now three. They went back to their home in Alexandria when Germany invaded Poland and England and France declared war. The Non-Aggression Pact had been signed by Hitler and Stalin while the Führer had also signed with Japan.

Here at home the Bund held rallies in support of their new Germany. Bryan traveled more about the country. During the large rally in New York, one of the chief members became suspicious of his activities, seeing him conversing with a stranger he had also seen in Washington D.C. A few members were assigned to track Bryan who also became suspicious, having noticed various unknown people who seemed to be following him, even though by now the membership was falling. The House Un-American Committee damned the Bund, causing people to leave. Then by 1941, Fritz Kuhn was indicted for embezzling.

One night in 1941 when the Bund was now failing, one of these strangers confronted him. "Bryan Wilson."

Bryan's hand went to his pocket where he held a pistol. "Yes, that's who I am. What do you want?"

"You are a traitor." The man strongly pulled at the lapel of his coat. "We've been watching you. You are a spy." The man's hand went to his pocket and pulled out a knife. "You are a member of the FBI."

"You're crazy. Let go of me." Bryan pulled away, as they began to struggle in an alleyway. The stranger raised his arm ready to strike. Bryan grabbed, the man's knife grazing Bryan's face. Bryan struck the man's chin with his fist, knocking him backward. They struggled, striking at one another. Bryan was able to get out his gun as he shoved the stranger farther away from him. Pointing the gun at the man's breast, he shouted, "You are under arrest. Move any more, and I'll shoot if I have to. Raise your hands high in the air."

A police officer happened by, hearing Bryan's shout. Bryan turned slightly toward the policeman, reaching with his left hand in his breast pocket, pulling out his FBI card. "Call a car and get this man to the station. I'll go along in the car." Bryan was now trembling a bit, trying hard not to show his emotion but could not resist, "You fucking Nazi sympathizer. You will be going to prison for assaulting an officer of the United States Government."

After this encounter, Bryan was withdrawn for his safety. He met with his father. "I'm sorry this happened, Bryan. You will explain to Kathryn Anne."

"That's fine. We've been apart too much. I have hardly seen Andrea grow."

"Things are getting bad. The Germans: the occupation of

Austria, 1938, and the taking of the Sudetenland in 1938, then all of Czechoslovakia, then Poland and now attacking Russia. The President has started his Lend Lease to Britain. I fear we may be drawn in. In the meantime, go home to your family. We are not going to call on you for a while. Obviously you'll have to explain to Kathryn Anne the slight scar on your face and why you have moved back to Alexandria.

So now all of us will be close again. Your mother has so enjoyed being with her and Andrea." He laughed. "I have sneaked in too to see Andrea. Has she grown."

"Dad, she's 5 years old."

"Well go home, son and see your women."

Saturday evening, December 6, Bryan let himself into the house wanting to surprise Kathryn Anne and Andrea. They were in the parlor, Andrea sitting with her back to her mother who brushed Andrea's light brown hair.

Andrea saw her father and leaped from her mother's lap. "Daddy," she screamed, running to him as he leaned down and kissed her on the cheek, hugging her. "My goodness Andrea Louise Wilson, pretty soon you'll be as tall as mommy. He hugged her again. "My beauty, those green eyes and beautiful hair. I saw mommy brushing."

By now, Kathryn Anne had risen and hurried to him. "You surprised us, darling." They firmly kissed, he remembering her soft lips. She pulled back. "Let me look at you, my handsome husband." As she did, she noticed the scar. "Bryan, that scar. It's not from shaving. What happened?" She felt her hear beat more rapidly.

"I'll tell you a little later, all right?" He did not want Andrea to hear.

After dinner and when they both placed Andrea in her bed, they went to the living room. Kathryn Anne looking at his face, trembled a bit. "Bryan . . . you have been in danger. I have always been scared for you." She felt tears in the back of her eyes and tried to force them back. "I can't stand it when you are away as you have been." Some tears fell to her cheeks that she wiped at.

"I haven't enjoyed being away from you. I'm sorry. You know I'm with the FBI." He hesitated. "I guess I can tell you now. I have been undercover with that damned German Bund. Those bastards with their heil salute and anti-Semitism, their praising of Hitler. We'll have to watch them closely now for spying on us. Well before I get myself angry, I did have a little run-in with one of them." He placed a finger on his cheek. "This is a remembrance."

"Bryan. You could have been killed."

"Not quite dear. Here I am with you. Come closer so I can hold you."

She moved to him, placing her head against his chest. "Bryan, I miss you so when you are gone. I love you sweetheart." She whispered, tears again forming.

He raised her head. "Darling, there's nothing to cry about," as he wiped at her cheek, kissing it. "I'm here with you and Andrea. Isn't she a beauty?"

Kathryn Anne smiled seductively. "I made her, oh with some help from you, and that gives me an idea," as she rose, taking his hand. "You can tell me more in bed." She put her fear temporarily at rest.

She lay on the bed, turned on her stomach. "Unbutton this please."

He did and pulled it over her head while releasing her bra. She turned, pulling it off. "You like what you see?"

"Love it." He bent placing his hands on her soft, round breasts, his lips to her nipples.

"That's good," she whispered. "Undress so I can see you." As she said it, she pulled off her panties.

He quickly shed his clothes and gently raised himself upon her. They made love for hours until they fell asleep, with

Kathryn Anne holding him to her.

Sunday, December 7, the family walked to a park as they watched Andrea on the playground, Bryan pushing her on the swing. "Me too," Kathryn Anne shouted. And as her voice rang out, they played about, while in Pearl Harbor men and women died or were wounded, ships sunk, planes destroyed. The Japanese had sworn to defeat the United States.

At home, as they often did in the afternoon, they turned on the radio. On CBS they heard at 2:30: "The Japanese have attacked Pearl Harbor at Oahu Hawaii and the Philippines. The attack occurred at 7:35 A.M. Hawaii time."

They also heard on another radio that they excitedly turned to and on NBC: "The Island of Oahu attacked at Pearl Harbor. The attacks then moved on to Hickman Field. There has been considerable damage at Pearl Harbor. The Oklahoma was set afire. There is damage to shipping."

And from Hawaii Station KGU raised NBC: "Hello NBC . . . We have witnessed this morning severe bombing of Pearl Harbor. This has been going on for 7 hours."

The nation then heard that President Roosevelt would address a joint session of Congress on Monday, December 8, while the *New York Times* headline that same day read in enlarged print: JAPAN WARS ON U.S. AND BRITAIN - MAKES SUDDEN ATTACK ON HAWAII.

President Roosevelt before the Joint Session: "Yesterday, December 7, 1941 – a date that will live in infamy – the United States of America was suddenly and deliberately attacked by naval and air forces of the Empire of Japan. . . . Yesterday the Japanese Government also launched an attack against Malaya.

"Last night Japanese forces attacked Hong Kong.

"Last night Japanese forces attacked Guam.

"Last night Japanese forces attacked the Philippine Islands.

"Last night the Japanese attacked Wake Island. And this morning the Japanese attacked Midway Island. . . .

"I ask that Congress declare that since the unprovoked and dastardly attack by Japan on Sunday, December 7, 1941, a state of war has existed between the United States and the Japanese Empire."

Kathryn Anne held tightly to Andrea while Bryan grasped Kathryn Anne's arm.

"Mommy, you're hurting me"

"I'm sorry, sweetheart." She took her arms from Andrea, turned to Bryan, tears in her eyes, "They'll want you for dangerous missions. This is horrible. Those fuc . . . ." She stopped, remembering Andrea and rarely using the word unless she was truly upset. She continued. "They'll take you, Bryan." She felt her heart beating faster. "Oh, Bryan."

"Well now, don't get excited about me. I'm an old man."

"Old," she told him sarcastically and punched him in the arm. "You know very well they could send you on some mission; well look for those Fifth Column people I have heard about."

"We'll see what happens."

In the meantime, on December 11, Germany and Italy declared war on the United States. This freed the President to help Great Britain in any way possible.

As it was, Bryan's father now growing old but still of service at FBI headquarters called his son and asked Bryan to report to him. "Bryan, we're placing you in charge with a team to watch for German and Japanese saboteurs. You'll probably be traveling. We worry about our munitions factories, air and tank factories, for example, as well as power plants etc.

"You'll probably be traveling about so you may as well tell Kathryn Anne, but she must keep your travels secret, tell people you're away on business."

"She'll understand. I also appreciate the faith the FBI has in me."

Bryan left for Florida after information that Nazis had

landed in the state. Agents there started tracking. When Bryan arrived, they moved in. The house was isolated where the Germans were making their plans. Suddenly gunfire erupted when a German agent saw movement.

The fire was intense. A bullet lodged in the muscle of Bryan's thigh. He fell, until one of the men bent to help him up. As he hobbled, the Germans surrendered. "Get them shackled," he shouted. The intended saboteurs were taken into custody.

At home, Kathryn Anne answered the phone. Every time it rang it frightened her, because Bryan was away again. "Kathryn Anne, it's your father-in-law."

She tried to laugh as her heart beat faster and her hand shook as she held the receiver, her voice shaky, "I know your voice, dad."

"I'm aware of that. Nothing escapes you. You sure got that brain from your mother."

"Tell me, dad, what's happening?"

"Bryan . . . Bryan has been wounded."

She interrupted, starting to cry. "Is it bad? Where is he?"

"He's fine, considering."

"Considering what, Andrew?" She usually did not use his first name though both Margaret and Andrew had told her to call them by their first names. Being, though, that she did not know her father and rarely saw Olivia, though they talked, she called them dad and mom.

"He bravely confronted German saboteurs and was shot in the leg. He'll be at Bethesda Naval Hospital. So don't worry. You'll be able to see him. Margaret will be coming over to be with you and Andrea." He tried lightness. "Think of it. Andrea is almost 7. I can't wait for her birthday party." He hesitated, thinking he shouldn't have said that, for it was possible Bryan would still be in the hospital. He heard Kathryn Anne, crying. "Dearest. Don't cry. He's all right. I assure you. He's your hero."

"I don't need a hero, dad, just my husband." She sobbed.

"Kathryn Anne. Please. I assure you he's good. Think of seeing him soon."

When they hung up he thought, *My son is so fortunate to have married such a woman. Good heavens. My hands are shaking. We could have lost him.*

In the meantime, with 1942, Nathaniel and Kathryn Anne heard from their half-brothers. Albert was with the Army Medical Corps and Edward a Naval officer.

Nathaniel called his sister. "Think of that. Our brothers in the service. I wish I could go. I guess I'm too old." What he didn't tell her as yet, he was considering an invitation to join the Naval Medical Corps with a promise with the rank of Commander and that he would not be sent overseas. He would be at Charlestown Navy Yard. Then he called back.

"Kathryn Anne. Hi. It's me again. I'm going to be stateside in the navy. Evelyn and I agreed. I have told mother and I want you to know."

"I'm proud of you, Nathaniel. Think of it. I told Albert and Edward they must write. I want to be closer with them."

Thus it was with so many families affected, rationing, war work, Hollywood stars eventually going overseas to entertain the troops.

Then, in 1942, President Roosevelt created a new service: the OSS. Bryan would join. Kathryn Anne would be with the FBI Investigative Service but near home. Her mother-in-law would look after Andrea. Olivia decided she would retire and spend as much time as possible in Alexandria. So Andrea had two grandmothers to look after her.

Chapter Three

Home Front and War

Bryan, in June 1942, without first informing Kathryn Anne because he believed he couldn't, became a member of the new service without mentioning the designation. It was the secret OSS (the Office of Strategic Services), he being chosen for his Ivy law background. He felt as though he had deceived her. He had never done that and embarrassed, he came home one evening and shyly said, "Kathryn Anne. I have to tell you something. Please don't be upset. I have become a member of the OSS, a secret service. Obviously, this is secret. For all intents and purposes, I'm still with the FBI. You must never, never tell anyone."

"You're a sneak. I've heard rumors about that service." Tears came and fell to her cheeks at which she wiped. "You're always scaring me, Bryan. Now you become a member of a secret organization that practically no one knows about. Heaven knows what you'll be doing next."

"Please don't cry." He wiped at her cheek where tears continued to flow. "I'll take care of myself. I'll be teaching others because of my background."

"Is that all? I'm not sure I trust you after that gun battle you were in."

"We'll have to see."

She suddenly forced a smile. "Well, I'm with the FBI now. I guess we're both going to serve. But they promised I'd be in an office evaluating reports etc." Now she did laugh. "I hope your mother and mine get along well. They'll both be with Andrea when I'm not home. What better protection?"

As they ate their dinner, however, Kathryn Anne wondered what might happen, felt a quiver of uncertainty in her body as she occasionally subtly glanced at Bryan when they weren't speaking directly. Andrea spoke up. Now 6 she was in grammar school. "Mother, I saw you crying. Why?"

Frightened she heard them talking, Kathryn Anne asked, her voice unintentionally raised some, "What did you hear?"

"Just you and daddy talking, but I didn't sneak a listen. You just seemed upset."

"It was nothing, dear. Just daddy and I having a talk."

"You're not mad at each other are you? One of the girls at school told me her parents argue a lot and that she heard the word divorce. What exactly is that?"

Bryan tried to answer. "Andrea . . . Andrea. It's when a mother and father do not get along too well and . . . Goodness, you'll find out later."

Kathryn Anne truly laughed for the first time that evening. "Andrea. You know daddy and I love each other and you."

"Yes."

"Sometimes a mommy and daddy decide they don't love each other like we all do and they . . . they think they'll live away from each other."

"Oh well, mommy. I'm not sure I understand. But it's not like you and daddy who are away from home but always come back."

Bryan and Kathryn Anne laughed, particularly when Andrea told them, "I like being with grandma Margaret and Olivia."

The dinner and all conversation ceased. Later in the night, Andrea asleep, Bryan and Kathryn Anne glanced at one another after listening to the late news about the war. It was now mid-1942. They decided they had enough news as Kathryn Anne leaned to him, kissing him. He turned and followed, their tongues seeking. She pulled back. "I want to seduce you, Bryan Wilson. I feel it coming on," as she took his hand to her breasts that he pressed.

"Let's go to our room," as he felt himself growing hard. Kathryn Anne slowly slipped from her dress and stood before him in her bra and panties, slowly unhooked her bra and pulled down her last cover and stepped out of them. She turned from him and back. "You like what you see?"

"Come here," as he also quickly undressed.

"Ooo. You're hard. I can't waste that." She sat atop him, stimulating him with her hand then placing him inside her, moving, moaning, hearing him in his pleasure. For some time it would be one of their last nights of such rapture.

OSS & FBI

While Bryan was busy learning and then training new members about wireless, codes, how to avoid detection, and escapes if possible, Kathryn Anne had become involved in tracking German saboteurs who had been landed in Long Island, not only Florida, and eventually in Maine, their mission to destroy anything that would limit our war effort. The Andrew Sisters, Frances Langford, or Peggy Lee, Glenn Miller calmed some with their singing and he with his band music. But these Nazis, if possible, wanted to cripple our ability to build planes, to shatter rail traffic and water lines.

She sat at her desk, getting news and tracking information. Suddenly she tells they have them in the FBI sights, what cities they have spread to. She almost shouted out the information to her superiors she was so happy. Suddenly she thought, *We've got those fucking bastards. They want to blow up New York's water supply, aluminum plants that can harm our bomber and fighter ability. Yeah, affect out plane manufacture to protect your fucking Reich. Not on your life Nazi bastards – killers* and then under her breath, "Jew Killers. Me. Nathaniel. My mother. Oh God,

Andrea. Thank you lord for placing us here, me where I am right now despite the ant-Semitism among some of our population."

As it was, eventually all the intended saboteurs had been caught, their money gone to the United States and most of them executed as spies. Kathryn Anne was extremely pleased, felt she had helped bring down some Nazis even if she couldn't actually fight in battle. She thought of North Africa. What she did not know was that Bryan was being sent to that desert, although he told her he would be away for a while, that she should not worry if she did not hear from him. Somehow he would get word to her, thinking the people in Washington could forward notes.

The Desert

Bryan, who had been given an army uniform to protect him from being caught as a spy, began to erect a network of informants in North Africa. He spent the better part of early fall moving back and forth across the desert but always close to the sea, thinking of how the British fleet could cause problems for Rommel. He could transmit messages to the naval commander. Also, as he became more knowledgeable about the desert, he knew it was good for bouncing signals to London without distortion and for quicker reporting back to troop commanders. This was of rewarding help in the Second Battle of El Alamein that would eventually beat Rommel, while the Americans and British were invading North Africa. With the code name he had been given, he continued reporting German movement that intelligence sifted, studied, and verified. Not actually knowing what was happening in battle, he worried after Tobruk if the Germans had reached the Suez Canal. He believed however he would have heard from London if this had happened.

One night as he moved about with his volunteers from the

Jewish Brigade fighting with the British, they heard the firing of guns. They moved toward the sound, watching the light from the sky, search lights and the explosion of ammunition dumps. They moved closer watching the British demolish the depot. Suddenly there were silhouettes of running German troops. Some fell. Others had seen them and approached. They hit the ground but too late. The Germans fired at them. Bullets hit one of the Jews. Moments later. Bryan who had raised himself slightly to see what had happened to one of his men, felt a stab in his leg. "Oh, fuck, not again," thinking of when the Nazi at home had fired at him. He dragged himself along the ground. As a German approached him and was about to fire again, one of Bryan's Jewish allies leaped with a knife, thrusting it into the German. The man fell. The Brigade member who stabbed, his name David, pummeled the German as he fell to make certain he was dead. He then quickly went to Bryan, wrapping his leg with a tourniquet, whispering to a friend. They dragged Bryan far enough away from the German depot. They lifted him and struggled toward their home base. They managed his wound. Bryan then radioed about his crippling. The British sent a small observation plane to pick him up and take him and the members of the Jewish Brigade to the British lines.

David with whom he became friendly started talking about his family, telling Bryan how his great grandmother left the United States with one of her sons, after whom he was named, and who had fought in the American Civil War.

"What was his name?" Bryan asked, suddenly aware of the history he had heard of Kathryn Anne's family.

"The same as mine. Blumenthal."

"My Gracious Lord. He meant this to be, for you to save me from imprisonment or death by firing squad if those Nazi's had captured me."

David smiled but could not quite follow Bryan's excitement until he heard, "You are a relative of my wife Kathryn Anne and her family going back to before the Civil War. Wait until they hear this, and my mother-in-law, Olivia, particularly whose father was your great, great uncle's brother."

"I don't believe this," David answered, laughing. "We must stay in touch."

"We will. I'll make sure of that and tell everyone at home how you saved me from those bastards." They then exchanged addresses.

Eventually, after this conversation, the British took Bryan to the Americans from where he was sent to England for recovery. While in the hospital a general appeared. He spoke to Bryan about his activity and then bent over and pinned a Purple Heart on his pajama top. He did not tell Bryan what more awaited him.

All this time Kathryn Anne kept busy at the FBI headquarters, receiving notes assuring her he was safe. She did finally hear directly from Bryan, telling her about being in a hospital recovering from a wound, that she should not worry, that he had met David, that he thought he would soon be home.

When they flew him home, Kathryn Anne met him along with ranking officers, some from OSS in civilian clothes. She would not wait for a gathering but ran to meet him, her arms pulling him toward her as she cried. They pulled a bit apart to kiss firmly, assuring one another they were once more together.

"You have a cane," she told him in a hushed voice, then hiding her head in his shoulder as more tears fell that she wanted to hide from everyone. When they parted, she was wiping at her cheeks. She then pardoned herself and brought Andrea to her, now 8, her green eyes shining, her light brown hair shoulder length. She was already close to five feet and growing, "Daddy. Oh, daddy. Where have you been? I thought you left us." One of the men standing close by laughed a little, bit his lips to stop while watching this loving family. Andrea excitedly asked, "Daddy, when are you coming home?"

As he kissed and hugged her, smiling, he told her, "Very soon, dear. Look at you, so beautiful." She blushed, laughing, smiling. "Well, I do look like mommy, don't you think?"

"I certainly do."

While Kathryn Anne and Andrea stood beside him, one of the officers told him he would be receiving another honor at which his family could be present. Within a few days, at the White House, with his family present, Bryan stood at attention before General Marshall as he pinned on Bryan's breast a Distinguished Service Cross for his bravery in aiding what became the victory at the second battle of El Alamein and the defeat of General Rommel in this battle. The eventual victory came in Tunisia in1943.

As battles raged, the American troop contingents in Great Britain grew. It seemed to some of the English that the Americans had taken over their island. Among these was Albert, Kathryn Anne's and Nathaniel's half-brother, who had become part of a medical field hospital attached to an anti-aircraft unit. The men and officers guessed at and wondered when there would be an invasion of Europe. Finally there was movement of troops and equipment through the English towns toward the channel. Normandy Invasion. Of course Albert did not know of the action to come. For some reason, unknown, his unit did not as yet become part of the invasion. At home, the radios and the newspapers flashed the news.

The Bangor Daily News Report
Allies Land in Europe on Gigantic Scale

Within a few days, however, Albert's unit lay off the coast of France. It was a momentary sense of unreality, for they knew now from the wounded flowing back to England and the many dead on the beaches, his war, what he called 'our war' . . . 'is just around the corner.'

It came faster than he imagined, for one day, when it appeared quiet, despite the admonition not to be careless, he walked along a tree-lined road from his medical tent with another doctor. Soon they heard a plane. Albert glanced upward, saw it was German and yelled to his friend who had jogged ahead. Albert dived for a ditch, yelling at his friend. Suddenly the plane flew off after machine gunning where they had been seen. When Albert cautiously rose, he looked for his friend, ran forward seeing the man lying in the path. He was face down, blood flowing. "Oh shit." He tugged at his friend, turning him. "My God. You fool, you damn fool," and Albert crouched over him crying. This was his war. It came closer yet, for Hitler ordered an offensive in the Ardennes that came to be known as The Battle of the Bulge. Albert was with the Ninth Army as it moved past Aachen, Germany. They were the northern flank. The Germans slaughtered the men at Malmédy. Then, suddenly, as the Germans pushed to get to the River Meuse, the anti-aircraft guns of Albert's battalion became anti-tank guns. Albert stood a little way back listening the incessant pounding.

The Germans pushed faster and harder. Now they were close to the Germans, shooting at their tanks, while Albert operated in a tent. An eruption. He fell, knocked unconscious for a moment. When he woke, his arm flared with pain. There was little left around him. Several of the medics and nurses lay wounded; someone was dead, he was sure. He crawled toward the man. *The wounded man. Where is he?* Albert crawled to look at the man. He was dead.

Albert felt his pain, looked for some bandage and wrapped his arm. Men came running. Someone raised him. "You'll be all right, doc. Just hold on a minute."

Another doctor came and looked at him. "It's not bad, I believe"

"It hurts, more pain than I expected. I guess I won't be able to operate for a while. Damn. You need me."

"Just try to relax." The doctor gave him medication. "Hah," he loudly exclaimed, "The Jew finally got it." Albert heard just before becoming groggy, mumbling, "You son of a bitch."

What the Jew hater doctor did not know was that Albert would be in charge of a group that went to investigate and report on a concentration camp. He thought back to what he heard not only recently but when he was first in the service from some of the men at Fort Bliss and how they were insulted for their religion.

All this news regarding Albert not only went in letters home to Philadelphia, but knowing Bryan had been involved, he wrote Kathryn Anne and Nathaniel, knowing they would understand, that this war was far from over. It went on until May, 1945. The allies defeated the German army. Germany in ruins, and Adolph Hitler lay dead with his mistress, married just before the poison killed them.

Near the War's End

"When you enter the army, be prepared," one of my uncles told me. "Matthew, you are going to confront anti-Semitism." He was a doctor, had already been discharged because he had enough points to come home after his war in Europe. The wounds he had suffered and the medals for bravery he received.

"Oh. C'mon. In the United States Army! That's impossible." I had to go, was anxious to, having just turned 18 and been drafted. It was the idea of experiencing what my uncles did, joining them in a common venture. The fighting with Japan was about to end, although the war was not officially over until December, 1946. But I was excited, because I would be joining my uncles who fought. They were my heroes, and the army was my great adventure.

"I just left it, didn't I? I saw all those Jews from the concentration camps. Don't forget, I was a leader of one group to examine the camps, look for war-crime criminals, and to report on the survivors. Do you think that made a difference? Well perhaps some. But there are those men who will taunt you. Yes, in our army."

Well, my day came. I was sworn in with many others. I was a United States soldier. They shipped us to a camp. I had heard German prisoners were there. I did not want to even see them, for what they had done to my people. Of course, I didn't consider them mine, but life taught me they were. I didn't even give much thought to being Jewish when I was growing up. Of course, eventually growing up meant being in the army at eighteen, an adult.

Then, one morning, after we had fallen-in for roll call, three of us were back in the barrack. Two were down the columns of beds a little way, whispering out loud, and I heard it. "He's a Jew, but he seems O.K." Startled, I did not know what to do, but just stood by my bunk, pretending I didn't hear. Cowardice not to have said something? Even as I tell this story, I'm not sure.

But then on one of the following days, a peculiar thing happened. A sergeant entered. "Hey, Levine." I hesitated. "Hey, you, Private Matthew Levine. You. Come with me."

"Huh? O.K., Sergeant. I'm comin.'" I followed him outside to the mess hall. Standing there with a guard were three German prisoners. They looked gigantic to me, but the hatred swelled. My heart beat faster.

"Take these guys back to their compound."

I looked at him, wondering. They were taller than I, more muscular. "Go on. Take 'em."

I don't know. Was he testing me? As we walked along to the compound, I was thinking, *What's to keep these guys from jumping me and trying to escape?* Of course, that didn't happen. They knew better, but I also figured they knew I was a Jew, and I was happy, making sure these shit-heads entered the high barbed-wired top fencing through the gate where a soldier with a rifle took over. "Here. Take these bastards." I turned and walked back to my barrack, a smile on my face. We had beaten them, ground them down, bombed the hell out of them; and my uncles, my heroes, helped do all that to those inhumane Jew killing fuckers.

When I returned to the barrack, one of the guys who had said something about me being a Jew, waited until I was near my bunk, and yelled, "Hey, Levine, did you kill any Germans today? I bet a Jew would love to do that."

My face turned red with both embarrassment and anger. I faced around, clenching my fists, my voice loud enough for everyone to hear. "You know, asshole. If you saw a German over there, I bet anything you would have turned and run. And listen, Anderson, don't play games anymore with my religion and me. I'll flatten you."

"You will huh." as he started walking toward me. "You damn Jew boys in the army or anywhere are cowardly crumbs."

I thought of my uncles, ran toward him as someone stopped and held me. "Cut it out, guys. The sergeant will throw all of us in the guard house."

Just about that time, the sergeant entered. "What's all the shouting here?"

Hesitantly, turning toward him, my voice trembling, I told him, "We were having a loud discussion."

"It was more than loud. Any fighting in here, I'll teach you before they send you out. What the fuck was going on?"

No one answered.

The sergeant walked up to me. "I asked what was goin' on."

"Ander, Anderson, was kidding me about being Jewish."

"Anderson." He went straight for the man, facing him. "We're all in the same army. Get that?"

Softly, "Yes, sir."

"And don't 'sir' me. Do you know anything about Levine or his family?"

"No," almost a whisper.

The sergeant turned toward me. "Levine, how about a little background for these guys?"

"What kind of background, sergeant? I don't understand."

"Your family, Levine. Even about you. Tell us how you were born," and he faked a laugh.

"Well." I didn't want to tell anyone I had already gone through one year of college on those fast track programs they had then because of the war. There were even a couple of veterans in one of my classes. I used to look at them, they looking back, I wondering what they were thinking, asking myself what they had gone through.

"Well, what?" the sergeant waited.

"Well, my uncles were in the ETO, one in the navy, one a surgeon who was decorated. Ah, he was right near the front lines, got wounded twice, once in the Battle of the Bulge, then went into Aachen, and, well," I was embarrassed. Why should I have been? "We'll he got a bronze star and two Purple Hearts. My other uncle was all over the Mediterranean. He was on one of those wooden, small minesweepers, in North Africa, Sicily, Italy – ah like Anzio, Sergeant. He's a naval officer." I felt my face warming. About what was I embarrassed?

"Ya mean, no runnin' away when the Germans shot at 'em."

"Yes, Sergeant."

The barrack was completely silent.

I looked toward Anderson, also red-faced, then at the sergeant standing almost over me. He was a tall, lanky fellow. I was tall too, but he seemed inches above me.

"That's quite a story. Did any of them see one of those concentration camps?"

"Yes," quietly.

"Ya mean like I did."

"Well, I guess so. I thought maybe you had already been there, sergeant but just guessed."

"I was and I saw and, in one of those coincidences, met your uncle who treated me. But no favors." He turned away from me, faced the whole barrack. "Have you heard enough, wise-asses?" looking straight at Anderson whose appearance was funny, his face really red. Then the entire barrack complement answered. "We heard it, Sergeant."

After he left, Anderson came over to me and held out his hand. "How about it, Mat?"

I took his hand. "O.K., Jerry. Let's forget it." From then on and for a long time we became close buddies until something happened.

So what else could happen in the army?

We gathered in the rain waiting for a troop train to take us someplace. They never told us where. All, I knew was that I was cold and shivering in the heavy rain, despite the rain proof sack covering me. It was supposed to be a raincoat, but damned if it felt that way. Finally the train pulled into the small station and a sergeant bellowed. "On board." We climbed into the car nearest us. We shoved and pushed one another trying to get a seat. Andy and I got one and threw our duffle bags on the floor, slipping out of raincoats, water spilling on the floor. Later, after the train started rolling, the car was loud with talk and shouting, "We're on our way." But where was our way? I remember seeing a station sign and knew we were somewhere in the western part of the state. When the train stopped, there was the wrenching and movement of either cars or engines until the sergeant came in and shouted, "Out of the car and follow me."

We went to another car, pushed and shoved some more to get seats. It was dark. I was weary from carrying the heavy duffel bag and just because it was late. Sleeping? On the car floor as the train rolled again. I lay on the floor, my head on my duffel bag I had dragged down to use as a pillow. All night long our sergeant or another or some guy wanting to use the bathroom shoved or stepped over anyone trying to sleep.

The morning was bright. We scrambled for our seats. When we looked at the farther end of the car, we saw a sign reading "White." It was like a roll. Andy got up and played with it, showing either White or Negro. He left it on Negro. We all laughed. A conductor, from wherever he got on the train, came through, looked up and changed the sign to White. Anderson waited until he left and changed it back. The game went on until Anderson wearied of it. We were riding on a White only train, obviously going South.

I then realized that perhaps there was something worse than being a Jew or kike, as I heard some bastard whisper. It was being black, but I didn't know how bad until we knew we were in the South where blacks were the enemy, not the German prison camp that was just being open to American troops for basic training. Were the Germans worse than the blacks? It was a question that haunted me, because in my mind no person could be worse than a Nazi bastard.

I guess because of my military training in high school, the tall, lanky war-knowing sergeant made me a platoon leader. I had a room in the barrack with one of the other guys who had been a high school graduate from a military academy, a Texan. There's always a Texan, of course. But it suddenly came to me one night while trying to fall asleep.

* * *

Five or six years old, spoiled brat, who was always turned over to a black maid, Harriet, or a nanny, Mrs. Goddard. We were on the back porch overlooking the hill we all coasted down in winter. She didn't like the way I was talking.

"You do as I told you. You tie the shoes and keep them that

way. And when I tell you to wash, from now on you do that too." I angrily looked into her dark eyes, glared at the black face. If older, I may have noticed her shapely figure and attractive face. Maybe my mother hired her because of her looks, ignoring her blackness.

I glared more, my mouth tight, refusing to move.

"C'mon now. Do what I told ya."

Looking straight at her, I shouted, "I don't have to do what you tell me. You're a nigger."

She stepped quickly toward me, slightly raising her hand. "Don't you ever, not ever use that word again. It's one of the worst things you can say. It's – it's horrible," stuttered, her eyes showing tears that she blinked back, dropping her hand, preventing herself from slapping me.

I lowered my face, tears also coming to me. I looked up, wiping my eyes, studying her in my young way. "I . . . I'm sorry, Harriet. Don't cry. I won't ever say that word again. I promise." I then ran to my room, fell on the bed crying. I never wanted to hurt anyone. I never used the word again.

* * *

Then there we were back on that train and the posting one could hatefully turn from white to black to white. That conductor with the grimace on his face and making certain it stated white. What was the difference among all the southerners I trained and would be with? And now the Germans. We hadn't called it holocaust where I trained, but I knew it. Every time I saw a German there was that hatred and even fear that one could kill me if I got too close. I didn't have enough training as yet to fight back, not the way they had been taught. Black, white, Nazi and what my uncle had told me about the camps. Every time I saw one, it rippled through me and the hatred would rise. Is this the way the southerners felt about the black people, hating them? For what? What did they do? Help to destroy the South in the Civil War? What did I know and what would I learn?

We saw black troops now, but they were never near us, until that night. We were on a bivouac in the Virginia forests. It made me think of the Civil War and the Battle of the Wilderness. I imagined being a northern soldier fighting in these woods. With nightfall, I imagined the fear the soldiers must have experience.

One night, the sergeant told me I was to stand guard. He marked out my area of patrol in that dark forest where one could barely see the sky. I was to march from one trail to another where it forked into two trails. I held my bayoneted rifle on my right shoulder like a good soldier, back and forth, braver and braver, because I was a Northern Infantryman guarding against the rebels. Suddenly it occurred to me. My ancestors. They came here before that war and some served. Well here I was in my imagination protecting them from the Rebels and fighting off the impression of the disgusting Jews who were supposed to have been nothing more than moneymakers during that war. No question, Abraham Lincoln was one of my heroes. So I was here protecting him from Lee and the – good heavens, from the blacks. Orders were they were never to come anywhere near our encampment. I was to stop them if they tried. But didn't their freed ancestors fight in the Northern Army and die for freedom? What freedom did they have? Here in this modern army having defeated the fucking Germans they had what? I marched back and forth. Suddenly at the fork, I heard voices. In that dark forest some enemy was coming toward me. The black troops. We were told to keep them out of our area. There were five of them appearing suddenly, talking loudly, laughing until they saw me with my rifle pointed at them.

"Halt. Who goes there?"

No one answered. They just came toward me, walking

slowly, confronting me.

"Halt."

"Who says so?"

"I do. We were told not to allow anyone into our area. So halt and go back where you came from." It never occurred to me, "where you came from" until years later. They told that to my ancestors. From where did they come? Go back to what? Hatred and fear for their lives.

But for now, I was only thinking of myself and these five black men surrounding me, Oh, they moved so slowly about me. I felt my heart beating faster.

"We're going through," their apparent leader told me. He was about as tall as I, probably stronger. But who could see in that dark forest? I moved very close to him, pressing my bayonet close to his throat. "I said you're not coming through. Those are my orders." I was aware they circled me and felt certain they would jump me. "I pushed the bayonet so it touched his throat. "You're not coming through. Get me?" Suddenly I was no longer afraid but certain of myself. "Now go back to your area." Perhaps he felt the bayonet. I'll never know. But someone gave a false laugh as their apparent leader turned and they followed, walking down the trail through which they had come. Perhaps it was Robert Frost's "The Road Not Taken." But I was scared now, feeling my heart pounding until suddenly I was smiling. I was a soldier who had done his duty and done it well. I turned and walked slowly back to my starting trail. My ancestors would have been proud of me, especially my Great Grandfather and Great Grandmother. We turned back the Rebels.

Sometime after that, I decided I would make it up to those soldiers who had obeyed me. For they were soldiers even if they were black. Yet, there was more with these troops that the United States services refused to admit . . . they could fight alongside whites or that they were comrades, despite the story of the Black squadron that escorted B-17s on missions over Germany and never lost a bomber.

The black troops were stationed somewhere on the road above us, we being at the bottom of the hill on which were our barracks. One night someone came running into our barrack yelling, "Hey the niggers are beginning a fight with us."

I blanched, thinking back to Harriet. I had come to despise anyone who demeaned black Americans. Andy came into the barrack after the other guy had left. "Matt. Aren't you comin'? C'mon. We gotta fight 'em. They have no right to be comin' into our area."

I was disappointed listening to him. "No, Andy, I'm not."

"Well I 'm not lettin' the other guys down." He grabbed his cartridge belt as more men ran in to the barrack and grabbed theirs. Soon there was yelling outside. I wondered who would be hurt.

I may have stopped thinking about it, except that our M-1s were in a stack, although they had no bullets. Just then, an officer entered. He ordered me to help gather the belts and the rifles. Other officers, I heard later, black and white, had rushed to the hilltop, pushed between the groups of quarreling troops, separated them, and the worst was averted. Some of the men from my barrack wandered slowly in, staring at me as though I were either a coward or deserter. I felt my face turn red with anger, waiting for one of them to say something. No one did.

Sometime later, we received passes for a day. Andy and I went to the southern town to enjoy ourselves, not knowing what we would do. We did take a bus ride to see the city. I had to sit behind Andy because the bus was full except for the back where the blacks sat. At one stop, the passenger beside Andy left while at the same time a black, elderly woman, hobbling, got on. She saw the vacant seat beside Andy. And sat. Suddenly Andy, grimacing, pushed her off the seat. She just managed to keep her feet, struggling toward the end of the bus. "Andy.

What the hell are you doing? You're no Southerner. He turned toward me. "She's a black bitch. She belongs in the back of the bus."

"Well, shit on you. You spend the rest of the day by yourself. I will too." We never spoke to one another again.

The rest of my sterling army experience had little to do with my Jewish heritage, I assume. Eventually, when black troops partly were integrated in the services, I became friendly with two black soldiers who worked with me occasionally. I had a room and shower all to myself in a clinic way at the end of the hospital, my having been transferred to the Medical Corps because I did not care to go to O.C.S. Having an extra bunk, I invited them to switch off and on nights. We had good times together, making certain no one saw us together outside the hospital. Then it happened. The commanding officer, a southerner, ordered me to report immediately.

"Levine. You've been using your room as something like a hotel. Starting today, move your gear to barrack (whatever) and sleep in the room with a white man. Do it now." I had a feeling he did not like me, just generally.

"Yes, sir." I hated the man from then on. Perhaps I was growing to hate Southerners, but how would that be any different than I being despised as a Jew. When I went into the barrack area some southern medics were shooting craps. I went to watch, listening to their yelling. When they looked up, they grimaced, never said anything to me, stopped shooting, and walked to their bunks. Was I now black-skinned or just a despised kike, as I had heard one call me in a whisper some time ago?

And yet, I was to have another experience that reminded me where I was. I had a pass and decided to go to Williamsburg, having heard how lovely it was and how it retained its past. Families that lived in the old homes took in servicemen for a small fee. I waited anxiously for the bus. It stopped, I got on with a black soldier. Taking my seat near a young woman, I saw him sit a few seats away. The bus driver looked back. "Hey, you. Get in the back of the bus."

"No, sir. I'm sitting here."

"Well, then this bus ain't movin' until you do."

The soldier looked. Of course, I couldn't see whether his skin changed color. He must have been embarrassed though. I was also thinking of his daring and silently cheered him for trying to defy the Southern rules. Yet, he did go to a seat in the back. This was just another occurrence, though not directly aimed at me, I thought back to the past and what my ancestors must have gone through and how in these modern times, a war still on, there was the hum, if one heard it or tried to, that echoed, "Stop trying to Jew me down on that price."

Yet, Williamsburg was not ended. I loved the sight of it, the retention of our Revolutionary past, the Governor's Palace with its broad English lawns and flowering. It was in town, though. I noticed, how could I not, the bubblers for drinking and their signs "White" and "Negro." Could the left over from a black mouth poison the white? I turned and looked back to the Palace thinking, "Patrick Henry 'I know not what others may think, but as for me, give me liberty or give me death.'" Such did it resonate. Those words had always made me shiver and understand what my country meant, as did George Washington's to the Rabbi in Newport, Rhode Island, when he told him this country for which he was fighting, welcomed Christians, Jews, and Moslems. Nor was there in our history anything such as the French lying about an officer for handing military secrets to the Germans, Dreyfus, then sent to Devil's Island to waste away.

But our camp was an island for German prisoners. We were supposed to stay away from them. They had an encampment practically hidden by woods from the main areas but guarded. I did find a Jewish friend, not that I was looking for one. I had never even thought of that growing up. We just happened to meet and liked one another. Saul and I decided one day to go to the German wired area, to look at our enemy of the United States and of the Jews, now beaten. And I thought, *Why hadn't more of them died, maybe the whole country. Are all Germans guilty of Jew hatred and murder*? I said little to Saul. We just stood there looking at them until several came toward us. They spoke English, probably learned in captivity. I don't know. But there was that German accent.

"Hello," one of them muttered.

"Hello."

"Are you new guards?"

"No. Just came to look."

"You are pleased to see us prisoners. No?"

"Yes. And we're wondering, just how many Jews you killed, gassed."

One of them shouted at us. "We kill Jews? We knew nothing about that. We never. . . ."

I looked angrily at him. "You lie," I shouted. "You not only killed Jews but murdered our troops at Malmédy."

"You think all German are guilty?"

"Aren't they? You were all Nazis. You are a Nazi killer."

"You are stupid," He shouted back. "We are not criminals like those you keep in Germany or some other country waiting to put them on trial and perhaps to death."

How they got their news, I wondered, about the formation of tribunals. But as I looked at them and the man speaking, I thought, *You saw the trains transporting Jews and Gypsies and undesirables to those camps, selecting those, most of them to die, children, as well as adults.* I was getting very angry and wanted to reach through the wire and choke that German. I remembered my uncle. Not only had he told me about anti-Semitism in our army but about his being chosen to lead a group into one of the camps and to take back their report to the headquarters. He described the horror to me, the emaciated survivors barely able to walk, throwing up food if they ate it too fast. Oh, how I wanted to choke, to kill that German.

"You're a fucking liar." My face was hot, coloring. Turning to Saul, I growled, "Let's get out of here. I can't stand anymore of these fuck-heads. They should all die. Let's get out of here."

He was also angry, his hands clenched, his eyes glaring, although he hadn't said anything, except now he was pulling me and somehow quietly, telling me, "Enough."

Yet, aside from the Germans and what my uncle had told me of the concentration camp, and thinking of my experiences, he had been right. Anything said about my ethnicity was always just within my hearing. In fact, when I left the commanding officer that day, I wondered, as I still do, how much my religion had to do with my move back to the barrack. However, yes, I was happy and proud to be honorably discharged with memories fond, disquieting, disgusting.

* * *

There was an ache about my heart. From what? I was thinking of her, the anticipation of meeting again. I varied my pace from the elevated train, occasionally faster than more slowly. The anticipation, imagining a kiss. Arriving, my heart beat faster. I could see her face, her body. She was shorter than I, slender, breasts I had never seen but imagined when she dressed for a cocktail lounge or nightclub. A lovely face, not a beauty, the green Irish shining, inquiring eyes, as I always thought of them. Oh, how I remember. She was always quick with questions or answers, smiling, showing her dimples, laughing when she knew she had surprised. This night she had asked me to meet her in the OR, for she was on duty. I forgot. It was my first year of medical studies. This evening was more important.

I stepped from the elevator into a semi-darkened hall, a light showing from the supply room not too distant from where I stood. She was there, waiting, a white gown.

"Come in here." She reached for my face touched it, turned her back to me, leaning against the high shelves. "Rub my back." Without hesitation I started above, moving my hands downward but just enough to feel the beginning bulge of her buttocks. My hands moved slowly, touching the edges of her hips, inward again, rubbing gently up the small of her back until I felt her bra strap, and hesitated. She bent slightly backward from her waist to encourage my hands, softly in a quiet, plaintive moan. "That's good."

Bending, I went below her hem, following her legs to her thighs when she turned, her legs spreading slightly, pushing against me just below her mound. She unclasped her bra that fell to the floor. She moved about in rhythm with my hands as they went to her breasts. My fingers wrapped about and massaged her hardened nipples, then the round softness. She turned as she loudly moaned and reluctantly, I'm sure, softly spoke, "Stop." She reached for her bra and pulled down the hem of her hospital gown. "No more. Not here, not anywhere."

"But."

"You think I'm teasing. I'm not. I want to . . . but . . . We just can't go any further." She took me in her arms, raised to her toes for her mouth to meet mine.

"Maureen," I whispered. "I love you, want you to know it."

"We have to wait," even though she had gone to and held my hard penis, rubbed, stopped. "I'm sorry. We just have to wait until . . ."

"Why?"

She hesitated, "My beliefs. You know that. It's a sin."

Her religion, Catholic like my beautiful red haired mother who at least adhered to her beliefs while I was growing up and until my studies for my Bar Mitzvah. So I know Maureen truly

417

believed, and in part, it drew me to her. Sometime from the long past, I knew the story of my forebears, the proof being there. It was part of me although my mother had allowed my father to raise me Jewish which began to have an effect on her. But early on I went to church too with my mother. I remember the first time. I was five or six. The church was so quiet as we entered. I looked about at the altar, at the candles and started to ask my mother, but she had let go of my hand and was kneeling, crossing herself. When she rose, she led me to the burning candles. Taking one, she lit it, knelt again and prayed. "Mother, what are you saying?"

"I'm asking God to protect us, to forgive . . . ." And she stopped. What was forgiveness and for what?

"What do you mean? Did you do something bad? Daddy would forgive you. My sister loves you too and would."

She smiled. "I want God to know that anything I may have done wrong should, oh well. Look, Matthew. We may do something that we think is all right but may be wrong. It's hard to explain. Your father and I. Well, we have different beliefs. When you're older, you'll understand and when you begin to learn new ideas that won't agree with mine. But that won't separate us. People have different ideas about life. Oh. Matthew," she whispered. "We can't talk here. Let's go home."

I didn't know it then, but even though she took me to church, my mother had begun to think she would become Jewish. That came when I was 13. It was then my mother also began to go to the temple and study Judaism so she could become Jewish. In the end though, she didn't. So many conflicts and so much love.

Maureen's soft voice interrupted my thoughts. "I've talked to the priest about us."

It surprised me. "But why?"

"For a thousand and one reasons, most of which you know, and why I won't go further. I want to, but we can't. What if I...

Even though I love you too." She took my hand and led me to a small but long room with windows all along the wall looking out over the city, its lights. We leaned on our elbows. "It's so beautiful in the dark. I love the quiet, and we are above the sounds of the world," as she turned, pulled me toward her, kissing me. "There'll come a day for us."

When would that day come? I have always felt strangeness as though it were possible for me to go to the past. That thought often made me stir after I met Maureen.

Then, for some reason, it occurred to me. "Maureen. If we were to have a daughter, what would you name her?"

She laughed. You're already getting prepared. Ruth."

"Ruth?"

"Why not?"

My mind suddenly grasped a faint echo, "Ruth," as though I had left that peaceful interlude above the dark, lighted world. Maureen and I were separated.

Chapter Four

Renewal

The apparent loss of Maureen came as a blow, as though a war were still being fought, this one regarding my heart. Yes, I Matthew did not know how to take this. There may have been the end of the shooting war, but officially it ended with President Truman's proclamation officially calling for the cessation, as I said, in 1946. That was a number of years back. And also that year in July, 1946, the Irgun, as we heard from David who had kept in touch with my Uncle Bryan told him in a letter about the destruction of the King David Hotel and his loss of a brother being sadly killed while walking by. My family and I did not know this man, but he was related. So how much of us, the family, also died? I never figured that out. Did it make me sad? Not really, but for some reason in the early 1950s it reminded me of watching Maureen who I saw in the train widow on her way to Chicago, leaving me behind. Watching that train disappear there were only forlorn tracks before me seeming to say, "It's too late. It's too late. You didn't stop her. The stretching, devoid tracks appearing to be my empty heart."

Well, my cousin Andrea Louise was now 16. She appeared to be such a lovely maturing young woman whose heart I would hope would never be broken, just as I thought of my sister Natalie a year older who was about to enter college.

Did we Jews multiply? Obviously. And did we inherit a history of diverse multiplication as we would prepare to renew our inheritance? Of course. I see this in my sister, my cousin, and Maureen who seemed to have disappeared. Was there another Maureen? That Irish blood flowing away. I would find another, or it would be the one I thought I lost. It was my inheritance. I must re-find her.

* * *

It was during the fall. My friends and I had discovered a soft lighted, plush cocktail club. One of them had a date and asked me if I would like to join them. It was a cool fall night. When I was finally free from my first year medical studies in Boston, following the medical heritage, I went and sat across from her by a fireplace, making it brighter despite the soft lights. The flame shown on her green eyes that seemed to focus on mine, the same color. I watched her the entire time we were there, talking some and telling myself this was the woman for me. I wanted to see her again, to be able to enjoy her company alone with me. She was about five foot four I guessed when she stood. I also loved the glossiness of her black hair, the shape of her, the swell of her breasts, and the way her slim waist widened to her hips. Her ankles were also slender, her shapely legs showing below the hem of her dress. Her voice was so softly pleasant and distinct. I must see her again. Oh, and her name, Maureen Meyer. This was how we met and what eventually brought me to her that night of her duty in the OR.

Well, of course, we did meet again. We would go out to eat, visit the art museum, and go to plays, ballet and, movies. Was I repeating my remote ancestors in reverse, the history my great-great grandfather left for all to know and about whom to read.

Eventually I met her parents. Her father did not seem to like me much. I could see him thinking she has brought us a Jew. Her mother, though, was pleasant to me. Eventually, despite everything, Maureen invited me to dinner to meet her brothers and sisters. It went well too, except for the coldness of her father. He would be my nemesis. Was he the one who sent her away, believing we would never meet again as when I watched those empty tracks that curved away under the bridge on which I stood watching as the train moved more swiftly carrying her from me?

It was then I thought of my ancestor of long centuries ago meeting his Jewess Ruth. Was that why I told Maureen a child, a girl, we would name Ruth?

Ah well, for some reason I thought then of my old, frail Grandmother Olivia. Why? Because she was left with a broken heart. Perhaps Maureen's heart was like mine, broken. My grandmother. But her brother, Joseph, was still going strong. My great Aunt Millicent, though, sadly lost her husband.

Why do I think of these things now? It's a wonder. My great-great grandparents, their courage, Benjamin and Constance. I wish I had known them and could talk to them. Oh yes we have old photos, you know those stiff ones of the time. Constance was so lovely, stiff as she had to sit and Benjamin standing beside her, his hand on her shoulder, telling all and future generation, "She's mine."

Maureen, but my grandparents of old, their courage leaving behind our heritage of Jews in Europe and then in America that was mine. Oh how they left us with the independence they had learned and handed down, almost like the Founding Fathers.

I decided. I would bring back Maureen. We had talked on the phone. She asked, her voice tearful, "Matthew. I miss you. Please come see me, and at Christmas we can go back together to Cambridge. I don't care what my father thinks." Then she told me. "Matthew. I must tell you. My father sent me away. I felt I must obey him. He would not, he said, have his daughter, any daughter marry a Jew. Matthew, I don't care anymore. Please come to me."

"Maureen, I will. Just keep believing in me." And I sang to her:

Oh! I will take you back, Kathleen
To where your heart will feel no pain
And when the fields are fresh and green
I'll take you to your home again!

She laughed as I did. "No I haven't the voice, Maureen, my love, but do change Kathleen to Maureen."

And that is how it happened. I went to Chicago and brought her back with me. Before we left, I asked, "Will you mind changing your last name to Levine?"

"Foolish man, my future doctor. Maureen and Levine rhyme, do they not?"

We laughed. "Maureen, before we leave here, let's marry. If you want it to be a church, I won't object." I was thinking of the stories of Benjamin and Constance. *I must tell Maureen about them.*

"I do care, Matthew, but I believe we must settle that later. I am a good Catholic and will not be allowed to take communion, may be excommunicated if . . . Your mother is Catholic." She struggled silently, then, "Yes. Settle it later. It will be easier to find a Justice of the Peace, and then we could marry in the church. It's our secret."

We did. But before that I went and bought a ring and knelt before her. I took out the small box and asked, "Maureen Meyer, will you marry me?"

"I will, Matthew Levine."

I brought out the ring and placed it on her finger.

"We are betrothed. I love you with my life, Maureen."

"And I love you also."

We did marry and took the train back to Boston. Her mother softened her father. We went to Portland. My parents adored her. She also made certain she would be a friend to my sister Natalie.

And, yes, we did have a daughter named immediately by

Maureen who smiled at me. "We'll name her Ruth. You know, Matthew. She signifies, 'Abiding loyalty and devotion.'"

The End

Bibliography

Alcott, Louisa May. *CIVIL WAR Hospital Sketches,* Mineola, NY: Dover Publications, Inc., 2014.

Devine, Shauna. *Learning from the Wounded: The Civil War and the Rise of American Medicine.* Chapel Hill: The University of North Carolina Press, 2004.

Levinsky, Allan M. *The Night the Sky Turned Red.* Carlisle, MA: Applewood Books, 2014.

McGaugh, Scott. Surgeon in Blue: *Jonathan Letterman, The Civil War Doctor Who Pioneered Battlefield Care.* New York: Arcade Publishing, 2013.

Montefiore, Simon Sebag. *Jerusalem: The Biography.* New York: Alfred A. Knopf, A Borzoi Book, 2011.

Sandburg, Carl. *The Prairie Years: Vol II.* New York: Harcourt, Brace & World, Inc., 1926.

Schultz, Jane E. *Women at the Front.* Chapel Hill: The University of North Carolina Press, 2004.

Skinner, Carolyn. *Women Physicians & Ethos in Nineteenth Century American.* Carbondale: Southern Illinois University Press, 2014.

Wear, Andrew. *Knowledge & Practice in English Medicine, 1550 - 1680.* United Kingdom: Cambridge University Press, 2000.

Wood-Allen, Mary. *Almost A Women.* Middleton, DE., 2015.

Wood-Allen, Mary, M.D. *What A Young Woman Ought To Know.* Middletown, DE., 2015.

From Google:
1941 Declaration of War: Franklin D. Roosevelt Presidential Library, 2015.

"George John Dasch and the Nazi Saboteurs": The FBI Federal Bureau of Investigation. (FBI), 2016.

World War II: German Saboteurs Invade America in 1942: Net History on Line, 2015.

Jewish Brigade Group: United States Holocaust Memorial Museum. Washington, D.C.: Encyclopedia Britannica, on line, 2016.

ABOUT THE AUTHOR

Richard Shain Cohen of Cape Elizabeth, Maine, is originally from Boston. He retired from the University of Maine at Presque Isle after serving as Vice President of Academic Affairs and Professor of English. He holds B.S., M.A., and Ph.D. degrees. Richard served in the military and is a U.S. Army veteran.

His own publications include: Fiction—*Ecstasy and Distress; Our Seas of and Love; Monday: End of the Week; Be Still, My Soul;* and *Petal on a Black Bough. Non-fiction---Healing After Dark: Pioneering Compassionate Medicine at the Boston Evening Clinic; The Forgotten Longfellow: Man in the Shadows;* Poetry---*Only God Can Make a Tree.* He also wrote chapters for *Aroostook: Land of Promise;* academic reviews and articles, and – with the aid of a Shell Grant – a monograph on Samuel Richardson that can be found in major library holdings.

He served as editor of the journal *Husson Review* and was principal participant in a National Endowment for the Arts Grant for "Images of Aroostook" that was exhibited throughout the State of Maine.

www.ingramcontent.com/pod-product-compliance
Lightning Source LLC
Chambersburg PA
CBHW020926020726
47495CB00002B/368